UNDER COVER OF STARS

DANIELLE PRICE

Under Cover of Stars

Copyright © 2025 by Danielle Price

Published by PocketVerse Press. All rights reserved.

Edited by Casey Jones and Ana Hansen.

Title design and character art by Sofía Sanz.

No AI was used in the creation of this book.

ISBN: 979-8-9997186-0-0 (ebook)

ISBN: 979-8-9997186-1-7 (trade paperback)

*For anyone who's ever felt stuck, lost, or ready to give up: keep going.
There's always a way through.*

CONTENTS

Systems & Planets

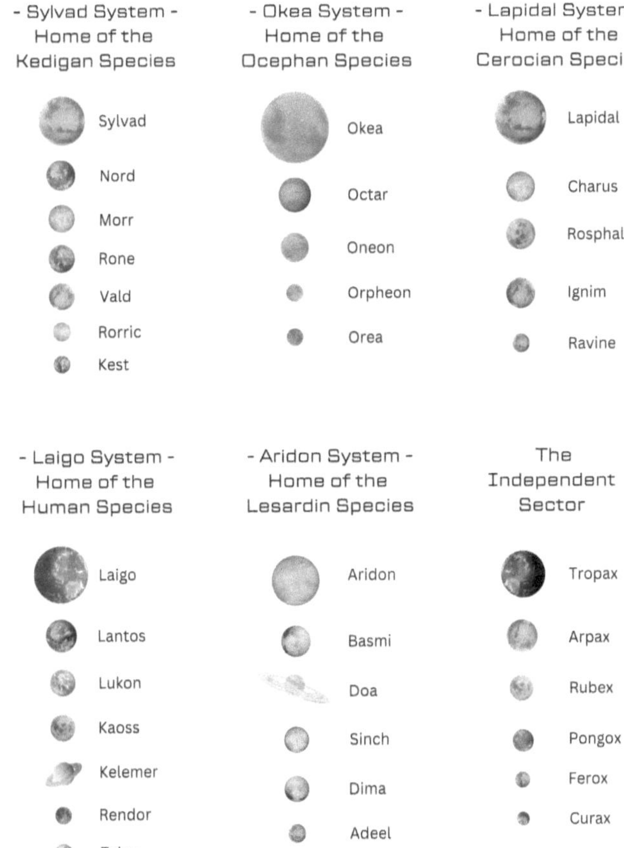

- The 7th Sector -
[Planets Unknown]

PROLOGUE

REPORT: SECURITY BREACH, THEFT

Classification: Clearance Level 8

Incident Overview:

At approximately 0300 hours Galactic Standard Time, an unknown assailant breached multiple layers of security at the Galactic Union Museum, located on the planet Lantos. The suspect executed a highly coordinated operation, infiltrating the museum's perimeter undetected.

Night shift security officers reported hearing a disturbance coming from the other side of the building, drawing them away from their post to investigate. The disturbance was later found to be caused by multiple low-impact explosive detonators, strategically timed to divert security personnel away from the museum's Early Artifacts Gallery.

Once the gallery was clear, the assailant accessed a specialized case housing the rare artifact, the **Egg of Arpax.** (Valued at this time at over 100 million Galactic Credits.) The perpetrator bypassed the case's security measures using a data-encryption key, a trammel beacon, and intimate knowledge of the case's security mechanics. It is believed this knowledge was obtained through unlawful methods on the open vector wire. After the Egg of Arpax was removed, the thief left the scene without further incident. Attempts to locate the artifact have so far yielded no results.

Currently, there are no definitive leads regarding the identity of the assailant. However, preliminary analysis suggests that this incident fits the emerging pattern of high-value Union vault thefts across multiple sectors over the past six months. Involvement by the Independent Sector, also known as "Free Sector" is not being ruled out.

Upgrades to the museum's security system have been initiated. However, the immediate focus of Galactic Union investigators is to track down the responsible party. As head of the Security Division, I am proposing an aggressive approach to all inspections over the next few weeks in an effort to recover the artifact and deter future offenses.

My official recommendation for media positioning is as follows:

Report the museum's security officers as having been killed during the incident in order to discredit the suspect and discourage public support. Maintaining a media narrative in which this crime hurts the state and all of its citizens is of the utmost importance at this time.

Report Filed by: Inspector Daran Markens, Galactic Union Security Division

Stellar Date: 3367.182.9

1

———————

HADRIN CITY

ACROSS THE GALAXY, PEOPLE WERE FACING THE CRUSHING tyranny of our age with courage and resolve. *I* was hiding in a lavatory.

This lavatory only had four stalls, and I was holed up in the one furthest from the door. I had changed the status screen on the door from *Vacant,* to *Out of Order,* and now I was crouching awkwardly on the back of the cistern to keep my boots out of sight. Technically, you needed a data key to be able to set a stall to *Out of Order,* but I'd found that if you held the power and reset buttons down simultaneously, you could force the screen to cycle through the display options. With practice, I had gotten the process down to twenty-three seconds. Twenty-one if I kept calm.

A low, grinding rumble vibrated the lavatory walls as a ship in the yard outside fired up its engines. They wouldn't be allowed to take off, not with an active inspection in effect. I exhaled wearily, daring to relax for a brief moment, and felt my boot slip on the slick surface of the cistern. A sharp gasp escaped me as my balance faltered, and my hands shot out, slamming against

3

the walls of the stall to steady myself. *Great, Fenn. That's what happens when you let your guard down.*

Twenty minutes, I decided. I'd give it twenty minutes, just to be safe. I'd be docked a portion of my pay for "excessive lavatory use," but I'd decided I would rather be short on drinking money that week than come face to face with a Union officer on an investigative walk-through. *Welcome to life under the Galactic Union.*

The "random" workplace inspections were becoming more frequent. I could tell my coworkers found them annoying, but no one seemed to fear being investigated as much as I did. The inspecting officers, if they were still there, would be menacing their way around the shipyard, looking for anything not up to code. Anything *off*. The last inspection had been brief, almost perfunctory, perhaps meant more to keep us on our toes than to actually uncover anything.

They could already be gone. Maybe I was hiding in here like an idiot for no reason at all.

Just as I was considering stepping down from my perch, the lavatory door swung open, hitting the wall with a sharp *crack* that echoed through the tiled room. My breath caught, and I instinctively pressed a hand over my mouth to muffle the gasp that almost escaped. I'd never seen an officer step into the lavatory before. It's why I'd picked it as my hideout. Low-risk, unnoticed. *Are they becoming more thorough?*

I closed my eyes and listened to a pair of boots thud into the room, followed by the unmistakable *smack* of the door slamming shut. *Gryta, protect me. Is this how it ends?* My heart pounded and adrenaline flooded my veins. Questions. Suspicion. Arrest. Prison. Execution. Or worse, maybe the officer would decide to shoot me here and now for the hell of it. I'd heard the stories.

I flinched as the boots took a step forward.

Bracing myself, I waited for the sound of those heavy boots to start kicking in the stall doors. Any second now.

I waited, but heard nothing. Silence. Whoever had come in was standing still. The automated tap hadn't kicked on, so they weren't washing their hands. *What in the seven sectors are they doing, staring in the mirror?* That's when I heard a very familiar sigh of exasperation.

"Rego?" I said without thinking.

Rego's voice reached me from across the stalls, assuring me with great relief that I hadn't just made the dumbest mistake of my life.

"Oh, hey, Fenn," he muttered flatly.

Something's wrong. I stepped down from the cistern, unlocked my stall door and opened it to see my best friend hunched over the sink. His hands were planted on the counter and his shoulders slumped as if under the weight of the galaxy. His work goggles were sitting on top of his head and he had pulled his face mask down.

Rego was exceptionally tall for a human, with a burly build that essentially made him a giant. His dark hair was drawn into a haphazard bun at the back of his head as always. He straightened up when he saw me, looming to his full height. "I forgot you always hide in here during inspections," he said with a tired smile.

"I wasn't hiding," I snapped, walking to the other sink. "I was…" It was pointless to deny it. Rego knew me too well. "Well, what are *you* doing in here?" I asked, rinsing anxious sweat off my hands and glancing at our reflections. I wasn't particularly small for a woman in her mid-twenties, but next to Rego, I always looked tiny. Rego shrugged and brushed at the thick layer of dirt coating his mechanic's jumpsuit.

"I'm using the lavatory," he muttered.

I flicked water from my hands and turned to face him. His shoulders were drawn up. He was lying. Something or someone had upset him. For all his size, Rego was gentle and passive. *Too* passive. My eyes widened as I noticed the mop leaning against the wall behind him.

"Oh no," I said, shaking my head. "Did Delm put you on lavatory cleaning duty *again?*"

"Fenn," he sighed, "it's not a big deal."

"It is a big deal, Rego! That's the third day in a row."

"Wait," he protested, but it was too late. My hands were already curled into fists as I turned and shoved the lavatory door open.

As I stepped into the shipyard, it hit me that I hadn't even checked to see if the inspection was over. Glancing up at the control tower, I was relieved to see the light was green. Takeoffs and landings were currently permitted, meaning the officers had left. I stalked across the yard, kicking up clouds of dirt with each infuriated step. I'd caught the faint scent of ship fuel on Rego, so I headed straight for the fuel terminal. Rego was deeply sensitive, and kinder than anyone I've met. That kindness had saved me once.

Nearing the fuel pumps, I saw two of our resident mechanics topping off the mobile fuel cart.

"Bastard," I muttered, quickening my pace.

Our mechanics spent so much time in the dusty yard, they had to wear jumpsuits, masks, and goggles. Once suited up, you could only tell them apart by their body shapes. I couldn't make out one of the guys at the fuel pumps, but the other one had a shape I recognized. Delm was as burly as Rego, but a whole foot shorter. Of the Hadrin City shipyard employees, I wasn't the tallest, strongest, or even the most senior, but I sure as hell was the angriest.

I thought about yelling to get their attention, but the sounds of the yard were too much to compete with. I spied a drink canister on the edge of the fuel pump next to me. Ksaba juice. Delm's favorite legal-to-consume-at-work drink. I picked it up and weighed it in my hand as I closed in on him. The canister itself was lightweight, but the dregs inside gave it a little heft. Not enough to harm. Just enough to make a point.

I aimed and launched it at the back of Delm's head, where it made an audible *plunk* before bouncing away and tumbling to the ground.

"Hey!" Delm yelled, dropping the heavy fuel hose and spinning to face me.

"You put Rego on lav cleaning duty again?" I asked, stopping just a foot from him. He lifted his goggles and lowered his mask.

"Greez, Fenn, was that really necessary?" He rubbed the back of his head and glanced down at the canister in the dirt. The other mechanic lifted his goggles and drew his own mask down. Delm's new trainee, Sam. *Perfect.* New employees needed to know that if Rego wouldn't stand up for himself, I would.

"You're supposed to rotate lav duty amongst all the mechanics, Delm. Not stick Rego with it three days in a row."

Delm threw his hands up defensively. "Relax, Rego doesn't mind lav duty!"

"He does mind! He just won't say anything. Is that why you keep assigning it to him?"

Delm hesitated, glancing over at Sam, who was quietly shifting his weight between his feet and watching us with passive curiosity. I watched Delm sharply, waiting.

"Fenn…" he trailed off. I knew he was trying to come up with an excuse. His shoulders slumped, an admission of guilt.

"I'm sorry," Delm muttered, "Rego's the only one that doesn't give me a hard time when it gets put on his schedule."

"He's too nice, Delm. He shouldn't be punished for it."

Delm scowled. I was attacking his character now, not just the back of his head.

"You're on the docking team. Why don't you let me handle maintenance team matters? I don't want to have to go to Giil with a report that you're making my job harder."

I shot him a cutting glance. "Go ahead, Delm. Let's call Giil. I'll tell him about the time you sideswiped that customer's brand new Stream-Hawk with the fuel cart because you were too hungover to drive straight."

That had been a tense day in the yard. The entire staff had covered for Delm, swearing that they'd seen the scratch on the racing vessel when it had arrived. I had never considered holding it over Delm's head. But there was nothing I wouldn't do to protect Rego.

Delm let out an exasperated sigh. "Come on, Fenn…"

"Try me," I said, tapping my foot.

He sighed and scratched his head thoughtfully. "Fine," he said sheepishly.

I nodded, and gave him some space. "Just be fair with the assignments, okay?"

"You got it, Fenn. Sorry."

A loud huff sounded behind me, and when I turned, I saw Rego had finally caught up with me. He panted, out of breath, mop in hand.

"Oh, hey, Rego," Delm said cautiously. "Actually, Sam is on lav duty today."

Sam looked as if he was about to protest, but when he saw me still glaring, he nodded begrudgingly. He dropped the fuel hose and took the mop from Rego.

I sighed, feeling better about Rego's work day, but annoyed that my own was steadily becoming more of a headache. As if on cue, a loud beep echoed from the speaker by the entrance to the fueling terminal.

"Ahem," A voice crackled over the intercom and echoed through the shipyard. *Jera.*

I squeezed my eyes shut and took a slow breath.

"Paging Fenn..." the voice continued. "Are you coming back to the station anytime soon? Over."

"I gotta run, boys," I said, turning to leave. "Enjoy your afternoon."

"Drinks later?" Rego called after me. "We're taking Sam out to celebrate the end of his first week."

I turned to face him, trying to think up an excuse not to go. I had a tendency to hermit, spending all my free time hiding away in my rented room. Rego was always making an effort to get me out. *After today, it might be nice to have a drink.*

"I'll be there," I said.

His eyebrows raised in surprise. "Promise?"

"Ugh, I've changed my mind," I said with mock disgust.

"Yeah, yeah," he grinned at me as I turned and left. Rego and I tended to fall back on humor when a conversation became too earnest.

I hurried back to the shipyard's control station—if Jera had paged me, something had come up. Hadrin's position in the galaxy made it a convenient place for pilots to refuel or get a drink, so our shipyard saw a lot of traffic. As a docking technician, I helped make sure incoming ships were logged in and assigned a docking quadrant.

I prayed that there were no officers waiting in the control tower when I arrived. My mind went to the woman who had run the maro soup shop across the street from our shipyard. Last month, she'd hung some printed pamphlets with anti-Union sentiments in the window of her shop. They were up for a whole day, but the next morning, she had disappeared and the shop had been shuttered. No one knew what happened to her, but according to Union laws, infractions like that could get you sent to a work camp on some outer-brink planet. The thought ran a chill down my spine.

I finally reached the station and pulled the heavy door open, mentally preparing myself.

"Fenn!" Jera shouted the moment I stepped inside. Her usually slitted pupils were dilated with excitement. "Where have you been? We just had another inspection!" *Excitement* was Jera's default setting. She always had the energy of someone who'd just had five cups of high kolo.

I glanced down at the dust I tracked in from the yard, then took a moment to shake out the wavy brown hair I'd loosely braided that morning. More dust fell to the floor, ready for the sweeper bot that would make its rounds at the end of the day.

"Did we?" I asked Jera, feigning ignorance.

Her tail flicked furiously behind her as she settled at her desk, a sign that she was excited. The feline-like Kedigans were largely known for their cool, detached personalities. Jera's relentless energy was definitely a quirk.

"Well, I handled the inspection all by myself," she said, her feline features pulling into a proud smile. "They asked for the travel logs from last week, and I managed to locate and transfer them without a hitch."

"Was there a reason you paged me?" I said, hoping to change the subject. I stalled by the door, kicking dirt from my boot.

"Oh, yes," Jera said, tapping her specially designed earpiece that linked to her console. "I've got a pilot on hold. He's requesting a manual scan. Is that something we do?"

"Ugh," I groaned, already dreading the idea of going back out into the yard after just coming in. "Are they asking for maintenance or fuel?"

"Neither," she said. "They just want to be scanned in manually rather than transmitting their docking credentials."

"That's odd," I muttered. "We usually only get manual scan requests when a pilot needs maintenance and has too many specs for a single transmission."

"So..." Jera mused, waiting for instruction.

I sighed and reached into my desk drawer, pulling out a hand-held scanner.

"Tell them we'll meet them in the yard."

Jera cleared her throat and picked the call back up. "Okay, sir, we can do that, please proceed to the northeast quadrant of the yard." Silence filled the room as she waited for a response. "No, thank *you*," she said, then giggled.

Great. The pilot was a charmer.

"Pause docking," I told her, watching as she nodded and flipped a switch on her console. "We'll be quick."

As she joined me by the door, she primped, smoothing her feline whiskers and tail. She stopped when she noticed me watching.

"He sounded cute!" she said with a guilty grin.

"Come on," I said, rolling my eyes and gesturing her out the door.

I took my time walking to the northeast quadrant, having learned early on in the job to let a ship land before approaching. It was partially for safety, but even more so to avoid being coated in the dust the engines kicked up.

"On the subject of cute pilots," I said.

"Go on…" Jera said with a smile.

"I don't want to tell you what to do, but good-looking pilots come through here all the time. They'll throw you a smile. Tell you some stories from their travels that are very exciting and *surely* not exaggerated."

"I'm waiting for the bad part," Jera said.

"Just know that they're good at breaking hearts, okay? Don't fall for it. If one of them asks you out for a drink, be careful."

"Oh I don't plan on going out with them," she said with a wicked grin. "I just like to flirt."

I peered at her sideways. Maybe she was savvier than I gave her credit for. "You might like this job then."

"So what's with all these inspections lately?" she asked. "Why are there so many?"

I squinted in the afternoon light, searching for a non-seditious answer.

"The Union wants to know exactly who is coming and going, and what they're bringing with them when they do."

"But isn't that a good thing?" Jera asked. "They're probably cutting down on intergalactic smuggling, stopping criminals."

I wanted to tell her that the *real* criminals were the ones at the head of the government, but I thought better of it.

"Yeah but they're also cutting down on fairly priced goods getting to communities that need them. And they're actively stopping donated food from getting to the places it needs to go."

"What? Why would they do that?"

I swallowed, lowering my voice.

"Because every time they starve a small, backwoods planet and then show up with loads of supplies and media coverage, they end up looking like heroes to the people who don't pay attention to what's going on."

Jera didn't respond, and stayed quiet the rest of the walk. We eventually reached the northeast quadrant, and I stopped, scanning the sky in the distance.

"What model is the ship?" I asked.

"Something called a Dawn-Wing?"

"A Dawn-Wing? Haven't seen one of those in a while."

The low hum of twin engines came into earshot, growing louder as a ship appeared on the horizon.

"That'll be it," I said, waiting to get a better look.

The vessel's sleek silhouette glinted in the Hadrin sun as it drew closer, revealing a silvery white craft with green accents. It circled the yard, slowing to a hover above a wide open space between two larger ships. The landing struts deployed and the ship lowered, inch by inch, onto the ground. I held my hand out, motioning for Jera to wait until the ship's engines had powered down. Once they had, I nodded, and we approached the vessel together. I tapped my scanner on, ready to scan the pilot's credentials.

I watched, waiting for the Dawn-Wing's side-facing door to slide open and reveal the pilot who had forced me to leave the station and stand in the hot, dusty yard. I scanned the craft while we waited, taking in the various visible mending jobs in its hull. This ship had clearly been patched up multiple times in lieu of more permanent repairs.

With a click, the door unlocked, and a sharp hiss filled the air as the ship depressurized. The door slid to the side and the pilot stepped out, his back to us. He took a deep breath, filling his lungs while grinding the soles of his boots into the dirt.

I'd seen many long-haul pilots do the same—it seemed to ground them after extended space travel. Whoever he was, he had traveled a long way. He turned to face us, and Jera made an excited noise under her breath. When he looked my way, I dropped my eyes to the scanner in my hand, pinching my eyebrows together and feigning interest in the screen.

I couldn't tell if Jera was good at judging voices over the transmitter or had just gotten lucky, but the pilot was as attractive as she'd suspected. I pretended to wipe dust from the screen with my sleeve, determined to appear like I hadn't noticed him. I'd dealt with handsome, charming pilots like him before. They were the worst.

2

―――――――――

I DON'T WANT TROUBLE

THE PILOT WAS TALLER THAN ME BY FIVE OR SIX INCHES, WITH A lean frame and subtly sloping shoulders. He carried himself with a slight slouch, as if he had a hundred things to worry about besides his posture. His hair, dark and wavy, had a shaggy fringe that he raked back with his fingers as he scanned his surroundings with a sharp gaze. His skin was a golden tan, deeper than my own by a handful of shades. I saw subtle shadows under his eyes that spoke of excessive time spent in the dark, endless void of space.

He wore a simple, fitted shirt, sleeves casually rolled up to his elbows, and a pair of dark pants tucked into thick-soled boots. Over it all was the same padded flight vest most pilots wore to protect them from their seat harnesses during flight. His vest was dark green and frayed around the edges from heavy use, a clue to just how much of the galaxy he'd seen.

As he strode over to where Jera and I waited, a broad smile warmed his face, and I noticed how dashing of a figure he was when you really took him in.

"Thanks for meeting me out here. My transmitter is down," he said, flashing a grin at Jera specifically. My annoyance must have been written on my face.

"It's no problem," she beamed.

"I wouldn't go that far," I said, drumming my nails on my scanner. "Anyway, how exactly did you hail our station with a broken transmitter?"

He leaned forward, squaring his shoulders in a way that drew attention to their shape.

"The comms work just fine, but it won't let me transfer data. I'm getting it repaired soon," he promised.

Close up, I saw that his eyes were a deep brown with warm bronze flecks. I would have studied them further if he'd been looking at Jera, but his gaze was focused on mine. I hadn't known brown eyes could be so *piercing*.

"Sure," I said, hoping my tone conveyed my doubts about his story. "I'll take those credentials," I demanded, my hand out.

He hesitated, but reached into his vest pocket and produced a vessel identification chip, which he held out to me.

I took it, still eyeing him carefully. I made sure Jera was paying attention, then scanned the chip, and waited while it entered his ship's ID into our system. He watched quietly. My device beeped, confirming that his Dawn-Wing was indeed registered, and not flagged as stolen. I handed him the vessel chip, which he pocketed.

"ID?" I asked, my hand still out. He handed me his personal ID chip, and I inspected it closely. The photo on his chip was indeed him, albeit with shorter hair, but it was the name listed that caught my eye.

"Kad Rand?" I said.

"Family name," he said, shrugging with a grin.

"It's a nice name," Jera giggled.

He gave her an appreciative nod.

I scanned his ID, watching the screen carefully.

"Have you ladies worked here long?" he asked. "I've been through here before. I'm sure I would have remembered you."

I almost looked up from the screen but resisted. The scan had finished.

"Not long," Jera said. "Fenn here is training me."

I handed him his ID chip.

"That's right," I said. "And what a great pupil she is." I smiled, sure I would have seen her blush if she was human. "Jera, why don't you head back to the station? I'm sure we have a ship or two waiting to land. I'll wrap up here."

"Sure," she said, then flashed a fanged smile at the pilot. "Enjoy Hadrin."

"Thank you," he nodded, and watched Jera turn to leave. I didn't take my eyes off of him, listening for her footfalls growing softer as she padded away.

"Thanks again for scanning me in," he said.

"No problem, *Kad Rand*," I said, wondering if he detected my sarcasm. If he did, he ignored it.

Nodding, he spun around, heading back to his ship. I glanced behind me, making sure Jera had gone.

"So who are you, really?" I called after him.

He stopped dead in his tracks, his posture stiffening. With a slow turn, he locked eyes with me.

"Excuse me?"

"The screen glitched when your data loaded."

"Your scanner must be faulty," he replied, smooth and steady, not missing a beat.

"No," I countered. "A glitch like that only happens with…interference." I paused, letting the weight of the implication sink in. "So what is it? A trammel beacon, maybe? Some device in your pocket that spiked my machine with external data? It doesn't matter. Your ID chip shows that it was issued on planet Kaoss five years ago, but *three* years ago, Kaoss overhauled their system and issued brand new chips. So either your chip magically time-traveled—or you put the wrong date down when you forged it."

He stood frozen, but I saw a flicker of recognition in his eyes, and a subtle shift in his demeanor. The bright, easy expression he'd carried off the ship with him faded away as his shoulders dropped.

"You know," he said, his voice taking on a darker edge, "no one's ever caught that before."

His eyes had lost their warmth, replaced by something colder. Annoyance?

"For a yard worker, you seem to know a lot about illegal tech," he said.

"I almost didn't notice," I said, "but your Dawn-Wing, your manual scan request, *and* an ID glitch? It's a suspicious combo."

He arched a brow. "What exactly about a Dawn-Wing raises suspicion?"

"Dawn Wings were built specifically to extract troops from battlefields."

His silence felt heavy, like he wanted me to go on.

"It's the way they're built," I continued, gesturing at the craft behind him. "Low body, no boarding ramp? Makes for a fast takeoff. And these days?" I locked eyes with him, my voice lowering. "Decommissioned Dawn-Wings are the perfect getaway ship. Especially for thieves."

He raised his eyebrows, then with a sigh, shifted his stance, watching me closely. *Studying* me.

"Alright, if you're so sure I'm a criminal, why aren't you alerting the authorities? What's stopping you?"

"I don't want trouble." I said steadily.

He narrowed his eyes. "Then what do you want?"

I lifted my chin, confident that I had the upper hand now.

"I don't want you docking here. You're obviously up to something illegal with that fake ID chip. There are good, innocent people working in this shipyard, and if the Union seizes you or your ship, we could all be in hot water."

I watched him as my words landed, trying my best to get a read on him. His gaze was cold and gave nothing away. He took a small but deliberate step forward. It took everything in me not to flinch. Backing down now would put me back at square one.

"Innocent, huh?" he grunted, still fixing me with an intrusive gaze, fully aware that he was unnerving me.

"I'm serious," I warned uncertainly. "I'll call the local officers—"

"No, you won't," he said, stepping even closer, catching me off guard. He took another step. He circled me slowly, looking me up and down.

My hands began to sweat as I glanced toward the station and realized just how isolated we were. Even if I screamed, it could take a full minute for anyone to reach us. A lot can happen in a minute.

"You're not going to call the Union's minions," he said, "for a number of reasons." His voice no longer came from behind me. I turned just in time to watch him amble over to his ship and slide the cargo door shut. "For one, your accent isn't Hadrinic. And that complexion, looks like you were born on a world with a colder climate than this. Elgo, or maybe Lukon?" He tapped a sequence on the door's keypad, locking it with a soft click. "Either way, you settled here at some point." He glanced back at me, waiting for a reaction.

"What are you getting at?" I shot back, hoping he wouldn't hear panic rising in my voice. His theory was too close for comfort.

His eyes made their way to my face, lingering over my features. "You're clearly intelligent," he said, then hesitated. "And you're… a decently pretty girl." His gaze moved down, taking in my frame in a way that made me feel exposed.

"Excuse me," I started, but found I didn't know what to say. He locked eyes with me again.

"My point is," he said, smoothly drawing his blaster from its holster. My stomach clenched. "Smart, pretty girls like you don't settle on backwater planets like Hadrin. No, no." He turned the blaster sideways and ejected the ion cartridge, checking its charge. He wasn't pointing it at me, but the message was still clear. "Smart, pretty girls like you move to metropolitan planets. They become chancellors, or chancellors' wives, depending on just how smart versus how pretty they are."

"Seems reductive…" I muttered.

Ignoring me, he slid the cartridge back into place with a snap, holstering the weapon, and meeting my gaze. "So, I have to ask myself, what's a smart, pretty girl like you doing in a place like this, unless she's…" He trailed off, letting the silence stretch as he gathered his final conclusion.

"Unless what?" I asked, voice even despite the knot tightening in my stomach.

He gave a casual shrug. "Unless she's hiding out."

Shit. He sounded so sure. *Too* sure. I tried not to react, but he searched my eyes, as if I might confirm his suspicion somehow. My heart pounded, and I forced myself to keep still as he stepped closer, looking down at me.

"I'm willing to bet that you're hiding out from the Union," he continued, his voice cooler than the ice rings of Kelemer. "You'd probably prefer to keep their questions to a minimum. That's why you haven't called them. And that's why you're going to let me walk out of here without a fuss." He closed the gap between us, his presence filling my personal space. I could smell the leather accents on his flight vest, and the faint musky scent of ship fuel that clung to him.

I had to hand it to him. He was *good.*

My finger hovered, trembling over the screen on my scanner. I didn't want to log his false credentials. I didn't want to put myself and the rest of my shift at risk. I *really* didn't want to lose this standoff.

"What will it be?" he asked. He framed it as a question, but I saw the smug look in his eye. He knew he had me.

I tapped the prompt on my screen, validating his credentials, and showed him the confirmation for good measure.

"Well, have a terrible stay on Hadrin, Mr. Kad Rand."

He searched my eyes, as if recognizing the unspoken agreement between us. His mouth curled into an arrogant smile of satisfaction, and it took every ounce of restraint I had not to take a swing at him. He'd called my bluff, and he'd threatened me. I hated him.

3

―――――――――

AN OLD FRIEND

After work, I rushed to my tiny apartment a little faster than usual. Rego was already at the bar, and I was anxious to tell him about my unsettling encounter with the criminal pilot who'd threatened to turn me in to Union authorities. He deduced my situation well, but there was no way he actually knew my past. Only Rego knew about my past.

I quickly changed clothes at home. Employees of the Hadrin City shipyard weren't permitted to be seen in their work uniform inside of a drinking establishment. Rego and the other mechanics would already be there, as they had recently devised a ridiculous workaround that let them go straight to the bar without changing.

The oyzo shop I lived above was already catering to the dinner rush, slinging bowls of steamed grain and bottles of fermented oyzo alcohol. They were in the middle of steaming a fresh batch, forcing me through a cloud of the savory-smelling vapor as I descended the rickety metal stairs affixed to the side of the building. The steam clung to the fibers of my clothing, and I knew it was bound to catch dust as I walked.

A hoverbus zoomed past me, and I threw my sleeve over my mouth to avoid inhaling the swirl of dirt from its wake. The dust meter that morning had indicated that today was a "mask not necessary day." *Lies.* Whoever calibrated the meter was high off Tranq. Of all the planets in the galaxy I could have fled to, how had I managed to land on one of the worst? The unrelenting sun darkened my freckles and scorched my pale skin if I stayed outside too long.

I stepped into Hollak's bar, tracking dirt in with me. One truth about our planet was that if you ever lost your job, you could always find work sweeping out establishments that couldn't afford a sweeper bot. My ears adjusted to the rowdy din of the place. I would have preferred to rotate bars throughout the week, but Hollak's was the favorite of Rego and the other mechanics, so we were regulars. It was a dark and dingy joint, but the drinks were affordable.

I scanned the place, knowing the guys would be unfortunately easy to spot if they were wearing what I thought they were. Sure enough, I spotted five guys draped in plastic sitting around a table with a bottle of liquor and a drinking glass each. Sam, the newest mechanic, was among them. *No Rego. Where is he?*

Over the noise of the crowd, I could hear Delm explaining the brilliance of the plastic waste bags they all wore like ponchos.

"See Sam? So even though we're not supposed to wear our work clothes in a bar, with these plastic bags over us, no one can tell what we're wearing. We're totally in the clear!"

I shook my head and couldn't help but smile.

"You might not get written up, but you sure as hell look stupid." I said, walking up to the table.

The guys all smiled and raised their glasses to me, crinkling their plastic waste bag ponchos in unison. Delm nodded at the empty chair across from him with a sheepish grin.

"Fenn! We were just wondering when you'd turn up. Have a seat, if you're not still mad about earlier."

I gave his shoulder a brief squeeze, letting him know I had already let it go. He poured a shot of liquor into a glass and held it out to me.

"No thanks, Delm," I said. "I need a clear head right now." I considered adding that I had once seen him using that particular alcohol to strip rust off of a ship's hull, but I held my tongue.

"Ah, suit yourself." Delm tipped the shot into his own mouth and grimaced painfully.

"Hey, is Rego around?" I asked. Delm wiped his mouth and jerked his thumb toward the back of the bar.

"Yeah, he's talking business with someone."

"Really? Who?" I asked, scouring the place.

"Never seen him, but Rego says it's an old friend."

My eyebrows knit together in suspicious concern. After ten years of friendship, Rego Velaan was my best friend, and I was his. An *old friend* of Rego's was most likely someone he had worked with during his criminal days. My jaw tightened in irritation. *It's going to be one of those nights.*

"Thanks, Delm. See you later." I slapped him on the back and made my way toward the back of the bar, anxiously scanning tables and booths for my best friend.

The day I met Rego, he told me that he'd done a stint in a Union prison. He'd been working as a getaway pilot for an interstellar thieves guild when he got caught. Rego had an impressive getaway reputation before going away, so every few months, someone would come by Hollak's bar trying to recruit him for illegal work.

Rego told me he wanted to stay out of trouble, and definitely out of prison. I did not take this lightly. It was my mission to scare the scavengers away. Rego would always turn the jobs down, but he was too polite; sometimes they didn't take *no* for an answer. Over the years, I had poured drinks on people, cursed them out, and even threatened to call for Union officers. Anything to get them to leave Rego alone.

If the *old friend* talking to Rego was one of those, I was fully prepared for the usual confrontation.

I finally spotted Rego at a dimly lit table with a human man who had his back to me. He and Rego leaned across the table, probably speaking in hushed voices. Rego wasn't smiling. *Definitely an illegal job pitch.* I made my way across the room, but as I neared, I got a better view of the man with Rego. My boots skidded on the dirt-strewn floor as I stopped dead in my tracks.

Shit.

Dark hair, tan skin, and a forest-green flight vest. *Kad Rand,* according to his fake ID chip, was deep in conversation with the one person in the galaxy that I cared about. I decided to eavesdrop.

The table next to them was overflowing with people invested in a game of dwind. I eased up to the card game, pretended to watch the round being played. Keeping my back to Rego's table, I tilted my head and listened.

"I'm sorry. I can't help you," Rego said.

"Can't…or won't?"

"If it was just my help that you needed, I'd do it in a heartbeat. Unfortunately—"

"Rego," the pilot snapped, cutting him off, "after all we've been through?" Maybe he *was* an old friend.

I couldn't stop myself from stealing a quick glance at the pilot over my shoulder. It felt safe to assume he hadn't spotted me. His brown eyes were fixed intently on Rego, his glare cutting through the haze from the rusticane smokers in the corner. Letting my gaze linger, I noticed that the dim light over the table flattered him, obnoxiously accentuating the shadows of his jaw and cheekbones. *Stop it, Fenn. He's a jerk.*

"Look, Tor, I'm sorry, but it's a *no*," Rego insisted.

Tor?

"Dammit, Rego!" the pilot growled, slamming his hand on the table. "I'm trying to help you."

I'd heard enough. Whipping around, I slid into the booth seat next to Rego.

Tor, Kad, or whoever he was, sat upright, alerted by the sudden presence of what he thought was a stranger. We locked eyes, and when he recognized me, he slouched. "Shit." he muttered, leaning back against the booth.

"Oh, good, you remember me."

"The sketchy docking technician," he said. "How could I forget?"

He can't be serious.

"*I'm* the sketchy one?" I said, my eyebrows arching high. He smirked.

"Wait…" said Rego, looking between the two of us. "You know each other?"

"We met just this afternoon, didn't we, Mr. *Kad Rand*," I said.

He looked me in the eye and answered Rego without breaking our gaze. "She scanned my ship in." I resisted the urge to roll my eyes. He made it sound like I had done him a favor, and not that he had strong-armed me into it.

"Yeah, under threat," I said, gritting my teeth.

"I never threatened you," he said, like he believed it.

"Rego, who is this creep?" I asked without breaking my gaze.

"What are you, a Union investigator?" he asked.

"No, still just a docking tech, but I know a con man when I see one." I glanced at Rego. "He made me log him in with false credentials. Said he'd turn me in to the Union if I didn't. Now that I know he's with you…did you tell him anything about me?"

Rego lifted his hands innocently. "I would never! He's just really good at reading people."

I searched Rego's face, but I knew he was being honest. He would never betray my trust.

The pilot inhaled and casually rested his arm along the back of his booth seat. "So," he said, looking back and forth between Rego and I, "how do you two know each other? Is she your girl-friend, Reeg?"

Reeg? This jerk was on nickname basis with the most important person in my life, and I had never heard of him. *Who the hell is this guy?*

"Very funny." Rego said. "She's a friend."

"His *best* friend," I insisted.

Rego turned to me, lowering his voice. "Fenn, just go. I'll find you later."

"No. I don't trust this guy, and I'm not leaving until I know what he wants." He and Rego shared a glance that only people with a history would understand. Jealousy began to redden my cheeks. I fixed my gaze back on the pilot.

"What's your name?" I demanded.

He paused. "Kad Rand."

"Oh, like that's your real name," I said, lifting a brow and leaning across the table.

"It's the one I'm giving you." he growled, leaning right back at me with a scowl.

The hostility of it was so sudden, and it set Rego off. "*Torren!*" Rego hissed, warning him.

The stranger sat back, shooting an irritated glare at Rego. *Definitely his real name.*

I watched him for a second. *Torren.* The name fit somehow.

"So, *Torren...*" I taunted, resting easily back against the booth seat. "How do you know Rego?"

"I'm an old friend of Reeg's. One who's offering him something valuable. If he's not *stupid*, he'll take me up on it."

"What's the offer?" I asked. Torren glanced at Rego, silently asking if I could be trusted. Rego gave a nod. Torren leaned in, dropping his voice.

"I assume you're familiar with the planet Talar?" he asked.

My eyes met Rego's, and I shifted in my seat. "I know Talar," I said. "Small forest planet in the Laigo system. Known for its mining industry."

"Well, it's very important that I get to Talar this week. The problem is, the Union has it on lockdown," he said. "Right now, the only ships permitted to land on Talar are those carrying Talarian natives, returning or visiting."

I'd heard of that ordinance. It had been instated earlier last year but no one seemed to know why. "So what do you want with Rego?" I asked.

"Basically," Rego interjected, "Torren here has a...business opportunity on Talar, but can't get there without a native Talarian on his ship. I very stupidly mentioned once that I had a friend from Talar. I don't know how he remembers these things."

"What's the opportunity?" I asked.

Torren glanced around for eavesdroppers, drumming his fingers on the table anxiously. I could tell he still didn't trust me. Real rich, considering he was the career criminal at the table.

"There is a piece of contraband hidden on Talar that a business associate of mine wants. It's all ready to go, I just need to retrieve and deliver it. The only hang-up is that—"

"That you need a native Talarian on your ship in order to get to it," I said.

"What I *need*," Torren said through his teeth, frustration

bleeding through his stony facade, "is for Rego to convince his Talarian friend to come with me so I can land on the planet."

"They won't," I said.

"And how would you know?" he asked, scowling.

"Because *I'm* his Talarian friend."

Torren paused, a glint of surprise registering for a mere moment before he blinked and returned to the stone-still face he'd had in the shipyard. I got the feeling he was dangerous to go up against in dwind or any other game that required bluffing. I'd seen him in action; this was a man who lied the way most people breathe.

"Tor, this is my friend Fenn," Rego spoke up.

Torren looked at me curiously, reassessing me. "So you're the one from Talar. Do you want to tell me a little more about that?" Torren asked.

"Not really." I said. Torren ignored my quip, but I saw the subtle eye roll. *Guess Mr. Stone Face shows emotions after all.* I watched him with a smirk and said nothing. The dynamic at the table was shifting in my favor. Now, Torren wanted answers from *me*.

4

ANYONE HIDDEN CAN BE FOUND

I GLANCED DOWN AT THE DRINK TORREN HAD PLOPPED DOWN IN front of me, my official invitation to the conversation. The amber-colored ale looked frothy and cool, but I didn't touch it. I didn't trust him, and I wanted my senses sharp.

"So," I said, "tell me more about this job so I can pretend to mull it over before telling you to get lost."

Torren stared at me with no trace of a reaction. *He's either soulless or has the thickest skin in the galaxy.*

"Okay, this is the idea," he said. "You fly to Talar with me, get me through the Union blockade with your ID. I locate this shipment and we leave Talar with it. My buyer will give me 6,000 credits once the payload is delivered, and I will split that sum with you and Rego."

"That's all?" I asked.

He nodded. "You just spend a week or so aboard my ship and you walk away with 3,000 credits." There was a hint of desperation in his voice so faint, I almost missed it.

I laughed and looked at Rego, but he was straight-faced and refused to meet my eye. He couldn't possibly be considering this, could he?

"Why do you get half, and Rego and I split a half?" I asked.

"Because this is my ship, my intel, and I'll be doing all the work. All I need you for is to flash your identification at the blockade," he said.

"3,000 isn't nothing," I said. "But Talar is locked down and most likely crawling with a heavy Union presence. I've spent the last ten years working hard to stay off the radar, I'm not throwing that all away now."

He scoffed, and I wanted to reach across the table and shove his drink onto his lap.

"Besides," I said. "Have you seen the news-wires? Someone robbed the Galactic Union museum on Lantos last month. They are going to be on even higher alert now than usual."

"I heard about that," Rego piped up. "Heard it might be the work of Free Sector."

Torren narrowed his eyes at me. "Free Sector's too busy surviving to plan heists," he muttered.

From everything I had heard, Free Sector lived without Union interference, but it wasn't an easy existence. They apparently spent much of their time fending off the marauders in the outer-brink territory. "But if Free Sector is the reigning theory, it helps us," Torren shrugged. "If the Union is busy monitoring the brink, they won't be looking too closely at us."

"It's still so risky," I said.

Rego stared down into his nearly untouched drink. Torren drummed his fingers on his own cup, no doubt trying to work out what angle might get me to accept. If he wouldn't take no for an answer, the conversation was finished.

"I'm sorry, but I don't need 3,000 credits that bad," I said. I gave Rego an apologetic shrug and stood up. I turned to leave the table, but before I could take a step, I heard Torren's voice over the din of the crowd.

"So you can afford to pass up 3,000. Good for you. The question is, can Rego?"

"Tor..." Rego warned, grumbling.

I stopped in my tracks, a cold sweat gracing my palms despite the heat in the bar. Turning slowly, I zeroed in on Rego, who was looking at Torren with pleading eyes. There was something in Torren's voice. He knew something that I didn't. Something big.

Stiffly, I returned to the table, dropping into the seat and staring at Torren. He met my gaze head on. I glanced at Rego, and for the first time ever, my best friend couldn't even look at me.

I didn't know which of them I was more upset with.

"What do you mean?" I asked Torren. I stared him down, but he was looking at Rego.

"Do you want to tell her or should I?" Torren asked.

Rego sighed and looked up nervously from the table. "There's...a small price on my head," he admitted in a soft voice.

I stared at him dumbly, my mouth dropping open as the meaning of the words solidified for me.

"I..." Rego struggled. "I owe an outstanding debt to the Hacks."

I was still speechless. The Hackal clan was a family-run crime syndicate, notorious for being the most ruthless in the galaxy. I floundered, opening and closing my mouth, desperate for words I couldn't find. *There's a bounty out on Rego?* It had to be a mistake. Why would the Hackal clan be after someone like Rego?

"Rego used to smuggle for them," Torren said, a smug look on his face.

Dammit.

My eyes searched Torren's. He was trying to hide it, but his concern for Rego was melting through. *This is real. No mistake. No joke.* I grabbed my brimming cup of ale and began to chug, no longer wanting a clear head.

"Fenn," Rego whispered nervously, almost grabbing the cup from me before thinking better of it.

My best friend, the only friend I had in the galaxy, was in imminent danger, and everyone around us was laughing and drinking like everything was fine. I downed the entire drink. As I gulped, I noticed that Torren had leaned away from the table, choosing to remain a silent observer in the drama unfolding.

Once empty, I slammed the cup down on the table. Sucking in a deep breath, I steadied myself, then glared at Rego.

"Rego…" I said as calmly as I could. "I knew you had worked as a smuggler years ago but...the Hacks? *Everyone* knows better than to get involved with them."

"I didn't. Not when I was younger," Rego said sheepishly. "They paid well, and that was enough for me at the time. I didn't know that if you lose a shipment of theirs and can't pay for it, they'll have you killed. Can you believe that?"

"Oh, I can," I said. "I'm close to killing you myself."

Rego's face fell, his head lowering. My heart continued to pound, and I found myself glancing around the bar. An open bounty meant professional hunters. If the Hacks wanted you dead, you were dead. End of story. It was a miracle from Gryta that they hadn't found him yet.

When I glanced at Rego again, he looked so crestfallen that it stung my heart. It was clear that he didn't need any more berating. We needed solutions now.

"How long has the bounty been out?" I asked.

Rego cleared his throat. "Well, the initial bounty was posted years ago, but I dodged it long enough that it eventually stopped trending on the hunter's wire. Unfortunately, Torren saw my picture going around again earlier this week. Apparently I'm not as forgettable as I thought."

Torren leaned in, ready to rejoin the conversation. "The Hacks just had a regime change," he explained. "Whoever heads the family now must be following up on old business. Making sure their reputation for taking care of transgressors is upheld."

I sighed. Rego was fairly hidden here on Hadrin, but given enough time, anyone hidden could be found. Especially by a good bounty hunter, and the Hackal clan could certainly afford the best.

"How much do you owe?" I asked.

"The 3,000 credits from Tor's job would more than cover it." Rego shrugged. "It's a pretty small amount, all things considered, but more than I can come up with."

I looked at Torren, who was watching me with an aloof curiosity, waiting to see what I would do. *Bastard.* He was astute, I gave him that. From the moment I sat down, he had been assessing how close Rego and I were, and I'd stupidly shot my mouth off about being his best friend. Torren *knew* Rego was the way to get to me. I stared down at the table for a moment, taking stock of the situation. *I can't believe this man has managed to corner me twice in one day.*

"Look, Tor, I'll find another way to get out of it—" Rego said.

Torren began to protest, but I interrupted. "No," I said, drawing both of their gazes. Rego was taken aback, but a victorious satisfaction glowed in Torren's eyes. "Is it a long trip?" I asked.

"No," Torren said. "My ship can make it there in a matter of days." *Of course.* I had made the trip from Talar to Hadrin once, but it had been so long ago, I'd almost forgotten. I shook my head slowly, already regretting the decision I was making.

"I'll do it," I said.

If there was anything in the galaxy that could get me to risk my life and freedom, protecting Rego was it.

I noticed a satisfied glint in Torren's eye, and a smug expression on his stupid, handsome face. My hands curled into angry fists. I hated him. I hated myself too, for being attracted to him. For noticing the texture of his hair and the angle of his jaw while the person I cared about most was in danger.

I returned Torren's gaze as coldly as I could. "When do we leave?"

5

I'D RATHER JUMP OUT AN AIRLOCK

I worried at first that Giil, the shipyard manager, wouldn't believe me when I said I had to miss some work due to a family emergency. The urgency in my voice must have been convincing. After all, it was technically true—Rego was my family, and this was definitely an emergency.

I stood in the shipyard, feeling strange to be at my workplace without my technician uniform on. Torren hadn't told me how to dress for the trip, so I had pulled an outfit together that was similar to what he had arrived in. I had on a simple shirt, dark pants, and a charcoal-colored utility jacket with plenty of pockets. I wore a pair of sturdy, mid-calf boots that were thick-soled and waterproof.

Gripping the strap of a canvas bag slung over my shoulder, I shifted my weight anxiously. Torren circled the ship, methodically checked the engines and compressors. I found his attention to detail comforting. His ship might be banged up, but he at least looked like he knew what he was doing.

Rego stood before me in his mechanic's gear, watching me with an apologetic brow. "You don't have to go, you know," he said, gesturing at Dawn Wing. "There's still time to—"

"To what?" I cut him off. "Back out? Fine. I didn't want to help you anyway," I said with a teasing smile.

His shoulders rounded as he looked down and kicked up dust from the yard. "I just feel bad. You shouldn't be dragged into my mess."

"No one is dragging me, Rego. You're my best friend," I assured him, playfully punching his shoulder to distract from the earnestness of my words. Rego and I weren't used to heavy conversations; we preferred to laugh. "Besides, I'll be perfectly fine," I said. "I went and bought a shock-blade in case I run into trouble." Flexing my foot, I felt the small weapon pressed between my ankle and my boot.

Torren opened the access door on the side of the ship, disappearing into the cargo hold.

"And you're sure I can trust him?" I asked.

Torren started the ignition sequence and the engines thrummed to life, blowing warm air over me like a breath.

"Tor is a good guy," Rego insisted, raising his voice to compete with the engines. "I think you two got off on the wrong foot, but you're more alike than you know."

Torren and I? Alike?

"I highly doubt that," I said, my eyebrows raised.

"This trip might actually be good for you," he said, "You can get off Hadrin for a bit and really stretch your legs, you know? *Live* for once."

The legs in question were still sore from crouching for too long in the lavatory stall the day before.

"I'm not really a *live life* person, Rego. I survive."

"That's a shame," he said.

I was thankful that the volume of Torren's ship engines filled the silent moment between us. I didn't know how to tell Rego he was wrong.

He shrugged. "In any case, don't worry about Tor. I trust him with my life."

I nodded emphatically. "Well, that's good. Your life is quite literally in his hands right now. Mine too."

"I'm serious," he squeezed my shoulder reassuringly. "He'll keep you safe."

"What do you mean?" I asked. I believed Rego, but it was hard to reconcile his admiration for the man who had threatened to turn me over to the Galactic Union just yesterday.

"What I mean is..." Rego closed his mouth and looked at me pensively. *What is he not telling me?* "Torren is very good at what he does," he said, glancing back at the Dawn-Wing.

"What does he do, Rego?" I asked.

He searched my gaze for a moment, then bit his lip.

"You'd better go." he said, cocking his head toward the ship.

I turned stiffly, struck with a wave of new concerns. *Is Torren part of a crime syndicate? Is he a cold-blooded contract killer?* Anything seemed possible. Pushing through my apprehension, I walked to the ship's side-access door and looked back.

Rego gave me one last wave and a smile, and then hurried off. He disappeared from view behind a row of ships in the yard, pulling his mask and goggles on.

I offered a silent prayer to Gryta, if she was real, that everything would go according to plan. I prayed I'd be back here in a week to have a drink with Rego in our dingy little bar on our boring little planet.

I climbed into the cargo hold, pulling the access door shut behind me, then took a look around. The ship was small, the kind a single pilot could handle without a crew. *Probably the way someone as cold as Torren likes things.* The empty cargo hold was spacious for a ship of its class, larger than my small apartment. Wandering toward the back of the ship, I met a narrow hallway that led to what I guessed was two tiny bunk rooms. In between them was a compact galley and a slim door that I assumed led to a lavatory.

"Do you always stand in the middle of a walkway?" asked an impatient voice behind me.

Turning, I came face to face with Torren. He seemed to have just exited one of the bunkrooms.

"Sorry," I muttered, looking around for somewhere to move. I had expected awkward run-ins on a ship this small, just not before we had even taken off.

I flattened my back against the wall as Torren stepped through the narrow hallway, his chest brushing against mine as he squeezed past. The feeling of him pressed against me, even for an instant, sent an unexpected flutter through my stomach. *Get it together, Fenn.* After years of drinking at Hollak's with a bunch of sweaty mechanics, bumping elbows with grown men usually didn't faze me.

To be fair, I'd never been in such close quarters with someone who looked like Torren.

"You have your ID chip?" he called back to me as he strode toward the cockpit.

"Yes."

"And it says your planet of birth is Talar?"

"Of course," I said, annoyed we were going over this. Again.

"Then we're good to go; come on, Sketch." he said, beckoning me impatiently. *Sketch?*

"My name is Fenn," I said firmly.

"Yeah, but you're kind of sketchy." He trailed off and busied himself with reading the fuel gauge on the console.

A professional criminal thinks I'm the sketchy one? I exhaled through my nose, calming myself and deciding that it was a good thing he was kind of an ass. It balanced out his good looks, and it would keep my head clear during all the time we were about to spend alone together.

I stepped into the cockpit as he threw himself into the pilot's seat and secured the seat harness over his chest and shoulder with practiced ease.

"Buckle yourself in for takeoff," he said. "You can roam the ship once we're up there, not that there's much to see."

"I noticed."

"The galley is stocked with fresh water and basic packaged food rations," he continued. "Your bunk is the one to the left."

I nodded, removing my bag and harnessing myself into my seat.

"Hold onto that," he said, nodding at the bag on my lap. "Everything needs to be secured during take off."

"I can handle it," I said, gripping the bag tightly.

We sat in silence while he prepped the ship for takeoff. I watched his impassive face as he flipped on switches and checked the console's readouts. He was so calm and focused, as if he was the only person on the ship.

He must have sensed that I was staring at him, because he addressed me without looking up from the console. "Trying to figure me out?" he asked.

I made a mental note that he was also *very* perceptive. *Rego was right.*

"*Trying* is the keyword," I said bluntly. "Rego trusts you. I just hope that trust isn't misplaced."

Torren turned in his seat, his eyes blazing despite his stoic features.

"The only thing you need to worry about right now is getting us through the blockade at Talar," he said.

"That's right," I said, leaning back in my seat. "You *need* me. If I were you, I'd think twice about being so callous to the person whose help I needed." I watched him smugly, hoping to see him pause. I didn't expect him to laugh.

"First of all," he chuckled, "it's cute that you think you have leverage here, but I know you're going to do what I say. If you don't, Rego's head is on the line." I glared at him. "And second, I've worked with bounty hunters, mercenaries, and spies. If you want to threaten me, you'll have to do better than that."

I scowled at him, wanting to snap back, but my curiosity won out. "Spies?" I asked.

"I know you've been living in the slow lane here on Hadrin but yes, spies are real."

"I know that," I shot back. "I also know that if you were really as good at this as you say you are, you wouldn't shoot your mouth off to a near-stranger about it. Correct me if I'm wrong, but isn't discretion the most valuable form of currency in the criminal world? Besides currency?"

He faced front again, but shot me an appraising sideways glance and made an approving noise. "Okay, Sketch, maybe you know a thing or two."

The transmitter on the console crackled to life with Jera's voice.

"Alright, pilot, your Dawn-Wing is cleared for takeoff!" she said cheerily. She knew I was off work at the moment, but had no idea I was in the ship she was patching through to. A part of me couldn't wait to get back and tell her that I'd flown to Talar with the pilot she had drooled over.

Torren flipped a switch on his transmitter, his face lifting with a smile. "Received, I'll be on my way then. I hope to hear that sweet voice of yours the next time I pass through," he said.

All I heard was a giggle from Jera's end before Torren dropped the smile and switched the transmitter off. *My god, he really does know how to get people eating from the palm of his hand.*

He fired up the engine thrusters, then pressed on the helm, vertically lifting our ship upwards. My stomach dropped as we rose above the shipyard. I glanced out of the viewport at the climbing overhead view of Hadrin City. It looked even smaller than it had felt the last ten years. When we reached the altitude we needed, Torren pushed a heavy lever forward to pivot the direction of the thrusters and pushed us toward orbit.

Rego had taught me the basics of flying once. He showed me how to lift and move a ship, and actually let me move a few small vessels under his supervision. Until I jammed the landing gear on a brand new Passerin transport. The mechanics had banned me from boarding anything in the yard after that. I almost laughed out loud at the thought; I was certainly on board now.

Watching Torren, I admired how effortlessly he manned the helm while making all of the little adjustments he needed on the console. His hands were quick and dexterous, and a strand of his dark hair escaped from behind his ear and fell across his temple. *Why does he have to look so cute?*

The ship accelerated, and we shot toward the atmosphere with a steadier glide than most ships I'd seen leave the yard.

"You're a pretty good pilot," I acknowledged. A peace offering.

"You didn't know that?" he asked.

"Why would I?"

He was quiet as our ship continued to climb further from the city and higher into the air. He eventually gave me a sideways glance. "What did Rego tell you about me?"

"He said you're good at what you do, but refused to say exactly what that is," I told him.

He nodded, refocusing on the expanse of sky in front of us. "Good. That's about all that concerns you."

"For Gryta's sake…" I muttered. I don't know why I expected him to tell me anything more. *Mr. Kad Rand* hadn't been forthcoming once since I'd met him.

The ship began to travel through Hadrin's atmosphere, and the seat harness cut into my shoulders as the vessel pitched up and down in small shaky movements. Smaller ships get bounced around in the atmosphere as their engines fight the last pulls of planetary gravity. Torren's rig was much smaller than the one I'd flown in on years ago, and the incessant lurching made me sick to my stomach. I fixed my eyes on Torren, desperate to distract myself.

"You know," I said above the groan of creaking metal, my nails digging into the bag balanced on my lap. "If you're flying unsteady on purpose to disorient me or teach me some kind of lesson, I can assure you it's not necessary."

"Wow, I've never been accused of creating turbulence on purpose," he laughed. "Greez, you're really not good with people, are you?"

I wanted to tell him that I used to be good with people. That I used to be friendly—sweet, even, before things got bad. Hardening my voice, I opted to deflect before I could think too hard about it.

"I'm not good with people I don't trust, and I definitely don't trust you," I said. "In fact, I have a hard time picturing Rego even being friends with someone like you."

"Well, lucky for me, you're not here for your input." He glanced my way, making deliberate eye contact. "You're just here to show that ID. You're a prop and nothing more. Do you understand?"

My heart dropped into my stomach, and not from the turbulence. *Does he have to be so mean?* I had to get away from him.

"I see," I muttered. "Then since I'm just an object, I guess I'll go stow myself in my bunk room until I'm needed." I unbuckled my seat harness.

"Stay seated," he warned me. "We're not out of the atmosphere yet."

"Save the safety lecture," I said, slipping free of the harness and rising to my feet.

I threw the strap of my bag over my head and across my chest, then turned to leave the cockpit in a huff. My balance on the tilting flight deck was already precarious, and I was completely unprepared to handle the ship's sudden lurch beneath my feet. What little balance I had was lost, and my body pitched backwards. As I braced myself to hit the deck, something caught the collar of my jacket, keeping me half upright. Whipping a look back, I saw Torren had taken one hand off the helm and grabbed the scruff of my jacket to keep me from falling. He quickly turned his attention back toward the helm as the ship continued to rumble.

"Thanks..." I muttered through clenched teeth. I was embarrassed, but nonetheless grateful for his Kedigan-like reflexes. I moved to head to the back of the ship, but stopped when I realized he was still grasping my jacket.

"Not so fast," Torren said, pulling me back into the cockpit.

"Hey!" I protested, stumbling.

He ignored me, dragging me backwards until I collided with the console. He used his grasp on my jacket to push me into a seated position on the floor, then slipped his boot through the strap of my bag, bracing it against the metal panel behind me. The strap pulled tight across my chest, pinning me in place.

"What are you *doing*?" I yelled, pulling at the strap to no avail. I pressed my elbow against his heavy boot, but it didn't budge.

"Securing you," he said. "I told you, everything needs to be secured during take off."

"Well, *unsecure* me! This is ridiculous!" I shoved at his leg, but he didn't take his eyes off of the clouds we were barreling through. The bag strap cut painfully into my collarbone and I winced, still grappling with his firmly planted boot.

"This turbulence would throw you across the ship like a ragdoll," he muttered.

I knew turbulence was dangerous. I just didn't want to spend another second around him. I felt trapped and panicky, and thrashed my legs against the flight deck. Torren took his eyes off the viewport to watch me squirm. "Stop that," he said. "You'll hurt yourself."

I continued to try to break free, my animal instincts drowning out the logical part of my brain.

He fixed me with a stare. "Look at me," he said.

I didn't, focused instead on trying to slip free of my bag's strap.

Taking one hand off the helm, Torren leaned forward, hooking a finger under my chin and forcing my gaze up to meet his. "Sketch," he said in a softer voice, his brown eyes relaxed and sedate despite the groaning of the ship around us. "You're sitting there, or on my lap where I can hold onto you. What would you prefer?"

I stopped struggling and went still, glaring up at him coldly. "I'd rather jump out an airlock than sit on your lap."

"That's what I thought," he said, sitting back and focusing on the helm again. There was an amused smile on his face. I kept still, knowing we would clear the atmosphere at some point. I could wait it out. "Well, seeing as how I've got you here," he said. "I'd like to take this opportunity to get something dead straight with you."

"Yeah, what's that?"

"You don't have to like me, Fenn Kensie," he said. "I'm not even asking you to respect me, but you *will* listen to me when I give you an order on this ship. Are we clear?"

We locked eyes.

"Fine." I said, taking a breath and reminding myself that we had a common goal. We needed to work together. Also, on the floor, I was quite literally in no position to argue with him.

I adjusted my posture, hoping to lessen the pull of the bag strap across my chest. I waited. The rumbling ceased as we slipped into the vast openness of space. A multitude of white stars came into view, and the interior of the ship darkened and quieted all at once. *Thank Gryta.* Torren shut off the thrusters and put the ship into auto-cruise. He finally took his boot off of the console, releasing the strap of my bag. I scrambled to my feet with my head high and my shoulders back, desperate to regain my dignity.

Releasing his own seat harness, he stood up to face me with a glare so intense that it was difficult to endure. He must have seen the unwavering defiance in my eyes, because he relaxed his posture and softened his voice, trying a different angle. "Look, I'm not here to order you around like I'm on some power trip. It's for your own safety. I've been doing…" he searched for the word, "*all* of what we're about to do, for a long time. I'm good at it, and I will keep you out of harm's way *if* you listen to me. All I'm asking for is a little trust here, Sketch."

He's good. Persuasive. I took a deep breath, feeling my own body relax. "Alright," I muttered.

He sat back down and began setting a course on the ship's navigation. "Just do what I say, when I say it, then we can get through this and part ways. In fact, when this job is over and done with, we should agree to never cross paths again."

"Oh, I'd love nothing more," I said. "Glad we can agree on something."

He grunted and continued punching in coordinates. Thick silence lingered.

Feeling dismissed, I turned and left the cockpit, stomping through the cargo hold and to my bunk room at the back of the ship. The door slid shut behind me, and I threw myself onto the tiny bed, dropping my bag onto the floor with a sigh. Here I was, trapped on a ship, soon to be in the middle of space, with the most infuriating man I had ever met.

I pressed my fingers to my collarbone, which now felt sore from the force of the bag strap. I understood now firsthand why pilots wore padded flight vests. I rolled onto my back, and before I could think better of it, I was recalling how Torren's hand had felt under my chin. The way he'd softly drawn my face up and looked into my eyes. I recalled now that even through all my anger and resentment, it had felt...exciting. Definitely exciting enough to replay in my mind a few more times.

A sound outside of my room pulled me back to the present, and I realized it was the sound of Torren's boots approaching my door. I sat up, listening closely as he stood outside the door for half a minute. I wasn't sure, but I couldn't help but think he was trying to think of something to say. An apology, perhaps? For being so dismissive and imprisoning me with my own bag? After a while, he walked away, heading back to the cockpit.

As my head cooled, I thought again about his finger under my chin. Those deep brown eyes. I shook my head as if to clear it. It was the sudden change in my routine that was throwing me off.

I was in a new place, soon to be far from home and my best friend. *Of course* I was having weird thoughts.

I flopped back onto the bed. "This better be worth the trouble," I said softly to myself.

52

6

WHAT ARE YOU HIDING?

I SPENT THE ENTIRE FIRST DAY OF THE TRIP HIDING OUT IN MY bunk room, figuring that the less Torren and I interacted, the better. I readied a set of biting responses in the event that he tried to come talk to me, but to my satisfaction, and a little bit of disappointment, he never did.

Eventually, hunger set in, so I crept from my room to the ship's galley to see what kind of packaged rations Torren had stocked. The first drawer I opened held nothing but a flashlight and some kitchen shears. Upon further searching, I found some protein blocks and canisters of water. I searched for powdered kolo, but there was none on board that I could find. The only stim-beverage Torren had was kelp tea from the ocean planet Okea.

I scoffed out loud in the tiny galley and shook my head. *Who doesn't drink kolo?* Most adults I knew couldn't get through a morning without a cup of high kolo to wake them up.

I spent the rest of my time in my bunk acquainting myself with the shock-blade I had brought. If I was going to have it, I needed to know how to use it. Shock-blades were generally used as non-lethal self-defense weapons, more for deterring attackers than causing harm. The blade was shorter than a classic knife, more like the blade of a med scalpel. There was a button on the handle that discharged a jolt of electricity that could render someone unconscious. I didn't relish the thought of stabbing and shocking someone, but I would rather be prepared than dead.

It took some time to get used to the feeling and weight of the small weapon in my hand, but by the second day, I felt confident that I could wield it safely and effectively. I was sitting on the edge of my bed practicing defensive strikes when the small speaker on the ceiling of my room crackled. Torren's voice patched through, invading the only space I had all to myself.

"Come to the cockpit when you get a minute," he said flatly. The speaker clicked and went dead again. No discussion. Just an order. I groaned, remembering that I had agreed to follow his orders while aboard his ship.

I sighed and retracted the blade back into its handle, then slipped it into my boot. Dragging myself to the cockpit, I dropped into the copilot's seat and waited.

He glanced at me as if he hadn't expected me to have come the first time he asked. "Give me just a second," he said, tapping at the console.

I studied his pensive face and set jaw. If he wasn't so cold, the man could probably cruise the galaxy getting *anything* he wanted from *anyone. A little bit of charm with those looks? He could run an outer-brink planet if he wanted to.*

"Okay," he said, finally looking my way. "We're making a small detour."

"A detour?" I sat up.

"I have to drop something off on Laigo."

"Laigo?" I crossed my arms, wondering what could possibly need our attention enough to derail the plan. "This wasn't part of the deal," I said. "I agreed to fly with you to Talar. You said nothing about any detours."

"Relax," he said. "It'll only take a couple of hours from touch-down to takeoff. Besides, we need to refuel anyway."

I surreptitiously eyed the fuel gauge on his side of the console to see that we did indeed need fuel. I couldn't argue with that.

"Fine." I sighed.

"Get comfy," he said, gesturing at the seat I was in. "We'll be coming up on the planet shortly."

"Is that an order?" I snarked.

He ignored me. I thought about going back to my room just to be defiant, but realized I was interested in watching the planet come into view. I harnessed into the seat as a speck in the distance appeared. We continued towards it, and the globe of green and silver began to grow in size. Laigo was the most important planet in the center rim, its capitol city a bustling metropolis nearly one hundred times the size of Hadrin's. I had seen pictures of it on the vector-wire. It looked like the kind of place you could lose yourself in, for better or worse.

Our ship broke through the planet's atmosphere. I craned my neck to look down at the gargantuan city sprawling below. Out of the corner of my eye, I could see Torren watching me curiously. Hopping from planet to planet was probably routine for him, but this was the first new place I had seen in years.

"You really haven't been here before?" he asked.

"I was raised on Talar, then moved to Hadrin. I haven't been anywhere else," I said, scanning the terrain beneath us. "Embarrassing, I know."

"That's not embarrassing," he said, adjusting the ship's thrusters to account for the planet's gravity. "Many people never leave their homeworld. You're braver than most."

I held my tongue, not ready to admit that it was fear, not bravery that had inspired me to leave Talar.

We burst through a layer of clouds, gaining an aerial view of the city. It was stunning. I could see why people from all over the galaxy visited every year. I had seen some drab cities on the vector-wire, stark environments devoid of foliage. Laigo City was blossoming with lush greenery. Here, there were tall buildings standing next to giant trees of the same height, while the shorter buildings were covered in vines or moss. The seat harness cut into my shoulders as I leaned hard toward the viewport to take it all in.

"You can unharness," Torren said. "The turbulence is behind us." I looked at him, and saw no smirk on his face. *Is he...being nice?* Tentatively, I released myself from the seat and leaned forward, placing my hands gently on the console to look further out.

As he carefully eased the ship into a stream of air traffic meant for vessels of our size, I drank in the sights below. It was all so beautiful. There was more nature below me than I had seen in years, and it reminded me of home. I heard a high-pitched engine crying for attention, and a sleek red luxury ship whizzed past us at breakneck speed.

"Woah!" I turned in my seat to catch a glimpse of it. "A Tanager Dart? I've never seen one in person."

"You know your ships," Torren said.

"Believe me, it's against my will."

"How so?"

"It's just this game we play at the bar. We'll pit two ships against each other, then talk through a theoretical battle or race, debating the winners according to each ship's features and capabilities."

"Sounds fun," he said.

"It can be," I said. "But Rego will play all night if no one breaks it up." I rolled my eyes, but there was a smile on my face. It wasn't my favorite game, but Rego loved it, so I always paid attention. I wondered how he was doing, and I looked out the window to distract myself from the worry.

Running alongside our mid-air traffic stream were floating holoboards, hovering lazily in anti-grav fields, their neon surfaces pulsing with an array of advertisements. I ignored them for the most part, until a video began playing on the one ahead of us that grabbed my attention. The image showed a zoomed-out rendering of the planets in our galaxy. The transmitter on Torren's console crackled to life, and audio began playing. I knew the tech existed, but brands weren't allowed to push audio to your transmitter. The only entity permitted to do so was the Galactic Union itself.

A woman's bright, cheery voice filled the cockpit.

"*Enlist today!*" she said proudly.

"Here we go," Torren groaned.

"What?"

On the screen now was a row of armored Union Officers standing at attention, holding their weapons reverently as they looked out over a picturesque Laigan sunrise.

"Serve the galaxy, secure order, and protect your place in a united, prosperous universe!"

"Secure order?" I said in disbelief, glancing at Torren.

"Oh, is this your first Union propaganda?" he asked. "Lucky you."

I leaned forward, feeling sick to my stomach. Union officers terrorized the whole galaxy. I couldn't handle seeing them portrayed as conscientious heroes. The holoboard went blank before displaying an advertisement for a new brand of Ksaba juice just as our ship passed by it.

"That was disturbing," I muttered.

"Welcome to life under the pesking Galactic Union."

The next holoboard in our view was a news-wire, and since no audio was being patched in, I squinted to read the headline.

"They're still reporting on the Union's museum break-in," I said.

"Oh," said Torren. "Did they say what was taken?"

Circulating on the holoboard's screen was a video of a deep blue, semi-translucent orb. I recognized the famed gem instantly. It was one of the most well-known exhibits in the Galatic Union museum.

"Looks like someone stole the Egg of Arpax. They're asking for anyone with information to come forward."

"Good luck," Torren said. "That thing is probably long gone by now. Hey, we're coming up on the plaza if you want to see it."

I leaned forward, eager for a glimpse of the famous Laigo City Plaza. It was half park, half city center, and one of the most visited spots in the galaxy each year. I had always wanted to see it with my own eyes. The circular plaza was wide, with a lush carpet of grass. The space was dotted with benches and fountains and surrounded on its rim by large, ornate buildings. There were many citizens strolling around the plaza, at a glance, it seemed as if every upright species in our galaxy was represented.

As our ship passed over the plaza, I shook my head, stretching my neck to watch it all slip out of view behind us.

"You should get out of Hadrin," Torren said.

"Excuse me?"

"You're too smart for that unchallenging shipyard job of yours."

"Hey, that unchallenging shipyard job is *safe*."

"I'm serious," he said. "If you went into my line of work and came to a planet like this, you could make some serious credits on grifts."

I slowly sat back and harnessed myself in again. "Well, I can't leave Hadrin—Rego's there," I said. "Besides, I'm not a criminal."

He chuckled at me.

"What?" I snapped.

He exited the air traffic lane and slowed our speed. "I hate to break it to you, Sketch, but you're on the run from the Union and on an illegal job with me. You're *definitely* a criminal."

"You said this job was about picking up a shipment on Talar."

"Yes, an *illegal* shipment." He chuckled again.

I frowned and looked down at my boots. *This whole trip keeps getting worse.*

"Don't be so judgmental," Torren laughed. "Being a criminal by the Union's standards is hardly difficult to achieve, and it doesn't make someone bad. Hell, Rego went to a Union prison. Is he not the best person you know?"

I shrugged. He had a point.

Torren got on his transmitter and hailed the docking bay. When he transmitted his vessel number, the tech on the other end immediately gave him a docking assignment. None of the back and forth he and I had gone through the other day.

"Wait," I shouted. "That's *it*? They didn't even ask for your ID!"

"This city has over a hundred docking bays and shipyards. This is one of the few that doesn't ask you for your ID. Some kind of loophole. I didn't want to risk running into some insufferably persistent docking technician." He grinned and watched me for a reaction. I shook my head.

Torren piloted the ship to our allocated area and brought the vessel down gently. I'd never seen someone so competent at the helm. As the engines powered down, he unharnessed from the pilot's seat and stood up. "Alright, I'm going to request a fuel refill. It might take a little while. Then I'll come back here and grab some things I need for my business meeting."

He said he needed to drop something off. Now it was a business meeting? *What exactly are you up to?*

"Should I go with you?" I asked.

"It's a discreet meeting with some business partners, confidential. They wouldn't approve of the unexpected company," he said, adjusting his flight vest. "Just wait here. If you get bored, you can open a vector-wire on my tablet. There's some touristy stuff about the city you can read."

I thought about what I could possibly glean from going with him, versus what I could gather if I didn't. "Fine," I said, slouching down in my seat and grabbing his vector tablet from its sleeve on the console. I opened a vector-wire and was immediately greeted with location-targeted vectors about Laigo City's popular attractions.

Torren stepped out of the cockpit, but paused and rounded back. "Try not to touch anything. I mean it, Sketch." he said with a stern look.

I held my hands up defensively. "I get it. I won't touch anything." I said.

He searched my eyes, seemingly convinced by what he saw, and walked back to the cargo hold without another word. I resisted the urge to twist in my seat and watch him, instead scrolling on the tablet aimlessly. He opened the access door, hopped out, and shut it behind him. I craned my neck, peering out the viewport to watch him make his way toward the maintenance bay.

Once he was out of sight, I jumped into action. Dropping the tablet into my seat, I sprang up and went straight to the cargo hold. I didn't trust Torren for an instant, and this was possibly my one chance to snoop around and see what I could find out about him. I hurried to the galley and threw open a supply drawer, digging around until I pulled out the flashlight I had seen last night. Torren was hiding something, and I was going to find it.

I'd already inspected my bunk room, the galley, and the lavatory, so I went to Torren's bunk room door, hit the control panel, and stepped inside. His room was indistinguishable from my own, save for some storage bins. There were some clothes and an extra pair of boots in a locker, but otherwise, no personal belongings of any kind. *Strange. Doesn't he live on his ship?* If he did, he didn't seem to have any kind of life outside of his work. I checked the floors, knocked on the walls, and even stood on his bed to press on the ceiling in case he had a hidden panel up there. I found nothing, so I moved on.

I stalked to the cargo hold with urgency. It was now the only area I hadn't inspected, and the biggest one by far. I surveyed the various storage shelves and bins, then moved on to the panels of metal that made up the ceiling, walls and floor. There was too much space to cover quickly, and I wasn't sure how much time I had left. I needed a hack, something to speed up the process.

Scanning the room, I sighed in frustration, desperate to find dirt on Torren. If I had something I could hold over his head, it would give me a little leverage—or at the very least, I would know what I was actually dealing with here. *Dirt. Dirt. How do you find dirt on someone?*

I thought about the pollutant-screening module installed in the galley, and I froze. *It's not a crazy idea.* I assessed the flashlight in my hand, hoping the bulb was the same size as the one in the PS module.

Scurrying back to the galley, I approached the metal cube bolted to the narrow countertop. The module was a small, oven-looking unit that screened fresh food for unwanted oils, dirt, and other contaminants. I opened the end of the flashlight and unscrewed the bulb, setting it gently on the counter. Opening the module, I reached in, unscrewing the PS bulb carefully. It was the length of my forearm and made of milky blue, tinted glass. I fitted it into the flashlight and smiled when it screwed in neatly. *It's going to work.* If the bulb was built to reveal oils on food, it would certainly show oily fingerprints on metal.

I practically skipped to the front of the ship, where I searched the overhead console, found the switch I was looking for, and shut off the ship's interior lights. Striding to the center of the cargo hold, I held my improvised PS lamp up and peered around. There were no prints on the floors or ceiling, and the first two walls I checked were clean. I was about to give up, but as I held the bulb close to the wall on the other side of the lavatory, something caught my eye—a small, light blue oval glowing on the metal. Bringing the bulb closer, I traced more of them. There they were; Torren's fingerprints, accumulated over time in a rectangular pattern on what looked like a solid sheet of metal.

I knew exactly what I was looking at. Rego and the other mechanics found them sometimes during interior ship repairs.

"The smartest thing you can do when you find a smuggling compartment is to pretend that you didn't," Rego had told me once. It was good advice, but I wasn't about to follow it. I noted the placement of the print-marked rectangle on the wall, then rushed to the cockpit again and flipped the interior light back on. Returning to the wall, I inspected the metal closely. There was a barely visible seam that I otherwise would never have noticed. Gently setting the lamp on the floor, I put my hands on the panel and pressed. Nothing happened. I applied more weight to it, pressing inward until I heard a mechanical *click*. The panel popped away from the wall just half an inch. Enough for me to pry it open.

I looked at the ship's access door warily, but it was still closed. I wasn't sure when Torren would return, but this was probably the only chance I'd have to investigate. I reached for the panel of metal, and it swung toward me. There *was* a compartment inside.

There were a handful of items in the compartment, but my eyes went right to a small black case with a handle on it. *Torren, what are you hiding?* I released the case's lid, opening it with a flourish. Inside was a blue orb the size of my fist. It was glittery and semi-translucent, truly stunning to behold. I was so mesmerized by it that I barely heard the ship's door slide open behind me.

I glanced back. Torren stood in the doorway, his eyes fixed on me. *Well, there goes my secrecy.*

I thought I saw fury building behind his gaze, but he blinked, as if trying to appear casual and calm. I braced for him to yell at me, but he didn't say a word. He crossed the cargo hold with a restrained urgency, slowly closing the case's lid and pushing it to the back of the compartment. He glanced at me out of the corner of his eye, gauging my reaction to what I'd just found.

"Hey, that looks like..." I stopped short.

It didn't just look like it, it *was* The Egg of Arpax. The Union was instructing the entire galaxy to look for it, and here it was in Torren's cargo hold. I didn't know what I had expected to find in the compartment, maybe dark-market drugs or illegal weapons, but this was worse.

Finding it was one thing, but letting on that I recognized it was my mistake. Maybe Torren wasn't the thief, maybe he was just the middleman transporting the stolen Egg.

Glancing into the compartment again, I saw what looked like detonators. Every news-wire I'd read about the break-in said that the thieves had used detonators as a distraction. Everything Rego had told me about Torren suddenly clicked into place. He *was* good at what he did. He was a thief and a smuggler, and right now, he was holding on to one of the galaxy's biggest secrets.

Torren was eerily quiet, still watching me. The sudden danger of my situation plunged into my chest like a knife. I had stumbled upon an unfortunate truth, one that put me in danger. *Maybe I can play dumb?* He was too perceptive for that. He knew that I knew what I had just found.

I needed to run. I could see the open ship door in my peripheral vision, but I avoided looking at it. I smiled at him like there was nothing wrong, hoping to disarm him. He tilted his head, warning me.

I bolted.

He moved the second I did, having anticipated it. I had fear on my side, and made it to the doorway before him. Before I could jump out, he grabbed the collar of my jacket and yanked me back inside.

7

MEDDLING KILLED THE KEDIGAN

THE EGG OF ARPAX WAS NO MERE GEMSTONE. IT WAS A cherished antiquity the Froxian species had safeguarded throughout the many hardships they had faced. Two centuries prior, the Froxian's primary planet, Tropax, had died. Rivers turned to swampland, crops moldering to mud. The amphibian species had no choice but to abandon the system, moving inward and scattering themselves across the galaxy. Marauders had taken over the system in their absence, the abandoned planets ideal for conducting criminal activities.

Froxians were now a displaced people with no real home to speak of, their culture subsisting on half-remembered traditions and the occasional relic. The glittering Egg of Arpax had been enshrined by the culture's historians until a few years ago, when the Union had seized it. They'd stuck it in one of their museums, as an example of our galaxy's *recovered treasures*—really just proof of their ability to take whatever they wanted.

The jewel was even more stunning in person than on the newswire. Its black case loomed at the edge of my vision as Torren pushed me against the wall next to the open compartment door. He held his forearm against my throat, pinning me in place. I could still breathe, but his arm made it painful to move.

"Hey!" I protested. I gripped his forearm with both hands, trying in vain to ease it from my throat. I knew there was no way I could get to the shock-blade in my boot without him noticing. On second thought, I didn't want him to have a blade on hand. Not with the angry look I saw in his eye. "Well," I muttered, "Rego was dead wrong when he said I'd be safe with you." I hoped that mentioning Rego would buy me some goodwill, or at least remind Torren that *someone* would notice if I went missing.

Torren stared at the open compartment door, his face stone-still, as if thinking through his options. He was currently in the possession of the most wanted artifact in the galaxy. If he was smart, which I knew he was, he'd come to the conclusion that there was only one way to be sure that information didn't get out. My stomach dropped as I realized that I was quite literally at Torren's mercy, and that my life depended on where his morals fell on the scale.

Movement outside the open door caught my eye. There was a man walking past, a pilot by the looks of his flight vest, and he happened to glance into the cargo hold. He stopped when he saw us, and I thought about what he was seeing; an angry man physically threatening a woman. The pilot got a panicked look on his face, and he turned and hurried away. *Incredible. Thanks, man.* Torren's deep brown eyes finally flicked back toward me.

"Have you ever heard the phrase *meddling killed the Kedigan?*" he asked.

"Have *you* ever heard the phrase *get the hell off me?*" I snapped, hoping to disguise how scared I was.

He shook his head at me. "You really shouldn't have touched anything," he said with a hint of what sounded like regret. Eyeing the open compartment door again, his brows furrowed. "How did you—" He stopped, spotting the PS lamp I had rigged. His scowl eased and he shook his head.

"Clever. It's a shame you have no interest in a life of crime. You'd be great at it."

"Thanks," I breathed sarcastically.

"I came back because I saw the ship's lights cut out from the maintenance bay," he said. "Makes sense now."

I wanted to snap back at him, but his arm was starting to press against my windpipe, and I struggled to get a full breath.

He noticed, quickly dropping his arm from my throat. He planted his palm against the wall near my head as he towered over me, letting me know he was poised to grab me again if I tried to move. I coughed, then took a deep breath.

"So what happens next?" I asked. "I'm guessing you're going to off me and get rid of my body?"

His eyes met mine, his dark brows knitting together in an indignant scowl. "Oh greez, do you really think I would *kill* you?" he asked, his eyes narrowing. Was he that offended? There was a slight rasp in his voice, and he took a shallow breath.

"I don't know," I snapped. "I don't know you."

He shook his head. "I'm not—" He stopped, his gaze shifting to the wall behind me. His breath became short and labored. *What the hell?* He tried a few times to get a deep breath, but it seemed as if his lungs wouldn't allow it.

"What's happening?" I asked.

He ignored my question, reaching into his pocket with his free hand. He pulled out a small, metallic, disk-like object, a device I recognized was a Respirin cartridge. Usually used by people with some kind of lung condition. I felt a sting of pity for him, but it was soon replaced by the realization that he was vulnerable at that moment. I could make a break for it. *He might even be easy to knock down.*

I tensed, preparing to make a move, but he took his hand from the wall and gently grasped my shoulder, his breath wheezing loudly now. Since I was trapped again, I studied his face, and was surprised at how bad I felt that he looked...*scared*. He fumbled with the Respirin cartridge, tapping at the unlock button with a shaky thumb.

I don't know what moved me to do it, but I put my hand over his and pressed the button firmly, unlocking it for him. He brought it to his mouth and inhaled, the device emitting a blue light and a soft whirring noise as he breathed deeply. He closed his eyes and slowly let the breath out, the anxious look on his face dissolving.

"Are you...sick?" I asked.

He shook his head *no*, then gave a slight cough.

"Thanks for helping. This device is on its last legs, and the button sticks." He threw the cartridge back in his pocket.

"No problem," I mumbled, wondering if it was the last act of kindness I'd perform.

He dropped his hand from my shoulder and straightened his posture, looking at me as if nothing had happened.

"Where were we?" he asked.

"You were going to kill me?"

"Oh, for Gryta's sake, I'm not going to hurt you," he said. "I'm not a killer."

I rubbed my throat, slightly sore now from the pressure of his arm. "The news-wires said you killed two museum guards."

"They're lying," he said. "They don't want citizens like yourself idolizing the person who robbed them."

I considered it. It wasn't past our government to push false narratives. *Besides, Rego wouldn't have sent me off with someone that dangerous. Unless he didn't know...*

"Does Rego know you stole the—" His glare stopped me mid-sentence. "Does he know?" I asked.

He nodded stiffly, then gave a smile despite himself.

"Rego knows I'm a professional thief."

"Thief?" I asked. "A thief walks out of a shop with a vector tablet under their coat. You robbed the pesking Galactic Museum!"

He stole a quick glance over his shoulder before locking eyes with me. "I'm a damn good thief, alright? Will you keep your voice down?"

Rego had almost told me Torren's secret in the shipyard. *He's good at what he does.*

No shit.

"Look, I don't know your last name, I don't know where you're from," I said. "And you called it the moment we met—I'm hiding from them too, Torren. Your secret is safe with me. Can we just carry on with the job as planned?"

"No offense, but I'm going to need more than that to trust you, Sketch."

"Okay, then what do you want?"

He looked down, considering it a moment. "What I want," he said, leaning in, getting uncomfortably close, "is to know *your* secret. Why is the Union after you?"

I scowled at him, resenting the too-familiar way he looked down at me, and I shook my head. "Out of the question," I said. I had spent the last ten years pushing all thoughts of my past deep down into the dark recesses of my mind. *I would rather die here and now than take that trip down memory canyon.* I glared at him, refusing to answer.

Our tense silence was interrupted by a man's voice. "Is there a problem here?"

Torren and I looked over to see a Union officer standing next to the open door. *Shit.* The pilot who saw Torren threatening me had gone to get help. I appreciated the gesture, but Union officers were the last people you should summon if you wanted to be helped.

I swallowed, watching the officer assess us with a stern expression. He had on the shiny yellow armor and helmet that all Union officers wore. The Union called it gold, but everyone thought of it as yellow. *The color of cowards.* The officer held a heavy-looking plasma blaster in one hand, supporting the weight of it with his other one. Union officers were not to be taken lightly. Most of them were mean and overall unhelpful, but the really bad ones would beat you if you looked at them wrong.

Torren and I both instinctively straightened our postures as we turned to face him, and Torren subtly moved to block the officer's sightline to the smuggling compartment.

"No problem here officer," Torren said coolly. He kept his body language fluid and easy, but standing next to him, I could see his jaw was clenched.

The officer peered into the ship and looked around. "A pilot just reported a disturbance coming from this vessel. He says he saw a man and a woman fighting."

Torren and I glanced at each other. This was my opportunity. I knew I could say any number of things that would get me out of there and away from him. The downside was that it would leave Rego with the bounty still on his head, and the Hacks still hell-bent on getting their dues with interest.

Still, if I thought Torren might hurt me, outing him to the officer would give me immediate safety. The words were on my tongue, eager to spill out of my mouth. My palms began to sweat as I went back and forth in my head.

"Hello?" the officer shouted, furious that we failed to answer him. He moved to step up and into our ship.

"You're right," I said, taking a step forward, causing the officer to pause where he was. I could practically feel Torren tensing up beside me. "My husband and I were having an argument, but we resolved it." I glanced at Torren. "Haven't we, darling?"

Torren met my gaze, and one of his eyebrows twitched, but he nodded at the officer. "Yes, we're fine. Thank you for your concern, sir."

The officer gave us both a leery glance, apparently not convinced. *We need to sell this.* I moved closer to Torren and put my arm through his, curling my hand over his bicep. He was so warm to the touch.

Torren forced a smile and leaned in closer to me.

The officer looked me up and down, searching for any nervous behavior that might indicate I was in trouble. I smiled at him and prayed like hell he couldn't hear the way my heart was pounding.

"Alright. Keep it down," he said.

"We will, thank you."

The officer nodded dismissively before walking away. We waited until he was out of sight, and Torren and I both let out a shared breath of relief. He eyed me cautiously, then yanked the handle on the door, sliding it shut with a *clank* and sealing us inside.

"*Now* do you trust me?" I asked.

He let out a deep sigh and leaned against one of the cargo bins, still watching me. I got the sense that he wanted to believe me, but his line of work had taught him to be wary.

"You know how much Rego means to me. I'm not about to turn in the only other person in the galaxy who is trying to clear his bounty. I'll keep your secret about..." *Being the galaxy's most wanted.* "...you know."

He nodded slowly. "Okay," he said, finally seeming convinced.

"Great." I moved to head back to the cockpit, but as I passed him, he grabbed my wrist. I stopped and looked up at him.

"I'll take your word that you're game to follow through with this job as planned," he said, "but know that I plan to find out what it is you're hiding."

"Good luck with that," I said.

He let go of my wrist, and I headed for my seat. I wanted to get off of my feet, decompress, and try to shake off the stress of the last ten minutes.

"Let's go," Torren said behind me. I froze, slowly turning around. He began to unbuckle and remove his flight vest, setting it aside and opening a cargo compartment. He fastened a weapon holster around his hips and slid a silver blaster into it.

I blinked at Torren, still not understanding.

"I still have to make this drop," he said. "You're coming with me."

"Excuse me?" I asked. "Drop? I thought you had a business meeting."

"Oh, I think that song and dance is over by now, don't you?" he said, glancing at the smuggling compartment. He was here to hand the Egg off to someone.

"Okay, but why do you need me?"

"I trust that you don't want to turn me in," he said. "But I don't exactly trust you to stay on the ship alone without getting into more trouble." He smirked, crossing to the open compartment. I followed, watching him pull the black metal case out and checking that the Egg was still safely inside. He secured the case's lid and closed the smuggling compartment's door, effectively obscuring it once again.

The last thing he did was pull a long grey taurvid-leather coat out of a cargo compartment and shrug it on. I had seen thousands just like it, and figured that was its appeal to him. The grey coat would let him blend in more than his forest-green pilot's vest. "Come on, it's almost time for the hand off," he said.

If he was so secretive about his work, I didn't get why he

wanted me to be a part of it. "You're serious about me going with you?" I asked.

"Deadly."

I began to formulate an argument against him in my head, but I had nothing.

Torren slid the door open and gestured toward it with a jerk of his head. We exited the ship, and once he had secured the door, we were off. His hand gripped my arm, pulling me along with him. I was about to walk into the system's biggest city, with the galaxy's most wanted criminal.

Great.

8

ACT NATURAL

THE SIGHTS AND SOUNDS OF THE CITY HIT ME EVEN BEFORE WE
stepped out of the docking bay. Torren and I walked past a crew
of Cerocians. They were the largest, strongest sentient species
in the galaxy, and were loading heavy cargo containers onto a
ship with ease. They towered at least a foot and a half above
Torren, their thick, muscular limbs rippling. I knew it would be
rude to stare, so I tried not to, but I couldn't help but sneak a
glance as we passed. Their eyes were glassy and dark. Each one
of them had a configuration of small keratinous horns running
from their snouts to the tops of their heads. I noticed the
texture of their grey skin as we got close. Their dermis, I knew,
had evolved to withstand the scratchy rock and gravel of their
home planet. They were beautiful.

Torren led us out of the bay and onto the street. He gripped the
handle of the case firmly, the hand on my arm just as tight. I
quickly made peace with the fact that I was being dragged
along; I was seeing the city up close, and there were wonders
everywhere I looked. Wide streets of smooth, white stone were
lined by shops and restaurants. People bustled throughout the

sleek, clean avenues, unfazed by the glistening architecture around them. I took it all in, jealous of the grandiose setting. There was little beauty on Hadrin, where everything was function over form.

As evening settled over the city, its vibrant nightlife began to stir. The restaurants and bars flickered to life, their bright neon signs illuminating the walkways in a dazzling display of ambient color. The rich, savory scents from the oyzo shops drifted out onto the street, mixing with the lively bursts of laughter spilling from the bars. It was so tempting, so alive that for a brief moment, I lost myself in the atmosphere.

Torren led me through the streets at a brisk pace, stopping periodically for hoverbuses or to let groups of pedestrians pass us by. Though his touch had an odd way of reassuring me, his grip had begun to hurt.

"You can let go," I offered. "I'm not going anywhere."

He looked at me blankly for a moment, as if remembering I was there. It made me wonder just how many steps ahead of his tasks his mind moved.

"Stay close," he warned, his eyes ahead. "The city is beautiful, but not without hazards."

"Do you come here a lot?" I asked, my head buzzing from over-stimulation.

"I know my way around," he said, leaving it at that.

I watched him as we walked, noticing how desensitized he seemed to the sights around us. He had been to Laigo City more often than he wanted to let on.

Eventually, we stepped onto a long, winding promenade, leaving the hum of hover traffic behind. Low hedges lined the path, dotted with perfumed orchera blossoms, while the frosted street lamps above cast a gentle, dreamlike glow. The promenade was less crowded than the streets, and people strolled at an easier pace. In the distance, the sparkling city skyline stood like a jeweled backdrop. I found myself gazing in awe, wondering what it would be like to live in a place so beautifully alive with possibility.

"I need you to do something," Torren said, breaking the silence between us.

I hummed in reply, still mesmerized by the view.

"There are usually a couple of Union officers stationed ahead, and I'd like to avoid looking suspicious."

"Sorry, what are you asking me to do, Torren?"

His shoulders tensed. "For a start, don't use my name when we're in public."

"Sorry…*Kad*," I said.

He threw a glance behind us, then fixed his eyes on mine.

"Could you take my hand, or my arm?"

He wanted us to look like a couple. It was better than looking like a thief and his accomplice. I almost circled my arm around his, but remembered how it had felt when I'd done it in front of the officer earlier. It was too cozy for my taste.

"Fine. Give me your hand," I said quietly, reaching out.

When he curled his fingers between my own, I immediately regretted my choice.

The feeling of our hands clasped together was suddenly the most intimate thing I had experienced in years. I'd had a few flings on Hadrin, but nothing with a real connection. I swallowed, trying not to betray how affected I was by Torren's touch. His hand was warm, and softer than I'd expected, but still firm and strong, clearly accustomed to work. I could feel each finger, strong and dexterous, woven between mine.

"Just stay calm and act natural," Torren whispered.

As we walked, two yellow-armored Union officers came into view, standing illuminated under one of the street lamps. They eyed the pedestrians that walked past, the light glinting off the blasters in their hands. As we got closer, I saw that this pair had more advanced-looking equipment than the officers on Hadrin. Their helmets were sleeker and their guns bigger.

My palms began to sweat as we neared them. I felt embarrassed to be holding Torren's hand now, especially since his own palm was drier than the red deserts of Aridon. *How often does he do this kind of thing?* We neared the officers, our pace unchanged, trying to look casual. My heartbeat increased, and I took a deep inhale in a futile attempt to calm myself.

As we passed by the officers, I felt their eyes. Their armor clinked as they shifted in place, turning their heads to watch us. I tensed up, all of my muscles stiffening in fear. Torren had to have felt it in my grip. He brushed his thumb over my knuckles, and my heart nearly stopped. I flinched, involuntarily squeezing his hand as I fought for control of my nerves. He did it again, the action steady and sure. I wanted to look at him, but kept my gaze ahead.

Is he reassuring me, or was that for show? Whatever the reason, it worked. I took another breath and steadied myself. We left the officers behind as we headed down the walkway. When we had gotten far enough away, Torren flexed his fingers and dropped my hand. I let it fall to my side and shook it out.

"You okay?" he asked.

"Yeah," I said. "I'm just not accustomed to getting that close to Union officers. I avoid the ones on Hadrin as much as I can."

"You did great," he said. "We're almost through this. The drop point is just up ahead."

We continued down the promenade in silence. I let my nerves return to normal, and flexed my hand, which now felt cold in the absence of his.

We came to a small structure at the edge of the walkway.

"That's it," he said, jutting his chin toward it.

As we drew closer, I read its neon sign and realized that it was a kolo stand. The rich scent of freshly roasted kolo wafted through the air, making my mouth water. The kolo on Hadrin was passable, and sometimes even decent, but it was never fresh. The small building was sleek and white, with a large oval serving window. On either side of the stand, patios extended from the main walkway, each holding several small groupings of tables and chairs. Most of the tables were full of people sipping their hot drinks and enjoying the evening.

"Do you drink kolo?" Torren asked. His eyes cast around, his body rigid and ready. I suspected it would stay that way until the drop was over.

"*Everyone* drinks kolo," I said.

"Not the Ocephans."

He was right—Ocephans drank nothing but salt water. But since Ocephans rarely left the ocean planets of their home system, they weren't usually factored into *everyone*. I got the feeling that Torren had visited the Okea system and had seen Ocephans in person.

We walked up to the window at the stand, where a female Kedigan was taking orders.

"Do you want high or low kolo?" he asked me.

I glanced at the simple menu. The high version was brewed from kolo beans, an energizing drink that got most of the galaxy through their mornings. Low kolo utilized the kolo plant's leaves, producing a drink with a calming effect.

"Um, low," I said, hoping to ease my nerves.

"One high, one low," he said to the Kedigan, and tapped a credit marker at the till.

The Kedigan poured two cups and handed them over with a smile so charming, it made me miss Jera for a moment.

What am I doing here?

Torren passed me one of the cups and jerked his head toward the tables, indicating that I should follow. We skirted a table where a lone girl sat. She had soft purple hair, and was utterly absorbed in her vector tablet. When we passed, she looked up, and I saw her notice Torren. I would have bet one hundred credits then and there that she was reading a romance chronicle, and that the swish of his long, dashing coat had caught her eye.

We stopped at an empty table, and I sat, setting my kolo carefully in front of me. Torren didn't join, instead scanning the area with a practiced gaze. I assumed he was plotting a quick escape route if things went sideways. Dropping into the seat across from me, he relaxed into a slouch.

"We're a little early. My contacts won't be here for a while."

I took a sip of my drink, letting it settle on my tongue. It was the best kolo I'd ever had. Now all the kolo on Hadrin was going to taste even worse by comparison. *This trip is ruining my life.* I noticed that Torren's hands were curled around his cup, but he didn't lift it once.

"You're not drinking?" I asked.

"I don't drink kolo," he said, turning in his seat to scan the promenade.

"You're weird."

I thought about his ship's galley, and how he had stocked kelp tea but no kolo. He really didn't drink it. The cup in his hand was just a prop, something to help him blend in.

As we sat in silence, I took in the beauty of the promenade. Everything was so clean and aesthetically pleasing. The lamps along the walkway slowly shifted in unison from soft white to a warm pink.

"I can't believe I'm here," I said

Torren twisted to face me, fixing his intense brown eyes on mine.

"Why *are* you here?" he asked. "I mean, I know you and Rego are close, but I'm surprised you actually agreed to come."

"Rego saved me," I murmured, dropping my gaze to the steam rising from my cup.

He raised a curious eyebrow and waited.

"When I was fourteen, about a decade ago now. I landed on Hadrin with no belongings and less than twenty credits to my name. I was so lost; I didn't even know how to exit the shipyard."

"The one you work at now?" he asked.

"Unfortunately, yes," I chuckled. "One of the shipyard mechanics saw me wandering around looking completely hopeless. It was Rego. I should have been more scared of him, as big as he is, but he had such a gentle energy." The corner of Torren's mouth twitched, a small smile forming against his will.

"He asked if I knew where I was going, or if I knew anyone there. When I told him I didn't, he laughed at me, then bought me a bowl of oyzo."

"Sounds like Rego," Torren said, the smile softening his expression.

"I was lucky. A fourteen-year-old girl lands all alone on a new planet, nowhere to go?"

I shrugged. "It could have gone poorly for me. I just happened to run into the kindest person in the galaxy," I said.

Torren nodded in agreement.

"Rego gave me the lay of the land on Hadrin, which areas were safe, and which ones to avoid. I think he was eighteen when we met? He had a boyfriend at the time, seemed like a sweet guy, but Rego kicked him out so I had a place to stay."

"That idiot always did put his friends' needs before his own," Torren mumbled, a spark of affection in his eyes.

"Always." I murmured. "He got me a job at the shipyard when I was old enough, and I eventually got my own place." I put my cup down and looked Torren in the eye. "I don't know where I might have ended up if it wasn't for Rego's big heart. I'll do whatever it takes to keep him safe."

Torren sat back, letting the story sink in. "You're loyal," he said. "In a way that's hard to find."

I didn't know how to respond, so I distracted myself with another sip of hot kolo.

"So how did *you* and Rego meet?" I asked.

He looked away, watching the promenade again.

"That's a story you're not getting." His voice was flat.

"Are you serious?" I sputtered. "I just told you the entire history of my friendship with Rego."

"I didn't ask for that," he said. "I simply asked why you were here."

"I thought we were making conversation," I said through half-gritted teeth.

"Weird assumption," he said dismissively.

This man is infuriating. I sat back against my chair with a huff and crossed my arms.

"You've got some *serious* walls up, you know that?"

"And you've got a temper," he said.

I uncrossed my arms slowly, but I knew I couldn't argue. People without tempers didn't throw bottles of Ksaba juice at their coworkers' heads. They didn't unharness during the middle of a bumpy flight just to spite someone. I was embarrassed, and felt the urge to deflect.

"So says the guy who had his arm at my throat earlier."

He nodded.

"I wasn't angry, I was trying to keep you from running off. But you're right, the force I used was over the line. I'm sorry."

I sat stunned. I hadn't expected him to agree, let alone apologize.

"Okay," Torren said, standing up. "It's time. I told my contacts that I would be alone, so I need you to stay here."

I looked around, but didn't see anyone approaching the kolo stand or the patio.

"This should be quick," he said. "Wait here until I come get you."

"Alright," I said.

He met my gaze with laser-focus. "You'll stay right here?"

"I said I would, didn't I, Tor—" I stopped myself. "*Kad?*"

"You also said you wouldn't touch anything on the ship either, Sketch." Torren leaned over the table towards me. "And we both know how that went."

I couldn't refute that. "I'll wait right here," I assured him.

He nodded, picking up the metal case and his cup of kolo and heading for an empty table a few yards away. I shifted my chair, scraping its feet on the patio surface, getting ready for the show. From this angle, I could pretend to focus on my drink but watch the transaction out of the corner of my eye. He placed his untouched kolo on the table and set the metal case on the ground between his boots, sitting down casually. I sighed to myself, waiting.

I was supposed to be on Hadrin, deciding what type of shitty alcohol to numb myself with after work. Now I was about to be an accessory in the illegal sale of a stolen artifact. I looked down into the cup between my hands and caught my reflection in the dark liquid. *So much for keeping my head down and staying out of trouble.*

9

THERE'S ALWAYS A WAY THROUGH

Torren sat calmly at his table, studying the people walking along the promenade. I was about to go back to my drink when three approaching figures caught my eye. Two human males and a reptilian Lesardin came ambling down the walkway. All three wore dark clothing made of taurvid leather, and there was something in the way they carried themselves that I immediately didn't like. The word *menacing* came to mind.

They stepped off the walkway and headed right for the kolo stand. I saw Torren take stock of them for a moment before looking away. The trio walked right past Torren and seated themselves at an empty table next to the purple-haired girl.

I brought my cup to my lips and drank, subtly watching them. The three of them sat around the table and immediately began cracking crass jokes. None of them looked twice at Torren, caring more about their banter than anyone else on the patio.

The other kolo patrons shot wary glances at the increasingly rowdy trio. The girl who was reading glanced up from her tablet and quickly went back to her screen, shifting nervously in her seat. From what I understood, it took quite a lot to rattle the inhabitants of big cities, but everyone was uncomfortable now.

The taller of the human men was pale and gangly with long black hair, slick with grease. The Lesardin was female, based on her dark green scale coloring. She had orange eyes with dark slitted pupils. She scraped her clawed finger against the tabletop absentmindedly while she spoke, scrawling deep grooves into the soft wood. The third one, a shorter human male, was the loudest of the bunch. He had spiky hair dyed the color of human blood and a scar across the side of his face, running from temple to cheekbone. All three of them had neon green stains on their fingertips and nail beds; common on those who smoked cheap synthetic rusticane sticks. The real rusticane was fairly safe to inhale, but the fake stuff could kill you if you overindulged. If these three didn't care about their own safety, they likely cared even less for the safety of others. Directing my gaze back to my cup of kolo, I remembered all the bar fights I had seen kick off because someone *looked* at someone else too long.

I glanced back at the promenade, wondering what was taking Torren's contacts so long to show up. As if on cue, two more figures slowly approached the kolo stand. Out of the corner of my eye, I saw Torren sit up. He tapped his foot against the metal case, reassuring himself it was still there. These *had* to be his buyers, but I hadn't expected them to look like this. The pair walking over were both Froxians, a male and a female. Older ones, judging by their slower pace and the way they hunched over. Their wide mouths were pensive, and their large amphibious eyes darted around anxiously.

I knew next to nothing about the criminal world, but I could tell these two were not seasoned crooks. They could be affluent artifact collectors, but looking at their clothing, they didn't appear to be rich. They approached Torren's table, and he gave them a nod as they sat down.

Froxians, of course. The Egg of Arpax rightfully belonged to their species. My heart sank as I realized that Torren was here to sell a relic back to the displaced culture the Union had seized it from.

"Bengax, Marax," Torren said politely. "I appreciate you meeting me here. I know it was out of your way."

"We understand," croaked the female, her words hardly above a whisper. "You wanted a secure location."

"You have the Egg?" the male asked.

"The *item* is right here," said Torren, his voice clipped.

"Before we begin…" the female hesitated, her eyes darting around the area. "We just wanted to thank you, on behalf of our organization. For getting the…item back."

I knew immediately what organization she meant—The Froxian Collective. They were dedicated to recovering Froxian artifacts from before they were forced to abandon their planets. Some of their most famous relics were in the hands of the Union, not likely to be relinquished anytime soon.

"I don't know who you think I am, but I did not procure the item. I am merely the messenger," Torren said, his voice stern.

Both Froxians gave an apologetic croak, their cheeks deepening in color.

"Though," Torren said with a softer voice, "I will be sure to pass your thanks along."

They bowed their heads in respectful appreciation.

Before I could hear anything else from their conversation, the murmur of a man's voice rang in my ear.

"I said *hi*. Are you going to ignore me?"

I looked to my left and saw the human with spiky hair staring at the purple-haired girl.

"What?" she asked, looking up from her tablet wide-eyed.

The spiky-haired man smirked. Warning sirens went off in my head. I had met guys like this back at Hollak's bar—they got bored easily and entertained themselves by bothering people. The poor girl just happened to be the nearest person sitting alone, making her an easy target.

The spiky-haired man pointed lazily at the cup on her table. "Is that high or low kolo?" he asked.

She sighed. I knew she didn't want to talk to him, but didn't want to provoke him either. To me, she looked eighteen or nineteen. I only had a few years on her age-wise, but all the time I'd spent working with grown men and drinking in a dingy bar had toughened me. She seemed sheltered. I envied her for it.

"It's high," she said flatly, hoping he would get the hint that she wanted to be left alone. I watched as she looked back down at her tablet, probably hoping that was the end of it.

It wasn't.

He stood up and walked over to her table, sitting down in the chair next to her.

"You waiting for someone? Looks like you got stood up," he drawled sarcastically.

Torren was still in conversation with the two Froxians.

"Well, I…" the girl stuttered. "I was about to leave." She looked like she wanted to grab her bag and dash, but she was frozen to her seat.

The spiky-haired man looked her up and down. "You look nervous," he said, glancing over at his buddies. The other man smirked, and the Lesardin tilted her reptilian head and blinked. "We're not making you nervous, are we? We didn't even do anything."

The other human man laughed like it was a joke. "You're such a pesking bastard, Spike," he said with a grin.

"Too good to talk to us? Is that it?" Spike sneered at the girl, encouraged by his friend.

I scanned the patio. Most people were too wrapped up in their own conversations to notice the girl being harassed. That, or they were purposefully keeping their eyes on their drinks, minding their business.

Great. This is the last thing I need right now.

"Hey!" I called out to Spike.

All three of their heads swiveled my way.

"Leave her alone," I said firmly. "She doesn't want to talk to you."

For a split second, I met the girl's eyes and saw her relief. Spike scoffed, stood up, and swaggered over to my table, completely dropping his attention on the purple-haired girl. The Lesardin and the other human followed him.

The girl grabbed her bag and slung it over her shoulder. She darted toward the walkway, disappearing from view just as Spike dropped into the chair next to mine. He stared at me with an amused look on his face.

"You trying to tell me what to do?" he asked. "That doesn't usually go well for people."

Up close, I saw just how jagged the scar on his face was. He leaned forward, resting an elbow on my table. His jacket fell open, and I caught a glimpse of a blaster holstered at his side. Blasters weren't outlawed on Laigo, so the concealed nature of his wasn't a good sign. It was either an illegal model, or his blaster rights had been revoked.

My nerves prickled as the other man and the Lesardin seated themselves comfortably beside him. I glanced at Torren, but kept it brief, not wanting to draw attention to him. There was no good scenario if they found out he had something of such high value in his hands. I cracked my knuckles anxiously. *I'm going to have to handle this myself.*

"Look, the three of you are very tough, I get it," I said, gesturing around the patio. "We all get it."

Spike narrowed his eyes at me, waiting to see what I was getting at.

"I'm sure you feel very powerful right now, but is intimidating the patrons of a kolo stand really a flex? Why don't the three of you hit up a dive bar on the rim of the city and see how you hold up against a *real* tough crowd?"

Spike sat back in his seat, exchanging a glance with his companions. They knew I was right.

"This part of town *is* a drag," the other human muttered. Spike cocked his head, as if actually considering moving their games somewhere else.

I glanced at the Lesardin, but saw she was no longer looking at me. Her eyes were now fixed on Torren and the two Froxians. I saw the amphibian couple handing him something small and rectangular. It had to be a credit marker, a portable payment method that the Union couldn't track.

Shit.

Lesardin were sharp, with excellent vision and hearing. I didn't like the odds of her picking up on the important deal happening over there. Spike and the other man noticed her focus had drifted and began to follow her gaze. I needed to draw their attention away from Torren. I needed their attention on me.

Clearing my throat, I offered a wry smile. "Actually, why don't the three of you go ahead and go to hell?"

That did it.

All three snapped their heads toward me. The surprised looks on their faces were so ridiculous, I would have laughed if the situation weren't so tense. Spike knocked my cup off the table, sending it flying to the ground. Kolo splattered everywhere before the cup bounced to a stop. The other patrons went quiet, nervously watching the sudden commotion.

Spike leaned toward me, getting so close that I began to lean away on instinct.

"Stupid girl. You think you're funny, don't you?" he asked, his eyes flickering with rage.

I flexed my foot, discreetly checking for the small shock-blade still in my boot. This was the second time tonight I needed it, but couldn't get to it. It was also the second time a man had threatened me, and it was quickly getting old. I made a decision to go for it, dropping one hand beneath the table and sliding it down my leg toward my boot.

Spike noticed the movement. He grabbed my wrist, yanking it back above the table. His grip was brutal, tightening so hard I could feel my pulse and see my fingers beginning to turn red. The pain was far worse than when Torren had grabbed me back on the ship. In that moment, I realized Torren had held back, probably doing his best not to hurt me. I winced as Spike twisted my hand, forcing sharp pressure on my wrist.

"Still think you're funny?" he asked. He twisted my hand again, and I clenched my teeth to avoid crying out. Before I could think of what to do next, a hand descended on Spike's shoulder. I heard the scrunch of Spike's leather jacket as the hand increased its grip. Torren was standing over us, his eyes dark.

"Let go of her," Torren said.

I glanced back at his table and saw the older couple were still seated, but now held the metal case between them. They watched us with worried faces.

"Or what?" Spike sneered, still holding my wrist.

Torren removed his hand from Spike's shoulder, slowly drawing it back to rest casually on the grip of his blaster. A warning. "Take your hand off her. *Now.*" He chose each word with deliberate precision, his eyes never leaving the red-haired man next to me.

Spike rolled his eyes, but conceded, unceremoniously dropping my wrist. He stood up, and his buddies followed his lead, all of their focus now on Torren. Spike reached into his jacket, resting his hand on his own weapon.

The crowd on the patio got the hint. They quickly vacated their tables and scurried away, down the walkway and out of sight. *City folks certainly know when to clear out.* Within moments, the patio had emptied. The kolo stand employees were hurriedly closing up the service window, and the two amphibians were still watching Torren.

Torren looked at the Froxians, then jerked his head toward the promenade. They bowed their heads at him and tottered away with the metal case clutched between them. Torren watched them go, making sure they got away safe before turning back to our dilemma. He wordlessly held his hand out to me, a lifeline I didn't think twice about taking.

I placed my hand in his and Torren pulled me to my feet, his face rigid. Once I was standing, he smoothly guided me behind him, his gaze tracking the three aggressors.

"There are Union officers posted just down that way." He jutted his chin toward the direction we'd come. "I suggest you let us leave now, without a struggle. One blaster shot and they'll be here in under a minute."

Spike scoffed at him. "You're bluffing."

"Would you like to find out?" He stared at them, unblinking and confident. The hand on his blaster steady and waiting.

Spike held Torren's gaze for a moment, but he took his hand off of his blaster and sat down. The other human and the Lesardin reluctantly joined him.

"You're lucky we're in range of Union goons," Spike growled.

"You're lucky I'm not putting a blaster hole in your face," Torren snapped. "See you around."

He pushed me in front of him, guiding us to the walkway.

I said nothing as he ushered me down the promenade. I glanced back at the patio, and the trio was watching us hurry away, their faces the picture of contempt.

Torren kept one hand on his holstered blaster and the other on my arm. "We should get off the walkway," he said through clenched teeth, once the gang was out of sight. He looked back to make sure we weren't being followed, then yanked me onto a smaller stone pathway that branched off to the right. "We'll get to the docking bay faster if we cut through the park."

The Laigo city park was surrounded by a stone wall about eight or nine feet high. There were four main entrances to it—I had seen them from above as we had flown over the city. This entrance was flanked by ornate stone pillars, and as we approached, I saw there was a waist-high metal gate barring the way in.

"It's closed?" I said.

Torren holstered his blaster, planted one hand on the top of the gate, and hopped smoothly over it. *Of course. Why did I think a locked gate would stop him?*

"Come on," he said, turning to me and holding both hands out.

I let him lift me by my waist and help me over it.

Inside, the park stretched out before us, an expanse of grass and trees divided by decorative stone paths. The stone walls softened the sounds of the city, and I noticed there were fewer lamps lining the walkway here. I didn't like the feeling of being so far from the safety of the promenade. We walked for a few minutes, and Torren must have felt confident we hadn't been followed, because he stopped.

"Are you okay?" he asked, looking me up and down. "How's your wrist?"

"I'm fine," I said.

He stepped closer, taking my hand and examining it. Brushing his thumb over my wrist and flipping it over, he turned my palm up to face him. His touch was surprisingly delicate for someone who'd had his arm against my throat just an hour earlier. I felt a buzz running through my hand and arm. He stood so close. My eyes unconsciously flickered over his tan neck and angular jaw, a soft heat sparking inside my chest.

"I said I'm fine," I repeated, whipping my hand out of his, my words coming out harsher than I had meant them.

Torren's eyes locked on mine for a moment, searching my expression.

"Just making sure you're alright," he said. "That guy was rough."

I shrugged. "I've survived worse."

Torren looked a little taken aback by that, knitting his brows together curiously. When I didn't elaborate, he nodded and jerked his head forward.

"Come on. This way back to the ship." He continued down the stone path in front of us, and I followed him, easily matching his pace. "What happened back there?" he asked. "Why were they so mad at you?"

"I told them to go to hell." I said.

He shook his head in surprise. "That was really stupid, Sketch, you know that?"

I'm not about to be scolded by the man whose ass I just saved. "Yeah well, the Lesardin was catching on to you, so I got their attention. You're welcome, by the way," I said.

He walked silently for a moment. "That was good thinking," he muttered, "But so reckless. Don't do it again. I can handle things."

I clenched my fists. Would it kill him to say thank you? Or admit that he's not the only one capable of problem-solving? I was so frustrated that I decided to take a shot at him. "So the Froxians have their Egg back," I said, "Which is good, but…"

"But what?" he snapped, sensing that an uninvited opinion was coming his way. He was walking faster now, and I found it difficult to keep up.

"Don't you feel bad about taking their money?" I asked.

"Excuse me?"

"The Egg rightfully belongs to the Froxian people. You just sold their own artifact back to them for a profit. I just want to know how you sleep at night."

Torren stopped walking and faced me. "You *really* don't know what you're talking about."

"Then enlighten me," I said.

He stared at me as if weighing what to say, then shook his head. "We don't have time for this. Come on."

We continued down the stone path in a tense silence. Eventually, the foliage on either side of us thinned and the path opened up onto a garden. Ahead of us was a half-lit body of water shimmering in the starlight. By the look of the sun lilies floating gracefully on its surface, it was some kind of tranquility pool. It was hexagonal in shape, with tiled walls and flat polished stones on the ground at its edges.

Our path met and merged into a stone bridge with a gentle arch that stretched across the water.

We stepped onto the bridge. We were making our way across when a noise behind us made us both jump and turn around. At first I saw only darkness, but movement caught my eye. A Lesardin stepped forward, green scales glinting in the dim lamplight.

She followed us.

Without a word, Torren took my arm and ushered me forward, continuing our way across the bridge. Two more figures materialized from the dark ahead of us. Spike and the greasy-haired man stepped onto the opposite end of the bridge, blocking our way. Spike stood tall, blaster in hand, a smug grin slowly spreading across his face. Glancing back, the Lesardin had stepped onto her end of the bridge. We were boxed in.

"Shit," I whispered.

Torren slowly drew his blaster out, holding it low and checking the fire settings with a measured composure. He returned the weapon to its holster, apparently not wanting to start a firefight just yet.

"Don't worry," he whispered, leaning close to me. "There's always a way through these things."

"Well, let me know when you find one," I said.

"Hey," he said in a reassuring voice before meeting my eye. "I've survived worse."

I thought back to what Rego had said before I'd boarded Torren's ship. *'He'll keep you safe.'*

As the gang closed in, I hoped that Rego was right.

10

IN CASE OF TROUBLE

THE TWO MEN IN FRONT OF US SLUNK CLOSER, SMIRKS ON THEIR faces. Torren shifted to stand nearer to me, putting one hand on my arm and making a show of resting his other hand on his blaster.

"What do you want?" Torren asked.

Spike gave him a coy smile. "After that little showdown back there, I was going to take the loss and move on," he said, looking past us toward the Lesardin. "But my associate there *swears* she saw that Froxian pair hand you a credit marker. That it looked like some kind of deal."

Torren's hand on my arm flexed. I thought I felt his pulse quicken, but it could have been mine. He let go, reaching into his pocket with careful movements, then pulled out the marker and tossed it to Spike.

"Take it," he said.

Spike caught it and handed it to the other human. He crossed his arms and tapped his blaster against his bicep, waiting.

The man smiled as he pressed the display tab on the side of the marker, but his face fell when he saw the amount. "300 credits?"

Spike looked at Torren in disbelief. "You're kidding me. That's all?"

I looked at Torren's stone face in utter confusion. The Egg was worth *thousands*.

Spike uncrossed his arms, tapping his blaster against his leg in agitation. I took mental stock of our situation. Torren had his blaster and I had a shock-blade. But there were three of them.

"Well," said Spike, "I suppose that explains why you were so quick to hand it over."

Torren nodded. "Keep it," he said, putting his arm around me. "We'll be on our way now." Torren moved as if about to push past them.

"Hold it!" Spike snarled.

Torren and I froze. I glanced behind us. The Lesardin lay her hands on the railings of the bridge. The way was blocked.

"We saw you hand off something valuable in exchange for money," he said. "I know you have more on you than this. I'm not going to ask again."

Shit. They think we're holding out on them.

Torren inched closer to me. It was a subtle movement, perhaps an unconscious one. Spike saw it. He swiveled his wrist, taking full aim at me instead. My breath caught in my chest.

"I told you I wasn't going to ask again, pretty boy, now hand over your credits or I'll paint the pavement with your girlfriend here." He leveled his eyes at me, his finger twitching near the trigger.

"I just did," Torren said through his teeth.

The gangly man leaned toward Spike. "We could try and track down the Froxians. See what they walked away with."

Beside me, Torren bristled. Spike kept his blaster on me and leaned towards his buddy. They whispered back and forth, weighing their next move. Deciding what to do with us. *Clack. Clack.* The Lesardin's claws drummed impatiently on the bridge's metal railing. *They'll attack. And if they win, they're going to kill us.* I leaned towards Torren, lowering my voice.

"Can you fight?" I whispered.

"Enough to stay alive," he shrugged. "Can you swim?"

"Enough to stay afloat," I shot him a look. "But—"

"Good," he nodded.

Reaching up, he shoved my shoulder. Hard. I slammed against the railing and toppled backwards over it. The goons shouted, and I saw Torren pull his blaster and take aim. The world disappeared as I plunged into the water.

The sound of rushing bubbles filled my ears. I was grateful to be away from the blasters, but the sudden rush of cold took my breath away. The water enveloped me, pooling into my clothes to kiss my skin. I flailed blindly, fighting to orient myself in the blue dark of the pool. I heard muffled shouting and muted chaos above me. Opening my eyes, I saw glimmering light. I swam. Breaking through the rippling surface, I inhaled, filling my lungs to the sounds of the chaos on the bridge. My feet touched the bottom of the pool, the water reaching my shoulders. I heard a grunt, and something hit the water next to me. A blaster. I recognized it as Torren's. I reached for it but disrupted the water, losing sight of it as it sank.

A groan of pain drew my attention to the scuffle. Spike lay on his back at one end of the bridge, eyes closed but fluttering. A stun blast had clipped him. At the center of the bridge, Torren was locked in a battle for control over a blaster with the other man. Both clung to the weapon, grunting as they each tried to wrestle it away from the other. The Lesardin watched them struggle, waiting for a moment to step in.

The men grappled, shifting positions. Torren's back was wide open and facing the Lesardin. She stalked toward him, brandishing her claws. Torren struggled for control of the blaster, concentrating only on the man in front of him.

Those claws will slice him to the bone.

Splashing awkwardly, I began an embarrassingly slow swim toward the bridge. I gripped one of the bars that supported the railing as the Lesardin strode past. I reached up, grabbing her ankle tightly. I pulled. She tripped, falling hard onto her front with a pained exhale. Both men looked back at the sound. Torren took advantage of the moment, letting go long enough to take a swing at the man's chin.

My view was interrupted by a scaly green head, the Lesardin turning to scowl at me. I shuffled my feet, slowly floating away from the bridge. She pulled herself up by the railing and then climbed over it, looking down into the water.

She's not coming in, is she?

Letting go of the railing, she dropped into the water below with a splash.

Shit.

She surfaced with a snarl. The orange slitted eyes were fixed on me. Water droplets bled from the tips of her razor-sharp claws as she took a step, moving towards me in the pool. The fear I'd felt from Spike's blaster was nothing compared to this. Panicked, I attempted to maneuver away from her and reach the place I'd seen Torren's blaster sink. I treaded water, feeling around the bottom of the pool with my foot. The Lesardin pushed through the water towards me. Her claws ready to strike. When she was an arm's length away, I gave up on trying to locate the weapon. I darted backwards right as she swiped, her claws slicing cleanly through the water in front of me.

I watched the seething reptile with wide eyes. She swiped again and I dodged it. Over her shoulder, I could see that the man had pinned Torren against the railing. He'd gotten his finger on the trigger and was attempting to point the muzzle under Torren's chin while Torren fought to keep it away. *If he takes Torren out, I'm next.*

I swam backwards, fear and adrenaline giving me an unexpected boost. My back collided with something solid. I'd reached the far edge of the pool. The Lesardin surged towards me, her needle claws backlit from the lamp over the bridge. I'd seen how easily they'd slivered through the wooden table back on the patio.

"Torren?" I called toward the bridge.

He looked my way. Letting go of the blaster entirely, he drove his elbow hard into the man's jaw. The man blinked once, dazed. Torren twisted the blaster from his attacker's hand and aimed the muzzle at his shoulder, pressing the trigger and sending a blue blast of stun energy right into him. The man crumpled, falling into a heap. Torren twisted around, leaning against the railing and aiming at the Lesardin. The weapon hummed again, ready to dispense a charge.

Even at a distance, I heard it *click* and power down. It was out of energy. He cursed and threw it aside. He stood over Spike, frantically searching the ground for the blaster he'd been holding when he'd been stunned.

I tore my eyes from Torren. The Lesardin was quickly closing the gap between us. I was an easy target in the water, but knew I might stand a chance on land. I braced my hands against the edge of the pool and hoisted myself up, scrambling to climb out. I crawled over the bed of gravel that surrounded the pool. I wasn't fast enough. When she grabbed my foot, I winced, bracing myself for pain. The leather of my boots was fortunately thick enough not to be pierced, but her grip was inescapable. I managed to grasp a handful of gravel before she dragged me back into the pool. I turned, flinging the rocks at her as hard as I could. She let go of my foot and raised her arms to shield her face.

"Torren!" I screamed.

Behind her, Torren gave up on finding Spike's blaster. He hastily ripped his coat off, then stepped up onto the bridge's railing and dove headfirst into the dark water. *There's no way he'll make it here in time.*

I lifted my foot and reached into my boot, my fingers wrapping around my shock-blade. By the time the Lesardin had lowered her arm, I had the blade flicked out. I readied myself to stab or slash. She waded closer, either oblivious or unbothered by the knife in my hand. Torren had been underwater for longer than I expected. *Probably looking for his blaster.*

She was on me. I raised my blade as she raised her claw, both of us ready to strike. I flinched as a loud yelp erupted from her throat. I watched in surprise as she jerked backwards and disappeared beneath the surface. Something had pulled her under.

Her head resurfaced with a shriek. She sailed to my left. By the way she thrashed, I could tell it wasn't of her own volition. She was being pushed. When she met the nearest wall, Torren burst from the water, slamming her against it. His hand was at her throat. He had to be an experienced swimmer, to get to us so quickly and push her away from me all in one breath. She flailed, coughing up water. It gave Torren a chance to grab her wrist, flip her around and pin her arm behind her.

She reached her free hand over her shoulder, swiping at him. He dipped his head away in time. Mostly. One of her claws clipped his chin, leaving a bright red scratch. She wasn't going to stop fighting, and he didn't have a weapon on him.

"Knife!" I yelled.

When he looked my way, I tossed him my shock-blade. He caught it by the handle and plunged the blade into her shoulder, pressing the shock button. Electricity crackled around the point of entry. Once she went limp and her eyes closed, Torren retracted the blade and let go. She slid, unconscious, into the water, the weight of her tail keeping her face-up. *Good.* I wanted her subdued, but I didn't want to see her drown. She drifted peacefully among the sun blossoms at the corner of the pool, like a painting of a heroine from some forgotten myth.

It was over. I let out a massive sigh of relief and found myself eyeing her buddies to make sure they were still out. Despite knowing we were safe, my body still trembled from adrenaline.

Torren swam over to me. He stood, putting his hands on my waist and examining me for injuries.

"Are you okay?" he asked, water dripping from his hair into his eyes.

"Never better," I said, hoping to hide how shaken I actually was.

"Sarcasm, that's good. It means you're not in shock." He pushed away from the wall and swam to the area his blaster had hit the water. "Wait there," he said. Taking a deep breath, he ducked beneath the surface, leaving me alone.

I shivered, less from the chilled breeze on my wet skin and more from the receding stress of the fight. It had all happened so fast, and I was still accepting the fact that we'd come away unharmed. Torren finally surfaced with a gasp, his blaster in his hand. He swam back to me and climbed out of the pool.

"Come on," he said, bracing himself and reaching for me.

I took his hands and he helped me out of the pool, pulling me to my feet on the grass. In the dim light of the streetlamp, I noticed how his soaked white shirt clung to his chest. The wet fabric was sheer, vaguely revealing the muscles of his shoulders and abdomen. I let my eyes linger.

"Are you sure you're alright?" he said, holding the back of his hand to my forehead and then reaching for my neck to check my pulse.

"I'm fine, I swear," I said, gently brushing his hand away and hoping he wouldn't notice that I was blushing.

"Sorry," he said. "The body can do weird things when it experiences fear."

A raspy breath escaped his lips, followed by a wheezing inhale. He headed toward the bridge and I followed, wringing out my wet hair. He picked up the coat he'd thrown off, pulling his Respirin cartridge out of a pocket. One deep inhale set his breathing even again. *Hell, I could use an assisted deep breath right about now.*

He held the dry coat out to me, and after a moment's hesitation, I took it. The chill biting through my wet clothes had overpowered my urge to appear tough. As I pulled it on, he smacked his blaster against the heel of his hand, seeing if it would power up despite having been submerged.

"I'll have to take it apart and clean it. Here, keep this handy," he said, passing me my shock-blade. "That'll be our only defense until we reach the ship."

I nodded, slipping it into my pocket.

"Where did you get the knife anyway?" he asked.

"I bought it on Hadrin before we left, in case of..." I paused, "trouble."

He nodded. I had a feeling he knew I'd brought it along to potentially use on him. Our dynamic had certainly shifted since the start of the trip.

"Let's go," he said. "Someone will have reported the blaster fire. Officers are probably on their way."

We made our way to the end of the bridge. I stepped over the unconscious men delicately, but Torren stopped and crouched next to Spike. He reached into the man's jacket, retrieving the credit marker and stowing it in his pocket. I had forgotten all about it in the excitement.

We hurried toward the park's exit, but I couldn't keep my curiosity contained. "You only charged the Froxians 300 credits?"

"I didn't charge them anything," he said, his stony expression back in place. "But they insisted on giving me something, *to cover my fuel costs,* apparently. I didn't have the heart to tell them that 300 wouldn't get you halfway to Pentelos from here."

I shook my head, wrapping my brain around the answer. "You

gave the Egg to the Froxians instead of selling it to some rich collector?" I asked.

He shrugged. "You said it yourself—selling an artifact to the people it belongs to? I'd prefer to sleep at night."

I glanced at him as we walked.

"I don't get you," I said.

"I know."

When we hopped over the gate at the exit, the city was just as we'd left it. I felt an immediate sense of safety now that we were back amongst the crowd. We stepped onto the busy street and merged with the foot traffic, aiming to blend in. A few people took note of our drenched state with confused looks, but Torren and I smiled awkwardly and kept going.

We neared an advertising holoboard, where a small group of people had gathered around the screen. As we passed it, I caught sight of a news-wire showing the glittering Egg of Arpax, followed by a shot showing the exterior of the Galactic Museum. The feed cut to a female news-dealer sitting across from a smartly-dressed man with grey hair.

"Inspector Markens," the woman said, "as the head of the Union's Security Division, what can you tell us about what you've discovered so far? I'm seeing reports that you have a lead on the unknown suspect, or suspects, in this case?"

I glanced at Torren to see if he was watching the feed as we walked. His eyes were ahead, but from the look on his face, he was listening closely.

"I cannot disclose much while the case is still open, but take a look at history. No one evades the Galactic Union for long."

We passed by the holoboard, and though I could no longer see Inspector Markens, his voice followed us down the street, snapping at our retreating heels.

"We have no shortage of manpower, and every resource in the galaxy at our disposal. Rest assured, we *will* catch the culprits, and deliver justice so swift, it will redefine the cost of defiance."

11

LET ME DO THE TALKING

THE NEXT FEW DAYS ON THE SHIP WITH TORREN WERE EASIER than the first. After Laigo, there was a tentative trust between us, and I didn't take it lightly. At one point, he headed to his bunk to grab some sleep, and asked me to watch the console for system malfunctions or approaching vessels. I settled into the pilot's seat, still warm from his body heat, and looked over the controls. I was beginning to see the allure of his life. It seemed a hell of a lot more freeing that working in a dusty shipyard.

The next morning I woke feeling rested, but more than ready to get off the cramped ship. I washed my face in the lavatory sink and made my way toward the cockpit, rebraiding my hair as I went.

"Morning, Sketch," Torren said when he heard my boots approaching.

"Are we close?" I asked, dropping into the copilot's chair and tying off my braid.

He studied the console. "Almost."

"Good."

Torren tapped a sequence into the console, and the ship continued on autopilot. He stood up and walked back into the cargo hold. "I have something for you," he called over his shoulder.

He retrieved a leather pack from a cargo shelf and pulled something out of its pocket. When he walked over to me and reached for my hand, I tensed up. I was getting used to his touch, but I didn't want him to know how much I was beginning to like it.

"Relax," he said, misreading my stiffness. He grasped my hand gently in his and began sliding something onto my finger. My stomach lurched when I realized it was a ring.

I yanked my hand away before he could finish, taking the ring off and inspecting it closely. Carved from reddish-brown wood, there was an intricate vine of tiny leaves etched into the length of the band.

"What is this?"

"We're married," he said. "If they ask at the Union blockade, that's our cover." He reached for my hand again.

"I can put a ring on without help, thank you," I said.

He held his hands away defensively and returned to the pilot's seat.

"Where'd you get this?" I asked, admiring the craftsmanship. I had to hand it to him; he'd done his research. Tree motifs and wooden jewelry were both customary on Talar.

"Don't worry about it," he said, refusing to elaborate.

I slid the ring over my knuckle and adjusted it in place, shocked to see it fit perfectly. "How did you know my ring size?" I asked.

"Luck?"

I narrowed my eyes at him, and he tapped something into the console.

"Okay, I sized you up that first night at the bar," he said, "the second you said that you were from Talar. I started planning our cover while you and Rego went back and forth about the bounty. I studied your hand and made an educated guess for the ring. Is that what you wanted to hear?" He turned back to what he was typing in.

"Creepy," I muttered, turning in my seat to face the console.

"Now, pay attention," he said, taking the ship off of autopilot and handling the helm once more. "We've been married for five years." He glanced at me, making sure I was listening. "We met on Laigo. You're a docking technician, and I'm an artisan wood-worker. Your parents didn't approve of me, but I proposed anyway. It was during the Festival of Gryta."

I nodded, mulling over my fictional life as the ship carried me closer and closer to my former one on Talar. "Why is my cover occupation the same as my real one? That's no fun."

"You need to be able to elaborate on your job if they ask you questions," he said.

"But *you* get a cover job? You're not a woodworker."

He sighed wearily. "I've been doing this a long time, I can handle a deep cover. The less you have to lie about, the better. Now, look at me. How long have we been married?" he asked, watching me, wanting an immediate answer.

"Five years," I said.

"Good," he said, the tightness in his jaw lessening.

"Are they really going to ask us questions that in-depth?"

"Hopefully, they just scan our ID chips and let us pass." He pulled a chip out of his jacket pocket and showed it to me. It was fake, but good—better than the one he had shown me on Hadrin. He'd updated the chip's issue date. The only reason I knew it was forged was because his picture was accompanied by my last name. Kad Kensie. *That was quick.* Unless he knew someone on Hadrin who forged ID chips, this was his own handiwork.

"You're certain this will pass?" I asked.

"They won't look that closely. All that matters is that *yours* checks out. It's why I needed a Talarian for this job and no one else." A beeping sound came from the console. Torren silenced it and peered out of the ship's viewport.

"Almost there," he whispered.

I leaned forward as our ship approached Talar. It was a small dot in the vast vacuum of space, its hazy white shape a ghost on my horizon. I felt a surprising tug at my heart. Talar was my entire childhood, my home, and I hadn't seen it in years. The closer we got, the more I could see of the thick verdant forests that covered most of the planet's surface. Those forests had been my playground, and the thought of seeing them again was overcoming me.

My nostalgia was interrupted by a sight that made my heart drop. A gigantic space barge sat in stasis over the planet.

The Union blockade.

An ugly block of metal dotted with observation ports and a hangar, the barge was the last thing in the immediate galaxy that I wanted to get near. I drew in a sharp inhale as Torren pressed on the helm and guided us toward it. There was an entire row of dormant pulse cannons running along the side of the vessel. With Talar on lockdown, they'd be monitoring incoming ships, and if we tried to land without clearance, they would most likely fire on us.

"They'll hail us when we get close," Torren said, gripping the helm harder, his knuckles going white.

I shifted uncomfortably in my seat as the risk of what we were doing hit me. I didn't notice my hands were shaking until Torren did. He glanced over, then took one hand off of the helm and placed it over mine. I thought he was comforting me at first, but he didn't squeeze my hand, he just held two fingers against my inner wrist. *Is he feeling my pulse? Assessing my nerves? Any normal person would have asked how I was feeling.*

"Stay calm," he said, withdrawing his hand.

"Because everything is going to be fine?" I asked.

"I can't promise that, but if your nerves are shot, this whole thing could go south really fast."

"What do we do if that happens?"

He pointed at a red dial under a hinged glass lid on the console.

"Then we punch our nova-drive and pray they don't catch us."

The fact that he had a nova-drive gave me a little comfort. If you could afford to install one on your ship, it gave your ion engines a quick boost that could put you miles away in the blink of an eye. They were good for getaways, but you had to be careful not to overdo it or your engines could burn out, leaving you dead in the water.

I hoped we wouldn't have to use it.

Ignoring the growing pit of fear in my stomach, I watched as Torren navigated our ship with a careful speed. Union gunners were notoriously trigger-happy, so we needed to be unmistakably compliant. When our ship was close enough for the barge to fill our viewport, the transmitter on the console beeped, and Torren flipped it on.

"This is Galactic Union Checkpoint S-54," a man's voice said. *"State your business or transmit your clearance code."*

Torren slowed our ship and switched on the inertial dampers, bringing us to a standstill. He pressed a button on the transmitter and spoke clearly. "Hello, we have a native Talarian onboard. Requesting permission to orbit and then land."

I held my breath, but no response came for a worrying amount of time. While we waited, I felt Torren looking at me, and I did my best to appear calm. We were so close to solving Rego's problem, but still seemed so far from it.

The voice came through again. *"Current security protocols require us to inspect your vessel. Have your ID chips ready and prepare to be boarded."*

"Received," Torren said, switching the transmitter off. He swore loudly and ran his hand through his tousled hair. I didn't recognize the language, but I'd spent enough time at Hollak's bar to know an expletive when I heard it.

"This wasn't factored into your plan?" I asked.

"I knew it was a possibility, but really hoped it wouldn't happen. Your job is about to get ten times harder." He unharnessed and stepped out of the cockpit. For the first time since I'd met him, Torren moved in a way that indicated a modicum of panic.

His breath became noticeably more shallow, accompanied by the wheezing sound from before. He pulled his Respirin cartridge out of his pocket, held it to his mouth and activated it, taking a deep breath.

"This is okay," he reassured himself. "We're prepared. Do you remember the cover I gave you?" He fixed me with a wide-eyed stare, and I nodded. His shoulders relaxed, and he glanced around the ship to make sure everything looked up to snuff. I got the feeling he wasn't nervous about getting through a Union inspection—he was nervous about getting through one with *me*.

A small shuttle exited the barge's hangar. As it sailed toward our ship, Torren grabbed my hand, rubbing his thumb over my fingers to make sure I was still wearing the wooden ring. I focused on deep breaths and tried to ease the worried lines I could feel in my forehead.

He turned toward me, looking me square in the eye. "Just stay calm and let me do the talking, unless they ask you a question directly."

"Okay." I bit my lip, glancing down and noticing that he too was now wearing a carved wooden ring that matched mine. I hadn't even seen him put it on.

The Union shuttle approached, and I tried to clear my mind and steady my hands, but my pulse was thundering in my ears. Torren ushered me into place, and we stood facing the access door on the side of the ship. At the sound of the shuttle's airlock sequence being completed, my body locked up, frozen with fear.

Torren leaned in toward me, his lips brushing my ear as he spoke.

"Can I hold you?" he whispered.

I stared at him, completely confused.

"It'll look good," he said, his eyes nervously darting back and forth between mine.

I was speechless, but there was no time to think, so I nodded warily. He put his arm around me right as the metallic door slid open with a loud hiss. I didn't have time to think about how good Torren's arm felt wrapped around my shoulders, because two Union officers stood in the open doorway. One of them stepped forward.

"Which one of you is the Talarian?" he demanded.

"That would be me," I said, lifting my hand awkwardly.

He held his hand out. "Identification chip?"

I held it out, and the officer shifted his blaster, pointing it up and resting it against his shoulder. He took my chip with his other hand and read it to himself, verifying my information before turning it over and studying it for signs of forgery. When it checked out, he nodded to himself and tapped it against a scanning device attached to his utility belt. The scanner dinged, and the officer looked at us once more.

"You're clear," he said, handing my chip back before lifting his gaze to Torren. "What is the nature of your association?" the officer asked, holding out his hand for Torren's chip.

Torren handed it to him slowly, making sure his ring was visible. "We're married," he said. The officer looked down at Torren's ID chip, and I held my breath. The man scanned it without any further inspection. *Torren was right—my ID was the one they cared about.*

Out of the corner of my eye, I could see Torren deftly reach into his pocket. He was activating the remote device that would spike the scanner and keep the fake ID from flagging. Torren would need to draw the officer's attention so he didn't see the glitch.

"Will this take long?" Torren asked at the right moment. Sure enough, the officer with the scanner looked up from the screen.

"It'll take as long as it takes," he snapped.

Torren nodded. The second officer watched us with a scowl, probably annoyed that he had to leave his post on the barge to come deal with us. The scanner dinged, and the first officer handed the chip back to Torren.

"How long have you two been married?" he asked.

"Five years," Torren and I said in unison.

"And what's your business on Talar?"

Torren looked at me, then gave my shoulder a subtle squeeze. He wanted *me* to answer.

I cleared my throat. "Just visiting home."

"How long are you intending to stay?"

"Two or three days? Is that right, darling?" Torren asked.

I nodded, leaning into him, more for comfort than for show. My nerves were grating on me, and I felt like I was going to be sick.

"You have family down there?" the officer asked.

"I did. Not anymore."

"Off-world?"

"Deceased," I said softly, my voice breaking. Torren looked my way, perhaps sensing that it wasn't a lie.

The officer nodded. "Your IDs are clear. We'll conduct a routine investigation of your transport, and if it checks out, you'll be free to make your way planet-side."

Torren and I stepped aside as the first officer strode past us. I assumed they were checking for undeclared passengers or illegal contraband, but when he began tapping on the bulkheads of the cargo hold, my stomach dropped. *They're looking for smuggling compartments.* My heart started racing, and I couldn't stop myself from glancing right at the hidden panel. Torren caught my eye and gave me a subtle shake of his head. I snapped my eyes away from the panel, and his arm tensed around me.

As the first officer moved back into the galley, the other one stayed behind to watch us, checking us for suspicious behavior. Torren pretended not to notice him, and turned to face me with an artificial smile. He stepped even closer and wrapped both arms around my waist. I leaned into him, hoping our illusion was good enough to get us through. My heart was beating faster and faster, and I was sure Torren could feel it. I couldn't tell how much of it came from the inspection, or how much from being held by him. My lungs felt tight and I struggled to fully inhale. What we were doing was incredibly risky; it would only take one slip up for this to all be over. If we were arrested, Rego's bounty would go unpaid and he would be found.

The second officer was still watching us. I felt myself getting dangerously close to panicking. The Egg of Arpax was gone, but there were still detonators inside the hidden compartment. By this point, distraction detonators were a widely known detail in the now-infamous Galactic Union Museum robbery.

My hands started to shake. I gripped Torren's jacket to steady myself. He could feel my anxiety rising, and he locked eyes with me, wordlessly urging me to calm down. I couldn't. This situation was too big, too impossible. The second officer surveyed us with eerie stillness, as the first officer rapped the knuckles of his armored glove on the bulkhead, getting closer and closer to the concealed detonators. Torren stared me down, cocking his head at me with a warning look that said *Don't*.

I couldn't help it. I glanced right at the hidden compartment again.

Torren grabbed my chin. Turning my face toward his, he leaned down, bringing his lips to mine. He kissed me. I understood the reason, so I didn't fight it. It was a distraction, for me, and for the officer watching us.

But as our lips touched, the world fell away. For a moment, nothing existed but him. What was supposed to be an act of deception suddenly felt so...honest. *Does he feel this too, or am I having an anxious breakdown? It's adrenaline from the high-stress situation. Has to be.* That theory didn't explain why it *felt* so nice. It didn't dull the fact that he smelled and tasted so good.

Torren eventually pulled away, staring at my lips before looking into my eyes. His expression was confusing. There was *no* way he had been surprised by that kiss. He wasn't surprised by anything. The officer watching us rolled his eyes and looked away. He must have been satisfied that we were who we said we were, because he turned and watched his partner, who was now in the narrow hallway at the back of the ship, visually inspecting the galley and lavatory.

My body relaxed, thankful for a reprieve in the intense scrutiny. *They bought it. We did it.* Torren turned away from me and watched the officer, casually keeping one arm around my shoulders.

The first officer strode back into the cargo hold, and Torren and I stood up straight. "You're clear to go," the officer said, heading toward the door. His partner gave us one last leery glance before turning and following.

"Thank you," Torren said.

Both officers marched through the airlock, tipping their heads goodbye and returning to their shuttle. Torren and I stayed still, holding position until our ship's door slid shut behind them. We exhaled, our bodies still pressing against each other. We quickly pulled away and listened to the sounds of their shuttle detaching.

We made eye contact for a fraction of a second, but Torren looked away first, striding back over to the cockpit. I stood back for a while, still shaken by the ordeal. He sat, flipped the thruster ignition on, and harnessed himself in.

I slowly returned back to my seat, feeling awkward. "You didn't tell me we might have to *kiss*," I mumbled.

He drew a sharp intake of breath. "That wasn't a kiss. It was a cover."

"I see," I said, looking away in feigned indifference. I had completely imagined the electricity. *It was adrenaline after all.*

"Believe me, if I kissed you for real, you'd know it."

I raised my eyebrows. If that meteor shower of a kiss was fake, it had me wondering what a real one was like.

"You did great, by the way," he said, clearing his throat.

"Oh. Thanks."

"Not everyone can handle the pressure of undercover work. You stayed calm right in front of two Union officers. Well, until the end there."

I blinked, trying to process his compliment. I hadn't been calm *at all*. I must have held my act together well. *Old habits really do die hard.*

"That's good," I said.

"You could do this for real, you know."

"What?" I asked, watching him at the helm.

"Smuggling, thieving. Even spying." He cut me a look. "You have the instincts for it."

"Oh," I said dismissively, not wanting to continue with the subject.

I harnessed into the seat and stared ahead, but I saw Torren glance at me out of the corner of my eye. I got the feeling he was trying to figure *me* out now, the way I had with him the first day of the trip. He wouldn't be able to. He had his secrets, and I had mine.

He was guarded, but I was picking up plenty. For instance, the tiny wood shavings the same color as my ring that littered the floor of the cockpit by the pilot's seat. *He must have stayed up all night carving it.* I fidgeted with my ring, leaning back in my seat and watching as we entered the planet's atmosphere.

Home sweet home.

12

THIS WASN'T THE AGREEMENT

A vast blanket of white was the first thing I saw. If you were new to Talar, you could easily mistake it for snow. Torren had clearly done some amount of research, because he confidently flew the ship right into the sea of cloud cover so perpetually present around Talar. When we burst through the other side, the sky was dull and gray. Beads of rain pelted the glass viewport and streaked away as Torren scouted the terrain below. The landscape of Talar stretched out before us, a rocky expanse covered in large swathes of green, arrow-straight fir trees.

Torren circled a clearing and gently brought the ship down, sending the trees swaying from the force of the engine exhaust. He had mentioned that he didn't want to dock in a city shipyard if we didn't have to, and I hadn't argued. The fewer people we saw, the better. Though odds were astronomically low that anyone would recognize me around here, I didn't want to take the chance. He shut the thrusters off, then powered down the engine and unharnessed.

"I need to contact my buyer for the exact pickup coordinates," he said. He opened a storage locker near the pilot's seat and took out a black metallic box and telescopic antenna. "It'll take some time to set these up and put the signal through."

"I can do it," I blurted, eying the equipment.

"Are you sure?"

"I've put these up at the shipyard," I lied. I had never set up a comms antenna, but there were only two pieces. I knew I could figure it out. I was desperate for fresh air and a moment alone. I needed to regroup after the stress of the checkpoint and the excitement of the fake kiss.

"Alright then," he said, handing both objects to me. "Be careful with them, they're not mine."

"Got it," I nodded. The black box, what I assumed was a receiver, was heavy for its size. I cradled it against my chest and balanced the antenna against my shoulder. Torren walked me to the door and hit the pressure release mechanism above it. Outside air flooded into the cargo hold with a loud hiss. Sliding the access door open, he looked out.

"Can you climb?" he asked.

I nodded my head towards the Talarian fir trees now visible through the open ship door. "I climbed hundreds of those as a kid."

"Greez," he said, eyeing the scale of them. "Okay, there are maintenance handles to the fore of the engine there. Let me know when the antenna is in place."

As he strode back to the cockpit, I jumped out of the ship, stepping foot on my home planet for the first time in a decade.

The ground was carpeted with a thick layer of fallen fir needles, dampening the noise of the ship as it cooled down behind me. I went to work, climbing the maintenance handles like a ladder with only the receiver under my arm before going back for the antenna. My boots had little traction on the metal of the ship's roof, so I moved slowly, but got both pieces to the center of the vessel. The craft's exterior was still warm from its travel through the atmosphere. Folding down the tripod feet of the antenna, I fitted it into the receiver with a *click,* then banged on the ship's roof with my fist.

"Good to go!" I called, figuring he would tell me if it didn't work.

I looked around, making good use of my vantage point on the ship. The trees blotted out the distant landscape, but I saw smooth rock formations within the forest around us, grey boulders draped in moss and lichen. I inhaled, and the crisp, earthy scent of the Talarian forest hit me like an asteroid. Memories of my life on Talar came flooding back, all begging to be remembered.

I immediately pushed the thoughts away, forcing them to the back of my mind. They weren't all happy memories. *We just need to locate the shipment, get it on the ship, and we'll be out of here.*

Torren's voice cut through my daze, drifting out of the open ship door. I realized he was speaking with someone over the transmitter. I crept to the edge of the roof to listen.

"We made it through the security checkpoint," Torren said, "and landed without incident. I just need those coordinates now."

A posh voice responded through the transmitter. It sounded male, but velvety and light compared to Torren's voice. I strained to hear it. *"Yes, well, about that. It looks like the initial intel I had was a little...off."*

"How off?" Torren said, irritated.

It was a simple miscalculation. No need to get snippy, Tor.

"Watch it," Torren hushed him. "I'm not alone." Whoever this buyer was, they knew his real name.

Torren lowered his voice, and I found myself straining to hear the rest of the exchange. I assumed he must have leaned closer to the transmitter and lowered the volume, realizing that I was probably listening in.

Something's happening. Something that wasn't part of Torren's plan. I took one more deep breath, glancing around at the gently swaying trees, then descended from the roof and climbed back on board. Torren was still talking to the buyer when I approached the cockpit. He threw me a brief glance, barely registering that he had seen me as he hunched over the transmitter.

"This wasn't the agreement," Torren snapped, running his hand through his hair in agitation.

"Yes...unforeseen circumstances and all that. You know how it goes," the voice said.

Torren paused. "Is this because I took the Egg to someone else?" he asked flatly. It struck me then that Torren hadn't just passed up a massive profit by giving the Egg to the Froxians, he may have jeopardized his business relationships too.

"I'll have you know I am appalled at such an accusation of pettiness," said the voice with hollow outrage. *"Anyway, you don't have to go through with this Talar job if it's too much for you. I can always hire someone else."*

"No, you can't," Torren growled.

"Fine, you called my bluff." The velvet voice was weary now. *"I don't know what to tell you. Get the shipment or don't."*

Torren sat back with a defeated demeanor, the wheels turning in his head seeming to turn as he calculated his next move. He sighed and leaned toward the transmitter. "I'll handle it," he said, switching it off without waiting for a response.

His shoulders slumped, and he raked his hands over his face for a moment. Then he sprung out of the chair, briskly brushing past me to get to the cargo hold.

"What's happening?" I asked.

Torren began grabbing things from storage bins and throwing them into a leather bag with more force than necessary. *What had rattled him so much?* His movements were mechanical, as if his body was on autopilot. "My buyer just dropped some last-minute intel on me that complicates this whole thing."

"What did he say?" I asked as he stalked into the galley. He was moving so fast, seemingly angry at everything and nothing. On Hadrin, I had learned quickly to steer clear of angry men, but I swallowed my instincts and followed Torren into the galley. He dumped a case of packaged food rations into his bag, then spun around and tried to push past me.

I stood firmly and put my hands out, pressing them against his chest and slowing him to a reluctant stop.

"Tor," I said, using Rego's nickname for him. The buyer had used it too, so I figured it would get his attention. I could feel his heartbeat pounding under my palm, his breathing a little more labored than normal.

He looked down at my hands on his chest with an expression I couldn't decipher.

I withdrew my hands. "What did he *say?*" I repeated calmly.

He shook his head, irritation simmering in his gaze. "The shipment isn't located near here, Sketch. It's miles away." He brushed past me and reached for the smuggling compartment, opening it and searching its contents.

"So? Can't we fly there?" I asked.

"Apparently," he sighed, pulling out the detonators and carefully placing them into his bag, "the shipment has been in its hiding place for a handful of years, and in that time, a Union outpost happened to be built nearby. Civilian ships are outlawed from flying near Union outposts, so it'll have to be reached on foot."

"I see."

"And according to the coordinates, it's a two-day walk from here," he said, closing the compartment and facing me. I paused, letting it all sink in. *This alters the mission entirely.* Instead of leaving Talar that afternoon, we would be leaving in four or five days.

"We can't land the ship any closer than this?" I asked.

"I'd rather keep my ship as far from the outpost as possible. Their security patrols could find it."

I nodded, for once agreeing with him. "Do you believe your buyer that this intel is last-minute?" I asked.

He looked at me curiously, as if impressed by my skepticism. "No, actually. I think he knew how involved this mission would be, but downplayed it to me. He knew that once I got here, I wouldn't back out."

Whoever this mysterious buyer was, they seemed to know Torren well. "And you're sure the shipment can be retrieved and brought back here on foot?"

"He was clear about that. It's supposedly a small crate, easy enough for one person to hand-carry."

I nodded, thinking it all through. Torren removed his flight vest, rolled it tight, and shoved it into his bag. He pulled a brown jacket out and threw it on, then slung his bag over his shoulder and jumped out of the ship.

"Stay here, Sketch," he said. "The ship has rations and water to last you a week, but I should be back in four or five days."

I stood dumbfounded. *He's leaving me here?* I imagined sitting around the ship for four whole days, either bored or racked with worry over him making it back. *What if he runs into trouble?*

I clenched my fists and followed him out of the ship. "Nope. No way in hell are you leaving me here. I'm going with you."

"I'm handling this," he said over his shoulder. "Just listen to me and stay here,"

"*Hold it,*" I said sternly, my voice echoing off the trees.

Torren stopped walking, begrudgingly turning around.

"I need this payout as much as you do Torren. For Rego." I stepped out of the ship. "I know you're the expert here, but face it, I know Talar better than you do. I know the culture, I know the terrain, and I *know* that you are going to need my help at some point."

He dropped his gaze to the forest floor, tapping his fingers against his leg. I could practically see him running every step of my proposed scenario in his head.

"This is a two-day hike," he said, "and another two days back. I'm not going to hold your hand, and I'm not going to slow down. You'll have to keep up with me."

"Fine."

"We'll be camping every night. So we'll have to share a tent."

"Whatever."

"It's a *small* tent," he added. It sounded like a threat. He slowly stalked toward me, waiting to see how I reacted to the information.

I relaxed my shoulders, meeting him with an apathetic gaze. "If it's not a problem for you, it's not a problem for me."

He looked down at me, scrutinizing me with soft brown eyes. I found myself looking at his lips, and I remembered the feeling of them pressed against mine. When I met his gaze again, he was still studying my face in the soft light of the overcast sky.

"Alright," he said, adjusting his bag and jerking his head toward the ship. "Go pack anything you'll need over the next few days, and make it quick."

I nodded and turned around, preparing to climb back into the ship.

"And uh, Sketch?" he said, his voice lowered.

"What?" I stopped.

He took half a step toward me and leaned in. "You should really stop thinking about that kiss."

13

———

TALAR CITY

I KNEW TALAR WOULD HAVE CHANGED IN THE TEN YEARS SINCE I'D lived there, but I was willing to bet that Talarian scarves were still in fashion. Before leaving the ship, I grabbed the blankets from each of our bunks, cut them up, and fashioned them into large, draped scarves that Torren and I wore around our necks and shoulders. I showed Torren how to wrap his scarf, standing in front of him and working the fabric around until it looked right. I could feel him watching my face as I did it, but I pretended not to notice.

As we plodded through thick Talarian forest, the trees towered above us like sentries. Talar's lush green ferns dotted the land-scape, a comforting sight after years spent in the flat nothing-ness of Hadrin. Torren's legs were longer than mine, but I kept up, breathing through my nose to hide how winded I was getting. His own breath seemed fine. Physical activity alone didn't seem to set his lungs off. From what I had seen, it seemed to flare up when he was stressed.

While we walked, Torren focused on the small device in his

131

hand, a sleek, high-end-looking nav-projector that plotted our course for us.

"You're sure we need to wear these?" he asked, tugging at the fabric around his throat.

"Hey, these scarves are a staple of Talarian fashion," I said. "This is a mining planet, remember? The scarves keep people warm on overcast days, and miners cover their nose and mouth with them."

He shrugged. "I just don't want to walk into town looking out of place."

Town? I stopped walking so abruptly my boots skidded across the fir needles on the forest floor. "Did you say *town?*" I asked, alarm making my voice higher than usual.

He stopped, looking at me as if I'd gone crazy. "Yeah, we're going into the city for supplies."

City?

I heard it now, beneath the serene ambience of the forest—a soft but distinct cacophony of man-made sounds in the distance. There was a low rumble from land speeder engines, clanging metal, and the hum of many voices.

"We can't go to Talar City," I said.

"Where else would we get supplies?" he asked, following the route.

I squeezed my shaking hands into fists to steady myself, then followed him. "Torren, we've got rations, we've got a tent. What else could we possibly need?"

We reached a break in the trees, and a dirt footpath stretched out before us.

Torren stepped onto the path, stowing his nav-projector without missing a beat. "A water canister, for one. An ion lantern, and a few more rations," he said.

"Comfort items," I said with a shrug. "I don't need them if you don't. Come on, we brought plenty of rations from the ship."

He sighed, but didn't slow his pace. "The ship's rations are calorically designed for sedentary travel. We're about to hike for days. We'll need something more substantial."

"So we'll forage," I insisted. "Wild Talarian mushrooms are to die for—"

"Sketch," he cut me off, raising his eyebrows and waiting until I looked at him, "I don't know if you've noticed, but I have to use a Respirin cartridge now and then."

"I noticed."

"I've only got one cartridge. We're about to venture off into the wilderness for four or five days. A lot can happen in that time, and I'd really like to have a spare. So yes, we're going into the city."

My shoulders slumped as I realized I couldn't argue without looking callous.

I walked beside him silently for a moment. "What's that about anyway? Your breathing thing."

"It's just something I live with," he said.

I swallowed, wanting to ask my next question, but unsure if I should. "Are you…dying?"

He laughed. "No," he said, the corner of his mouth cracking into a smile. "It's nothing like that. It's…it's a long story, one we don't have time for."

I could tell from his tone that he was finished with the subject, so I kept quiet, weighing my options as we followed the path for a while longer. As the city noises grew louder, the high stone walls that bordered Talar City rose up ahead. The dirt path we were on turned to cobble. My nerves got the better of me, and I stopped, my feet refusing to let me take another step.

"Okay," I said, "I'll wait out here for you."

He stopped and turned to me with his eyes narrowed suspiciously. "What is this about? Are you wanted by the Union authorities here or something?"

Or something.

"I knew you were laying low on Hadrin, but..." Torren looked me up and down, "what did you *do?*" he asked.

I rolled my eyes at him with a groan, knowing he wasn't going to let it go. "Nothing! Of all the pesking places. Let's just go and get it over with," I said, stomping toward the city entrance. I reached for my wrapped scarf and drew the fabric over my head to create a makeshift hood. It covered my hair and only some of my face, but it would have to do.

He quieted, and we walked through the entrance together. The sights and sounds of Talar City were so familiar, and yet so new. I felt half at home, half a stranger in a new land. It was the city I had known as a child, but ten years modernized. There were less shops than I remembered, and far more bars. *The Union's looming presence must be driving more people to drink than usual.*

"How well do you know the city?" Torren asked, glancing around.

"I know where we can get those supplies," I said, "if the place is still there."

To our left, two Union officers holding blasters were standing on the street corner, keeping watch on the bustling crowd. *Act natural.* I caught Torren's eye and tilted my head toward the street to our right. Now it was Torren's turn to follow my lead, and to his credit, he did without question. I noticed that more than half the people we passed were draped in large scarves.

"See?" I said. "Aren't you glad you brought me?"

"Oh, absolutely," he replied, his voice dripping with sarcasm as he adjusted his scarf for the tenth time. He was clearly still irritated by it.

I had completely forgotten how inviting Talar City was. Where Laigo City was sleek and shiny, Talar was charmingly rustic. The streets were still busy, but the pace here was relaxed. The older buildings were made of stacked grey stones, while some of the newer structures were built with boards made from strong Talarian fir trees. The whole city had a warm, earthy feel.

We passed a street vendor selling charred elger steak and roasted maro legs. I hadn't tasted either in years, and my stomach growled at me. *Get in, get out. We don't have time to stop and reminisce.*

Talar's mineral and gem shops were still open, though their once-vibrant displays had dwindled. The Union had confiscated many of the planet's resources, or so I had read on the wire. Seeing it firsthand hurt more than I expected.

I could see that Torren was taking it all in. He had never seen Talar before Union rule, but I didn't doubt that he recognized the effects of occupation when he saw them. I ushered him down a narrow side street, where the shops were nestled closer together. Half of them looked abandoned.

"You should be able to find everything you need there," I said, pointing out a general goods depot.

He looked it over. "Do you want to come with me or stay here?" he asked.

"I'll stay out here," I said, crossing my arms.

He nodded and headed in. I readjusted the scarf over my head and looked around cautiously, still afraid I might see someone who might have known me before. Someone who knew what happened. Taking another anxious look around, I realized that there was a comms booth near the corner. A sleek and shiny white box, just like the ones on every other settled planet in the galaxy. It looked pristine and out of place here. Hadrin only had two, but I had seen hundreds of them back on Laigo. I glanced at the depot, then turned and approached the booth.

When I stepped inside and closed the door after me, the sounds of the city were muffled by the booth's soundproof structure. There were glass windows in each wall, so I positioned myself to be able to watch the depot door in case Torren stepped out and was looking for me. I tapped the screen and began navigating to the location I wished to send a transmission. *Laigo System, Planet Hadrin, Hadrin City.* I had to let Rego know I'd be coming back later than planned. I considered what I should say once the transmission went through; *Hey, Rego, you know that family emergency? It's been extended by four days. Be home soon!*

A flash of yellow outside the booth caught my eye. A Union officer patrolled the street, clad in armor and cradling a blaster rifle. I wasn't doing anything illegal, but my pulse still raced. I'd seen officers on Hadrin stun civilians for standing in the wrong place. They always claimed they'd spotted criminal activity, but I suspected it was boredom. Maybe they just liked knowing no one could stop them.

This one was young for an officer, which could make him even more dangerous. The young ones were hungry to exert power. They wanted to see how it felt to cause pain with no repercussions. As he sauntered in my direction, I fought the urge to duck and hide. My hands began to shake as he approached the booth. I swallowed nervously, my eyes zeroing on the powerful blaster in his hands.

A knock on the booth window made me jump. Torren stood outside, scowling.

"What are you doing?" he asked, loud enough for me to hear while sealed inside the booth. I shrugged, my eyes drifting back to the officer passing by. Torren opened the door and leaned in, looking at the comms screen.

"I was going to send a transmission to Rego," I said.

He made a face and reached into the booth, tapping the screen and canceling everything that I had queued up.

"Hey!" I protested.

"Can't let you do that, Sketch," he said.

"Why the hell not?" I asked.

He glanced around, then shuffled into the booth with me and closed the door. I put my back to the wall to keep from being pressed up against him. Reaching for the control panel, he hit a button that caused all the windows to take on a frost-like opaqueness, a feature I didn't even know comms booths had. The sights outside were now just as obscured as the sounds.

"Open your mouth," he ordered.

"Excuse me?" I asked, my eyebrows as high as they could go. He dipped his head, making a show of trying to see inside my mouth.

"Just making sure you're not halfway high off of a Tranq tablet," he said with lilting sarcasm. "Don't you know the Union listens in on every transmission sent through one of these booths? Every. Single. One. I thought that was common knowledge."

"They don't exactly print it on the side of the booth," I mumbled.

"This isn't funny. Imagine if you had contacted Rego and mentioned info about the job we're on."

"I wasn't going to give anything away."

"Just don't do *anything* unless I tell you to," he said harshly. I huffed, watching as he looked me up and down, then glanced at the navigation screen. "Although," he said, drumming his fingers on one of the frosted windows, "you just gave me a *really* good idea." He inspected the screen and the control panels. "This could work," he murmured under his breath.

"*What* could work?"

Torren hit the privacy button again, rescinding the window frost and looking for the Union officer, who was now standing on the corner of the street. The man had shouldered his weapon and was staring at the vector tablet built into his wrist armor, clearly bored.

"We're going to tie up a loose end," Torren said, turning back to me. "I need you to go talk to that Union officer."

I searched his face for any hint that he was joking, but seeing nothing, I laughed out loud. "Like *hell* I am." My voice rang through the small space of the booth, bouncing back at me. "I thought we were trying to be covert here."

"There's no way around it," Torren said. "The officers at the blockade logged our IDs into their system. Normally, this isn't an issue for me, since I use a fake ID chip."

"You don't say," I muttered.

"Yours, *however*, is real, which means they now have a record of your arrival. If anything goes wrong with this mission, you won't be laying low on Hadrin anymore."

"What are you saying?" I asked.

He bit his lip, glancing out of the window before piercing me with his deep brown eyes. "I'm saying, we need to erase that record if you want to stay out of a Union prison."

My pulse spiked. The idea of approaching an officer to avoid being arrested by one seemed too backward to be true. "The blockade was one thing," I said, looking up at him, "but I'm not going to interact with one more Union officer if I can help it. You *know* I didn't even want to come back here. You know I have my reasons."

"Which would be?" he asked, cocking his head expectantly.

"Still not telling you," I said definitively.

His eyes darted back and forth between my own. "I'll figure it out sooner or later," he said. "Now, come on, I need you to distract him."

"Why me? You're the professional," I snapped. I would have crossed my arms, but there wasn't enough space to do it.

"You kidding me?" he said, gesturing at my face. "Look at you. You're so unassuming."

"I am?"

"You're pretty enough to disarm people, but not so striking that you'll draw unnecessary attention."

"Wow."

"You're also smarter than you let on. You're the perfect cover," he said. "The perfect spy." My stomach dropped. I'd heard that speech before. It had led to ruin.

"If I'm so unassuming, why do you insist on calling me *Sketch?*"

"*I* can tell you're hiding something," he said. "A Union officer won't think twice." Before I could argue, he put his hands on my shoulders and spun me around to face the window. "Look," he said in a low voice, bringing his mouth close to my ear, "it's just one officer. Trust me, Sketch, you can do this." I felt his whisper on the back of my neck as we stared out the window.

I took a deep breath, letting my chest fill up while thinking through the worst-case scenarios. "And this is absolutely necessary?" I asked.

"We *have* to wipe that record. That, or pray we don't run into any trouble. It's up to you," Torren said, leaning back and giving me space to think.

I didn't actually have a choice. He knew I'd want my name out of their system.

"I hate you," I said.

"I know," Torren replied without missing a beat. Opening the door, he gave me a gentle push out of the booth.

"What do I say to him?" I asked.

"Anything. Ask him a question. It doesn't matter, just keep his attention on *you.*" He pulled a small silver flask out of his bag and unscrewed the lid. A strong alcohol scent wafted my way. *He thinks* now *is a good time to drink?* I glanced over my shoulder at the armored officer, still lost in his vector tablet. I swallowed.

"Can I have some of that?" I asked. Torren took a large swig, swishing it around in his mouth, and shook his head *no*. I watched, confused, as he leaned forward and spat the entire mouthful onto the gravel street, wiping his mouth dry with the sleeve of his jacket.

He's actually insane.

"Alright, Sketch, you're on," he said, nudging me toward the street corner.

I stumbled forward, then paused and spun back to ask Torren another question, but he had already turned and was striding away. *Shit.* I was on my own.

I gulped, willing my feet to move. Reluctantly, I headed straight toward the very threat I'd been running from for most of my life.

14

THAT'S IT. WE'RE DEAD

MY BREATH SHUDDERED AS I PUSHED THROUGH THE TERROR gripping my limbs. I wiped my sweat-slicked palms on my jacket and took a deep breath, adopting the most relaxed expression I could. *Directions. I'll ask him for directions to the city center.*

The officer still had his eyes down, gazing at something on his vector screen. Clearing my throat, I stepped within three feet of the armored man, not daring to get any closer.

"Um…officer?" I rasped with a dry mouth.

His eyes flicked over me with the same look he might give a bug crawling across his polished boot.

"What?" he snapped.

"Uh…" I hesitated. Behind him, I saw Torren approaching from the opposite direction he had disappeared in. *How in the hell did he get all the way around the street corner?* I guessed that he must have taken a side street and cut through the alley behind the row of shops in front of me.

"Sir," I said, snapping my attention back to the officer.

"What is it?" he asked impatiently, glaring at me. His brows were lowered in an agitated scowl. Torren was still approaching slowly, watching the officer carefully.

Union officers were generally dismissive. If I asked for directions, he might brush me off and catch Torren in whatever it was he had planned. I needed something that would hold his attention.

"Could you tell me where the nearest Galactic Union post is?" I asked. "I need to report a crime."

He tilted his head at me. *That did it.* He looked at me head-on, interest sparking in his eyes.

"You can report any illegal activity directly to me," he said, his fingers flexing against his blaster, his voice filled with tempered excitement.

Torren came up behind him, moving way too fast. He bumped right into the officer, causing them both to stumble. *That's it. We're dead.* As the officer recovered his bearing, Torren's hand reached for the officer's belt, low and almost too quick to catch. He drew his hand back into his own jacket pocket, and by the time the officer had whirled around to face him, Torren held two empty hands up defensively.

"Hey!" the officer barked.

Torren began to tip forward, but caught himself and swayed in place. "Oh, officer, I didn't see you there," he slurred. The sharp scent of the alcohol hung heavy on his breath. It wafted towards me, and I could tell it hit the officer too, because the man leaned away in disgust.

The officer sneered. "Watch where you're going, you drunken idiot!"

"I'm sorry, sir." Torren mumbled apologetically. "Won't happen again." He shrugged and shuffled away with his head down.

I resisted the urge to watch him leave, keeping my gaze on the officer. *I can't believe he just pulled that off. Whatever that was.*

The officer's fingers twitched on his blaster handle as he glared after Torren's exit. When he turned back to me, he gave an exasperated sigh. "You said you had a crime to report?"

Yeah. Stealing from a Union officer.

"I uh..." I glanced around, my mind completely blank. "I saw a pickpocket, sir."

His scowl deepened. "Where?"

I guessed that he was a new recruit, probably itching to prove himself. If he thought a crime was still in progress, he might jump at the chance to intercept it. I jerked my head in the opposite direction Torren had gone. "In the city center. He's working the crowd over and not being subtle about it. If you go now, you should be able to catch him."

His head whipped in the direction I had indicated. "Bastard," he muttered, shoving past me and stalking away. He was clearly too excited to remember to ask me for a description of the thief. *Idiot.*

When I could no longer see him past the crowds on the street, I exhaled, letting my shoulders unclench. I could kill Torren for putting me through that. I looked around and saw him duck back into the comms booth, already moving forward with the next part of his plan. I stomped over, still running on adrenaline from the grift we'd just pulled.

"I sure hope you got what you needed," I said, placing my hands on either side of the booth door and leaning in. "I'm never doing that again, I don't care how important—"

He pulled something out of his pocket and held it up to me without looking away from the screen. I took the object and turned it over in my hands, squinting to make sure I wasn't seeing things. My stomach dropped when I realized just how audacious Torren had been. "You stole his *ID chip?*" I yelled, my voice raising in alarm.

"Shhh!" Torren said, glancing around to make sure no one had heard me. Grabbing my shoulder, he pulled me into the booth with him and closed the door behind me. He hit the privacy button, frosting the windows.

"Calm down," he said, his hand lingering on my shoulder. "It's really not that big of a deal. Union officers are stupidly easy to pickpocket. Every single one of them keeps their gear in the same specific pouches on their utility belts. It's standard uniform," he said. "The left side pouch is where they always carry their ID chips." He turned back to the navigation screen, casually tapping and scrolling as if he had just explained how he tied his boot laces. Pickpocketing an actual Union officer. I'd never even heard of someone trying it, let alone succeeding at it.

"Greez, how do you *know* all of this stuff?" I asked. He didn't respond, clicking through screens faster than I could keep up with. "Are you…are you ex-Union or something?" I asked.

He threw his head back and laughed, giving me the biggest smile I had ever seen on him, then shook his head. "No, but that's a good one," he said, still grinning.

"I paid a wire-phaser to download and send me all the official Union officer's codexes. I studied them until even *I* could pass the graduation exam. I find that it pays to know your enemy inside and out." He paused, his fingers hovering at the screen while he threw me a glance. "Believe me, I'd jump into a vat of corrovium before I'd join the Union."

I *did* believe him. Most of us hated the Union's corruption, but Torren's disdain rang of something deeper-seated. *Something* had to have caused it.

"Why do you hate them so much?" I asked. He was always asking me about *my* history. "What happened to *you?*"

His mouth opened as if he was about to say something, but he closed it with a snap and held his hand out to me.

"Chip," he said.

I placed the officer's ID chip in his hand, and he tapped it against the screen. This opened a special Union-specific access portal. Torren put the ID chip in his pocket and crouched down, bumping my leg with his knee. I tried to move back and give him room, but there wasn't any in the cramped booth. I was becoming less and less startled by his touch, and increasingly alarmed by that fact.

He ran his hand along the sleek white wall below the screen, searching for something. His hand stopped, and though I saw nothing, he must have found what he was looking for. He twisted toward me, still crouched, then reached for my leg. His hand was on my shin, then slid lower, into my boot. He drew my shock-blade out before I could stop him.

"Help yourself," I muttered.

"Thanks," he said. Flicking the blade out, he used it to pry open a small hidden maintenance panel, exposing a tangle of cables in a range of colors.

"Remember when I told you that the Union listens in on the transmissions made through these booths?" he asked.

"Yes," I said, as he used the tip of the knife to delicately sift through the mess of cables.

"That's because they *own* these booths. Union officers can make credit-free transmissions through them to report information. Which means—"

"These booths are connected to the Union's mainframe?"

He looked up in surprise. "*Very* good," he said, impressed. He went back to the cables. "Their Talarian mainframe, at least.

"So," I said curiously, "if information can go from a comms booth to the mainframe, then that means it's possible for info to be pulled from the mainframe to a comms booth?"

"Exactly. Unfortunately, the Union isn't completely stupid. There is a fence-connection installed in each booth to make sure no one, not even an officer, can access the information stored on the mainframe."

"Let me guess, you know how to disable that fence-connection?" I asked.

He smirked at me, then went back to the wires in his hand. "Like I said, it pays to know your enemy. Though, even after I got comms booth schematics, it still took a lot of trial and error to crack it." He was still picking through cables, and as I leaned in to get a better look, he paused.

"There," he murmured, catching the underside of two thick grey cables with the knife tip and separating them from the rest. "Cutting one of these cables gets us in. I just have to cut the right one."

To my eye, the two cables looked identical. Same width. Same light grey outer coating.

"What happens if you cut the wrong one?" I asked.

"The security alarm will blare, and we'll have five seconds to clear the booth or it'll lock us in."

"Great."

Torren bent one of the cables back and forth in his hands, and from where I stood, it looked rigid. He dropped it. When he picked up the second one, I saw it curve more easily beneath his fingers.

"That's the one," he smirked. Deftly folding a section of the cable into a loop, he slipped the knife through it, severing it.

A *beep* came from the transaction portal on the screen, and an option appeared that hadn't been there before. He shoved the wires back into the wall of the booth, hastily replaced the access panel, and stood up. I gave him as much room as I could, but our arms were pressed together intimately. He didn't seem to notice.

"Alright," he said, selecting the new portal option. The screen changed, going from a bright, consumer-facing vector, to a black screen full of plain-looking portals. This was something we definitely weren't supposed to see.

"This is it, isn't it? The Union mainframe."

"Yes. We have to proceed cautiously, or our activity will get flagged and we'll have officers surrounding this booth within minutes. It's best to get in, do the one thing you need to do, and get out, no messing around."

He navigated through the various portals, eventually finding a set of arrivals logged by the planetary blockade. It was a small list, and we quickly found our own arrival log from earlier that day. Both of our IDs displayed across the screen, clear as day. Torren highlighted our entry log and read through the options available to him.

"Goodbye Fenn and Kad Kensie," he said, tapping and deleting our IDs from the log.

I began to breathe easily, looking at the empty screen. Torren backed out of the portal and returned to the basic vector screen, ending the transaction. He turned to me, a spark in his eye now that he'd completed his objective. "We're good to go."

Opening the booth door, I wondered if part of him was enjoying having an audience to all this work he usually did solo —someone to witness the lengths he went to fulfill his objectives. We stepped out onto the street together.

"So if I hadn't given you the idea to use a comms booth, how were you going to delete my ID from the record?" I asked.

He shrugged. "I hadn't actually planned that part out yet."

I turned on him angrily, grabbing his arm. "You mean you let me come here, get my ID logged, and you didn't even have a plan for how to clear it?"

"I would have figured it out," he said, gently removing my hand from his arm. "If I've learned anything during my career, it's that there's always a way through a problem."

There's always a way through. It's what he had said to me when the gang had us surrounded in the park.

"Always?" I asked skeptically.

He nodded. "The way might not be easy, or obvious, but you can get through anything if you use your head and your resources." He held my shock-blade out to me, handle first.

I took it and bent down to stow it back in my boot. "Well, I'll try to remember that next time I'm in a high-security Union detention center," I muttered.

"Come on. Let's go," he smirked, heading down the street.

I hurried to catch up with him. "Why are you teaching me all this stuff anyway?" I asked. "You've shown me how contraband drops work, how to pass a checkpoint with a fake ID, and how to hack into the Union mainframe. You're one of the most wanted criminals in the galaxy. Why are you spilling your secrets to me?"

"I guess I hate seeing people waste their potential," he said. "Someone like you, Sketch? You're wasted in a place like Hadrin."

I scoffed. "Why do *you* care what I do with my life?"

"I don't know," he said, glancing my way. "There's just something about you…" he trailed off, letting his words hang in the air.

I screwed my brows together. *What the hell did that mean?*

Torren studied me for a few seconds as we walked. "You remind me of…well, me," he said.

I scoffed. "You're out of your mind, I'm nothing like you."

He lifted his shoulders in a lazy shrug. "We'll see, Sketch. We'll see."

Raised voices drew my attention to the street corner ahead of us. Two officers were accosting a kolo vendor, by the looks of it. Torren and I both slowed our gaits as we took in the scene. The vendor's customers darted away, knowing that the trouble brewing was stronger than the kolo they'd been in line for.

"Please," the man pleaded with them. "I swear, I wasn't bartering. I only take Union credits, per the law."

"Didn't look like it," said one of the officers.

The other officer grabbed his shock baton from his belt and fired it up, blue electricity sizzling at the end of the metal rod. Torren and I both stopped walking. Without a warning, the officer jabbed the baton towards the vendor. I heard a sickening sizzle, and the man fell to his knees in pain.

I looked away, focusing on the cobblestone street instead. I had seen officers enact their violence on people before, and I didn't want the image burned into my brain. Out of the corner of my eye, Torren was gritting his teeth, his eyes still on the violent spectacle in front of us.

"How can you watch?" I whispered.

He exhaled sharply through his nose, his jaw clenched. "It's important to watch," he muttered. "You can't forget what you're fighting. Besides, the least we can do is witness it. If this was happening to me, I'd want people to know."

I glanced up. The officers were still standing over the man, asking him questions with the baton still crackling.

"Okay," I said, my fists balling tightly, "how can you watch and not *do* something about it?"

"I am doing something about it," he said. Holding up the officer's ID chip in his hand, he snapped it in half before unceremoniously tossing the pieces into a nearby waste bin.

We passed the street corner, shoulders tense, and made our way out of the city.

15

____

YOU'RE PARANOID

WE FOLLOWED THE NAV-PROJECTOR THROUGH THE FOREST, keeping a steady pace as we pushed further into the wilderness. My mind kept going back to the ease and eagerness with which Torren had broken Union laws. As much as I admired what he was doing, crimes like Torren's wouldn't earn a simple prison sentence. Robbing the Union Museum, for Gryta's sake? He'd be made an example of if they ever caught him. The thought made me shiver.

"So you were able to get all of the supplies we needed?" I asked, needing to escape my thoughts.

"Nearly," he said. "They didn't have any Respirin cartridges. The shopkeeper said that the Union blockade has made it hard for cargo to come in. I've only got the one cartridge on me, and that makes me nervous."

"Oh, so the infamous outlaw *does* feel fear?" I joked.

He didn't crack a smile or look my way.

If he's not looking to connect, why is he teaching me things? Why is he being so hot and cold?

"Can I ask you a question?"

He looked up from the nav-projector cautiously. "Sure."

"How long have you been in this line of work?"

He thought for a moment without breaking his stride. Torren was a thief by profession, and a very good one. I knew he had gotten there by not running his mouth to everyone he met. Still, we'd been through a lot together in just a few days. I suspected he was beginning to trust me.

"As long as I can remember," he said distantly.

"So are you more of a thief or smuggler?"

"Right now, I'm a guy trying to navigate." He gave me a sideways glance before going back to the projector.

"Damn, I'm just asking a question."

"I'd prefer not to get into personal stuff," he said. "Besides, you're asking me a lot of questions for someone who won't share anything about their own past."

"Fair," I admitted.

We entered a clearing, the sky opening up in the absence of forest canopy. The clouds had parted, and sunlight poured down on Talar for the first time since we'd arrived. I tilted my head down, hoping to keep the sun off my face, knowing it would only darken my freckles. Torren closed his eyes and let it wash over him.

With the sun's warmth and the heat building in my leg muscles, I suddenly realized how long we'd been walking. Torren didn't seem out of breath, but it crossed my mind that he could be masking his fatigue the way I was.

"Can we stop for a minute?" I asked, slowing my pace.

He looked at his feet, thinking it over, but slowed and nodded. I headed for a fallen log at the edge of the clearing and took a seat, retrieving my water canister. Torren joined me, sitting an arm's length away. The dynamic between us felt familiar now, though still tentative. We caught our breath together in silence.

Taking a sip from my canister, I noticed a flash of purple out of the corner of my eye. I twisted and peered into the foliage behind us.

"Mmm!" I hummed excitedly with a mouthful of water, nearly spilling it down my chin.

"What?" Torren yelled, reaching for his blaster.

"Star Bonnet," I said, reaching for the blossoms nestled among the greenery. As he followed my gaze, I gently took one into my hand, careful not to pluck it. Each sprig was a cluster of small purple-blue buds that grew smaller as they came to a point.

"These are used in Talarian traditions," I said. He let go of his blaster and relaxed. "You can be gifted the flower three times in your life. There's even a rhyme," I looked up, searching my mind for things I thought I'd forgotten. "Star Bonnet when you're labored of, Star Bonnet found in love, Star Bonnet at the end of things, gifted from above."

"What in the seven sectors does *that* mean?" he asked, cocking his head at me. I studied his raised brows, realizing how refreshing it was to see him confused. He looked *vulnerable.*

"For someone so intelligent, you're not exactly *poetic,* are you?" I smirked.

He looked down and fiddled with the lid of his water canister before giving me a shrug.

I wondered what kind of rhymes he'd grown up with, what kind of homeworld had shaped him.

"Are you going to explain it or what?" he said coldly.

He's gotta be from an ice planet.

I turned my attention back to the flower in my hand. "It means, someone gives a sprig of Star Bonnet to your parents when you're born. When you're older, you may receive it as a declaration of love from an admirer, and as for *gifted from above,* it means—"

"Someone will lay the flower on your grave when you die? As they *stand above it,* so to speak?"

"So there *is* some poetry in you," I smiled. "Yes, traditionally, someone who loved you will lay a sprig on your grave when you pass away."

"That's...beautiful," he said. "And everyone keeps to the tradition?"

"People try, but the blooms can be hard to find. Depending on the season, you really have to go looking for them."

"If they are so sought-after, why not cultivate them so you always have them on hand?" he asked.

I ran my thumb gingerly over one of the blossoms. "It's about the effort. It means so much more to give someone a flower you spent two days searching for than one that's readily available, you know?"

"Fair point."

"Good question, though. People have tried to cultivate them, but they won't take root just anywhere." I shrugged. "They may be lovely, but they're stubborn."

"Sounds familiar," he said.

I snapped my head up and looked at him. "What's that supposed to mean?"

"Nothing," he said. I could see him studying me out of the corner of his eye. "So, how does the courting part work?"

"You're that interested in Talarian traditions?"

He shrugged.

"The flower is a declaration of love, so they're not given or accepted lightly. When you gift a sprig of Star Bonnet to someone, you're saying 'As I picked this, I chose you.'"

"Hmm," he said, nodding. "And did *you* ever receive a sprig of Star Bonnet from an admirer?"

"Me? I always hoped to, but I left Talar before I reached the customary courting age." I looked down at my hands and laughed. "I've had a few flings on Hadrin, but this fake ring for this fake marriage is actually the closest I've ever been to a serious relationship." Neither of us spoke, and I instantly regretted saying it out loud. It sounded so pathetic.

We sat in stillness for a moment, the silence punctuated only by the creaking of trees in the wind. As he screwed the lid onto his water canister and set it beside him, I wondered what he was thinking.

"What about you?" I asked. "Do you have a partner somewhere?"

"I'm not in a relationship, if you must know," he said. I

shrugged, pretending to be indifferent to the information. "Having a spouse would just complicate my work."

"You're right," I said. "If you *did* have a spouse, they probably wouldn't like you kissing the fake wife you're working undercover with."

"I didn't plan on doing that, by the way," he said, his face falling into a scowl. "Going undercover is dangerous, you have to operate by instinct or you'll end up in hot water."

"Ah," I murmured, "so your *instincts* told you to kiss me?" I couldn't stop the smile on my face. Torren sighed and threw me a look that made me feel like *I* was in hot water.

"We should keep moving," he said, standing and slinging his bag over his shoulder. He reached a hand into his pocket, I guessed to check that he had his Respirin cartridge.

I stood up, but paused when I saw he'd forgotten his water canister on the log. "Catch," I said, picking it up and tossing it towards him.

He turned in time to catch it with one hand. "Thanks."

"What's a fake wife for?" I said, shouldering my bag and walking past him.

We hiked for a few more hours without much conversation. He was so used to working by himself, the silence was easy for him. Eventually, I looked around and noticed the trees around us had thinned. We stepped through a break in the foliage and saw a wide dirt path before us. It snaked through the forest like a river, leading somewhere out of sight. I crouched down for a closer look at the trail, and noticed a distinct lack of footprints in the dirt. *Hover vehicles.*

"This is a land speeder path," I said, straightening up. "Probably used by mining crews to get between work sites quickly."

Torren looked it up and down, checking the nav-projector closely. "Looks like we could take this for the next handful of miles. It's more level, and less rocky than the terrain."

"My legs could use a break from the climbing," I said, shifting my feet.

"If we pass anyone on the road, we'll just have to pretend we're miners."

"Easy enough," I said, stepping onto it. We made faster progress on the path, and I gained a burst of energy. Finishing this job, protecting Rego, it all finally felt within our grasp.

I was lost in thought when I heard a noise. Torren's head lifted just as mine did. We stopped walking and listened in silence. It was an engine, and it was definitely getting closer. We couldn't see the vehicle yet, due to the curve of the road, but it sounded like the high whine of a land speeder.

"Whoever it is, just stay calm," Torren said.

He tucked the nav-projector away, and we continued down the path, preparing to look inconspicuous. The speeder in question rounded the bend, and Torren cursed under his breath. Even at a distance, we saw the sun glinting off of yellow armor. There were four Galactic Union Officers seated in an open-top vessel.

They must be patrolling the transport routes for suspicious parties. Parties like us. I glanced at Torren. He didn't look up to greet them, keeping his head down, so I did the same. The speeder approached, and I prayed that it would simply pass by. My heart stopped when I heard the engine decelerate. *How many times are we going to have to deal with these bastards today?*

I looked up, watching the speeder come to a hovering stop in front of us.

"You two," snapped the driver with an accusatory tone.

Torren and I looked up as if we had just noticed them.

"Where are you headed?" the officer asked, his face as hard as his voice.

Torren wasted no time putting his arm around me, clearly deciding to play the couple angle again. I leaned into him and put my arm around him as well, surprised at how natural it felt this time. When Torren failed to answer the man, I figured he was working out a passable lie. All four officers stared us down. If we waited too long to answer, it wouldn't look good. With a shaky inhale, I decided to go for it.

"We're heading to the river shoals. We heard there might be some solcite deposits there."

"*Really?*" asked the officer. Torren and I both nodded. The other officers said nothing, exchanging glances behind the driver. The officer at the wheel looked back and forth between Torren and I.

"That's weird," he said flatly, "because no one has found any solcite on this planet in over four years."

My heart pounded against my chest as I fought to keep my breathing even. Torren's arm around me tensed up. *Damn.* Solcite was popular throughout the galaxy, widely prized for its stunning green iridescence. The Union must have mined all of it out of Talar since I'd left. I could feel Torren's other arm reach slowly behind him, inching toward his concealed blaster. I reached down and put my hand over his behind his back, warning him to stop.

"Well, yeah, that's what everyone in town says," I shrugged. "But can you imagine the price we could get if we *did* find some? We'll get lucky one of these days."

Torren gave them the weary smile of an exasperated spouse. "I keep telling her it's a long shot," he shrugged, "but here we are."

The officers glanced at each other again, this time their body language more at ease. I guessed, and hoped, that they were suppressing laughter.

"Well, good luck with that. Carry on," said the driver, barely hiding his amusement.

Torren and I nodded in unison as the speeder kicked back into gear. I felt his body relax as it sped away, though his breathing took on a faintly labored sound. We turned and continued walking down the path with our arms around each other. When we could no longer hear the engine, he dropped his arm and stepped away.

"Well, the speeder path seems to be more trouble than it's worth," I said, stepping off the trail and heading for the tree line.

"Well done," he said, "getting them off of our backs."

"Solcite prospecting was big back when I lived here, I thought it would be a decent cover."

He murmured in agreement as he followed me into the woods. "Still, that was quick thinking, making us look like yokels too dumb to know we were wasting our time."

I shrugged. "Yeah, in my experience, feigning ignorance is an easy deflection. *Especially* with someone like that, an officer that already sees himself as superior to us? It was almost a psychological certainty that playing dumb would lower his guard."

He stopped walking. It took me a few steps to notice, but when I turned around, he was staring me down. I didn't like the look on his face.

"Your experience?" he asked. "Just how much experience do you have? And what is all this stuff about *psychological certainties?*"

"What's the big deal, Torren?" I asked, unsure of what he was getting at.

He grumbled, then brushed past me, his whole body taut with anger.

"What's up with you?" I snapped, feeling threatened by his piercing gaze and what it implied.

He looked like he was going to walk away, but he paused and turned sharply to face me. "Why are you so good at this?" he demanded.

"Good at what?" I asked, taking half a step back.

"I thought back at the blockade, maybe you were just a natural. The same with the officer you distracted in the city. Now it's starting to look a lot like you've done this a lot more than you've let on."

"What are you talking about?"

"Lying. Maintaining a cover," he said. "That first night we met, you eavesdropped on my talk with Rego without me even noticing. Not a lot of people can do that."

I let out a laugh and shook my head. "So what? What if I do have experience with this stuff? Why do you care?"

He leaned in, his face getting close to mine. "Because *this* is a dangerous business. I've seen crews on a job like this slit each other's throats for a bigger cut of the profit. There's a reason I usually work alone." When he straightened back up, I saw his eyes flick down to my boot, the place I stowed my shock-blade.

Who does he think I am? A rival thief? Some undercover Union agent sent to infiltrate his little operation? It would have been funny, if the weight of his suspicion wasn't so offensive.

"You're paranoid," I muttered, brushing past him.

He grabbed my arm roughly, his fingers digging into my skin. He spun me back around to face him, his voice a low, threatening growl. "You're giving me reason to be."

I wrenched my arm free of his grasp. "What the hell's your problem?"

He took a step back, now holding himself with an eerily calm composure. He looked ready to snap any second, depending on what I said next. Slowly, deliberately, he slid his blaster from its holster. He kept it low, hanging at his side, but I understood the warning.

"I'm going to ask you something," he said, his voice devoid of emotion, "and I need you to be honest."

I glanced nervously at the weapon in his hand before forcing my gaze upward to meet his. The tension was as thick as smoke. We had come to an understanding after Laigo. We'd even built some trust. Now it seemed we were back at square one.

"Tell me," he continued, "which is my dominant hand? Right or left?"

My stomach twisted as my gaze fell again to the gun in his hand. I had an answer, and I knew he wasn't going to like it.

"Come on, Torren. What is this?"

"Answer me," he said gruffly.

"Left," I muttered. "You're naturally left-handed. Possibly good with both."

He didn't react, but his eyes darkened as he pressed me. "Why do you say that?"

The blaster glinted in the sunlight as he held it up, showing me that it was clearly in his right hand. I took a breath. *He wants the truth? Fine.*

"You shoot right-handed," I said. "I saw it in the park. You intentionally use your right hand when we're in public, but I've seen you type with your left when you're in a hurry. When I tossed your canister, you caught it with your left. It's the hand you use when you're caught off-guard. You intentionally switch it up, but I'm not sure why. Maybe to have an extra advantage if things go down."

"I knew it," he breathed.

We stood in silence for a moment, but the tension quickly became unbearable.

"Knew what?" I asked.

"Observation like that takes practice," he said, tapping the muzzle of his blaster against his leg.

"What are you saying?"

"I'm saying...how hard could it be for a Union informant to pose as a docking tech?"

"You think I'm a spy? Torren, that's ridiculous and you know it."

"You may work in a shipyard, but you've had some kind of intelligence training. I know the skill set when I see it. You need to give me some answers."

"Hey!" I shouted, my voice startling a maro bird in its nest nearby. It flapped its wings as I seethed. "I thought we weren't going to get into personal stuff!"

"How do I know you're not planning to double-cross me?" he asked. "I don't even know who you are."

He can't be serious.

"Like I know who *you* are? You're the one with a fake ID chip. You're a good liar too, I've seen it. In fact, I'm starting to have some suspicions of my own."

"Like what?" He said, adopting a skeptical tone.

"Like maybe this so-called *bounty* on Rego isn't even real. I've seen how you move your pieces on the board. I wouldn't be shocked if you fabricated Rego's bounty so I'd come along and get you into Talar for your contraband."

"I didn't," he muttered.

"Doesn't feel good to be doubted, though, does it?"

He looked down at his boots, giving himself a moment to think. The mention of Rego's name must have snapped him back to reality. The trust between us was balanced on the edge of a knife, one clasped in the hand of our mutual friend. Rego was the only thing protecting us both from each other.

Torren exhaled, then turned, taking out the nav-projector. "Let's just get to the pickup point so we can be done with this," he said, walking away.

The sudden rift between us made me feel hollow. I'd thought at the start of the trip that I didn't want anything to do with him. Now that I felt him drawing away, I suddenly realized how accustomed to him I had become.

I was about to call after him when he stopped abruptly, freezing in place. His head was cocked to the side, listening carefully. I glanced around, looking for clues as to what had spooked him.

"Sketch," he whispered, "what do you know about Talarian wildlife?"

"Everything," I said, keeping my voice just as hushed as his.

"Does this planet have any large predators?"

"Male elgers can get territorial just before mating season, but other than that, there's nothing out here that would harm us."

He threw me a worried glance. "I was afraid you would say that."

"What?"

He reached for me, placing a hand on my shoulder and the other over my mouth. "Shhh," he said softly, the look in his eye indicating that now wasn't a good time to argue.

I went still and listened, breathing through my nose as quietly as possible. All I heard was wind rustling the trees. *What did he hear?* I gently shrugged his hands off of me, pointing to my closed mouth to let him know I wasn't going to speak.

That's when I heard it—the unmistakable sound of a twig snapping. I realized with a sick feeling that we weren't alone. A rustling noise came from the underbrush, the distinct sound of someone treading carefully.

With fluid, quick motions, Torren turned toward the sound, pushing me behind him with one hand and pulling out his blaster. He aimed straight at the brush ahead of us.

"What do you want?" Torren said loudly, lowering his voice and standing at his full height.

The rustling stopped, sending a chill up my spine. There was only eerie silence for a minute, but then a male voice spoke up from somewhere in the foliage.

"Holster your weapon and put your hands up," the voice demanded.

Torren used his thumb to switch his blaster setting from stun to lethal. He definitely wasn't the surrendering type. *No surprise there.*

"We have you fenced in, so you'd better comply," said another voice, this one female.

We? How many are there? Two? Twenty? More twigs snapped around us. There had to be at least a handful of them. We were definitely surrounded, and most likely outgunned. Maybe Torren's *there's always a way through* philosophy was too ambitious. I didn't like our odds, but I had an itching feeling that I knew who we were dealing with.

I thought about how quickly Torren had moved to shield me, even after the argument just moments before. He *wanted* to trust me, despite my constant refusal to open up to him. I just prayed that I was right about who it was that had us surrounded.

16

THAT'S WHAT A SPY WOULD SAY

"Holster your weapon and get your hands up," the voice from the foliage commanded again. Whoever it was meant business. I slowly raised my hands to shoulder level. Torren shifted his feet and tightened his grip on his raised blaster.

"You tell me who you are, or I don't do anything," Torren said.

Who talks like that when they're outnumbered and surrounded?

The female voice spoke up this time. "Cut the act. We know you're Union."

"We're not with the Union," Torren said calmly. "We're just miners."

"Since when do miners carry weapons?" The woman's voice was shrill now, impatience undercutting every word.

"Holster your weapon. *Now*," the male voice demanded.

"Not until you show yourselves," said Torren.

He's not going to back down.

"We won't ask you again," said one of the voices, the threat clear.

I understood why Torren didn't want to give in. Had we been ambushed by some kind of bandit group, the last thing we wanted was to be unarmed, but I was pretty sure I knew who we were dealing with. I didn't want anyone to open fire.

The sound of another blaster being primed made the hair on the back of my neck prickle. Torren's finger twitched against his own trigger, but he didn't move another muscle. He had no intention of complying. I stepped around him and gently put my hand on his blaster, signaling for him not to shoot. He tensed, his eyes meeting mine, but he didn't resist.

"Wait," I said in the general direction of the voices. "If you are who I think you are, then I promise, we are on the same side."

Silence. The distant trill of a maro bird sounded somewhere beyond our standstill. Choosing to trust that I was right, I slowly lowered Torren's blaster, easing his arm to his side. I was relieved that he let me do it, but I felt his stare burning into me.

"We're not miners," I admitted, prompting an irritated sigh from Torren, "but we aren't Union. We have no quarrel with you." It was risky to abandon our cover, but we needed to level with them if we were going to get anywhere.

"Until we determine that...hands up," a voice commanded over the sound of rustling brush.

They're moving in. I slowly put my hands back up, but Torren hesitated, probably fighting his body's fight or flight response. He shot me a sideways glance, but then he holstered his blaster and begrudgingly raised his hands. The foliage around us shuddered with movement, and people materialized out of the greenery. Each was armed with a blaster of various sizes, and each was taking careful aim at Torren and I. There were three men and two women, all wearing practical clothing in shades of green and brown. Each had on the same large Talarian scarves Torren and I wore, but theirs were mottled shades of green, providing excellent camouflage in the surrounding flora. I wondered if there were more of them still concealed.

The tallest of the men looked us over, sternly sizing us up. He was square-jawed and broad-chested, his textured brown hair long enough to tuck behind his ears. *Well at least we know they're not Union.* Every Union officer I had ever seen had a cropped haircut.

I glanced at the thin woman standing next to him. She was tiny, at least two feet shorter than the tall man. She had long, silky black hair and a small array of knives strapped to her waist. A very fitting choice for her, as she was staring daggers at me. The tall man jerked his head toward us.

"What's your business out here?" he demanded.

Torren glanced my way. He understood that I knew something here he didn't, and was giving me room to take the lead.

I cleared my throat, addressing the tall man and tiny woman I guessed were in charge. "We're just passing through," I said. They watched me with narrowed eyes, neither of them convinced yet.

"You're not from here," the woman said. "Your scarves are tied for shit."

I had done my best with the scarves, but it had been a decade since I'd wrapped one. We had passed as locals to the Union officer in town, but actual locals must have clocked us in an instant.

"You know," she said. "we wouldn't have even known you were out here if you hadn't been bickering so obnoxiously."

Blood rushed to my cheeks in an embarrassed blush. Torren's paranoia and my temper were a volatile combination.

"You gotta tell us something, or we'll have to assume you're Union spies," she said. "What are you doing out here?"

"That's none of your business," Torren snapped.

So much for letting me take the lead. The conversation must have gotten too tedious for him.

Rage sparked in the tiny woman's eyes. "Oh, yeah?" she said, stepping forward with her hand on one of her knife grips. I almost took a step back, but Torren didn't flinch.

"Wait, please," I said, holding up my hand defensively. "We mean you no harm, but we can't tell you why we're here."

The woman scoffed and looked at the tall man, who shrugged. She turned her steely gaze back to mine.

"You're really not going to tell us?" she asked.

I shook my head, my eyes never leaving hers.

"Then I'm afraid your fate isn't up to me." She gave the tall man a charged nod.

"Alright," he said loudly, addressing the rest of the group. "Let's take them to the boss."

They stepped forward, surrounding us completely without another word. They were well-trained and organized. One of them gently lifted Torren's blaster from its holster and took it away. He bristled, then cursed under his breath. There wasn't much he could do with weapons still aimed at us. Things were out of our hands now; we'd have to reason with whoever *the boss* was.

The tall man slung his blaster onto his back and approached Torren to search him. He slid his hand into Torren's jacket pocket, pulling out a tiny remote with a clickable button. "A trammel beacon?" the man said, surprised and a little impressed. "For jamming and interrupting signals."

He pulled out two metallic cards and a circular chip out of the other pocket. "A data encryption key, a data *decryption* key, and…greez, is that neural disruptor unit?" His eyebrows raised and he handled the chip gingerly. "You know these are banned on sixteen planets, right? Including this one."

Torren met his gaze but didn't react. The tall man handed the items off to a colleague and flipped Torren's jacket open, revealing an interior breast pocket. He reached in and pulled out a set of small metal tines in a clear case. "An analog lockpicking kit." he chuckled. "Just how many non-digital locks are you planning to come across?"

Torren watched him apathetically, his mouth closed. He wasn't about to explain himself.

The man walked away as the tiny woman stepped forward, eyes on me.

"Your turn, any weapons?" she asked, carefully patting my frame.

"Nope," I said quickly, with my hands still up, hoping she wouldn't think to check my boots.

She stepped even closer to me, coming between Torren and I. Evaluating me slowly from head to toe, she crouched and slipped her fingers into my right boot, searching. She switched to my left boot, pulling my shock-blade out. She turned it over in her hand with a smirk, standing and stowing it in her pocket.

When she stepped away, I saw the small knife sheath on the back of her belt was empty.

I glanced at Torren in time to see him slip his hand into his jacket pocket. *Fuck.* He winked at me. No one seemed to have noticed, thankfully. His confidence was short-lived, as we were both relieved of our bags, making Torren grumble.

The tall man gestured with his rifle, indicating that we could put our hands down. As the group whispered amongst themselves, Torren leaned toward me.

"You'd better have a plan," he warned me.

"I know what I'm doing," I whispered.

"Being relieved of our weapons and being taken to a mystery location is *not* what I meant by *there's always a way through*," he said.

"Just trust me," I hissed.

The tall man stepped forward. "You'll have to go dark for the trip there," he said, "Security reasons."

Someone behind me lowered a dark length of cloth in front of my eyes, tying it around my head tightly.

"And now we're blindfolded," I heard Torren say. "Great plan." A slight rasp crept into Torren's breath, but he kept himself together. If I had to guess, he was more annoyed than scared.

"We'll take those off when we get there," the man assured us.

I believed him, but my fingers still itched to rip the blindfold off and regain my sight. I jumped when a hand landed on my shoulder and began guiding me forward. The scrape of Torren's boots on the ground let me know the same was being done to him. They pushed us through the surrounding brush and onto what I guessed was a small trail. All I could hear were our footsteps and the occasional clank of gear. As we walked, a hand closed gently around my wrist. *Torren.* I knew the feel of his hands by now. He gave my wrist a squeeze, and I wasn't sure if he was trying to comfort me or simply make sure we hadn't been separated. Either way, it made me feel better.

As we walked, the ground morphed under our feet, shifting from soft tree needles to a steeper, rockier landscape. No one spoke. The group weaved deftly through the terrain, making eerily little noise. With his hand still on my wrist, Torren seemed relatively calm, but I sensed a facade. I knew that like me, he was wondering how far off from our original route they were taking us.

After a while, we began to tread downhill, and our captors whispered quietly to one another. There were voices in the distance, and a crackling fire. Underneath it all, the quiet hum of some kind of machinery. *A power generator?* We had definitely arrived.

Torren and I were pushed forward, through the midst of the voices. There were multiple fires going, their heat warming me as we passed by, heading deeper into what I assumed was a camp. Whoever was holding my shoulder suddenly let go, and I froze at the loss of direction. If these people were who I thought they were, there were two *very* different ways this could go.

"On your knees," the tall man's voice boomed.

I hesitated, but slowly knelt, pressing one knee and then the other onto the damp ground, feeling completely powerless. *I hope I'm right about this.* Torren must not have complied as quickly, because I heard him being pushed to his knees next to me.

"Have they been swept?" a new female voice asked, her tone clear and authoritative.

"We secured their weapons. They had a blaster and a shock-blade, but nothing else. No transmitters, no tracking beacons, just a nav-projector and a small vector tablet."

They went through our bags on the walk here. They made no mention of Torren's detonators, but I had definitely seen him pack them. *Does he have a hidden compartment inside his bag?* He *was* a thief and a smuggler after all.

"Alright," the confident woman said, "let's meet these peskers."

My blindfold was abruptly pulled from my head. I blinked at the sudden return of harsh daylight. My hair had fallen into my face, but I resisted the urge to shake it aside. Anonymity felt safer for the time being.

A cursory glance confirmed we were indeed at some kind of camp. Off to our right were three small campfires flanked by log benches. Each fire had a smoke vacuum positioned nearby to inhale smoke before it could waft up above the treetops and give away the camp's position. This group, whoever it was, had gone to *great* lengths to remain hidden.

Past the campfires, a wide piece of canvas stretched across the ground, arranged on which was an impressive collection of handheld blasters and larger rifles. They looked as if they were being cataloged.

This isn't a camp; it's a base. A couple hundred men and women stood around us. I noticed no children or elders. Everyone looked sturdy. Whatever this group did, it was probably danger-ous. By now, the residents of the camp were all quietly gathered, watching the kneeling prisoners before them with interest. Torren and I were a spectacle.

We were facing the mouth of a large cave, where a young woman stood framed by the rocky entrance. Her honey-blonde hair was plaited into a tight braid that trailed over her right shoulder.

My chest tightened at the sight of her, and I kept my head down, peering through the strands of my hair. She had sharp, attractive facial features, and a deadpan expression that gave Torren's a run for his money. Her green eyes flickered back and forth between Torren and I. She looked confident. She looked *good*.

Her arms were crossed, and a holstered blaster rested on her hip. She wore the same green-and-brown-dyed attire as the rest of her comrades, but by the way she held herself and the way the others watched her, I guessed she was in charge. The tall man and tiny woman were standing off to the side, watching us cautiously with blaster rifles at the ready.

I gulped when the statuesque blonde woman finally moved a muscle, shifting her stance casually.

"My scouting party tells me they found you wandering across Gedeon Ridge," the woman said. "They also said you were armed, and that you don't appear to be locals."

I glanced over at Torren, but he was glaring back at the woman in front of us.

"What are you doing on Talar?" she asked, uncrossing her arms and tapping her nails against the grip of her blaster. "And don't try to feed me lies. I know their taste too well to be fooled."

Torren lifted his chin and looked her in the eye. "We're just cargo handlers," he said.

The blonde woman nodded at him, her mouth curling into a smirk. "First you were miners, now you're cargo handlers. Which is it?"

"We're here to pick up cargo," Torren explained, his voice hard. "It's the truth. How's that taste?"

She raised her eyebrows at his snide tone. "Oh, well, if it's the *truth*, then I guess we should let you go." The crowd around us laughed, all except the tiny, stern woman still glaring at us. I did a double-take, and if I didn't know any better, I could have sworn she was glaring at *me* specifically.

The blonde woman allowed herself a small smile, but shook her head.

"Unfortunately, we've had a bit of trouble recently with Galactic Union spies." She began to circle Torren and I, looking us up and down. I swallowed as she studied our clothing and the shoddy scarves I'd made for us. I had never felt so exposed. "The Union has their lackeys dressing like locals," she said. "They usually hang out in the city, hoping to catch us. Looks like they're finally branching out."

"We're not Union," Torren growled.

"That's what a spy would say. Try again." She stopped circling and stood in front of Torren, her green eyes locked on him. He remained defiant, returning the intensity of her gaze without flinching. A puzzled smile lifted the corners of her mouth. "Well," she mused, "if you *are* a spy, the Union certainly sent their most attractive."

Their gazes locked for a moment, Torren tilting his head as they both did their best to get a read on the other one. They were both strong, assured personalities, and though they were at odds, I got the sense they were impressed by each other's fortitude. A pang of jealousy hit me, and I nervously shifted my knees, now sore from kneeling on the ground.

The blonde woman turned around, returning to her initial spot at the mouth of the cave. With a bored expression, she lifted her hand and began to pick at one of her fingernails. "Now, we're fully prepared to beat the truth out of you," she said, a wicked smirk sharpening her features, "or you could save yourselves the discomfort and tell us everything right now." My head jerked in alarm, my hair falling away from my face. She looked at me, as if remembering Torren wasn't alone. "This is your last chance to come clean or—"

She stopped. Her expression went blank as she stared at me with a new intensity, her eyes raking over my features.

Shit. Here it comes.

Her carefree posture melted away, her face going white as if she'd seen a ghost. Stepping forward, she reached for me. She grabbed my chin and turned my face, studying me in the light.

"Fenn?" she whispered in disbelief. Torren whipped his head in my direction, his composed mask slipping.

I exhaled silently, knowing I couldn't hide any longer. "Hi, Canda," I muttered.

She lurched forward, throwing herself toward me, and I braced for the feeling of a blaster bolt in my chest or a knife between my ribs. *She blames me for what happened.* Torren jumped to his feet, ripping the stolen knife from his pocket. The tall man and the tiny woman aimed their rifles at Torren, ready to fire if he made another move. Canda's arm went around my neck, and it took me a few seconds to realize she was embracing me. It was a *hug.*

"Great Gryta, Fenn! I thought you were dead!" Canda yelled. She hauled me to my feet and looked me up and down in amazement. It wasn't the welcome I had expected, but it boded well. Torren slowly lowered the knife.

Canda glanced at the guards and put her hand up. "Mab, Markos, lower your blasters." They complied, but stood by on high alert.

"Everyone, false alarm. These two are friends," Canda said. The crowd around us murmured in acknowledgment as she held my face between her hands. "I mean, we are still friends, right?"

My heart melted seeing how nervous she looked while waiting for my answer.

"Of course, Canda," I said.

With a smile, Canda shooed the crowd away. "Alright, back to work."

The crowd broke up, most of them walking off with mild disappointment on their faces. I guessed that seeing a Union spy take a beating would have been good for morale.

Canda turned back to me, gripping my forearms as if she was afraid I'd vanish into the air if she didn't hold on tight. "Fenn, what are you doing here?"

"It's a long story," I sighed.

"I've got time to hear it. Stay here tonight," she said excitedly. "We've got food and a place for you to sleep." Canda looked to Markos, still standing by with his rifle at the ready. "Will you see to the preparations?" He nodded and stalked away, leaving Mab still glaring at us.

Torren cleared his throat. "Sorry to interrupt, but what the hell is going on?"

"Kad," I said, using his cover name, "this is Canda Tirell. We grew up together."

"I see," he said, relaxing slightly. "Nice to meet you," he said, offering Canda his hand.

She shook it firmly and smiled. "A pleasure."

Mab's face went red when she recognized the knife in Torren's hand. She reached a hand back to the empty sheath on her belt to confirm it was hers. Torren extended the knife toward her handle-first, a peace offering. She ground her jaw, fury emanating from her tiny form as she took it, shoving it back in its sheath without a word.

Canda chuckled, then turned back to me enthusiastically. When we were younger, we had been the same height, but looking at her now, she had surpassed me by at least three inches. "Wow. Fenn, I can't believe you're here." she whispered, her voice faltering with emotion. "After all these years."

"Where is *here*, exactly?" Torren asked, scanning the camp.

Canda tilted her head at him. "She hasn't told you about us?"

He slipped me a side-eye before giving Canda a shake of his head.

She smiled and looked out at the organized outfit around us. "Kad, let me welcome you to the official base of operations for the Talarian Resistance."

17

BACKED INTO A CORNER

Canda, Torren, and I stood on a rocky ridge, looking down at the camp. Below, the Resistance members moved about their duties in an organized fashion. Mab stood behind us, a large blaster slung across her back, her hand resting on the handle of one of her larger knives. They had given our bags back to us and returned Torren's blaster, but Mab still had my shock-blade. I wanted to ask for it back, but decided to wait until she looked more at ease. Which I realized might never happen. She was downright scary for someone her size. With the way she shadowed Canda, I figured she was her personal security guard.

Canda looked out over the camp, her hands on her hips. "We used to move the operation every six months, just to be safe. But we've grown in the past few years. Nowadays, it's gotten much harder to move the whole camp."

"I guess that's a good problem to have," I murmured. "More people for the Resistance."

"We'll see," she shrugged. "Just means more people you have to trust. We've got some people in town too, tapping into official Union channels. We use that intel to rob their supply convoys."

"Convoys?" Torren asked.

"The Union has outposts near major mining sites, to 'oversee' things," Canda explained. "Supplies for the troops come into the city, and delivery convoys transfer them to each post." She scoffed, and let her gaze fall to the people below. "They're stripping the planet of its resources, taking anything of value from the ground. That's why the planet is on lockdown—they don't want anyone seeing the extent of what they're doing here."

"And you've successfully robbed them?" Torren asked.

"Oh, yeah," said Canda proudly. "All of our weapons were originally meant for those Union outposts. Don't worry, they'll see their guns again, just not in a way they're going to like." She winked, and Torren's mouth curled into a smile. He was *impressed*.

"You're in charge now?" I asked.

Canda shrugged. "Someone needed to do it."

"Looks like you're doing a great job," I said, looking out over the camp. "Everything seems so organized, especially compared to the old days."

"Old days?" Torren asked, staring at me.

"Fenn and I were founding members of the Talarian Resistance," Canda beamed. "Well, our parents were. How old were we? Eleven, twelve?" A look of pride crossed her face. "The group was much smaller back then, but things have gotten so bad with the Union the last few years, recruiting has been a breeze."

"I had a feeling your scouts were with the Resistance when they found us," I said.

She turned to me, cocking her head in confusion. "Why didn't you say anything when they brought you in? Or when you saw me?"

Torren was silent, watching me for answers. I swallowed and shifted my feet nervously.

"I wasn't sure I'd be welcome here…after what happened," I said. My heart palpitated at the words coming out of my mouth. *I can't believe I'm talking about this.*

Canda looked me dead in the eye. "That wasn't your fault, Fenn. You haven't been thinking that all these years, have you?"

I looked down at the ground, hoping to hide how uncomfortable I was. Torren tensed up. I could tell he was itching for answers, but he kept still. Listening. Scheming.

"Where *were* you all this time, anyway?" Canda asked.

"Hadrin."

She shook her head and made a face. "Ugh, I'm so sorry." Turning to Torren, she studied him with an approving eye. "So, Fenn, who is this handsome devil? Kad, was it?"

Torren met her gaze with a subtle smile, and a sting of jealousy hit me. Before I could think, I stepped closer to him, placing my hand on his arm.

"We're married," I blurted, holding up my other hand, presenting the carved wooden ring that matched Torren's. He gave me a curious look, but nodded, corroborating my lie. Canda raised her eyebrows, looking him up and down. Her eyes raked over his lean figure, his toned forearms and angular jaw.

I knew the jealousy was irrational. *You can't be possessive of someone who isn't even yours.* Torren and I weren't together, I reminded myself; we were just pretending to be.

"Sweet Talarian Tundras, Fenn; how'd you snag a cat like *this?"* Canda said, as if he wasn't standing right there. Torren's mouth cracked into a hesitant smile as he pretended to be embarrassed by the praise. *He loves it.*

"Must have been my winning personality," I said flatly.

Canda laughed and gave me a playful shove.

"Oh Gryta's paws, I've missed you," she said. "Let's go. Dinner will be ready soon."

Mab joined her as they walked down the rocky ridge, the two of them chatting about camp business.

I began to follow them, but Torren hung back, grabbing my arm and pulling me close to him.

"You have some explaining to do," he hissed in my ear.

"Come on," I said dismissively. We followed Canda and Mab, but stayed out of earshot.

"Don't think our little discussion from earlier is over," he whispered, his stride keeping pace with mine. I let the silence between us linger, deciding not to reply. *It won't kill him to be in the dark for a while. Let him see how it feels.*

As we descended the steep hill, one of my boots slipped on the dirt and I teetered. As annoyed as Torren was with me, he held his hand out to help me down. I would have refused him, but his boots had better traction than mine. I placed my hand in his and let him steady me; his touch felt so natural by now.

"And what's with the cover, Sketch?" he asked.

Is he mad that I let Canda think we were married?

"What does it matter?" I snapped.

"I like to know what's going on," he said. "You're still hiding something, but I'll play along if it's what you want."

"Thanks," I said, and left it at that. I wasn't going to admit why I had been so quick to stake a claim on him. He didn't need to know that I'd been jealous.

Canda apologized multiple times for the simplicity of the dinner, but it was a welcomed break from the rations Torren and I had been getting by on. The freshly roasted maro meat and Talarian mushrooms pulled me back to childhood. I saw myself at twelve years old, plucking mushrooms from the forest floor and gathering them into a bag. I would always rush them back to camp so I could be done with my foraging duties and play with Canda. Together, we would climb trees and pretend we were warriors, protecting our land from all manner of imaginary villains with wobbly sticks we called our spears.

Both of our parents had refused to give us a knife to sharpen the ends of our sticks. I had snapped mine in half out of sheer frustration, but Canda had kept a cooler head. She'd spent the better part of an hour sharpening the end of her stick against a rock, forming it into a fine point.

I watched her now while we ate, hardly surprised that she was heading a rebellion and had scores of people looking to her for leadership.

After dinner, I asked for a place to stash our bags, and one of the resistance members offered to show me where we'd be staying that night. Canda stole Torren away to show off her cache of commandeered weapons. I was led to a large cave at the edge of the camp, where rows of padded bedrolls were laid out for the night. It explained the absence of tents around their camp.

Someone handed me two bedrolls, and I found an empty spot at the back of the cave to spread them out. I placed them side by side, tossing my bag onto one and gently setting Torren's bag on the other. I was certain he had those detonators hidden inside. Before I left, I examined the bedrolls one last time, then pulled them closer together. We had to keep up the illusion of marriage after all.

I left the cave as the sun was setting and saw that everyone was gravitating toward the three fires at the center of the camp. I wandered over. Canda was sitting at the center of a log that served as a fireside bench. Mab sat nearby on the ground, her back against the log while she quietly cleaned her rifle. As I took a seat next to Canda, I followed her gaze to see what she was watching. Across the fire from us, Torren was seated and playing a round of dwind with three Resistance members.

The four of them quietly studied their cards, until one of them confidently placed one down on a stack of cards at the center. The rest leaned in to see what it was. Before anyone could move, Torren ripped a card from his hand and threw it down onto the pile. The other players groaned loudly, realizing they'd lost, but they laughed all the same and congratulated Torren.

Is he having actual fun? Hopefully this means he's not still mad that I kept him in the dark about the Resistance.

"Who's winning?" I whispered, leaning toward Canda.

"That husband of yours," she said, narrowing her eyes and studying him. "I've watched him play for half an hour now. He's very good." She sounded almost suspicious.

I forced a casual-sounding laugh, praying the tension in my body didn't show. "Yeah, Kad's pretty good at bluffing."

"It's strange, though," she added. "I can tell he's holding back."

I could feel my face turn pink, and hoped the glow of the fire-light was masking it.

"No one playing has noticed it, but I'm pretty sure he adjusted his technique to match the skill level of the table." Canda cut her eyes my way. "Why would he do that?"

Of course Canda would be the one person around who could spot Torren making bum moves to let the others win. Canda had been incredible at dwind when we were growing up, able to beat some of the adults we knew.

"He's just being polite," I smiled. "You're so graciously giving us a meal and a bed tonight. No need for him to embarrass your crew at dwind, you know?"

Canda shook her head. "Good man," she said, then smiled at me. "I should have known someone amazing would fall for you."

"Yeah," I muttered, looking down at my boots. I couldn't tell her I had been alone all these years with just one close friend to my name back on Hadrin.

When I looked up again, Torren had looked away from his game and was watching me from across the flickering fire. One of the other players threw a card down, and the rest of the table cheered or groaned, depending on what cards they'd had ready to play. Torren congratulated the winner and laid his cards down.

"That's it for me. Thanks for the game," he said, standing up. The other players thanked him for playing and began dealing the next round. Making his way around the fire, Torren came to sit next to me on the log bench. At the other end, Mab had finished cleaning her blaster and was now methodically sharpening one of her knives on a whetstone.

"I think it's time for a drink," Canda said, pouring an amber-colored liquid from a bottle into a set of wooden cups. She handed one to Torren, one to me, then held one out to Mab, who waved it away. Canda shrugged, pouring Mab's portion into her own cup.

"What is this?" Torren asked, smelling the drink.

"It's fermented sap liquor," Canda said. "Markos makes it."

Torren and I both took a delicate sip and grimaced.

"It's *strong*," I coughed.

"Yeah, and not too smooth either," Canda laughed. "But it gets the job done." I set my cup on the log bench beside me, but Torren dared another sip.

"So how long have you two been together?" Canda asked, her head cocked curiously.

Torren smiled and caught my eye. The mischievous glint I saw there immediately put me on edge. *Uh-oh.*

"Two whole years," he said, setting his cup down.

Our cover at the blockade had been five. *Why is he changing it?* He leaned toward me and looped both of his arms around my waist. I gave a performative smile, my heart racing from the heat of his chest pressing against me. His arms tightened, and before I knew it, he was pulling me onto his lap. I tried very hard to act like it was not the first time it had ever happened.

"Two years," Canda repeated. "And how did you meet?"

Torren nuzzled my neck with his nose. It sent a shiver down my back, and I resisted the urge to flinch. This level of affection was not necessary for our cover. *He's going way over the top.*

"She was my docking tech. Can you believe that?" he quipped. I stayed quiet, my body rigid against his. He was attempting to teach me some kind of lesson. I had to roll with it, or Canda would know I'd lied to her.

"Oh, really?" Canda asked, raising her eyebrows.

Torren nodded emphatically, fixing his piercing brown eyes on me. "Yep. There was some discrepancy in my credentials, and she really gave me hell for it."

Canda chuckled, charmed by his story. "Good girl," she said.

Torren nodded. "Oh, she infuriated me. But it was hard not to be completely taken aback by her." He reached up and brushed my hair away from my face. "This beautiful, intelligent, confrontational woman," he whispered.

I whipped my head forward to stare at the crackling fire. *What is happening?*

"So a confrontation that turned into love," Canda laughed. "What a great story."

"He tells it *so* well," I laughed nervously, wriggling off his lap to sit on the bench again. He let me go, but settled for resting his hand on my upper leg as he sipped his drink. I plastered a half-smile on my face, my mind racing. *What is his game here?*

Canda leaned forward to throw a log onto the campfire. "Then what *are* you two doing all the way out here?"

I glanced sideways at Torren. As much as I trusted Canda and her group, they didn't need to know about our mission. The hesitance in his eyes agreed with me.

"It's business. Of a private nature," I said. "But I promise you, what we're doing in no way aids the Union."

She threw a second log onto the fire and brushed the bark scraps from her hands. "Fair enough. I trust you." I suddenly felt monumentally guilty for having lied to her. "I'm glad you're on our side. Their presence has gotten so bad here," she said, glancing up at the stars.

"It's happening all over the galaxy, Canda," I said. "Not just here. They're even on Hadrin, where there's no profit to be had. They just want control."

Canda looked at the fire and sighed. "So I've read on the wire," she said. "Speaking of, have you two heard about this break-in at the Galactic Union museum? It's incredible. Someone is out there throwing a grenade into the Union's gears in a big way."

"Oh, yeah," I said, resisting the urge to look at Torren. "I saw some news-wires about that." I stared at the dancing flames.

Canda nodded slowly, a thoughtful expression crossing her face. "Well, whoever it is, they're doing the work of almighty Gryta," she breathed, her body reverent and relaxed. "I just wish they'd been around back when...well, you know." I stiffened. "With what happened the *last* time you were here."

I swallowed nervously, but Torren cleared his throat, finally removing his hand from my leg. "You know, my darling, I still don't understand what exactly happened last time you were here," he said innocently, watching me over the rim of his cup.

There it is. The reason he made our marriage cover two years and not five. He needed it to be more plausible that I hadn't shared my entire life story with him yet.

"You're kidding?" Canda said, puzzled.

As I sighed in defeat, Torren gave me a small smirk, knowing he had me backed into a corner. *Bastard.*

He'd done the same thing at Hollak's with Rego and I—laying a trap for me and waiting for the perfect moment to leverage it. I bit my lip, worry spiraling through me.

"I never got around to talking about it, I guess," I said with a dull voice, staring dejectedly into the fire. "Why don't you tell him, Canda?"

He wanted to know the truth? Fine. Let him.

"Are you sure?" she asked. I gestured for her to go ahead, and she leaned forward, resting her elbows on her knees. He lifted his head, watching her hungrily for the answers he wanted so badly. Mab was barely listening, still sharpening her knife. Unless it was a second one.

I picked up the cup of liquor next to me and stared into it. The prospect of my history being dredged up made me want to be anything but sober. I took a huge gulp and winced as the liquor burned all the way down my throat.

"I guess I need to start at the beginning..." Canda said, taking a breath and resting her cup in her lap.

I glanced at Torren, eagerly waiting next to me. *He has no idea what he's in for.*

18

———————

THE TRUTH

"About nineteen years ago," Canda began, "The chancellor of Talar permitted the Galactic Union to come in and start overseeing our mining industry. There's no proof, but it's widely believed that he accepted a bribe for it. The Union's presence here started small, just a few regulations here and there. They helped us optimize our mining industry in exchange for a small percentage of the profit we made on exports. Well, profit came in, and they used that to start making demands."

Torren nodded, knowing where this part of the story was going.

"There were protests, of course, as the people here fought for Talar's right to govern itself. But at the end of the day, it was Talarians who chose to keep the Union in control. Too many people bought into the dream they'd been sold. The Union promised that the new regulations would protect the workers, increase productivity, make Talar into the best version of itself, blah, blah, blah." She rolled her eyes.

"And then it went downhill," he said.

Canda nodded. "Less than three years later, the Union had control of the entire planet. Our miners were being overworked and getting injured while trying to meet the Union's impossible export quotas. Meanwhile, they took the bulk of the profit and allowed *us* a cut. That profit came from our own labor and resources, and they just took it. Pesking bastards." She shook her head.

"Sounds familiar," Torren murmured.

"Yeah, if you've read a history codex, then you know that once their *planetary assistance program* worked on Talar, they moved on to other settled planets. It's a shame, once people realized what was actually happening, it was too late."

"When did the resistance group begin?" Torren asked.

"Well, once all the legal channels were exhausted…alternative methods became necessary. A group of concerned citizens formed. They sabotaged Union equipment, disrupted supply lines, and vandalized mining sites, just generally made things hell for the commanding officers. It worked for a while—the Union presence lessened and there was talk of them pulling out of Talar entirely due to the financial losses they were suffering. It was a brilliant strategy, and the brains of the *entire* operation were the Kensies." Canda glanced my way, and Torren followed her gaze.

"Kensies?" he asked, even though he knew.

"Fenn's parents," Canda said.

My knuckles went white around my cup, and I focused on a glowing ember that had landed on one of the stones around the fire pit.

"The Kensies were professors at the university in Talar City," Canda said. "Fenn's father taught psychology, and her mother…" she trailed off. "I can never remember, something to do with technology?"

"Mechanical engineering," I said, just above a whisper.

"Oh, that's right," Canda nodded. "The Kensies were the ones who organized all the protests. My dads helped, since they were longtime friends. Anyway, once more drastic measures were needed, they founded the Resistance. They laid the groundwork for Talarians to take *some* kind of control over our planet, if only from the shadows. It was the Kensies who built our very first camp. They moved the group out of the city, where homes were being raided, and into the forest."

I watched the errant ember flicker and gasp for life as my eyes glazed over and I retreated inside of myself. I could barely feel the cup in my hands. It was surreal to hear someone talk about the things I had adamantly pushed out of my mind for the past ten years.

"Now, at a certain point," Canda continued, "the Kensies and the others in charge decided we needed to take a more…*offensive* approach with the Union. Why should we simply react to their actions when they could prevent them?" She looked to me, waiting to see if I had any objections. I gritted my teeth and gave her a hesitant nod. She took a deep breath, sitting up straight. "That's when we began actively spying on Union officers. The only problem was that they were suspicious of adults. We needed a spy who was both inconspicuous and smart, someone who could talk their way out of things if they were noticed. Someone the Union would never expect. That's when the Kensies decided to utilize Fenn here." Canda jerked her head toward me.

The ember on the stone pulsed, fighting to stay alight in the cool night air. Torren shifted tensely next to me. I felt him staring. "Your parents had you spy for the resistance?" he asked. "How old were you?"

I swallowed the lump forming in my throat. "Thirteen," I said numbly.

"Fenn was amazing." Canda smiled. "She was really able to think on her feet. She'd go into town, eavesdrop on the officers at their posts, sometimes even follow them through the marketplace picking up whatever info she could. She was just a teenage girl, you know? They didn't notice her, and if they did, it never crossed their minds that she was feeding their conversations straight to the Resistance. It worked like a charm." Her smile fell, her shoulders rounding as she leaned over her drink. "Until it didn't."

The loose ember had succumbed, laying cool and black on the stone. I swirled the liquor in my cup and took a clumsy gulp, spilling some of it on my shirt.

"What happened?" asked Torren, his voice already tinged with regret. He'd heard me tell the officers at the blockade that my family was deceased. He knew where the story was heading.

"I wasn't at the camp at the time," said Canda. "I only saw the aftermath. Fenn, you were there. What exactly happened? I know there was a shootout."

I opened my mouth, but the words caught in my throat. A quick glance at the other two campfires assured me that everyone else was too focused on their own conversations to pay attention to ours.

Torren laid a hand on my arm. "Fenn, you don't have to—"

"It wasn't a shootout." I muttered, silencing him. My voice sounded far off, as if it wasn't my own. "Back then, the Resistance didn't have weapons. We just sabotaged Union equipment and gathered intel. My parents thought that if we weren't armed, it would protect us if we got discovered. That the Union would arrest us, not attack."

"Oh, that's right," said Canda. "Yeah, now that I think about it, we started building our weapons cache *after* what happened that day. Wait—then how did the shooting start?" she asked.

I swallowed, my eyes falling to the drink between my hands. "I made a mistake," I said. Tears formed in the corner of my eyes. "I was eavesdropping on two officers in the marketplace. I guess they had seen me hanging around one too many times. They… they followed me back to camp. We tried to surrender, but the officers just…opened fire. It wasn't a shootout. It was a massacre."

The three of us fell still and silent, letting the roaring fire and the distant chatter of the rest of the group fill the air. Even Mab paused her knife sharpening and quietly stared ahead. The deaths of all those we'd lost hung in the air. Heavy. Stifling. My eyes met Torren's briefly, and he looked uncharacteristically uncomfortable. *Good.*

"Yeah, one of my dads took a blaster hit to the knee, but they both managed to escape. Half the camp escaped, actually. It's just a shame the other half didn't."

"I'm glad your dads made it out," I said, trying to keep my voice from quivering.

"They're doing fine," she shrugged, as if the subject was nothing. "Losing your parents was hard on them. They stayed with the Resistance, but my dad's knee injury prevented him from being able to live out here in the wild. They live in the city now, feeding us regular intel about Union movements happening there."

"That's good," I said numbly.

"Fenn, we all thought you died along with your parents," Canda said. "What happened?"

I blinked back tears before they could spill down my cheeks. "I…I hid," I admitted, shame burning through me, as I shook my head. "I saw my parents go down. I couldn't bear to see the rest. So I ran. I ran back to the city, hoping I could blend in with the crowds. I didn't know what else to do. I was scared that the officers were looking for me. All it would take would be a description of a teenage girl with brown hair and freckles." I swallowed hard. "My family was gone. I couldn't think of a reason to stay."

"So you left…" Canda murmured.

"I found a cargo pilot who was about to leave. Bartered everything I had with me for passage off of Talar. I didn't care where I landed. I just needed it to not be here. That's how I got to Hadrin." I shook my head, remembering the ship touching down on the dusty planet. "He was dropping off a crate of elger jerky, then heading to Rendor to find work."

"There's nothing on Rendor but clones and crime," Canda muttered.

"Now you see why I got off the ship at Hadrin."

"I'm glad you got away," Canda said, her eyes glassy. "I just wish I'd known." She smiled, reaching over and putting her hand over mine. "You have no idea how happy it makes me to see you alive and well. Happily married, at that." I gave her a weak smile, and squeezed her hand before she let go. Torren was quiet. Canda took a breath and perked up. "After that day, we had a hell of a time trying to reorganize. But hey, ten years later, we're still here."

The lightness of her voice while describing the worst day of my life grated on me. Taking a deep breath, I quelled that feeling. I had run away and put it all behind me. Canda had stayed and helped rebuild in the aftermath. She had processed the trauma of it by now, in a way I hadn't let myself. I couldn't hold that against her.

I looked at Torren and saw that his shoulders were slumped. *I hoped he regrets dragging the truth out.* I knew he was skilled at manipulation, but to do it to me, after what we had been through? It hurt.

Tears stung the corners of my eyes. I stared into the darkness just past the firelight. *I need to get away.* If I was going to break down, I wanted to do it alone. I flicked my wrist, emptying the last few sips of my drink into the fire, where it hissed and evaporated.

"I need some fresh air," I grumbled, slamming the cup to the ground and standing up.

"But we're outside," said Canda.

"Smoke's getting to me," I said, my voice about to break. "I need to take a walk." I turned to leave.

Torren jumped to his feet. "Wait—" he said, starting to follow. I turned back, and we locked eyes. We stared at each other for an uncomfortable moment.

As I was about to leave, a high-pitched beeping sound broke the silence. Everyone in camp stopped talking and froze. Behind Torren, Canda stood and looked up at the sky with a hard, focused scowl.

"Incoming ships," she grunted. "Union scout vessels." Mab stood up, holding out the beeping device and showing Canda the screen. There were three blips on the display radar, drawing closer to our location with every passing moment.

Markos was suddenly next to me, eyes locked on the pinging radar. "I *told* you," he growled at Canda. "Yesterday's hit was too soon after the last one. They're *pissed.*"

"Not now, Markos," Canda shot back. She cupped her hands around her mouth. "Get the fires!"

Organized chaos broke out around us. Each of the campfires was doused with water, the smoke vacuums whirring to a higher setting to inhale the subsequent smoke clouds. Resistance members began gathering up any man-made items sitting out, concealing them under the trees. Most of the group hurried toward the large cave, surprisingly orderly despite the underlying urgency.

Torren and I quietly watched it all, our eyes adjusting to the moon as our only light.

Mab shut off the beeping device and began arming her blaster rifle with a practiced precision. She moved close to Canda, meeting her gaze and jerking her head toward the woods north of us. Canda's eyes flicked toward Torren and I—and Mab, after a moment, nodded.

I have no idea what they just said to each other, but a decision was made.

Canda turned to us. "Come on, you two. Let's get you somewhere safe."

Torren and I glanced at each other, then followed Canda as she led us into the woods with confident strides. The lack of light barely slowed her down. Mab clicked an ion lantern on, illuminating our way. The sounds of the anxious hustle died away as Canda took us further and further from camp. I disliked not knowing where we were going, but since we didn't know the area half as well as Canda, we would have to trust her. Torren rested his hand on my arm as we walked, and though I could feel concern in his touch, I ignored him.

"There," said Mab, aiming her lantern ahead of us.

The light fell on the forest floor, next to a large tree stump. Canda crossed to it and crouched down. We watched her make a pulling motion, and the entire patch of ground in front of her crumpled and moved. Shocked, I realized there had been a matte brown tarp laying hidden under dirt and fir needles. As she whipped the tarp away, I saw a very intentionally dug hole in the ground. It was large, with a series of six or seven stone steps leading down to a metal door. Canda took the steps carefully in the low light, lifting the rusted latch on the door and swinging it open on well-oiled hinges.

"What's this?" I asked.

"It's a bunker," Torren whispered, peering inside.

"Come on," Canda said, gesturing for us to go inside. Torren and I descended the steps and stepped through the door, but Canda and Mab didn't follow us. "Wait here," Canda ordered, "We'll come get you when it's clear."

"You're not staying?" I asked.

"It was only built to hold one or two people. Don't worry, Mab and I will join the rest of the crew in the cave."

My mouth dropped open as I realized the bunker had probably been built specifically for Canda—to keep the leader of the Resistance safe, in case the Union dropped down on the camp.

"Canda, we're not taking your bunker," I argued, starting to come back up the steps. She held out a hand, signaling for me to stop.

"Fenn, I just found out you were alive after ten years of thinking the Union had killed you and cleared your body away with all the rest. I'm not letting them find you now," she said, "Besides, my scouts are the ones who dragged you here. The least I can do right now is keep you safe." She looked past me at Torren. "There are lanterns next to the door, plus rations and water if you need them."

Torren took an ion lantern from the wall and flipped it on. Canda gently pushed me back inside the bunker and grabbed the heavy door.

As it started to swing closed, Torren reached over my shoulder and braced his hand against it. The door stopped abruptly against his palm. "Hold on," he commanded loudly.

Canda paused, and Mab's hand calmly moved to one of her knives.

I had a suspicion that he'd downplayed his height and strength all evening to politely make his female hosts comfortable. He wasn't downplaying them now.

Holding his lantern near my face, he looked me in the eye. "Do you trust her with your life?" he asked, jerking his head at Canda. *I shouldn't have expected Torren to voluntarily enter a place without a sure exit.*

I searched his eyes, my mind racing. Canda took her hands away from the door and stood back. *Would she turn us over to the Union? Does she blame me for what happened ten years ago? For getting half the camp killed?* I met her eyes, weighing my entire history with her in a matter of seconds. Torren's inability to trust had probably protected him countless times, but I knew Canda.

I gave him a nod, and he took his hand off the door.

"Sorry, I just had to check. I'd rather burn a bridge than willingly walk into a trap."

"Smart boy," said Canda, nodding her approval. "Don't worry, it only locks from the inside, and believe me—I would have taken your blaster first if I wanted to corner you."

Torren tapped the weapon at his hip, reassuring himself it was still there. He pulled the metal door closed, plunging us into deeper darkness. The lantern in Torren's hand illuminated the back of the door enough for him to bolt it. I heard Canda and Mab lay the canvas tarp back down and cover it with dirt. Soon, the sound of their footsteps faded away, and only silence remained.

The faint hum of a Union ship buzzed overhead. I took a breath and tried to calm myself, but dread hung heavy on my heart. The searching Union ships made me uneasy, but my recently unearthed trauma felt worse. I didn't even want to see Torren, much less speak to him, and he happened to be the one person I was locked in an underground bunker with.

Fucking perfect.

19

———————

EXTINGUISHED ENTIRELY

I GLANCED AROUND AT WHAT I COULD SEE IN THE SOFT WHITE glow of the lantern. The bunker was a tiny space, barely bigger than the rooms on Torren's ship. There were a few supply crates in one corner, and a sleeping cot in the other. Torren sat down on the largest crate, setting the lantern beside him as he ran his hand through his hair. I stayed near the door with my hands shaking, weighing the pros and cons of throwing the bolt aside and fleeing.

You can't run away, Fenn. Not this time.

"Fenn…" Torren said behind me, trepidation in his voice.

Shit, I guess we're doing this. I inhaled slowly and prepared myself for the confrontation. If I couldn't leave, I was going to speak my mind.

"You had no right to do that, Torren" I said. My voice broke, but I looked him dead in the eye.

"I'm sorry," he said. "I had no idea."

"Exactly. I was trying to keep it that way."

"Fenn," he sighed wearily, lifting his shoulders. "What do you want me to say? Getting answers, figuring things out, it's what I do."

"Don't give me that shit," I snapped. "You are remarkable at what you do, Torren, but people aren't comms booths. You can't just hack into them whenever you want info."

"That's not what I was doing," he said, gritting his teeth.

"Isn't it?" My voice raised. "I *told* you I didn't want to talk about my past. Multiple times. I practically begged you to let it go. But as soon as you saw an opportunity to back me into a corner, you took it."

He scowled and stood up. "Hang on, aren't *you* the one who poked around my ship after I explicitly told you not to?"

I laughed out loud. *He wants to go there? Fine.*

"I did that, yes," I admitted, lifting my chin. "And I *am* sorry, but this is different."

"How?" he asked. "We both pried into each other's business."

"It's different because when I pried, I discovered what you do for a living," I said. "You pried and made me remember why I hate myself."

He stilled. We stood silently, watching each other for a few moments.

"My parents were killed," I said. "A lot of people were killed. And it was my fault. My mistake. I don't deserve peace. I don't deserve a friend as good as Rego. That's why I'm here. If I can save his life, then maybe...*maybe* I'm not as worthless as I thought."

"Fenn—"

"No, Torren, I don't want to hear it. You have no idea what it's like to lose everything!"

The tears finally overcame me, rolling down my cheeks. I gasped, holding in a sob as I looked at the door again. The distant buzz of a Union patrol ship permeated the space, reminding me that I couldn't leave anytime soon.

Defeated, I sank down onto the edge of the cot, wrapping my arms around myself, and I stared at the floor. I didn't know what else to do. I could feel Torren watching me. A pang of guilt struck me for having yelled at him, but the tears I'd refused for years were finally here. There was nothing I could do about it.

I hate everything. I hate the Union. I hate Rego for getting himself into trouble. I hate myself for being so weak. I hate—

A sound drew me back to the present. When I looked up, Torren had seated himself on the crate across from me. Slowly and quietly, he positioned himself to face me, resting his arms on the tops of his thighs and leaning in toward me.

"I'm sorry, Fenn," he whispered. "Truly, I am." He sounded genuine, and I saw a pained look in his eyes. His hands fidgeted as if fighting the urge to reach for me.

I nodded, wiping tears from my cheek. We sat in silence for a moment, and I suddenly felt very self-conscious.

"I know what you're thinking," I muttered. "How can I be falling apart over something that happened years ago?"

"I wasn't thinking that."

"Well, I wouldn't blame you if you did."

"Fenn…" he whispered, then paused. My eyes traced his silhouette, waiting. Nothing.

With a sigh, he leaned back on the crate, bracing his back against the wall behind him, and we mired in silence. I buried my face in my hands, feeling the dark overcome me.

"When I was fifteen…" He cleared his throat and looked down at his hands. "The Union occupied my planet." His voice was numb. I lifted my head and stared at him.

"I was born in the Sylvad system…a planet called Rorric," he continued.

I racked my brain for everything I'd ever heard about Rorric. The Sylvad system was home to Kedigan species, and had many planets with biomes similar to Talar. Rorric, however, was tropical. Torren came from islands and lush jungles, white sand beaches, and ocean as far as you could see. I recalled his speed and agility in the tranquility pool back on Laigo. It suddenly made sense.

"Shortly before I was born, my parents were looking for work. Rorric needed workers, so they packed up their life and immigrated." I watched his gaze drift off as he went home, if only in his mind. "We were kolo bean harvesters. We worked in the jungle, and sometimes on the beach. I enjoyed climbing, but I loved the sea. Every afternoon, I'd run to the beach and dive for stone clams until I had enough for dinner." He looked down at his palms, his fingers curling with the buzz of nostalgia. "The clam shells cut up my hands, but it never stopped me. Nothing made me prouder than bringing back a net so heavy with clams, my mother needed both hands to lift it."

My gaze raked over him in the light of the lantern. I pictured him at sixteen, climbing kolo trees and collecting bean pods. I saw him emerging from the surf, shaking his wet hair out of his face with a smile. I could barely match it to the stoic man that sat before me.

"It was good work. Hard, but not grueling. We had each other, and everything we needed," he said. "Until the Union came in."

My heart sank. I understood now why Torren didn't drink kolo. It reminded him too much of home. A wave of guilt hit me as I remembered telling him he was weird back at the kolo stand. *If I had only known.* I watched as he looked down and absentmindedly picked at the edge of the crate with his fingernail.

"They found some untapped corrovium wells on Rorric," he continued. "And since the Union needs corrovium to power their ships, things changed. They took over. Cleared thousands of miles of our jungle, displacing hundreds of species of animals. They ruined something wild and beautiful. All for some fuel." His voice was flat. "They installed a massive drill to extract the corrovium, but they needed workers—cheap workers. Suddenly, all kinds of *problems* were found with Rorric's kolo industry, and they shut it down. Still needing a living, the locals had no choice. Kedigan locals and human settlers like my parents all had to take jobs at the extraction and purification facility. We had to leave our home near the beach and live at a crowded camp they'd set up near the drill site."

"Torren…I'm so sorry."

He shrugged. "The workers began to disagree with the whole arrangement. They started to gather each night to discuss it. There was talk of asking for higher wages and better living conditions. They began to plan a strike." He paused.

"What happened?" I asked.

"We never got the chance," he whispered, the weakness in his voice unbefitting of the stern image I'd had of him all this time. "The overseeing officers caught wind and put a stop to it."

"They punished everyone?"

He allowed himself a slow inhale, then shook his head. "Not quite. Punishment would have been meant to correct our behavior. They needed to stop the spark of revolution from fanning into a flame. So, they extinguished it entirely."

My heart dropped. I studied his face in the dim light, looking for hope that the story wouldn't end as poorly as I knew it would.

He reached his hand to the back of his neck, rubbing slowly as if subconsciously comforting himself. His eyes were fixed on the floor now, but his mind seemed a thousand miles elsewhere. "Our sleeping quarters were next to the drilling facility. Sometime late in the night, they opened the corrovium shaft and let the unrefined gas leak out."

Tears stung the corners of my eyes again.

"They poisoned the entire camp while it slept," he said.

My stomach turned, twisting into painful knots. I had thought Talar had gotten it bad all these years, but we had at least gotten a resistance movement going. Rorric hadn't even had the chance.

"I would have died that night," Torren admitted, "but I was shaken awake by someone, a young Kedigan who nearly jumped out of her fur when I opened my eyes. She and three other Kedi were awake. We think that because we were teenagers, we didn't succumb to the gas the way the children and the older people had. My parents..." He trailed off, suspended in thought. "Anyway, the five of us went to work trying to wake people up. All the while fighting to breathe and having coughing fits that brought us to our knees. We shook as many people as we could, but no one else woke up. They all just lay there. They looked peaceful. As if they were sleeping and might wake up any minute."

I sat quietly, imagining their desperation and terror. Tears silently flowed down my cheeks. I couldn't believe I'd told him that he had no idea what I'd been through.

"We might have died ourselves, but the Kedigan who woke me, she forced us out of camp and into the jungle. Once we could breathe again, we ran. We ran, and ran, only stopping when our legs could no longer move." His eyes focused again and he leaned forward, bringing his hands into his lap and looking down at them. "To tell you the truth, the Kedigan could have kept going, but they stopped when *I* could no longer make it. Their anatomy had repelled the corrovium gas better than mine. I coughed and retched for hours afterward, and it permanently weakened my lungs."

"That's why you need Respirin," I said.

He gave me a subtle nod, making me realize how lucky I was. I had no physical scars from my battle with the Union—just awful memories and the occasional nightmare. Every breath Torren took was tinged with a permanent reminder of our enemy's cruelty.

"We sat awake in the jungle the rest of the night, huddled together in horror. We were too scared to sleep, and too numb to grieve. All of our friends and family…everyone was gone. We should have been relieved to be alive, but the truth is…we weren't."

I closed my eyes and steadied my breath so I wouldn't burst into tears again. I knew *exactly* what he meant. When I looked up, he was listlessly raking his hair out of his face, eyes still on his lap.

"We waited until sunrise, then crept back toward camp. By then, the Union had shut the corrovium vent and were removing the bodies. We had a feeling they would simply write it off as an accident and find a new crop of workers. We weren't sure if they were looking for us or not…so we left."

I sat in a stunned silence, dabbing at my eyes with the back of my hand. I let the new reality take hold. *His story is mine.* We had both fled our homes, and had everything taken from us. We had both survived. I thought about what Rego had said as we were leaving Hadrin. *You two are more alike than you know.* Rego had been right.

Eventually, he inhaled and glanced my way. "I am so sorry, Fenn." he said, meeting my eyes. "For dragging your pain out into the open like that. I never imagined the truth would be something so awful. That was naive of me. But at least you know now, you're not alone."

My breath caught in my throat, and new tears stung my eyes.

"I know how those memories creep back up," he said. "I know what it feels like to push them back down. You do it again and again, knowing it'll just be back."

I stared at him. The lonely labyrinth of my heart wasn't as isolated as I thought. Torren knew it too.

"And the guilt?" I asked, my voice breaking.

He cocked his head, then pushed himself off the crate and knelt in front of me, taking my hands gently in his.

"Fenn…" he whispered, "all survivors carry guilt. But you're not going to make it if you don't let yours go. Especially when you did nothing to earn it."

The tears flowed freely down my face as I shook my head.

"But I led them right into camp," I sobbed. "I should have been more careful-"

"Stop it," he said.

I blinked at him through my tears, and watched him soften his brow and his voice.

"I mean no disrespect to your parents, but you were a *kid*. They put you into a dangerous situation. What happened wasn't because of anything you did."

I sobbed openly, my vision blurring through my tears. "But if—" I choked out, the hurtful words slamming around in my head, buzzing louder than the patrol ships outside.

He reached up, putting his hands on either side of my face. "Look at me," he said.

My eyes snapped to his, and I held my breath.

"It didn't happen because of you, or your parents. It happened because of the Union. Because they see citizens as disposable. Fuel for their machine. Don't blame yourself for their cruelty." He took his hands away, his eyes studying my face. "You did *nothing* wrong."

I drew in a desperate breath, suddenly aware of how badly I'd needed to hear those words.

When I cried this time, my body shook, releasing years of pent-up grief. Torren put an arm around me, pulling me toward him. I went willingly, desperate to be held. We collided, sitting with our arms around each other on the cold bunker floor. As I cried into his shoulder, he cradled my head gently against his chest with one hand, caressing my back with the other. He held me tight, keeping me afloat with the surprising tenderness of his touch. He knew I didn't need kind words in that moment; I just needed to feel less alone.

After a few minutes, I caught my breath and the tears subsided. I lifted my face away from his chest and sat back, giving both of us space to breathe. I patted my eyes delicately with my sleeve, feeling guilty for having fallen to pieces right after he had told me his own tragedy. He'd told me the harrowing details; I had to know how it ended.

"So," I said once my voice was usable again, "what happened next?"

Sighing, he leaned his back wearily against the supply crate behind him.

"Well," he said, "our little group stole a ship, a rickety little Dawn-Wing, and we left Rorric."

The Dawn-Wing we flew here with. That battered ship was the very symbol of freedom and escape to Torren and his friends. *He must be attached to it. I know I would be.*

Something flickered across his face—not quite a smile, more the suggestion of one.

"You should have seen Carrio trying to pilot it while the rest of us crowded around him shouting frantic instructions. None of us really knew what we were doing, but we figured it out enough to get away."

"Carrio was one of the Kedigan you escaped with?" I leaned against the crate, inching next to him. He lifted his arm, placing it delicately around me. My heart slowed at the nearness of him.

"Mm-hmm," he hummed. "We made our way into the galaxy together, looking for a place to lay low. We knew that if the Union went looking for us, we'd be easily spotted." He paused, then laughed.

"Did I miss something?"

"Spotted?" He threw me a glance, still half-smiling. "Just a joke. The Kedigan on Rorric are known for having spots in their fur."

I thought about all the Kedigan I had ever seen. They'd all had solid-colored fur, or stripes, like Jera. When the news-wires first broke about the museum robbery, there had been speculation that the thief had been a Kedigan. It had just been Torren—a human half-raised by his feline friends.

I suddenly fully understood why Torren had given the Egg back to the Froxians for free. *It hadn't even been a choice for him.* He knew the pain of having had everything taken away by the Union. He wanted to lessen that pain for someone else.

He was so different from the man I thought he was when we'd met. *What a sweet surprise.* I leaned my heavy head onto his shoulder, wanting to cling to his warmth and strength. "And then what?" I asked.

"We wandered around the galaxy for a bit, trying to make a living. Honest work goes out the window fast when you're starving," he chuckled, his muted joy filling the space. "We became thieves. It was risky work, but it kept us from going hungry."

"Sounds like the five of you are close."

"We were," he said.

Were.

"Where are they?" I asked.

He hummed, leaning his head against mine. "The others grew up and moved on to slightly more legitimate work. I might have too, but swindling and smuggling...they're all I know. I continued with petty crime for a while, which eventually grew in scale, which eventually became robbing Union facilities, like the museum."

"And then what?" I asked, lifting my head from his shoulder and looking up at his face.

"And then..." His arm around me tightened ever so slightly. "And then I met you," he said, looking down and meeting my gaze. His voice was hesitant, as if he was in unfamiliar territory and unsure how to proceed.

"Oh, yes," I said in a light voice, hoping to break the tension. "The girl who threatened to call the authorities on you the moment you met her."

He laughed out loud. It was a welcomed sound after all my sobbing, and it made me smile. I leaned toward him without thinking, putting both of my arms around him. Holding him. I wanted to thank him for guiding me through my grief, for shattering the chains of guilt I'd been carrying for years. I didn't even know where to begin to find the words. He put his arms around me as well, returning my embrace.

"I'm glad I met you," I whispered against his shoulder.

He opened his mouth, but didn't say anything.

I took a breath, remembering how painfully delicious he smelled. Though we had already kissed at the blockade, this embrace felt far more intimate. Here, there was no one to pretend for. We were on the floor of a locked bunker, our hearts pounding, our breath mingling as we held each other in the dark.

In the warmth of his arms, I felt a tension in his muscles, as if there were words on his tongue he couldn't bring himself to say. His breath deepened and his chest moved up and down in a way that hinted at the flurry of emotions underneath it all.

I pulled away, but he wasn't as quick to do the same, holding onto my arms as if reluctant to let me go. Feeling self-conscious, I dabbed at the tears on my cheek with the back of my hand

"Here," he said in a soft voice. He placed his hands on either side of my face, using his thumbs to gently wipe my tears away.

"Thanks," I laughed. "I think my face is a lost cause at this point." I saw a white, folded cloth poking out of the top of his jacket's breast pocket. I reached for it. "Can I borrow this?"

"Wait—" he said, reaching for it. I had already pulled it out of his pocket. A small object fell from the folds of the fabric, landing lightly in my lap.

"What's this?" I said, picking the object up and inspecting it in the light of the lantern. It was a flower, pressed and dried by the cloth it had been wrapped in.

"You have a sprig of Star Bonnet?"

He'd taken one of the blooms we'd found. Right after I told him about the courting tradition, and what gifting it meant. *As I picked this, I chose you.* He opened his mouth, but it seemed words wouldn't come. He shifted nearer to me, and when I looked up, our faces were close. Close enough for me to see the flecks of golden hazel in his eyes that reflected in the light. He was staring at my lips, his own mouth slightly open.

He's about to kiss me? Now? With my eyes red and my face tearstained? I tilted my face toward his, finding myself barely able to breathe. I wanted him. His arms. His breath. His mouth. I'm not sure which one of us leaned in first, but suddenly our lips were just inches away. I melted against him, eager to be even closer.

A rustling sound broke the silence, halting the heated moment.

We stopped, listening carefully. Someone was outside the bunker. Either Canda was back, or the Union had found us.

Footsteps clattered down the stone steps, and Torren and I sprang to our feet. A loud banging noise echoed through the bunker, a fist repeatedly hitting the metal door. Torren's hand fell to my waist, holding onto me as he reached for his blaster. He primed it and aimed at the door.

"It's me," Canda's voice echoed from the other side.

I breathed a sigh of relief, then looked up, searching Torren's gaze. He holstered his blaster and studied my face. Once that door was open, the moment would be over. *I don't want it to be over.*

"Fenn?" Canda said.

It was over. With a sigh, I stepped out of Torren's arm, crossing the room and unbolting the door. Canda stood outside, looking relieved.

"They're gone," she sighed. "Come on, let's get back to camp and get some sleep."

Throwing one more glance at Torren, I turned to her and nodded. Climbing the few stairs out of the bunker, I felt dazed. As Canda led us through the woods with an ion lamp, Torren stayed vigilantly close. He held his hand near me in the dark, ready to catch me if I stumbled. I can't remember who first reached for who, but by the time we reached camp, his hand was in mine.

20

REMIND ME OF THE STARS

I WOKE TO THE SMELL OF THE MORNING FIRES BEING COAXED TO life, and the sounds of the camp already buzzing. There was more noise than I expected for a place that had nearly been discovered the night before. I yawned, stretching out on my bedroll to stare up at the craggy cave ceiling. Last night after leaving the bunker, Canda had ushered us into the cave where the rest of her Resistance members were bedding down for the night. No one had seemed particularly rattled that the Union ships had flown right over the camp. *They must be used to it.* I didn't think I ever could be.

Before falling asleep, Torren and I had laid side by side on the bedrolls, unable to talk without waking our neighbors. We had both shared so much in the bunker, but there was something unsaid lingering between us as we lay there, shoulders touching in the dark. He had talked me through my pain in that bunker, and made my memories feel less heavy.

I didn't remember drifting off, but it was one of the easiest nights of sleep I'd had in years.

Now, breathing the crisp morning air, I remembered the kiss that had almost happened last night. I sat up, and something on my pillow caught my eye. The dried sprig of Star Bonnet. My heart skipped a beat as I reached for the delicate blossom. He'd left it for me to wake up to.

Slipping the flower into my pocket, I smoothed my slept-on hair as well as I could without a mirror. I pulled my boots on and stumbled bleary-eyed out of the cave.

I moved through the bustling camp, appreciating all Canda had done with the project my parents had begun. This was their legacy. *A fight for Talar.* I found my way to the trio of campfires, one of which was already roaring again. Torren was sitting on the same log bench as last night, talking to Canda while she stirred a large, boiling pot over the fire. When I approached, Torren shifted down the bench, making room for me with a gentle smile.

"Morning," he said. As I sat, he leaned in, giving me a gentle kiss on the forehead. It felt decidedly different from the performative show of affection he had put on after the dwind game. There was something about the way his lips brushed my skin now. The fact that he took his time leaning away.

I felt myself blushing as he handed me a steaming cup of high kolo in a clay mug. I cleared my throat and took it gratefully, acutely aware of the way our fingers touched as he passed it over.

"Good morning!" Canda chirped. "I wasn't sure if we should wake you, but he said you needed the rest."

"I did, thank you," I said, taking a sip of the kolo. Across the fire, Mab sat cross-legged on a tree stump stool. All her knives and guns must have been sharpened and cleaned, because she was idly smoking a rusticane stick and watching me intensely.

What did I do to piss Mab off?

Canda ladled something out of the pot and into two wooden bowls, handing them to Torren and I. From the aroma, I knew what the bowl held even before the steam cleared.

"Moat grass porridge?" I asked, taking a spoon from her outstretched hand.

"It's a bland breakfast," Canda said to Torren. "Nothing to wire home about. But it's filling and has a lot of nutrients. Plus, it's easy to forage. I'm sure you remember, Fenn?"

Canda and I had been raised on moat grass bread and porridge. After my parents had moved the Talarian resistance to the forest, there were days when it was the only food we had. I'd indeed found it bland all those years ago, but sheer nostalgia had my stomach rumbling.

"We're grateful to have something other than packaged rations," Torren said, barely examining the contents of his bowl, determined to eat whatever it was without complaint.

Mab threw the end of her rusticane stick into the dirt and stomped it out. She stood and stalked over to us.

"Hold on," she grumbled. "It needs something." Pulling a pouch out of her pocket, she gestured for me to hold out my hand. When she tipped the pouch, small, brown objects tumbled out.

"Bevelnuts?" I gasped, my mouth watering. The round nuts were one of the best things you could ever hope to forage on Talar; I'd once paid a pilot half a week's wages for a small jar of them on Hadrin.

"Texture for the porridge," Mab explained, pouring a few into Torren's hand as well.

We both threw them into our bowls and gave her nods of appreciation.

"Thank you, Mab," I said.

Mab flicked her eyebrows up and down in response. She walked away, tossing her long black hair over her shoulder and lighting another rusticane stick.

"Wow," said Canda, once Mab was out of earshot. "She picks those herself and never shares. She must like you."

She sure had me fooled.

I took a bite of my porridge and closed my eyes. Mab was right —the sweet, softened moat grass grains were delightful with the buttery crunch of nuts. It took me back, and for once, I breathed easy. After last night, memories from my life here came without the usual sting of regret.

"I suppose you're wanting to head out this morning?" Canda asked.

"We are unfortunately on a deadline," Torren said. "You mentioned that you had a vector map? I would love to get a look at it before we leave."

"Sure thing," she nodded. I saw her notice my sleep-matted hair. "I know you're in a rush, but would you like to have a shower before you go?"

I gasped, almost spilling porridge onto my lap. I had freshened up here and there, but hadn't bathed since we left Torren's ship.

I looked at Torren with pleading eyes. "I would do anything for a shower. I would *kill* for one."

He watched my face with amusement. "Easy, killer, calm down." He nodded at Canda.

"I think we can spare a few extra minutes."

The camp's shower area was, presumably for privacy's sake, just a short walk through a small stretch of woods. There were two open-air wooden stalls with doors, each with a metal shower-head and water reservoir suspended above them. The floor of each stall had a mesh grate to stand on, and trenches dug on either side to direct water runoff away.

"This is quite a setup," I said. "Much better than what the group had back in our day."

Canda grinned. "There weren't many things I insisted on when I took charge, but this was one of them," she said, sauntering over and resting her arm proudly on one of the wooden doors. "I find morale is better around camp if everyone has the ability to wash off the sweat and dirt after a long day."

"It will certainly improve *my* mood," I grinned.

She handed us each a clean, dry-cloth from a hanging basket. "Both stalls are stocked with soap, and there should be just enough water in each of the reservoirs."

"I'm sure we'll be fine," Torren said.

"I'm sure you will," Canda said, winking at me. "I'll leave you two lovebirds to it."

We waited until Canda was gone.

"Do you want to go first?" Torren asked.

"No need," I shrugged. "We can shower at the same time."

"I didn't realize you were so eager to see me without clothes on," he said with a playful smirk.

I paused. *Torren's cracking jokes now? Flirtatious jokes?*

"I meant *separately…*"

He let out a small laugh and entered one of the shower stalls. I stepped into the other one, shaking my head, pretending to be annoyed with the teasing. The walls of the stalls were short, about neck-high, meaning we'd be seeing a little of each during our showers. More than a little, if we weren't careful.

As we hung our bags up on the hooks outside our doors, I quietly sorted through my emotions. The dynamic between us was the most painless it had been since we met, but it felt far from simple. We both unlaced our boots, stepping out of them and setting them outside. I glanced over as Torren began to unfasten his shirt, and I quickly turned away, my face pink with embarrassment.

Why am I so nervous? This doesn't have to be a big deal.

I wanted to make some kind of joke to break the tension, but nothing came to mind. I pulled my clothes off, and it felt strange but freeing to be naked in the middle of a forest. Torren and I glanced each other's way at the same time, nothing but a wooden wall between us. At his height, if he got close to the wall, he'd be able to see right over it. Suddenly embarrassed, I crossed my arms over my chest.

"I won't look," he assured me with a smile, looking straight ahead at his shower handle.

The overcast pall Talar was so known for had dissipated, the sun now bathing us in warm light. I barely glanced in Torren's direction, but when I did, my eyes lingered on what I could see of his shoulders and chest. Sunlight kissed his tan skin, bringing out a beautiful golden undertone. My own skin was so pale that in the right light, you could see the thin blue rivers of my veins. Like my freckles, I had always been self-conscious about it.

Torren and I pulled the reservoir chains over our heads, releasing cascades of water down on ourselves. I closed my eyes, letting the refreshing water wash away the sweat and dirt. The sun had heated the metal reservoirs all morning, making the water comfortably warm. I let go of the chain and reached for the block of soap near me. It was handmade, dotted with dried petals that gave it a faintly floral scent. I rinsed the bar of soap off and began to lather up.

"So…" Torren said, massaging soap over his neck and shoulders.

"What?"

He shrugged his shoulders at me. "I suppose I should apologize for going so over the top with our cover last night," he said, "physically speaking."

My muscles stiffened, recalling the feeling of being on his lap, his arms holding me against his chest. I could still feel his breath warm on the back of my neck. My pulse quickened.

"No harm done," I said, my cheeks going pink. I pulled the shower handle and rinsed my face, hoping to hide that I was blushing.

"Why did you give Canda that cover anyway?" he asked.

I spat water out of my mouth and glanced down at the wooden ring on my finger.

"I don't know," I deadpanned.

"You don't know?"

I rinsed off silently, purposefully ignoring his question, glancing over at him when the silence stretched too long. His head was tilted back, his eyes closed as he let water run over his face and chest. I bit my lip, guiltily taking advantage of the moment to watch him. He stood, glistening before me, as the rare sun caught the water droplets clinging to his upper body. I watched as he reached up with both hands and raked his fingers through his dark, wet hair, his muscles flexing and pulling taut under his skin. He was *perfect*.

I can't lie to myself anymore. Not after last night. I had feelings for him. I was becoming dangerously used to his presence. I felt myself becoming attached. I only half-focused on lathering soap into my hair, too caught up in everything that he was.

"*Something* must have prompted you to tell her we were married," he smirked, refusing to let go of the subject. I realized I could make something up and keep denying my feelings, or I could tell him the truth. The truth was embarrassing, but I found myself wanting to be honest.

"I, uh...didn't like the way she was looking at you," I said, ironically aware that my own gaze was locked on his bare chest at that moment.

He opened his eyes, and I clumsily snapped my attention back to the soap in my hands. He finished rinsing himself off, leaning thoughtfully against the far corner of his shower stall. His smirk vanished.

"You were jealous?" his smirk deepened.

"I wouldn't go *that* far," I rolled my eyes.

"If you say so," he laughed.

I rinsed the soap out of my hair and squeezed out the excess water. I was about to start washing my feet when he spoke.

"Hey, Sketch?" he said, looking down at his own feet. "I'm going to come over to the divider, so if you want to hide behind it, you better do it now."

"What?"

He took a step forward. I rushed towards the wooden wall that separated us, crossing my arms over my top half again. He looked up, eyes on mine as he folded his arms over the wooden barrier and leaned on them. He studied my face up close in the late morning light.

"What is it?" I asked, watching beads of water drip from his chin and land on his chest.

"Look at that," he said wistfully, his gaze gliding over my nose and cheeks.

"*What?*" I repeated, mildly annoyed.

"Your freckles," he said.

I blushed and looked away. "Sorry, they're always noticeable in bright daylight," I muttered.

"Don't apologize," he chided me with a half grin. "I like them. They remind me of..." He trailed off, his smile fading.

"Of what?" I asked, my lungs tight with concern as he studied my face.

"The stars," he whispered.

Torren spent so much time traveling from one end of the galaxy to the other. The stars were his home. I swallowed nervously as his eyes darted toward my mouth and lingered.

He's going to kiss me. I bit my lower lip and began to lean in closer to him.

"Listen, I have this rule about my work..." he murmured, his eyes still fixed on my lips.

"Yeah?" I said softly. I continued to lean toward him, slowly lifting my face up.

He didn't lean in, but he didn't pull away either.

"I don't believe in," he gulped, his throat bobbing with the motion, "working together...while being together."

Being together?

"You don't?" I whispered, not particularly inclined to believe him at the moment.

"No matter how much I may like someone..." he said, his voice faltering.

"Is that so?" I stood on my toes, making myself more accessible.

"I..." he began, but trailed off.

Stop fighting it.

I angled my face towards his and looked at him dreamily, hoping I looked half as enticing to him as he did to me in that moment.

He slowly reached his hand to my face, cupping my jaw and brushing his thumb across my bottom lip.

"Damn it," he swore, giving in. "Come here."

I held my breath as he began to lower his face down to meet mine. *We are going to kiss.* His movements were achingly slow, but it was happening. I closed my eyes as he pressed his lips to mine with measured gentleness. My heart could have stopped completely and I wouldn't have noticed. I was too caught up in him. The sensation took me back to that charged moment at the blockade. *If I kissed you for real, you would know.*

He was right.

Pulling away for a moment, he broke the kiss, then immediately leaned in again. He brushed my mouth with his bottom lip, caressing the side of my face tenderly. The heat in my chest took over, pulling me toward him with a force like gravity. I slid my hand to the back of his neck, eager to draw him closer. His tongue teased mine, and I let out a soft sound of surprise. We pulled away to grab a breath before hungrily coming back together, our desire for each other evenly matched.

I had been touched before. I had been kissed. But never like this.

Right as I contemplated climbing over the stall divider to get to him, a muffled *ping* sounded from nearby. We both opened our eyes, freezing to listen. Another *ping.* It had to be coming from his vector tablet.

Torren panted, his eyes meeting mine. He growled in frustration and pulled away. I leaned after him as he did, desperate not to lose the closeness, but I was stopped short by the divider. He reached over his door, grabbing his bag and pulling out his vector tablet, not caring that his hands were wet. He opened the alert, his face falling as he scanned the screen.

"What is it?"

"I was afraid this would happen," he groaned. Handing me the tablet, he grabbed one of the dry-cloths Canda had left for us and hurriedly mopped the excess water from his limbs.

What could possibly be important enough to interrupt the moment we were having? I righted the tablet and was greeted by a photo of my best friend.

Rego.

A wave of guilt hit me as I realized my mind had been elsewhere lately, not on the job. The screen in front of me displayed a multitude of information. Rego's bounty listing. Torren had shown it to us back on Hadrin. It looked the same, except now the bounty amount was higher. *1,000* credits higher.

"How?" I asked, panic at the edge of my voice.

"The Hackal clan must be desperate to cross debtors off their list. They're starting to not care what the cost is."

"What does this mean for us? For Rego?" I asked.

Torren pulled fresh clothes from his bag and began dressing, his body stiff. When I looked up, he was fastening his pants and throwing a shirt over his head. Once he'd pulled it down into place, he took the tablet back and stowed it in his bag, barely looking at me.

"It means we need to go," he said, his voice flat. "The higher that bounty gets, the higher the skill will be of the hunters pursuing it. We have even less time now to keep Rego alive."

I stood in silence, realizing that if the bounty kept climbing, it could reach an amount we couldn't afford.

Torren grabbed my bag and tossed it at me. "Get dressed."

21

YOU REALLY HAD ME GOING

Torren and I followed Canda, matching her urgent stride as she led us into the cave at the edge of camp. We passed through the main cavern where we had all slept the night before, and veered into a dark recess in the corner. Once inside, I realized it was a tunnel, with a soft glow coming from further down the rocky surface. The light was dim, but Canda moved through it with confident familiarity, so we followed. The tunnel eventually opened up into another smaller cavern, and we were greeted by the low hum of a power generator.

At the center of the cavern, a large round table stood, its green, glowing surface painting the cavern ceiling with a soft, luminescent glimmer. It was a vector map, the largest I had seen in person. Canda had mentioned how hard it had been lately to move the camp to another location. This must be the reason. She strode right up to the side of it and rested her hands on the perimeter. Her concerned face was bathed in its neon glare as she beckoned us over.

"Nice map," I said.

"Thanks. We stole it," she said, confirming my suspicion that it had belonged to the Union. She looked at Torren, the planes of her face steady. "You got those coordinates?"

Torren stepped forward as Canda tapped at the control panel on the table.

"You can put them in here," she said.

Torren leaned over the control panel, keying in a series of numbers so long I could hardly believe he was pulling them from memory. When he was finished, he stepped back, and Canda configured the view to our current location. A vector-generated version of the surrounding terrain appeared across the map's surface. It showed an expanse of trees broken up by rock formations and streams. The first thing I noticed was that our path cut through rockier terrain than we had traversed yesterday.

There was a reason the Resistance was based out here, and a reason they hadn't been found; the wilderness here was difficult to navigate, even for native Talarians.

"Okay," Canda said, crossing her arms over her chest and surveying the map. "There are a couple of different routes you could take to get to…whatever it is you're trying to reach."

"Which do you recommend?" Torren asked, scanning the image.

Her lips thinned as she drummed her fingers on the table. She leaned forward and looked at the terrain. "It depends. Do you want a safe route through the forest? Or the fast route through the rocks?"

"Fast," Torren said. I could practically hear the worry for Rego in his voice. I studied the vector image and stepped over to him, standing close enough our arms brushed.

"Are you sure?" I asked. "The rocks can be precarious."

"We don't have time for anything else," he said.

"Fine." I glanced at Canda and saw her watching us quietly with narrowed eyes. She cleared her throat when she saw me notice, and looked down again, highlighting the second route on the map.

"Fast route it is." She tapped the display, sending a white streak across the image, a trail snaking its way from our starting point to our destination. Zooming in on what I assumed would be the first leg of the journey, she stopped and traced her finger across the surface.

"This first area should be easy, just follow your nav-projector through this dense bit of forest. When you hit this rocky outcropping here," she pointed to a spot on the map, "go south to get around it—it appears to be less steep."

Torren nodded, no doubt committing everything to memory.

Canda scrolled over to the second part of the route. "This area here could be a problem, but you'll be fine if you're careful."

"Problem?" Torren asked.

"Fenn knows," she said, glancing at me. "You remember what to look for?"

"I'll keep a sharp eye out," I assured her. "Kad, I'll explain it to you on the way."

He nodded, his lips tight.

Canda scrolled to our destination and made a disapproving noise. "Well, the good news is, if you don't run into trouble, this should take you no more than a day and a half. If you leave now, you can camp near the outcropping, then have half a day's journey tomorrow before you reach your waypoint."

"And the bad news?" Torren asked.

Canda enlarged the area at the end of the route. "Those coordinates of yours lead straight into a canyon, which isn't a problem in and of itself. The bad news is there's an active Union outpost nearby."

"My contact said something about an outpost. That's why we're going on foot," Torren explained.

"Did they mention that the outpost is at the entrance of the canyon?" Canda asked. "It might make it hard to enter the canyon without being seen."

Torren studied the image with a knowing frown. "Must have slipped his mind," he muttered, his jaw tensing angrily. He leaned over the map, searching the image. "There's got to be another entrance to the canyon."

Canda scrolled and zoomed. "Looks like there was, but it's blocked off now. Must have been a rockslide. Those happen around here." She scrolled back to the canyon entrance and paused, tapping her chin thoughtfully.

"Listen, I've seen this outpost in person. It's really not that big. I'd say there are probably no more than ten, maybe fifteen Union soldiers stationed there, with just one or two commanding officers. If you can draw their attention away from the canyon, you may be able to slip by unnoticed. It's either that, or you can inspect the canyon from the outside and see if there are any safe places to climb down."

"We'll make something work," Torren said. "Thank you for this. It gives us an advantage."

Canda nodded, erasing the map and deleting the coordinates. "Come on," she said. "I can take you to a trail that will put you right on track."

Torren and I shouldered our bags and followed Canda out of the cave, blinking against the sun breaking through the trees. She walked us quickly through the camp, dictating orders to people around her on the way. As demanding as she was, her people seemed eager to follow her. *The Talarian Resistance had chosen its leader well.* My parents would have been proud of her.

By the time we got to the other side of camp, Mab had joined us, carrying a woven bag full of supplies. Canda passed the items to Torren and I as the four of us walked into the woods.

"I know you have some rations but here are some more."

"Thank you," Torren said, putting them in his bag.

"Do you have a shelter?"

Torren patted his bag. "A small self-inflating tent. It'll be enough."

"Great." said Canda, shoving a bundle of fabric into my arms. "A couple of blankets too, in case it's cold. You know how nights around here can get."

"Thanks," I said, folding them into my bag.

"What am I forgetting?" she muttered, scratching her head.

Mab handed her a small case, and Canda nodded, passing it to Torren.

"Ah, yes, here's a basic med-kit, in case anything happens."

We reached a small break in the trees, and a faintly worn foot trail that disappeared out of view ahead. In unison, Mab and Canda stopped walking, staying under the cover of the canopy.

This is it.

My breath caught in my throat. I had gone so many years without seeing Canda, but I had gotten used to her presence again so immediately. It strained my heart to leave her now. It wasn't lost on me that my childhood best friend was making it possible for me to save my new best friend. *Maybe Canda and Rego can meet one day.*

"You have no idea how thankful we are for all your help," Torren said to Canda, filling the silence I didn't know how to break.

"No thanks required," she said. "Just take care of this girl for me, will you?" She smiled, giving my arm a playful shove.

"Of course," said Torren, extending his hand to Canda, and then to Mab, who both shook it in turn. "I'll get the nav-projector up and running," he said to me, stepping onto the trail and walking forward a few yards, watching his device. I had a feeling it was already calibrated, and he was tactfully giving me a moment to say goodbye to my friend.

Canda stepped forward and flung her arms around my neck in a tight embrace while Mab watched us stoically, her fingers drumming on her blaster rifle's grip.

"I'm so glad I could see you again," Canda said, her voice muffled by my shoulder.

"You too, Canda," I said, tears beginning to well up. "Thank you again for all your help."

She pulled away and smiled. "Of course. You're both welcome here anytime."

"I'll remember that," I smiled.

She faced Mab, the two of them about to walk away, but stopped as if remembering one last thing.

"By the way," she said, twisting back to face me, "you two are *very* good. You really had me going."

"What?" I asked, gripping the strap of my bag anxiously.

She looked down the trail, and I followed her gaze to Torren, who was now programming coordinates into the projector.

"You two. You're definitely *not* married," she laughed. Mab smiled too, and I stared at them both in surprise. *She knew I lied to her.* Panic surged within me.

"Canda, I—"

"It's okay," she raised her hand, cutting me off. "You don't have to explain. I'm sure you had your reasons."

When did she figure it out? Why didn't she say anything?

"I get the sense you haven't even known each other very long, but..." She stopped and pursed her lips for a moment, considering her answer. "There's definitely something between you two, something strong. You work well together, complement each other. You're like fire, he's like ice. Somehow it works."

I sighed. *At least she's not angry.* "How could you tell?" I asked, eager to know what had given us away.

"Mmm, just a hunch," she hummed. "That, and I know what marriage looks like." She stopped next to Mab and gave me a playful smirk. I looked between the two, gasping as it finally hit me. They were holding hands, their fingers interlocked in a gentle but affectionate clasp.

"Wow," I said with a surprised smile. "Congratulations."

"Thank you," Mab said, finally cracking a grin for the first time since I'd met her.

I regretted my assumption that she was just Canda's security detail. I'd been so caught up in my cover with Torren that I hadn't let myself put two and two together. Growing up, all the toughest, coolest, boys and girls had always fallen for Canda. Mab was just her type.

"Why didn't you say anything?" I asked.

"We're not big on public displays of affection," Mab said, winking at Canda. "We weren't even going to have an official ceremony, but everyone at camp insisted. They threw us the best wedding a ragtag group of freedom fighters living in the woods could have possibly thrown."

Canda laughed.

"I wish I had been here for that," I said.

Mab grinned again, offering a glimpse of the charming young woman behind all the scowls.

"Well, you're here now," she said. "I'm glad I got to finally meet *the* Fenn Kensie. Canda talked about you so much over the years."

I grinned back, and thought about how in sync Canda and Mab had been last night when the Union ships arrived. They were *perfect.*

"How do you two make it work?" I asked. "Working together while…being together?"

They exchanged a look.

"Trust," Mab said, pulling something out of her pocket and handing it to me.

I smiled, recognizing the weight of my shock-blade.

"The kind that only comes when you really let each other in."

"I'll keep that in mind," I sighed, pocketing the weapon and glancing down the trail at Torren.

"Good luck out there," said Canda, almost turning to leave. She paused. "Hey, if things don't work out between you two, can you let me know? That man is a *specimen*." She glanced in Torren's direction.

"Okay! Time to go!" Mab said, playfully rolling her eyes. She took Canda's arm in hers and ushered her away.

"See you," I laughed, watching Canda and Mab head back to camp. Before they disappeared, I saw Canda put her arm around her wife's shoulder, and Mab snuggled into her as they walked.

I shouldered my bag and walked down the trail to where Torren was waiting, Canda's words ringing in my head.

He looked up from the projector, his eyes searching mine. "Everything okay?" he asked.

"Yeah. Let's go."

We headed down the trail side by side. I knew we had a job to complete, but thoughts of affection and steadfast relationships were all I could think about.

22

DANGEROUS GROUND

WE TRAVELED IN SILENCE MOST OF THE AFTERNOON, TORREN focusing on the nav-projector, making sure we kept our pace steady. When I did talk to him, I received one-word answers. Rego's increased bounty price had us both on edge, so I decided not to take it personally. We stopped at one point to fill our water canisters from a stream, then ate some rations, and went right back to hiking. It wasn't until early evening that I was sure he was actively avoiding me.

"Is there something bothering you?" I asked as we moved through a thicket of trees.

"No," he murmured. The ensuing silence was loud.

"Well, *that's* reassuring," I said sarcastically.

He sighed and kept walking. If I wanted the conversation, I would have to force it.

"Let me guess—you're panicking because we kissed this morning and you don't know how you feel about it," I said.

His body went rigid and his pace slowed. I'd struck a nerve.

"I'm not panicking," he snapped, avoiding my gaze.

"Then talk to me."

He exhaled slowly, then stopped walking. As he turned to face me, I planted my feet and looked up at him, waiting.

"Fine," he said. "There were a lot of feelings happening last night, and again this morning."

I didn't respond, I could tell there was more coming.

He dropped his gaze to the ground. "But this alert about Rego's bounty was a wakeup call."

He's lying. To both of us.

"A wakeup to what?"

"That I let myself get distracted," he said. "I can't let it happen again."

"Let *what* happen? Feelings? Greez, you make emotions sound like some kind of disease."

He stared at me. Another non-response.

"Why did you give me that flower, Torren?" I asked. "I told you what Star Bonnet meant. What made you take it in the first place?"

"I don't know," he said, shaking his head. "I didn't have a plan."

"That doesn't sound like you."

"Look, Sketch," he said, putting his hand on my shoulder.

Sketch? We're back to the nickname now?

"I'm sorry. The truth is, even though there are some feelings between us, we'd both be better off if we put those feelings aside."

I stared at him blankly, and he looked away, focusing instead on the nav-projector. It recalibrated, struggling to keep a signal through the tree canopy. When it resumed, he followed it, climbing a hill in front of us that led toward a rocky ridge. I followed him numbly, feeling rejected and dismissed.

The ridge we strode across steepened on both sides the further we went. Towering up ahead was a massive bluff of stacked grey rocks. It blocked our route, and looked far too high and sheer to climb.

"So, where do we go from here?" I said, thinking about more than just the trail.

He met my eye with an almost apologetic look before turning to examine the rocks.

"There," he said, pointing ahead.

There was a rock ledge that led around the side of the bluff. We walked forward and inspected it. The ledge was narrow, with a steep drop-off into a rocky ravine below. I leaned forward, swallowing nervously at what I guessed was a thirty-foot drop. The whole thing stretched about seven or eight yards long. As risky as walking the ledge would be, we could both see level ground and woods on the other side—our path forward.

"We can make it," Torren said. "We'll go slow and hug the wall. Packs off."

I nodded and we both shrugged off our bags, holding them in one hand as we approached the rocky shelf. Torren went first, stowing his nav-projector and stepping tentatively out. I followed. We put our backs to the rock wall and began a slow, measured side-shuffle across the ledge. The sun was setting, casting a golden light onto the surrounding area, making me squint as I watched where I was placing my feet.

"You know, I wasn't just talking about the route when I asked where we go from here," I said.

"Oh, I put that together," he assured me.

"I just want to know why you're shutting me out."

"It's not that complicated. I work best alone," he grumbled. "Now can we focus on helping Rego?"

Rego. It felt like an excuse to change the conversation. I knew we were on dangerous ground, but I felt the urge to rattle his cage.

"On the subject of Rego," I said combatively. He tilted his head, listening to me, but didn't stop or look my way. "What kind of friend are you? You're never there for him."

"What do you think I'm doing out here?" he asked, gesturing at the landscape. We were more than halfway across now. My foot hit a loose rock, and it tumbled over the ledge. I didn't like how long it took to hear its impact on the stones below.

"I don't know. Absolving guilt?" I said. "I don't know how you and Rego met, but I'm assuming he went out of his way to help you like he helped me. What happened?"

"Why don't you ask him?" he muttered.

"Well, all I know is that *I'm* the one taking care of Rego," I seethed. "I'm the one who looks out for him. I'm the one chasing away criminals like you so he can stay out of trouble. And he's supposedly one of your best friends? If that's true you must be one lonely bastard."

He stopped walking. It was so abrupt that I bumped into him. He couldn't turn to face me on the narrow ledge, but his head and neck twisted enough for us to lock eyes.

"What?" I asked.

"So that's what you think of me?" he asked, his shoulders slumping. "Some heartless bastard who has no real friends, just contacts?"

I opened my mouth, but I didn't know what to say at first. "That came out wrong. I'm talking about criminals."

"*I'm* a criminal," he said, letting the words hang in the bitter tension between us. The angry spark in his eye faded, his gaze becoming hollow and cold. Mistake or not, I had cut him.

"Torren—" I began.

He raised a hand and cut me off. "It's fine. It's good to know where I stand with you." He looked away and carefully continued walking. I followed him cautiously.

"Torren, wait..."

"Don't worry about it," he said softly. There was a forced lightness to his voice that didn't match his crestfallen body language.

I followed him, desperate to repair things. I stopped in my tracks when a glimmer in the rocks caught my eye. I squinted, studying it for a few seconds. There was something in the rock under our feet, flecks of silver that glittered in the light of the evening sun.

My heart dropped to my stomach. *Shit.* Canda had warned us about this area. I slowed but kept moving, keeping my steps careful.

"Torren," I said, as calmly as I could.

"What?" he sighed, refusing to turn around.

"Stop moving," I said, my voice betraying the fear rising within me.

My tone caught his attention, and he stopped. When he looked back, his irritation had been replaced with concern.

"Don't move," I said, keeping still, my body tight to the rock wall. "We shouldn't have gone this way, the rocks are—"

"What is it?" he said, fully turning his body and reaching for me. That movement did it.

CRACK.

A horrifying noise filled the air, the sound of rocks dislodging from earth and stone. The ledge shuddered under our feet.

"Go," he said, pressing himself against back tightly and gesturing for me to move past him.

I did, making a dash for the solid ground at the other end of the ledge. It took me six large, hurried steps, but I made it. Dropping my bag and spinning around, I watched Torren. He tossed his bag onto the ground next to me, and took a step forward. The ledge buckled, cracking at the center. He stumbled, arms out to keep his balance, but the ledge tilted under him. It didn't fall, but it angled, threatening to send him sliding backwards and down into the ravine. He fell to his hands and knees, managing to grab onto the top edge of the slab.

The ground I stood on seemed solid enough, so I threw myself down, lying flat on my stomach. I reached out to him.

"Torren, grab my hand!" I shouted. A sheet of rock behind him tumbled free and dropped thirty feet down.

"Come on!" I said impatiently, shaking my outstretched hand for emphasis.

Steeling himself, he let go of the jagged rock long enough to grasp my wrist. I wrapped my hand around his wrist, locking onto him as firmly as I could. Flattening my body against the rocks, I let my muscles go dead, making myself heavier.

"Climb!" I shouted.

He scrambled against the rocks as I slowly inched myself away from the edge, both of us creeping toward safety. A sharp pain stung my arm where it dragged against the unyielding rock, but I gritted my teeth and ignored it. *If I give in, we're both going down.* I would fall before I let go of him.

Torren slowly inched himself farther from the cliff's edge, and when he was close enough, I grabbed the collar of his jacket and hauled him toward me with the last of my strength. He collapsed on top of me, and I held his full weight as we gasped and watched the cliff's edge, waiting to see if we were truly safe.

It had finally stopped crumbling. The ground we were on was solid.

I pushed Torren off of me and sat up. He propped himself up on his elbows, catching his breath while staring at the broken cliff's edge. Adrenaline was coursing through our bodies, the sudden, delirious relief of safety.

His eyes met mine and he let out a short laugh, which caused me to do the same. I shook my head at him, still panting, and that was when I heard his breathing become labored.

Shit. Of all the moments.

I clambered to my hands and knees, going back on high alert.

He struggled to take a full inhale, and his eyes went to mine again. *He can't breathe.* The shock of nearly falling must have been too much.

I crawled over and knelt next to him, putting my hand on his shoulder to let him know I was there.

"It's going to be okay, Torren. Don't worry," I said with a calm I didn't feel. I reached into his jacket pocket and felt around for his Respirin cartridge. *Nothing.* I checked his other pocket while his breath took on a wheezing sound. It was the worst I had ever heard it. "It's okay, I've got you," I promised, continuing to search. There was nothing in his other pocket either. *It's not here.*

I took a breath. Falling to pieces right now wouldn't help Torren. His face was starting to turn red. I began to panic, but I held it in and steadied my shaking hands.

"Torren, where's your cartridge?" I asked, before realizing he couldn't answer.

I grabbed his bag and ripped it open, scrambling through his supplies for the small disk. He dipped his head forward, trying to gulp in air, but his constricting lungs wouldn't allow it. *We don't have time for this.* I turned the bag upside down, dumping its contents onto the ground beside us and frantically searching through everything that clattered out.

"Torren?" He couldn't speak, the color on his face growing deeper by the minute. *Please, Gryta, don't let this be happening now.* The cartridge was gone. It must have fallen out of his pocket while he was scrambling back up the cliff.

Shit. Shit!

His inhales were becoming shorter and more rapid. He lay flat on his back, one hand clutching his chest as he tried to focus on drawing in a breath.

"It's alright, we don't need it." I said with a deeply feigned confidence.

His eyes met mine again, pleading for help.

I had never seen him this vulnerable before, and it lodged my heart in my throat. His lungs were failing him, and there was nothing he could do. I couldn't let him die like this. Rego needed him. *I* needed him. Leaning over him, I placed one hand on his chest and looked into his eyes.

"Relax, Torren," I said softly. I could feel his heart pounding, his body begging for oxygen. "Breathe," I coaxed.

He met my eye, relaxing his body as best as he could. He inhaled as deeply as his lungs would let him. It wasn't much, but it was more than before.

"Out," I said lightly, and he slowly exhaled. "Good," I reassured. "Come on...breathe in."

He inhaled steadily. His heartbeat didn't seem as frantic now, but it was taking too long to get back to normal for my liking. *He'll pass out at this rate.* If he panicked and went back into short breaths, I could lose him.

I thought about the Respirin cartridge and how they worked. Along with a small dose of muscle-relaxing medicine, the device simply pushed a bit of air into the lungs of the user.

Shit. I have to try it.

I inhaled, then leaned down to him and pressed my lips to his, making sure to seal our mouths. The taste of him enveloped my senses, and I gently breathed into his mouth. *I need to keep him going.* His chest rose under me, so I sat up and pressed on his sternum, pushing the air back out. I took another breath and repeated the action, gently pushing air into his lungs with my own and pressing on his chest to force the exhale. I did this for a few minutes, monitoring him carefully.

Slowly, his face began to return to its usual color, and his heartbeat evened out. *He's recovering.* I stopped breathing into his mouth, but stayed hovering over him as he started to draw deep breaths in on his own.

"That's good, Torren," I said in a soothing voice. "Keep that up." Relief flooded through me when after a few minutes, he was still shaken, but stable. I sat up and wiped tears away from my eyes I didn't know had even been there.

He weakly pushed himself into a half-sitting position, one arm propping himself up. I didn't know what to do with myself, so I sat back on my knees and started gathering the things I had dumped out of his bag.

He sat forward, grabbing my arm as I reached for a ration bar. He pulled me toward him. I fell against him, and his arms went around me, embracing me as tightly as he could after what he'd just been through.

I put my arms around him as well and we held each other, breathing deeply. I couldn't tell if he was thanking me or seeking comfort. Either way, I didn't let go until I felt him pull away first.

"What *was* that?" he asked, looking at the broken cliff's edge.

"Moonslab," I said, still catching my breath. "There are random veins of it in grey rock like this. It's beautiful, especially when light hits it, but it makes the rock fragile. You can't walk on it."

"No shit," he said, staring at the jagged precipice. "Was this the problem Canda mentioned?"

"Yeah. I was going to tell you about it, but—"

"But I wasn't easy to talk to today," he said.

"It's not your fault," I mumbled. "It slipped my mind."

We put his things back in his bag and slowly picked ourselves up off the ground. I felt lightheaded, but chalked it up to adrenaline. Torren was up first and held his hand out to me. After he pulled me to my feet, he put his hands on my shoulders and began looking me over to see if I was alright. *Me?* I blinked. *He was the one who had almost just died. Twice.*

His face fell. "Damn," he said, looking at my left arm. I held it up.

While pulling him back over the ledge, the jagged rocks had sheared clean through the sleeve of my jacket and cut my arm. The skin that was visible through the torn fabric was bright red and slick with blood. I felt the pain then, sharp and stinging. Clamping my other hand over the cut, I stood there, unsure of what to do.

Torren looked at the lowering sun, then back at me. "Come on," he said. "It's time to stop for the day."

"Are you sure?" I asked, taking in the terrain around us, "There's still daylight, and we're not at the halfway point yet. If we—"

"Hey," he said, putting a gentle hand on the side of my face.

I met his gaze.

"It's okay. Let's camp for the night and continue in the morning. I need to look at your arm," he said, dropping his hand to my shoulder and gripping lightly.

The pain in my arm was searing now. I nodded in agreement, and Torren slung his bag over his shoulder. We headed into the forest to find a secure spot to camp, adrenaline still coursing through us like a storm about to break.

23

IT'S A SMALL TENT

The late evening sky was overcast, and soon a cold drizzle began to fall. By the time we had decided where to camp, darkness and heavy rain had found us. Torren pulled the tent from his bag, letting it inflate on its own as he secured the corners with rocks.

I tried to help, but Torren wouldn't let me, given my injured arm. The bleeding had stopped, but the pain was relentless. I gritted my teeth, determined not to show how much it hurt.

Once the tent was set up, Torren gestured to the entrance. I dropped to my knees and crawled inside. He hadn't been kidding about how small it was—there was no standing room, and the sleeping arrangement would be cramped. Before I could process that, the pain in my arm flared, cutting through everything else. I pulled off my bag and muddy boots, tossing them in the corner, then sat down, trying to inspect my injury in the dim light.

Torren ducked inside, his wet hair plastered to his forehead, droplets of rain tracing down his face and neck. He fastened the entrance, the sound of the storm outside blending with the rhythmic tapping of rain against the tent.

He kicked off his boots, ignoring the damp clothes clinging to his body, and reached into his bag. The soft light of a collapsible lantern bathed the space, casting shadows that danced along his wet skin.

He knelt, unbuckling his blaster holster and shedding his soaked jacket, setting the gear aside. He rolled up his shirt sleeves and shifted closer, settling on one knee beside me.

His voice was low, almost hesitant. "Can you get your jacket off?"

I shrugged it off my shoulders, sliding my good arm out first. Gingerly, I attempted to pull my injured arm free, but winced as the fabric scraped the wound.

Torren put his hand on my shoulder, stopping me so he could take over. He cautiously pulled the sleeve off, then retrieved Canda's med kit from his bag.

In the light of the lantern, he inspected our medical supplies. His shirt collar hung open, a few buttons undone, revealing his neck and part of his chest, both glistening with raindrops. I felt the same magnetic pull towards him as I had that morning at the showers. *He has no right to look this good while soaking wet.*

When Torren found what he needed and turned to me, I suddenly felt very exposed in my sleeveless top. He reached for my arm and I lifted it towards him. He placed his hands delicately on my forearm, inspecting the cut. His touch was light and soothing, sending an excited shiver down my spine.

"It looks worse than it is," he said. "Do you want a Revivor shot for the pain?"

I shrugged, but he searched my gaze, looking for the truth.

"Fenn," he said, his voice soft, "you just saved my life tonight. Twice. I couldn't think any less of you if you said the pain was getting to you."

I had literally brought him back from the edge of death, yet here I was, wanting him to think I was tough.

"You can give me the shot," I said, dropping the pretense.

He nodded and rifled through the med kit for the powerful pain reliever. Pulling out a small canister, he examined it closely. I watched him, and saw that his cold demeanor from earlier had melted away, his expression now full of focused concern.

"Here we go," he said, maneuvering closer to me.

His fingers gently cupped the back of my neck to steady me as he assessed where to administer the shot. His wet hair was trailing into his eyes, but he shook it clear, his brow furrowing in concentration. With one swift motion, he pulled the cap off the canister with his teeth, his jaw set.

I could see the needle on the canister was only a few millimeters long, but my body tensed instinctively as he brought it up to my neck.

"Breathe," he murmured, the cap still between his teeth.

I took a deep breath, allowing myself to relax and sink into the warmth of his touch.

Pressing the shallow needle into my skin, he depressed the canister against my neck, dispensing its contents.

I flinched, but then exhaled in relief, the pain in my arm immediately beginning to ease.

"Good," he said in a soothing voice, brushing the back of my neck with his thumb before removing his hand. He put the cap back on the canister and gently took my arm again. I quietly relished the gentleness of his touch, wondering if the rest of him was as warm as his hands were.

This can't be the same man who put me in a chokehold back on Laigo.

"I'm sorry, by the way," he said, locking eyes with me for a moment.

"It'll heal," I said, focused on my injury.

"No. I'm sorry for being so callous today."

I looked at him in surprise and paused. *That was hard for him to say. Don't make a big deal out of it.* "It's okay."

"It isn't," he said firmly. "You deserve better."

I bit my lip, taken aback by his apology and impressed at how willing he was to own up to his own actions. "Well, I'm sorry I called you a bastard," I murmured.

He shook his head. "I was acting like one."

He began carefully cleaning the cut with a solution from the med kit. "I had just made a big speech about not needing anyone...but if it weren't for you, I'd be in that ravine right now." He dabbed my skin dry with a clean cloth, his eyes meeting mine. "Thank you for that."

I swallowed, considering my response.

"You're welcome."

He affixed a clean bandage to my arm with careful movements, his chest rising and falling as he breathed so close to me. His mouth was slightly open, as if he wanted to say something more but couldn't manage it.

I watched his hands wordlessly—grateful to be patched up, and acutely aware of how intoxicating his touch was. I didn't want it to stop.

He continued smoothing the bandage, brushing his fingers along my skin for what seemed like a few seconds too long.

Either I'm reading into things, or he doesn't want to stop touching me either.

He finally pulled his hands away, clearing his throat and packing up the med-kit.

"We should get some sleep," he said.

I murmured in agreement, taking a breath to steady myself. I needed to rest anyway.

Reaching for my bag, I pulled out the blankets Canda had given us. When I unfolded the bundle, I realized it wasn't two blankets, but one. Was it a mistake? Canda had seen through our lie, but she'd sensed something growing between Torren and I. She had sent the lone blanket on purpose. *Devious.*

"Here," I said, throwing the blanket to Torren.

"Just one?" he asked, brows drawn together skeptically.

"It's okay, I don't need one." I laid down on the floor of the tent, positioning my bag as a makeshift pillow and resting my head on it.

"You take it. It's cold." He held it out to me.

As much as I wanted the blanket, I wasn't going to make him sleep without one because my friend had decided to play matchmaker.

"I'm perfectly fine," I insisted. "I have Talarian blood. I was built to withstand cold nights." It wasn't true, but he didn't need to know that.

As he pulled his damp shirt off and laid it out to dry, I let my eyes trace his chest and shoulders for a moment before looking away and pretending to inspect the bandage on my arm. I took my damp hair out of its braid, shaking it loose to hopefully dry more quickly. I could feel his eyes on me. It felt like we were both waiting for the other one to break the tension.

When neither of us did, he laid down next to me, pulling the blanket over himself. He reached toward me. My heart nearly stopped, but I let out an exhale when I realized he was going for the lantern.

What did you think he was going to do? What did you want him to do?

He collapsed the lantern, plunging us into darkness. When my eyes adjusted, the interior of the tent was softly lit by clouded moonlight.

I turned away from Torren and wrapped my arms around myself, bracing against the cold. All I could hear was our breath against the melodic raindrops.

Just when I thought Torren had fallen asleep, I heard him whisper. "What's that noise?" he asked, his voice alert.

I cursed silently, realizing my teeth had been audibly chattering.

"Are you shivering?" he asked in disbelief, reaching over and laying his hand on my shoulder. It felt hot on my ice-cold skin. "You're freezing. What happened to Talarian blood?"

"I lied."

"Come here," he said with an exasperated sigh. Slipping his arm around my waist, he drew me toward him.

I tensed up as he grabbed the blanket and threw it over both of us. His body heat radiated over me, an instant comfort.

"You'll be useless tomorrow if you're sick," he said.

My back was pressed up against him. I felt the rise and fall of his bare chest, his breath on my neck.

We lay there quietly, sharing body warmth, both of our pulses pounding in a way that was impossible to ignore. A delirium washed over me. I couldn't tell if it was residual effects of the Revivor shot or merely the feeling of being held by him. His arm felt so strong, and his hand was curved protectively, intimately, around my waist. *How am I supposed to sleep like this?*

His fingers twitched, gripping me slightly tighter. I was fairly sure he wanted me, but the lack of certainty held me back.

Does he know I want him? Maybe he's waiting for a signal.

"You know, it's a bold move," I said, my voice low and airy, "going shirtless when you're sharing a blanket with someone."

"I'm just keeping you warm," he said. "I'm not making a move."

I paused, considering my response carefully. "Why not?" I asked.

He stopped breathing for a moment, and rain filled the silence again. *Shit.* Had I been wrong? Every second that passed made me feel more awkward.

He slowly removed his hand from my waist, and I realized how presumptuous I had been. Getting intimate with someone required a lot of vulnerability, and that wasn't exactly Torren's strong suit.

I closed my eyes tightly, praying to fall asleep. *Hopefully, we both forget about it by morning.*

Just as I was making peace with the fact I had embarrassed myself beyond all hope, his hand lightly grazed my arm. I stilled. His fingertips lingered over my skin. There was no mistaking the action. Trailing his fingers up to my shoulder, he brushed my hair away, exposing my neck.

I felt him lean in toward me. His lips were suddenly pressed right at the place where my neck and shoulder met. There was a burning in the pit of my stomach that screamed with want. I could feel him raise up onto one elbow behind me. He grabbed my shoulder and rolled me onto my back. Biting back a smile, I looked up at him while he hovered over me with hungry eyes.

He slowly leaned down to me until our faces were almost touching. The blanket had fallen away by now, letting warmth escape, but neither of us seemed to mind. He trailed one fingertip delicately along the base of my throat, watching my face carefully.

"What happened to your rule about not working together while being together?" I asked, hoping I wasn't tempting fate.

"I guess I lied too," he said. Raising an eyebrow, he traced his finger down to the neckline of my shirt, caressing the skin there. "Do you want me to stop?" he whispered.

"No," I said breathlessly, arching my back and pressing my chest against his.

His lips parted, and a ragged gasp escaped him. Normally, his heavy breathing would have concerned me, but I knew what was causing it.

"You're absolutely sure?" he asked, his eyes gliding eagerly over my neck and shoulders.

I appreciated his caution, but I didn't have time for it. "Do you need me to program coordinates into your nav-projector? I want you, Torren. I've wanted you since you kissed me at the blockade."

He licked his lower lip, eyes fixed on my mouth, but said nothing.

I gave him a playful eye roll. Running my hands over his arms and shoulders, I felt the beautiful smoothness of his skin beneath my fingertips. "Now's the part where you say when you first wanted *me*."

His sober expression gave way to the smirk I'd come to know, and he leaned down, ghosting his lips across my neck. "Mmm," he hummed thoughtfully, bringing his mouth to my ear. "Pass," he whispered.

Seriously? I huffed, ready to argue with him, but he pressed his lips against mine before I could utter a word. A moan escaped me as the final barrier between us melted away. His lips explored mine, delicately at first, then with a growing ferocity.

I reached up, running my hands through his damp hair. When he pulled away to breathe, I wrapped my arms around his neck to pull him back to me.

I can't believe this is happening.

With a deft hand, he slid the strap of my top down, then kissed my exposed shoulder. All I could do was make embarrassing little noises. He drew back to look at me. Slowly running his thumb along my lower lip, he searched my eyes with a cautious smile. He was being so gentle, so careful. I loved him for it, but I wanted *more*.

"You're tamer than I thought you'd be," I said with a smirk. I wanted to rile him up. To experience what I knew simmered beneath his cool facade.

His smile faded. He wove his fingers into my hair and tightened his grip. He pulled, forcing my head back to expose my neck.

"Fenn Kensie, you are playing with fire," he whispered against my throat. He grazed my skin with his teeth, giving me a playful bite. "Are you sure you want that heat?"

"Heat I can handle," I breathed. "It's the waiting that's killing me. Don't make me ask again."

He smiled. Leaning in, he kissed my mouth, then sunk his teeth into my lip. I laughed in surprise. He drew his kisses away from my mouth, moving down to my throat and not stopping there.

I closed my eyes in bliss, losing myself before opening them again to make sure I wasn't dreaming. The man I had once thought so cold and dismissive was now lavishing me with affection I had never experienced. Torren truly contained depths, and I wanted to dive into them. I wanted to drown.

We made the best of the space we had, grabbing at each other, impatiently pushing aside the blanket that had started it all. We slowly peeled our clothes off in between kisses, eager to explore each other. I knew it was a rare moment. He and I would never be in this forest, in this tent, and in this position again. I was determined to give him everything I had.

I did.

And so did he.

24

IN THE LIGHT OF DAY

I WOKE TO THE GENTLE TRILLING OF BIRD SONGS DRIFTING through the stillness of the forest. It was the second morning in a row that I had woken up after a night beside Torren. But this time, I didn't have to roll over to see if he was there. His arm was draped across my waist, and the sound of his breath told me he was still asleep. A smile tugged at my lips, and I nearly laughed with giddiness. I basked in his warmth and nestled closer to him, hoping to memorize the feeling forever.

May Gryta, in all her glory, bless Canda and her one-blanket scheme.

I never would have pictured this, not when he and I first met. We'd both been so cold to each other. Now, he was holding me, clinging to me in his sleep. It felt right. In fact, I was *alarmed* at how whole he made me feel.

I slowly drew my arms from under the blanket to stretch, and the movement woke him. He immediately tightened his grip on me, pulling me closer. His face nuzzled my neck, and he sighed deeply, his breath warm against my skin.

"I guess it's safe to assume you don't regret last night?" I asked, breaking the silence.

"I only regret mistakes," he said, his sleepy voice huskier than usual. He removed his arm from around me, brushing my hair away from my neck with a drowsy touch. "I'm pretty sure I knew what I was doing last night," he whispered in my ear. *He did indeed.*

As he placed a heartbreakingly sweet kiss on my neck, I swallowed silently, trying to contain the bliss teeming within me. I raised my arms to stretch again, but Torren grabbed my waist and burrowed his face into the crook of my neck. I shrieked at the tickling sensation and he shushed me, laughing. I twisted around and shoved his shoulder playfully.

"You're terrible," I said.

"I thought you knew that by now," he quipped, a smirk on his face. We both settled onto our backs, grinning like idiots. I laid my head against his shoulder, feeling the warmth of our bodies where they touched beneath the blanket.

I was happy. Possibly the happiest I had ever been. Something about that felt too good to be true. As I lay there, the realist in me began to wake up. *It was fun, but how long is this actually going to last?*

"Can I ask you a question?" he murmured, interrupting my thoughts.

"Sure," I said.

"Back in the bunker, you asked what was next for me, after we pay off Rego's bounty."

I waited for the question.

"Well, what's next for you? What's next for Fenn Kensie?"

I shrugged. "Back to Hadrin. Continue to look after Rego."

"That's all?"

"Of course, that's all. What else would I do?" I scoffed, glancing at him.

His brows twitched together for a moment, betraying his frustration. "You're too smart and too skilled to waste your life away in such a nothing place," he insisted. "You're too..." he trailed off.

"Too what?"

"Too many things," he mumbled, looking me in the eye.

I wasn't sure what he was getting at. "What, you want me to throw in with you? Start robbing the Union and smuggle stolen goods around the galaxy?" I asked, half-sarcastically.

"I didn't say that," he said, looking away.

"You never answered me, by the way." I said, masking my disappointment. "What's next for Torren...?" I trailed off, not knowing what last name to add.

Great, Fenn, last night you threw yourself at a man whose last name you don't even know.

"I'll keep doing what I do," he said resolutely, his expression empty. I waited for him to elaborate, but he didn't say another word.

I tried to picture things once the job was done, and found that I could see it so clearly. He'd be called away for work and I'd still be on Hadrin. We'd exchange some polite messages via the wire before he'd get busy and forget about me. The silence hung thick in the air, and I let out a breath. *With a great, wide galaxy at his fingertips, why would he ever choose me?*

Last night's fever dream suddenly felt a little foolish in the light of day. I shifted subtly, putting an inch of space between us. I could handle this being nothing more than a fling. But I had to forge my heart into shape for it now, and that meant skipping past the morning-after pleasantries. He moved to put his arm around me, but I pretended to yawn.

I pushed myself into a sitting position and began pulling my clothes on. "We should get going."

"Okay," he murmured. His voice was flat, as if he was surprised that I was in such a hurry to leave the bed we'd shared.

I dressed quickly and stepped out of the tent into the crisp morning air. A heaviness weighed on my heart, but I shoved it aside, determined to keep moving forward. The ground was still damp from last night's rain, so I picked my way carefully to the driest rock I could find. Settling onto it, I began lacing up my boots, my mind replaying last night over and over.

A sharp pain shot through my forearm, and I glanced at the bandage Torren had applied with such careful attention. He emerged from the tent, already dressed and pulling his own boots on. He walked over to me, his gaze fixed on my injured arm as I fumbled with my laces.

"Need a hand?" he asked.

I shook my head, but winced as I reached for the laces again.

"Let me help," he said, kneeling in front of me and lifting my boot carefully into his lap. He gently tightened the laces, tying them securely. Setting my foot down, he did the same with the other one, all while my heart pounded out an irregular rhythm in my chest.

I was about to get up, but he motioned for me to stay put. "I need to look at your arm. Let me grab the med kit."

I nodded numbly, and he stood, grabbing a packaged ration out of his jacket pocket and handing it to me. "Eat," he said, then headed back to the tent.

I sighed heavily and looked at the ration package in my hands. It was a pouch of elgar jerky he'd gotten back at the depot. I opened the foil package, shoving a few pieces into my mouth and chewing mechanically. I wasn't hungry, but I needed the fuel. *We can't screw up today. Rego is counting on us.* I managed to get a mouthful down by the time Torren returned with the med kit.

He knelt down again, carefully peeling the bandage from my skin. "Looks like we managed to avoid an infection, but it's still healing," he said. "I'll put on a clean bandage."

I looked away, trying to avoid his eyes. He cleaned the wound again and pressed a fresh bandage onto my arm, smoothing it with his thumbs. I could feel him watching me, but I kept my gaze on the trees behind him. Finishing with the bandage, he paused. He ran one hand down my arm, over my wrist, and gently clasped my hand in his. There was no mistaking the affection in it. It felt real. But if he had no plans for us once the trip was over, what was the point?

I slipped my hand out of his grasp and superficially busied myself with inspecting the new bandage.

Still kneeling in front of me, he cleared his throat.

"Seems *you're* the one who regrets last night," he said.

I opened my mouth, but didn't know what to say, so I looked down at my boots, scraping my toe in the mud. "I don't regret it, Torren. It's just…" The words caught in my throat. *You're going to dump me back on Hadrin after this is all done and fly off into the black without a second glance.* "I'm just anxious to finish the job," I lied, feeling his gaze on me.

"I see," he said, his voice devoid of feeling. He got to his feet. "Let's get it over with, then." He turned on his heel, stalking away to pack up the tent.

I sighed and massaged my forehead with my fingers. I hated that he was upset, but I was just expediting the inevitable. I had to rip the figurative bandage off now, before I got too attached.

Deep inside, part of me knew it was already too late.

Once we had everything packed up, Torren calibrated his nav-projector and got us back on course. After yesterday's run-in with moonslab, we steered clear of the rocky terrain, sticking close to the shelter of the trees. I followed a few paces behind Torren, neither of us making much conversation.

After a few hours, we heard the sound of running water, and since we needed to refill our canisters, we followed it until we located a small stream. Torren crouched on its pebbled bank and filled both of our canisters with the cold, clear water. He was just handing mine back to me when a distant noise caught our attention—the low hum of an engine drawing nearer. We listened intently, trying to determine if it was a ground speeder or an aircraft.

"Ship," he said, darting for the nearest tree. I was right behind him. We pressed our backs flush against the trunk, hoping the dense branches would hide us from any ships scanning the terrain below. The thrumming got louder, and through gaps in the branches, I saw the vessel. It soared overhead, clearing the treetops by just a few feet and vibrating the pebbles on the stream's bank.

"Union Air-Rook," I said as it sped away. I had seen them come through the shipyard on Hadrin. They were patrol vehicles, not fighter ships. *Did I see that right?* "Were those guns on the front of the craft?"

"I think so," said Torren, scanning the tree line. "They must be pretty spooked by the Talarian Resistance if they're equipping observation vessels with weapons. Canda told me their last supply raid was…destructive. We're getting close to the outpost, so we'll likely see more patrol vehicles from here on out."

I stepped away from the tree trunk, about to leave the cover of the branches, when Torren grabbed my wrist and stopped me.

"Wait," he said, eyes trained upwards. I cocked my head, listening. Sure enough, the ship's engine was growing louder again.

"Is it circling back?" I asked, stepping out and looking for the ship before thinking better of it.

Torren grabbed me by the waist and pulled me back under the branches, holding me against his chest. My breath caught in my throat as we waited silently. Another pass overhead that rustled the trees and shook the ground. Once it had moved on, he let go of me. I separated myself, fighting how much my body wanted to stay in his arms. The ship made another pass, but north of us now.

"We should hold our position for a minute," he said.

I nodded, watching the sky. The ship made multiple passes in the area, and we stayed put. After half an hour, we sat on the ground with our backs against the tree. Torren bent his legs and rested his wrists casually on his knees. He was calmer than me, as evident by the way I sat hugging my own knees tight against my chest. This was the second time in three days we had gotten pinned down by patrolling Union ships, a pattern I was not enjoying.

I opened my water canister and took a gulp, my mind hashing through the events of last night and the conversation Torren and I had that morning. I don't know why I had expected it to go any differently than it did. *He works alone by choice. Why would he involve another person?*

Torren was gifted. I couldn't imagine there being anything he couldn't do if he put his mind to it. There had to be more for him out there than flying around the galaxy alone, smuggling stolen goods. Stowing my water canister in my bag, I gazed over at the stream, listening to its continuous trickle. *You'd have an easier time diverting the direction of that stream than stopping Torren once he had a plan in motion.*

"Torren…"

"Hmm?" he grunted without looking up.

"Have you ever thought about joining Free Sector?"

He looked at me, his eyebrows raised, but didn't answer.

"Think about it," I said. "You're already sticking it to the Union. You have a real talent for hitting them hard and getting away with it. If *you* joined Free Sector? Hell, they could do anything."

He brushed at some dirt on the knee of his pants, his jaw tense. "You're not the first person to tell me this," he said.

The beat of silence that followed worried me. *Is he really not going to talk to me?*

"What I mean is," he said, his voice softer, "the word on the wire is that Free Sector is becoming more regimented. Sounds they're organizing into something the Union won't be able to ignore. Don't get me wrong, I'd like to see them succeed, but I don't see myself joining."

"But why?"

"After what happened on Rorric, I'm done with following orders. Free Sector might be better than the Union, but…" He picked up a smooth pebble next to his boot and tossed it into the stream. "I don't want to be a cog in anyone's machine."

I studied his face, seeing for the first time the subtle lines etched from years of harried survival. He was tired, and it wasn't from all the hiking we'd done.

The Union ship had circled further away, barely audible in the distance now. We would be moving soon, and I wanted to make the most of the moment.

"For what it's worth," I said, "I think sacrificing some personal freedom to fight the good fight might be worth it. Maybe it's even due."

"Due?" He tilted his head at me.

"We both lost our families to the Union. Maybe we survived for a reason. Maybe we *owe* it to them to fight."

"Maybe," he said, falling silent for a moment. "But if we die fighting the Union, then what was it all for? Maybe we just keep surviving, you know? Honor them by living."

"Fair point," I said softly. "It's just that I've spent ten years of my life keeping my head down and following every possible rule just to stay out of trouble. And it still found me. Maybe there *is* no living under the Galactic Union." I sighed, feeling helpless. "Why are they so evil?"

"That's the hard part," he said. "They're not."

I twisted my head to look at him.

"It's a comforting thought though; evil," he said. "Some abstract force we might protect ourselves from if we behave enough, or pray enough. But I don't think evil exists. There's just power, and the inevitable abuse of it."

"How are we supposed to fight that?"

He stared ahead, quietly thinking. "I wish I had answers for you, Sketch, but I just don't know," he said.

So *we're back at* Sketch. *Probably for the best.* The Union ship was gone now.

Torren powered the nav-projector on and watched it calibrate. "What I *do* know," he said, looking at the screen, "is that we're now less than an hour away from our cargo, and the Union outpost right next to it." He turned toward me. "I don't know how this is going to go, but I need to know if you're ready."

We were so close to our objective. The shipment we needed in order to save Rego was within reach. We couldn't screw this up, but there was no time for hesitation either. Not when the bounty price was on the rise.

I took a deep breath, then gave him a nod. "As ready as you are."

He stood, offering me a hand and helping me to my feet. Together, we ventured once more into the thick Talarian forest, the reality of what we were about to do weighing on me like a pile of bricks

25

SOUVENIRS OF THE UNIONS REIGN

CROUCHED IN THE SHADOWS BETWEEN TWO TOWERING TALARIAN ferns, Torren and I waited in silence. Our eyes were fixed on the Union Outpost that stood just yards away. Though it had been painted the same grey as the rocky outcrops around it, its unnatural modular shape only emphasized how out of place it was in the Talarian terrain.

To the side of the building was a small shipyard, but from our hiding spot, I couldn't tell how many vessels there were. There were three Union officers standing outside the structure's entrance, armored up and holding blaster rifles. They were engaged in a conversation, barely audible from where Torren and I waited. Torren studied them closely, but for what, I didn't know.

"What are we listening for?" I whispered to him.

"We're not listening; we're watching."

I was about to ask him what we were *watching* for, but he held up his hand as one of the officers nodded at the others and walked away.

"There," he said quietly, pointing at the two officers remaining.

The men didn't resume the conversation in the absence of their comrade, instead, facing forward and standing silently with their hands on their weapons. They were posted there.

"Looks like these two are on duty and guarding the entrance to the outpost. That means they won't leave that spot until the next shift comes to relieve them."

"That's going to be a problem," I frowned, looking past the outpost at what lay behind it.

A wall of jagged stone stood behind the ugly building, with a wide gap just a dozen or so yards from where we crouched. The canyon entrance. Inside that canyon was the crate we needed to extract and deliver in order to save Rego. If we tried to stroll in, the officers stationed out front would definitely notice us.

"Canda was right," Torren said, scanning the building with a monocular held up to his eye. "It's a small outpost. Judging by the size of what I'm assuming are the barracks over there, there are probably no more than twelve soldiers stationed here."

"You say that as if twelve Union officers are no big deal," I muttered.

"As long as they don't spot us, we're stellar," he said.

"But if they do, they'll have us outnumbered and outgunned."

"Let me tell you something about Union soldiers." He put his monocular away and started going through his gear. "One of the Kedigan I grew up with, Nilá, she uh…joined the Union."

He saw the look on my face even out of the corner of his eye.

"Relax," he said. "She did it for the training, to see how they operate." He stowed the gear back in his bag and pulled out his blaster. "She went in for two years, as a soldier, not a street officer. She got combat and weapons training, even rose the ranks for a while, then…left. Went off to Free Sector. She managed to smuggle out some of their training codexes, all of which I read."

The Union had a preference for human male recruits. If a young female Kedigan had risen their ranks, she must have been *quite* a soldier.

"So what are you saying? That you can fight as well as an experienced Union soldier because you read their training materials?"

"No. I'm just saying I can counter them pretty well, because I know what they're likely to *do* in a combat situation, especially lower-ranking grunts like these." He jerked his head towards the building. "The Union wants disposable damage-dealers, so they're not training them to keep themselves safe in battle. They don't check their corners, they charge in with guns blazing."

"If you're trying to convince me not to worry, you're not doing a great job."

"Listen, if we do this right, they won't even know we're here." He turned his blaster over, sliding the power cylinder out and checking the ion charges before reloading and priming the weapon to fire. Whether he had it on the stun or lethal setting, I didn't know. I didn't ask.

I lowered the fern fronds in front of me, looking over at our intended destination. "What's the plan?" I asked, looking at Torren for instruction.

"We've got two options. One, we distract the officers out front and slip past as quickly as we can," he said.

"Sounds terrible."

"Or two, we hike to the top of the canyon and look for a place to climb down. We might find a way in, or we might waste hours searching for one. What do you think?" he asked, holstering his blaster looking at me for my response.

I swallowed, pleasantly surprised that he wanted my input after taking the lead for most of the journey. I considered both plans. We could walk the perimeter of the canyon for hours with no guaranteed entrance. We didn't have time to waste. Not to mention that my arm was still healing, and I wasn't sure how much climbing I'd even be able to do.

"Let's make a run for it," I said. "It'll be quicker."

"My thoughts exactly," he murmured, drumming his fingers on his knee, formulating an idea. "We'll need a distraction then." He pulled a metallic object from his bag. It was round and flat, the size of his palm. One of the three detonators he had brought with him. He examined the disk, then slid it into his jacket pocket. "I'll attach it to the rock bluff on the other side of the outpost and start a countdown. If I can time it correctly, it'll work like a charm." He rose from a crouch, but stayed low. "Stay here, and be ready to run when I get back."

I didn't like the idea of him getting so close to the outpost, but before I could protest, he disappeared into the foliage behind me.

"Torren!" I whispered after him, but he was gone. I sighed, slinging my arms through the straps of my bag, and waited. Every second that passed danced on my nerves, and I found myself shaking. Needing something to do, I crept forward and peered at the outpost.

The two officers were still at their post at the entrance. They were at ease, no alarms sounding, so I knew Torren hadn't been spotted. As I was about to retreat back against the boulder, I heard static from one of the officer's transmitters and froze.

He unclipped it from his belt and held it closer to his ear, and fear warred through me. *Torren's been spotted. He's been caught.* The officer murmured to his partner, but neither of them jumped into action. They simply adjusted their uniforms and stood at attention.

I took one easier breath, but heard the low hum of a vehicle approaching. A ground speeder glided out of the forest and pulled to a stop in front of the outpost. *What's this? We don't need another complication right now.*

The man sitting in the back seat swung his legs out of the vehicle and stood up. He was no mere officer, I could see it right away. Tall, with impossibly straight posture, the man before me was middle-aged, with graying hair and strong facial features. He was not armored, a sign that he didn't enforce the Union's will. He dictated it. The man didn't carry a weapon: he just wore an immaculately crisp uniform and the same utility belt all Union soldiers wore.

"Inspector Markens," said one of the guard officers, throwing a sharp salute.

My stomach dropped as I recognized him. It was the Union inspector I had seen being interviewed on the news-wire on Laigo. The head of their security division. *What is he doing on Talar?*

He strode toward the outpost's door, and one of the guards scrambled to reach it before he did. The guard hastily punched a code into the control panel, and the hydraulic door slid open soundlessly despite its size. Markens stepped inside without ever breaking his stride. The door closed behind him, and the two officers let out a visible sigh of relief. The speeder pulled away, and the sentries went back to their post, neither looking half as imposing as they had moments before. They were terrified of Markens.

I sat back, and Torren appeared next to me. I jumped in surprise, doing a double-take as my lungs seized up. *I didn't even hear the ferns rustle.*

"Gryta's sake, Torren!" I hissed. "Do you know—"

"I'm counting," he whispered, looking aimlessly past me, his head nodding rhythmically as he concentrated.

He had set the timer on the detonator. The plan was in motion now. There was no going back.

Eventually, he caught my eye and raised his eyebrows, mouthing the words, "Get ready." Creeping up to the fern in front of us, he peered at the guards.

I tugged at my boot laces, making sure they were tied tight, then gripped the straps of my bag.

"We should see movement right about...*now.*"

At first nothing happened, but then—a small blast. It rumbled in the distance, followed by rocks grinding and sliding to the ground. *Part one, down.* The two officers turned and looked in the direction of the sound, their bodies stiff.

"What was that?" said one of them. The other shouldered his blaster rifle and hurried away from the door, heading in the direction of the blast.

I coiled into a crouch, getting ready to move, but Torren reached over and put his hand on my leg.

The second officer lingered for a moment, glancing between the door and the corner his partner had rounded. Eventually, curiosity won out, and he followed his partner.

As soon as they disappeared, Torren dropped his hand. "Go."

We took off. Our boots dug into the dirt as we crashed through the foliage and out into the open. I focused ahead on the canyon's entrance and sprinted forward, matching Torren's speed as best as possible. We moved as silently as we could, the only sounds our bags bouncing against us and our boots hitting the ground. Passing the outpost, we entered the grey rock canyon. *Almost there.*

The gravel floor of the canyon crunched under our feet. *We're in.* No blaster fire came. No voices yelled out. We kept running, aiming for a bend in the canyon that would hide us from view of anyone peering in from the outside. Rounding the bend, Torren stopped, glancing over his shoulder. I attempted to stop as well, but my boots caught on the gravel and I pitched forward.

Torren spun and shot his arms out, catching me while throwing his legs wide to steady himself and keep us both up. He walked backwards with me in his arms until his back hit the curved wall of the canyon. We stood still, catching our breath and listening carefully, our hearts pounding against one another. I expected to hear the footfalls of officer boots on the canyon floor at any moment, but no sound came.

He let go of me and exhaled, his body slumping against the rocks in relief.

"I think we're clear," he said, pulling out the nav-projector and calibrating our waypoint.

I took an anxious breath and met Torren's eyes as we began again, heading further into the canyon. As we walked, I saw that the walls weren't all that high. They were only ten or eleven feet tall in most places, with the floor of it averaging twelve feet in width. It was a small canyon, all things considered, but still would have been hard for us to descend into without any climbing equipment.

My fingers tingled in anticipation. The crate we needed was here; we just had to find it now. I couldn't believe we were finally nearing our objective. We had come so far and worked so hard.

We moved deeper into the canyon, watching the projector screen as the flashing waypoint drew closer. Eventually, we were standing right at the coordinates the nav-projector had given us. We stopped.

"According to the nav, it should be right...here," he said.

We both looked around, the canyon walls towering over us.

"It's a small crate?" I asked.

He nodded. "Yes, but it will be hidden somehow."

I looked for anything out of the ordinary, but saw nothing. Just rock walls and gravel.

Torren crouched, digging his fingers into the gravel canyon floor.

"Do you think it's buried?" I asked.

He sighed in response, and I knew he was thinking the same thing I was. We had neither a shovel nor the time or energy to start digging. He picked up a handful of gravel and let it slip through his fingers, the bits of rock scattering across the canyon floor as he hunched stiffly, lost in thought.

"It's got to be here."

"Or it *was*," he muttered. The thought hadn't even crossed my mind, but the crate having been found by the Union or someone else was not an impossibility.

I dropped my head into my hands and pressed on my temples wearily. After all this time, after everything we had been through, to think it may all have been for nothing was beyond disappointing. We needed to help Rego, and this alleged crate was supposed to be our ticket. Torren was quiet, no doubt running scenarios in his head, so I gave him some space.

Approaching one of the rock walls on either side of us, I leaned defeatedly against it. *What are we missing?* Whoever left the crate would have wanted it hidden, and whoever that was had done a great job. If I wasn't so worried about Rego, I would have been more impressed.

I closed my eyes and thought back to my childhood on Talar, leaning my head against the wall behind me. Growing up, I had played plenty of hiding games with Canda and the other kids. Canda had won just about every single time. *Why? It was because she wasn't afraid of climbing into...*

My eyes snapped open.

"Torren," I said, pushing myself away from the wall.

"Hmm?"

"Talar is full of caves. The one at Canda's camp is unusually large, but grey rock like this is full of them."

He stared at me blankly, but I saw a spark in his eye as he realized what I was saying. He shot to his feet. We both began inspecting the rock walls of the canyon, Torren taking one side while I took the other. We searched for anything that looked unnatural in the craggy surface, confident that we were on the right track.

"There." Torren pointed at a seam in the rock that had completely escaped our notice before. It looked like a small cave entrance that someone had blocked off by stacking slabs of rock.

My hands shook with giddiness. *This is it.*

Torren put his hand into a gap between two of the slabs. He pushed them, feeling for movement, but they seemed to be wedged tightly. Bringing a detonator out of his bag, he carefully affixed it to the center of the stack.

"You enjoy using these, don't you?" I asked.

He shook his head. "Not really. They're hardly subtle," he said, setting a timer on the device. "But do you remember when I told you there's a way through anything?"

"Yeah."

"Sometimes that way is a fucking explosion." He pressed a button that started a short countdown sequence. "Let's get back," he said, ushering me away.

We moved five or six yards down, watching as the numbers on the detonator's display ticked down.

"You'll want to cover your ears," he said.

"They won't hear it at the outpost?" I asked.

"This is a low-charge detonator compared to the last one, the impact will be small and controlled. I think we're far enough away from the outpost," he said, glancing down the canyon. I hoped he was right.

"Ears," he warned, refusing to cover his until I'd followed his instructions, holding my palms on either side of my head.

As the timer ran its last few seconds out, Torren lifted one shoulder and turned toward me, shielding me from any potential debris. There was no need—the detonator blast was as slight as he had said it would be. I heard the loud *clack* of stones hitting each other before cracking and tumbling to the canyon floor.

Torren and I waited for the dust to settle, then carefully approached. There was now a gap in the rock face—a few feet off the ground was a jagged entrance to a small cave. Torren wasted no time stepping up into it. I followed.

The cave was dusty and dark, but the newly-created entrance provided enough light for us to look around. The whole space was barely wider than my bedroom back at home, though rounded in shape with an uneven rock floor and low ceiling. My heart raced as we finally laid eyes on our prize—a small wooden crate sitting in the middle of the cave floor.

It exists. It's here.

Torren gave me a satisfied smile, quickly crossing and crouching next to the crate. Its lid was held in place by a long strand of rope wrapped around it several times. He blew a layer of dust from the lid. It looked no more than a foot and a half wide.

"It's smaller than I thought." I said, coming to stand next to him, my head ducked to avoid the low ceiling.

"I've transported a lot of stolen goods," he said. "The smaller the box, the more valuable the item. Remember the egg?"

He reached over and tapped my ankle, eyes still fixed on the lid. Pulling my shock-blade out, I handed it over. He flipped it open and slashed at the rope wrapped around the box.

"Just need to check something before we take it," he said, carefully loosening one end of the lid open with the blade.

"Are you supposed to open it?"

"I try not to move contraband without knowing what it is first," Torren said, prying the other end of the lid free. "Besides, my buyer lied to me about the risks involved with this job. I'm doing this my way."

As he removed the lid, we both leaned in anxiously to see what we had come all this way for.

Nestled in a bed of dried Talarian river reeds were four dark objects of various shapes. My eyes adjusted and I saw that they were stone carvings. Torren delicately lifted one out and turned it over, examining it. A brilliant green flash caught the light from the cave's entrance.

"Solcite," I said, breathless.

"This is the stone those Union officers said was depleted years ago?"

"Yes," I said, reaching forward to touch the carving. It felt beautifully smooth beneath my fingers. "And these are the biggest pieces of solcite I've ever seen, making these...priceless."

Torren turned the piece over again, and we watched the stunning green iridescence shift in the light.

"Someone wants to buy a piece of Talarian history," Torren said, "or souvenirs of the Union's reign."

"What?" I asked, tearing my eyes from the stone to look at him.

"There are some very wealthy people in the galaxy who get a kick out of owning rare artifacts from planets the Union has crushed and taken over," he said.

I thought of some rich baron displaying a piece of Talar on his mantle simply for the bragging rights. My blood heated as my breath shortened. "That's despicable."

"I don't like it any more than you do."

I studied the carving woefully. I hated the thought of handing the pieces over to a non-Talarian, but if I didn't, Rego would be in trouble.

"You okay?" Torren asked, seeming to know where my mind was.

"Doesn't matter," I said, taking the carving from him and nestling it back into the crate. "We came here to save Rego. We can't stop now."

He nodded and replaced the lid. Wielding my blade carefully, he cut the rope again and tied a few knots, creating a makeshift carrying strap. He stood and slung it across his chest like a bulky satchel. It would be clunky to walk back to his ship with, but we could do it.

"Let's go," he said.

We returned to the cave's entrance and stepped out. Before we could take another step, a distant noise made us both pause. Voices were coming from the canyon entrance. *Shit.* I heard the distinct sound of boots on gravel. They crunched closer and closer with every passing breath. Torren and I locked eyes. Maybe the officers had heard the blast? Or somehow pinged the nav-projector? Either way, they were coming for us, and this wasn't something we could talk our way out of. *Are we ever going to catch a break?*

Torren and I both took stock of our surroundings. The walls of the canyon were too steep to climb and too tall to reach.

My breath grew shallow. "Torren?" I asked nervously, hoping he had a plan.

His eyes flicked around the tall canyon walls, then returned to the cave gap we had just exited. He looked up with a focused expression, thinking.

His eyes scanned the rock faces, then landed on the jagged cave entrance that we'd blasted open. Dust still clung to the sharp edges of the fractured stone, and cracks splintered up the wall around it. The blast had left behind a craggy slope. It was irregular and rough, but looked climbable

"What did I tell you?" he said. "There's always a way through." Shifting the crate to hang behind him, he began to climb the irregular rock surface of the cave entrance, finding handholds and footholds with surprising ease.

I paid attention to the areas he used, preparing to follow it exactly. The sound of the officers marching grew closer.

Once Torren got to the top of the gap, he braced himself against the rocks with his legs, grabbing the strap of the crate and pulling it off. He pushed it up and over the top of the canyon wall. With a labored grunt, he clambered over the precipice, then turned around and lay flat, reaching his arm down.

"Climb to me. I'll pull you up," he said, out of breath.

The officer's voices were getting louder.

I began to climb. My fingernails dug against rock as I hoisted myself off the ground. Halfway up the wall, a severe pain shot through my arm. It was still weak from the injury. I tried to ignore it, but a searing ache overtook my senses every time I moved my arm. Grimacing, I reached up, almost grasping Torren's waiting hand. My reach fell just short. I stretched, my toes slipping against the steep rock as I strained for the few inches I needed. My fingers brushed his, but before we could grasp each other, my arm gave out. My breath caught and I slipped. My fingers and boots scraped the rough rock as I slid back down the six feet I'd managed to climb.

"Try again," he hissed, his voice low.

The concern in his eyes broke my heart. It wasn't going to work. I knew without having to try. I didn't have any grip strength left. My arm was useless.

"Fenn!" he snapped, abandoning his hushed tone.

My arm throbbed, and my heart slowed as I realized what had to happen now. I could hear the approaching boots much louder. *They're close.*

Torren began to look around behind him—searching, I assumed, for something to pull me up with. He still had hope. He began untying the rope holding the crate, but I knew there wasn't enough time.

"Tor," I said as calmly as I could muster, my voice barely audible over his frantic movements.

He stopped and met my eyes.

"Go," I said.

He didn't move, he just stared at me.

"*Go!*" I repeated, louder this time.

"Fenn Kensie," he said through gritted teeth. "I swear, if you don't get up here right now—"

Ordering me around again. I'm really going to miss that.

"Torren...whatever your last name is," I said, matching the

aggression in his tone. "Get to the ship, get off the planet, and get that bounty paid."

"I am not leaving you," he said through a clenched jaw.

I rolled my eyes at him. *We don't have time to argue.*

"I'll be fine," I said. "I'll use the mining cover and play dumb. Now *go*."

He hesitated, but must have seen in my eyes how unmovable I was. Eventually, he pushed himself away from the ledge and disappeared.

He was gone.

I knew I should have felt fear at that moment, but with Rego that much closer to being in the clear, I felt strangely...at peace.

"*Halt!*" a deep voice yelled.

Putting my hands up, I turned slowly. There were four Union officers standing in the canyon, all holding blaster rifles aimed right at me. I recognized the two guards from the outpost entrance.

"Don't shoot," I said calmly. "I was just prospecting."

"Keep your hands up," the squad leader barked.

"Okay," I said, stepping down from the cave entrance. My boots hit the gravel of the canyon floor, and I put my hands up again.

"What are you doing out here?" the squad leader demanded.

"I told you, just mining for minerals."

The squad leader reached forward and pulled the latch back on his rifle. It made a loud clacking noise, and I flinched. *He just changed his fire setting from stun to lethal.* The Union had the means to create silent weapons, so the clacking sound must have been added to the lethal setting as an intimidation effect. *Terrorizing bastards.*

"Is it illegal to mine now?" I asked defensively.

The squad leader raised his fist, giving the others a signal. Two of the officers lowered their weapons and walked toward me. I kept still, fully believing they would shoot me where I stood if they were ordered to.

"Put her down," the squad leader instructed coldly.

One of the officers approaching me pulled out a black shock baton. Electric blue sparks sizzled at the tip of the weapon, heating my skin as it drew near. Before I could say another word, the officer held it firmly against my neck.

I heard a loud *zap*. Every muscle in my body contracted, and everything went dark.

26

YOU'RE UNBELIEVABLE

I FLOATED THROUGH A COLD, DARK VOID. WAS IT A VOID? MAYBE it was a room. I didn't know where I was, but I could tell I was no longer in the canyon. *Am I awake? Am I even alive?* A sound caught my notice, and I listened closely.

Fenn.

It was my name.

Fenn.

Torren was calling my name.

Fenn!

The sound came again and again. *Am I dreaming?* I *had* to be; Torren was gone. A soft light glowed in the distance and I swam toward it, surfacing from the darkness. When I opened my eyes, I regretted it instantly. Wherever I was, it was devastatingly bright.

I was sitting slumped over in a metal chair, gaze angled down toward my boots. *Okay, not dead. So far, so good.* I tried to push myself up, but my movement was hindered, and I felt pain in my wrists. Looking down, I saw my hands were shackled together by a pair of metal cuffs. *Shit.* They pressed painfully into my wrists again as I tried to move. I held my hands up and saw why they hurt so much. The individual cuffs were bridged by a solid piece of metal, offering very little flexibility for the unfortunate wearer.

I weakly lifted my head, one eye still squinting, and glanced around. My chair was seated in the center of an empty room. I managed to get both eyes open and sat up slowly, taking in bare, beige stone walls and a grey concrete floor. At the center of the wall facing me was a window, the source of the glaring light. I turned my head to shield my eyes, drawing in a sharp breath as I felt a tender burn mark on my neck from the shock baton. *Bastards.* The stun setting on their rifles would have sufficed, but the baton was far more painful, and they knew it.

I lifted my arm to check on my injury and saw that my jacket sleeve had been rolled up to my elbow. The bandage Torren had put on was gone, now replaced with a fresh one. There was lightly printed text on the wrap that I squinted to read. *Issued by the Galactic Union. Great.* I was *inside* the Union outpost.

Studying the window again, I saw that it was tall and narrow. Too narrow to fit through, even if I could manage to break the glass. I wiggled my foot inside my boot, hoping to feel the handle of my shock-blade press against my ankle, but I felt nothing. Groaning, I remembered Torren still had it. *I'm so screwed.*

As I was still getting my bearings, the door facing my right side slid open with a hydraulic hiss. I snapped my head up as a man walked in. As soon as I saw the crisp golden-brown uniform, I knew. *Inspector Markens.*

I got a good look at him now that he was up close. Even if I hadn't recognized him, I would have known he was high-ranking because of his hairstyle. Unlike the cropped hair of the officers, Marken's hair was longer, parted with razor precision and combed neatly away from his face. He was sturdy, his limbs thicker and slightly more muscular than most of the higher ranking Union officers I had seen. The Union usually relegated men with his build to strength-forward jobs, like enforcement and combat. *Shit. He's probably extremely intelligent. Too valuable to waste in the field.* Though my mind was fuzzy, I remembered that the news-wire I'd seen had said he was head of the Union's Security Division.

I'd noticed the crispness of his uniform from my hiding place in the ferns, but now I could see that his utility belt was pristine and his boots were unscuffed. Polished within an inch of their life. I studied his face as he made his way in, his grey eyes fixed on me. He had a calm, detached expression that made his invasive stare all the more unsettling. Two Union officers entered the room, standing off to the side as Markens faced me, positioning himself in front of the narrow window. It backlit him with an ominous glow, slightly obscuring his expression. *This isn't his first interrogation.*

What would Torren do? He'd assess Markens. Try to locate his weak points. This guy is a hunter; don't give him anything to chase. Don't show fear.

"And are these really necessary?" I raised my shackled wrists. I had meant to sound confident and unrattled, but my voice came out weaker than I had anticipated.

Markens stood rigid, his eyes tracing over me with stoic interest.

"You were found in an restricted Union martial zone without clearance, around the same time multiple explosive devices were detonated within a stone's throw of a Union military building." He gave me a half-amused look. "You're looking at charges that come with words like *treason* and *terrorism* attached."

"There's been some misunderstanding," I said. "I was just tapping some boulders, looking for minerals. I didn't realize where I was."

"Talarian locals all know better than to mine outside of their permitted areas," Markens said. "We've demonstrated strict enough punishments to ensure that. So tell me, who are you, and what were you doing in the canyon?"

"I told you, I was prospecting," I shrugged. I decided to test his reaction to being given an attitude. "You're going to have to take my word for it, buddy."

I studied his face for a reaction, but saw nothing. Torren and I had manipulated the previous officers we'd run into because we could read them and find what made them tick. Markens was a brick wall.

Tilting his head, he stepped forward. I flinched. He circumvented the chair, walking behind me. I tensed, but resisted the urge to twist my neck and watch him. I kept my gaze on the window, trying to avoid the appearance of being nervous. He struck me as the kind of person who could smell fear.

"I am a very busy man," Markens said, circling me slowly like a hungry predator, one too calculated to strike without studying first. "I have little time, and even less patience. I'm in the middle of a galaxy-wide investigation, and suddenly, a person of interest is sitting in front of me. I'm going to need some answers."

With painstakingly slow movements, Markens made his way back to the window, where he faced me again.

"Are you Resistance?" he asked me with a piercing gaze.

"Am I *what?*" I asked, hoping to appear clueless.

"The Talarian Resistance group. Are you with them?" he snapped.

He doesn't like repeating himself. My heart pounded as I fought to keep my breath even and calm. *Maybe I can do something with that.*

"I don't even know what that is," I said.

He paused and narrowed his eyes, reconsidering the angle of his approach. Torren did the same thing when he wasn't getting his way.

"We found no ID chip on you. I have doubts that you're even a local." He clasped his hands behind him and looked down his nose at me. "So I'll ask you again—who are you, and what were you doing in that canyon?"

"You got me, I'm not a local. My husband and I just moved here to get in on the mining trade."

"Then where are you from?"

"Laigo," I said, glancing down at the carved wooden ring still on my finger. "I'm from Laigo. I'm a data tech, and my husband is a woodworker. We've been married for five years. My parents didn't approve of him, but he proposed anyway, during the Festival of Gryta."

He held his silence as he stared me down. We both knew I was reciting a cover.

"Was that a smuggling cave you were found in?" he demanded, his voice raising.

The reality of my situation hit me. A week ago, I had been a docking technician, following all the rules and staying out of trouble. Today, I was in Union custody and being interrogated. The thing I had been terrified of all these years had finally come true. I was no longer scared. *Talk in circles.*

"You know…" I said, leaning forward, "everyone raves about the Festival of Gryta on Laigo, but I actually think the one on Pentelos is better. The food is better anyway."

Markens exhaled slowly. It wasn't a sigh; he was far too practiced to show that I was beginning to get to him. But it was close.

"I don't think you've truly grasped the depth of the hole you've dug here. But you will."

He looked at one of the officers and jerked his head toward me. The soldier grabbed something off of his belt as he stepped forward.

I heard a familiar crackle, and my body instinctively tensed up.

The officer held up the sparking shock baton, the sight of it causing me to drop my fearless facade as I leaned away as far as the chair would let me. The soldier's face was blank as he pressed the electric tip of the baton firmly against my upper leg.

The shock wasn't as bad as the one at my neck earlier. The voltage seemed lower now, and the fabric of my pants created a minor barrier between my skin and the raw electricity. Still, I saw stars. My whole body constricted, and I spasmed forward in the chair, clenching my jaw and trying to catch my breath.

As excruciating as the pain was, I focused my thoughts. *Why use a lower voltage?* My hands began to sweat as I realized it was the same reason they'd treated and rebandaged my arm. They wanted me healthy and alert enough to feel *everything*. After all, you couldn't extract information from the unconscious.

"There was something in that cave. What was it?" Markens asked.

I shrugged and looked past him toward the other end of the room. *He's not getting anything from me.*

"We know about your partner," he sneered.

My heart dropped, and I searched his eyes. *Did they find Torren?*

"We discovered his footprints on the ridge above the canyon. We tried to follow his trail, but it disappeared," he said, desperation finally starting to bleed into his voice. "Looks like he left you behind. Abandoned you to save himself."

Torren had gotten away. I sighed in relief, my body relaxing enough for me to breathe better.

Markens bent at the waist and leaned down, putting himself level with my eyeline. "Tell me his name," he said, his grey eyes boring into mine.

Torren.

"I never learned his name," I said. It was half true—Torren had never told me his last name, and half-truths were easier to bluff with.

"Give me a name!" Markens shouted.

Torren, from Rorric, in the Sylvad system.

"I don't know!" I shouted back. My control on my emotions was wearing thin. I was so tired of the male inclination to intimidate when they were met with resistance. It was predictable.

Markens looked at me with barely detectable annoyance, then straightened up. Stepping back, he made eye contact with the soldier holding the shock baton and jerked his head toward me again. The officer pressed the electric tip against my rib cage this time.

The crackle danced in my ears as my body convulsed in the chair. My eyes clenched shut in pain. When I did get them open again, I saw Markens studying me as I writhed. He was indifferent to my suffering, objectively gauging my pain tolerance and calculating how long it would take to wear me down. I was simply an encrypted file to him, one he was going to crack.

I let out a labored breath as my dizzied vision slowly returned. I wasn't sure how many more of those I could take.

"I'll give you some time to think," he said. "I'll be back, and I will expect answers. You seem smart enough to know what will happen if I don't get them."

I didn't have a quip that time. It was just as well; I was too winded to speak. Still doubled over in the chair, I struggled to get a breath, my muscles screaming with pain.

He turned to leave but held up a finger, as if remembering something. "Oh, before I go—perhaps you can tell me the significance of this."

He held his hand out, waiting. One of his guards fiddled with the pouch on his belt, then stepped forward, placing something carefully in Markens' palm.

Star Bonnet.

It was the sprig Torren had given me. They'd found it in my pocket. Markens pinched the fragile bloom between his thumb and forefinger and held it up for me.

"Look familiar?"

I pursed my lips and stared at him.

"Strange thing for a criminal to be carrying," he said. "It wouldn't be of sentimental value, now would it?"

It seemed he was testing my emotional resolve now. I hated him.

"It's nothing," I lied. "Just a flower I picked."

"Mmm," he grunted. "I figured as much."

Rolling his fingers together, he crushed the sprig, grinding it to tiny pieces that floated to the floor. He watched my face while he did it, to see if he'd broken me yet. I inhaled slowly and kept still. He nodded, then turned on his heel and headed toward the door, the officers following him out silently.

The door hissed shut, and suddenly, I was alone again. I sat back up as best as I could and caught a full breath, ignoring my nauseous stomach and the sweat beading on my forehead.

My senses returned, and terror slowly set in. I was trapped. Torren was gone, and Canda was miles away. There was nothing anyone could do for me. If I didn't die here, they would send me to some cold, deep-space detention center or a deadly work camp on Lapidal. I let out a small laugh at the sheer irony of my fate. All these years, I'd worked so hard to make sure Rego didn't go to a Union prison, and in the end, it was going to be me that did. *Is that tragedy, or poetic justice?* It was *something*.

Biting my lip, I felt tears coming, and I squeezed my eyes shut. A wave of dizziness hit me and I tried to stay coherent, but I was losing the fight. I felt myself slipping back into the darkness again, steadily fading into a vast space without stars. My hands hung limp in the cuffs as I let my head fall forward.

The silent stillness was interrupted by a crackling noise. The sound jolted me awake, and I looked around frantically, expecting to see a shock baton coming toward me. After a few blinks, I saw there was no one in the room. *I'm losing my mind.* Giggling deliriously to myself, I felt disappointed at how quickly I'd broken. Sighing, I slouched forward in the chair again, my will to fight steadily evaporating.

"Fenn," a quiet voice sounded from nearby.

I lifted my head.

"Hey, are you awake?" the voice whispered.

Where is it coming from?

"What's happening?" I asked weakly.

"It's me."

Torren's voice.

"I hid a micro-transmitter in the collar of your jacket. I can't believe they missed it when they searched you," he said. I heard it now, the static clinging to his words.

"That was *you* saying my name when I was unconscious," I mumbled

"You weren't answering, and I panicked."

"Have you been listening this whole time?" I asked.

Torren paused, his silence saying it all. He had definitely listened to me being shocked. It couldn't have been easy to hear. *At least he heard me refusing to give him up.*

"Yes, Sketch, I heard," he said softly. He'd switched to my nick-name, I assumed, in case anyone overheard us or tapped into the transmission. "I'm so sorry." His tone of voice was odd. I had never heard him so worried.

I almost smiled at the thought, but I took a deep breath and cleared my throat. There was nothing he could do for me, so I needed to put on a brave show. *No sense in making him feel guilty about leaving me behind. There was no other way.*

"Yeah, I didn't have Union interrogation with a side of torture on my checklist for today."

"You're doing great," Torren said. "Just keep it up."

"Hey, I've got bad news," I said, shifting in the chair and wincing at the pain. "You know that inspector we saw on the holoboard in Laigo City?"

"Yeah, Markens?"

"He's here."

Silence. I knew what he was thinking, because I was thinking it too. *What are the odds the Union Inspector on the Egg of Arpax case, Torren's case, was also here on Talar?* There had to be some connection.

"The nav," he breathed. "Damn it. I used this same nav-projector during the museum break-in. On the whole string of Union robberies, actually. I never, across a hundred lifetimes, imagined it would be an issue. The Union doesn't sit around scanning for random nav-signals. They must have started. If that was Markens' idea..." He trailed off. He was realizing what I had when Markens stepped into the room—the man we were up against was no idiot.

"So," I said, changing the subject, "when exactly did you hide this transmitter on me without my knowledge?"

"The second night on the ship. You left your jacket laying in the cargo hold. I did it in case we got separated on Laigo. I swear I was going to tell you about it, but you were holed up in your bunk the entire flight. By the time you weren't, it slipped my mind."

"That's creepy," I said, wearily pushing myself into a better sitting position.

"Yeah, well, we can discuss the ethics of it later."

"Did you take my ID chip too?"

He was silent for a breath. "I slipped it out of your pocket before we entered the canyon. In case we got caught. I have a hidden pocket in my jacket for moments like this."

"You're unbelievable," I scoffed.

"We can discuss that later too. Look, Sketch, just hold on a little longer, okay?" he said with a pleading voice. "I'm coming to get you."

I paused. He *had* to be joking.

"Like *hell* you are. Reg…" I stopped myself from saying Rego's full name. "Our friend's life literally depends on that crate being delivered."

"And it will be, but right now, we need to focus on getting you out of there."

"Come on, this is my fault," I said. "I made you bring me, remember? You wanted me to stay on the ship."

"That was before I…" He stopped. "I'm getting you out of there,

Sketch, but I need your help," he said, leaving no room for argument.

"Out of the question," I snapped. I wasn't about to let him risk everything we've worked for, and Rego's life, on some harebrained scheme he came up with on the fly. "Just get out of here."

He was silent, I could almost hear him thinking over the transmitter. "Sketch, you know I've read their training codexes. There's an entire module dedicated to interrogation and torture." He paused. "Please, *please*, believe me when I tell you, they've only just started."

We sat in silence, and I swallowed nervously, taking a long, measured breath. The thought of receiving another electric shock made my blood run cold, let alone anything else Union condoned for of extracting information. I wanted out, but not enough to encourage him to do something stupid. He knew that, because he knew me by now.

Torren's calm voice through the transmitter broke the silence. "It was at the shipyard on Hadrin, by the way."

"What?" I asked, right before realizing. The answer he'd refused to give me last night in the tent.

"When I knew I wanted you. I wasn't lying when I told Canda." I could hear a smile in his voice.

Where is he right now?

"You were so *difficult* in the shipyard. It really pissed me off, to be honest," he said.

I laughed, an abrupt sound that rang off of the walls of the empty room. Of all the times and places for him to confess.

"But you gave me hell, and I couldn't help but like you."

"You *liked* that?" I asked, incapable of keeping the smile from my face.

"I liked that you weren't giving in. You challenged me, and you held your ground. I was impressed. There was something about you—I could tell you were on the run. Laying low, the way I was. I could tell you were like me."

I *was* like him. We were both stubborn, both bearing the scars of the harrowing events that had forced us to grow up too early. We both lived life on high alert, quietly observing the world around us, desperate to obtain a measure of control in the chaotic galaxy. *He saw it the moment we met.*

"Oh," I said softly, feeling heat blossom across my cheeks. "You sure hid all of that very well."

"Yeah, I'm good at that," he said abruptly, shifting focus. I could no longer hear a smile. "Now stop fighting me, and help me figure out where you are."

I let out a deep exhale, knowing there was no arguing with him. "Fine," I said at last.

"Did you see anything when they brought you in?"

"I was out cold."

"That's alright. How big is the room you're in?"

I sized it up. "Smaller than Hollak's bar, bigger than the cave we found earlier."

"Are there windows?"

"There's one, but it's too small to fit through."

"What shape is it?"

"It's a thin, vertical rectangle with rounded corners."

"Perfect. Is the light in the window cool, or golden?"

"What?" I asked.

"I'm trying to determine if you're on the east-facing side of the building or not."

"It's a golden light. Looks like the sun might be setting?"

"Okay, I know where you are," he said. "Hold on." The transmitter crackled and went dead.

"Hey," I said. There was no answer. "Are you there?" I whispered, but the transmitter was silent. I shifted in the chair nervously.

The outpost was guarded by officers, and I had seen the entrance. The door required a code, for Gryta's sake. There was no way in. I didn't know what Torren had planned, but a part of me hoped he would realize the risk involved and change his mind. I was tired and my muscles were so sore. When I felt my eyes closing, I fought it at first, but eventually gave in and drifted off to avoid the pain.

27

———————

I BELIEVE IN YOU

I DRIFTED IN AND OUT OF CONSCIOUSNESS. HAD IT BEEN MINUTES or hours since I'd spoken to Torren? Fear gripped me as I considered the possibility I hadn't even spoken to him at all. Perhaps the entire conversation had been a hallucination brought on by the painful shocks to my system. Maybe Torren had truly left and taken the crate, well on his way to paying off Rego's bounty. I closed my eyes, about to drift off again, when the hydraulic door slid open. I tensed up, knowing nothing good was coming.

Markens stepped into the room, but this time, the two officers didn't come in with him. I could see them standing outside the open door, holding their blaster rifles stoically, their backs to the room.

"I trust you've had time enough to consider your situation," said Markens. I sat up, wary of the fact that the officers hadn't come in with him. "Now, you will give me the answers I request, or you'll wish that you had answered me the first time."

Markens wasn't holding a shock baton. I immediately felt even more uneasy. He might be about to deviate from official protocol and was giving the officers plausible deniability by letting them wait outside. Cold sweat formed on my brow.

"I don't know anything," I said with hollow confidence.

"Well, I know something," he said, wielding the words like a weapon. "I know that either you or your partner, perhaps both, have some connection to the theft from the Union Museum."

Torren was right about the nav-projector. Markens had tracked us here.

"You don't know shit," I spat. "And you won't. Not from me."

"We'll see about that," he said, his mouth curling into a gleeful smile that sent a chill down my spine. He unbuttoned one of his uniform sleeves and casually began rolling it up to the elbow.

I studied his uniform again, noticing that it was sharper and more tailored than those of his minions. *Same utility belt that they all wear.*

He cleared his throat, and my palms began to sweat as I watched him lace his fingers together and crack his knuckles, his eyes glinting with anticipation.

This is his element. This is what he lives for.

"Do you know why the Union is so powerful?" he asked. "Why we win every time?"

"I'm guessing it's the constant unrestrained violence," I said, shrugging lazily.

"Wrong," he said with an amused half-smile. "Strength alone doesn't yield power; force must be wielded wisely." He calmly rolled up his other sleeve, keeping the folds as neat as possible.

"When an institution like the Union grows, there's temptation to drop old methods and embrace the new. It's a common misconception that the Union is cutting-edge in *all* of its operations."

I had pieced together where this was headed. He was going to hit me. A lot. And he didn't want blood on his precious shirt sleeves.

"Is this going somewhere?" I asked, feeling like I'd rather be struck already than have to listen to his self-righteous drivel.

"I'll give you an example," he said, stepping forward and cracking his neck. "The Union has access to the most advanced technology in the galaxy, and in turn, our scientists have engineered some truly innovative interrogation machines." He stood directly in front of me, his stocky frame completely blocking out the light from the window behind him. "But it's vanity, all of it," he said, dismissively waving his hand. "I've found that, for extracting information, the most effective methods are often the most rudimentary."

He looked down at me in the way that Rego and the other mechanics looked down at a faulty engine. I'd seen them take hammers to ship parts when nothing else worked.

I wondered again what Torren would do in my place, and wheels in my mind started turning. I had an idea, but it wasn't guaranteed to work. It all depended on how much rage lay underneath his calm surface, and whether he could be baited by unyielding noncompliance.

Markens pressed his fist into the palm of his other hand, cracking the joints in preparation for contact.

"Okay, okay," I said, adopting a panicky expression. "I'll talk."

He paused, as if surprised I was giving in so quickly—and disappointed that he hadn't gotten to apply his methods.

"I'm not really from Laigo," I said, sighing dramatically. "I was born on Oneon."

"Oneon?" he repeated incredulously.

I nodded emphatically, eyes wide.

"The water planet that can't sustain human life?" he asked. "Very funny."

I smiled at my own joke. "I certainly thought s—"

He cut off my response with a backhanded slap across my face.

My head snapped to the side from the force of the blow, my cheek stinging. *This is going to be a real bitch of a time.*

He stood back, watching me recover and flexing his hand with contained satisfaction.

"I'll start small," he said, "but don't think I won't knock all those pretty teeth out of your head if you keep this up."

My fists clenched in the cuffs, a helpless fear threatening to dissolve my determination. *I can't let him get to me.*

"Name?" he demanded.

My head was still spinning, but I collected my thoughts. "Your name?" I asked, feigning confusion.

"*Your* name," he growled. "Give it to me. Or the name of your partner."

"Oh," I said. *Someone's angry.* For my plan to work, I needed him *furious.*

"*Name,*" he repeated.

"Markens," I said, raising an eyebrow. He hadn't told me his name, and hopefully it would throw him off that I knew who he was.

There was a flash of surprise in his eyes, but it gave way to anger. He drew his arm back and delivered another solid smack to the other side of my face. His hand caught my jaw, and my upper and lower teeth knocked together loudly.

That's going to bruise. I found myself slumped over the arm of the chair, dazed as I sat back up, shaking my head to clear it.

"Who sent you here?" Markens asked, a hint of irritation in his voice.

"Your *mother*," I mumbled. My jaw felt numb.

He jabbed his fist forward. It collided with my mouth, knocking my head back. A flash of white streaked my vision. I tasted blood, then licked my lower lip and felt a cut where my lip had split. Markens was looking at his hand as if the action hadn't exactly been planned. *Perfect.*

I'd gotten him to lose a little control. Now I just had to get him within arm's reach. I slouched forward. Letting out an exaggerated groan, I hung my head limply, trying to appear disoriented.

He reached forward and grasped a handful of my hair, yanking my head up to look at him. I drew a sharp, genuinely pained breath through clenched teeth.

"You're going to tell me what I want to know," he said. "And you're going to want to do it while your jaw is still intact." He held my gaze intently, watching to see if I'd crumble.

I had read once that the threat of torture was as effective as torture itself. He wanted me to be terrified. Unfortunately for him, I wanted *him* just as scared. When I smirked at him, it must have been the last thing he expected.

"Who are you?" he swallowed. "Are you from the Independent Sector?"

The question itself revealed everything about the current state of Free Sector. *They must be even further along than Torren thought. The Union knows enough to be worried.*

"I'm not," I said. "But the fact that you're asking makes me wonder just how scared of Free Sector you are. Sounds like they've actually got you on your toes."

He pursed his mouth angrily, and seemed at a loss for what to do next.

I laughed out loud in the silence. It was a genuine laugh, but I hoped it would set him off. Hundreds of evenings spent in a dingy bar had educated me on how poorly some men reacted to being laughed at by a woman.

"What's so funny?" he sneered, his fist still gripping the hair at my scalp.

I winced at the pain of his agitated grasp. "It's just so ironic, isn't it?" I said, pushing through the pain and chuckling. "Here I am, helpless and injured, but *you're* the one giving up information." I laughed again, watching fury build within his gaze.

"You think you're in charge here?" he snarled, his voice about to break.

It's now or never.

"*You* sure aren't," I said, then spat a mouth full of blood onto his perfectly polished boots, hoping it would push him over the edge.

He trembled with rage, his neat composure finally slipping as he released my hair and closed his hand around my throat. He squeezed with a degree of restraint at first, but steadily increased the pressure. Though I struggled to draw in a full breath, I had him right where I wanted him. He was completely distracted. *Perfect.*

I tore my eyes away from him and glanced at the two officers in the hall. They both had their backs to us.

"Don't look at them," he said breathlessly, his eyebrows raised in a mock show of sympathy. "Look at me. I am the only thing that matters right now."

My pulse throbbed, my heart frantically pounding, desperate for oxygen. There was a ringing in my ears, faint at first, but growing. One of my legs kicked out weakly. My body was instinctively trying to fight. *Is this how Torren feels when his lungs betray him?* It was agonizing. I thrashed under Markens's grip, finally starting to panic. Had I gone too far? Miscalculated his desire to keep a prisoner alive? *Shit. At least I died fighting.*

As darkness began to creep into the edges of my vision, Markens released my throat. I fell weakly against the back of the chair, shocked to still be alive. I gasped, sucking breath in and coughing it out. *He's done this before. He knows exactly how far he can go without killing someone.*

Markens steadied his own breath, smoothing a fallen piece of hair away from his forehead with the heel of his hand. "Anything you'd like to tell me now?" he asked calmly, the uncontrolled rage in his eyes finally subsiding.

Outlast. Tire him out. Get him to leave the room. "Yeah, *fuck you,*" I said with a frail voice.

He pulled his arm back. He was winding up to deliver another strike when a muffled *boom* echoed through the building. It rocked the entire structure.

Markens froze. The officers standing outside the door jolted and looked at him. The transmitters on their belts began to go off, the chatter from the other end sounding frantic. There was shouting in the distance, followed by blaster fire. Markens lowered his hand, his brow furrowing. I breathed a quiet sigh of relief.

One of the officers raised his transmitter to his ear, then looked at Markens apologetically. "Sir, there appears to be a... situation."

Torren.

Markens stepped away from me without another glance.

"You two, with me," he said. The officers stood at attention as he strode toward them. "And lock this door," he ordered. "I don't want anyone in or out but me." He stepped into the hallway, and the hydraulic door slid shut after him. There was a beep from the exterior control panel, and a mechanical bolting sound from the inside of the door.

I held my breath, listening carefully until I heard three sets of boots march down the hall and out of earshot. Exhaling heavily, I sat up, holding up my shackled hands to examine the object I'd palmed discreetly a few minutes ago. I turned Markens' ID chip over in my hand.

"There *is* always a way through," I said to myself.

It may not be easy, or obvious, but you can get out of anything if you use your head and your resources, Torren had said after we hacked into the comms booth. He'd also been right that all Union officers carried their IDs in the same pocket of their utility belts.

Even a high-ranking inspector. Maybe regulation and conformity *would* be their downfall. I smiled, then winced, feeling my bruised jaw and split lip.

Pushing myself to my feet, I stumbled across the room to the door. It didn't open automatically, locked as it was. I hit the access button on the control panel. I tapped Marken's ID chip against the screen, and his commanding officer's portal opened. I navigated to the door's security vector and hit *unlock*. There was a clicking sound from within the mechanical door, and when I stood in front of it, it slid right open.

"Thank you, Markens," I grunted.

Peering cautiously into the hallway, I was relieved to see it was empty. I stepped outside and hit the control panel to close the door. If they thought I was still in there, they'd be less likely to go looking for me. I slid Markens' ID chip into my pocket and looked around, unsure of where to go next.

"Torren," I whispered, angling my mouth toward the transmitter in my collar. Nothing. I needed to get out of the open. I was still inside a Union facility, and still cuffed, but at least I wasn't a sitting maro bird now.

I jumped at the sound of blaster fire, seemingly much closer this time. *Move, Fenn.* An emergency klaxon went off. The alarm sounded again and again, echoing off the walls. The light above me went red, bathing the entire hallway in a crimson glow. Frantic voices shouted between the pulses of the alarm. The commotion, whatever it was, was moving closer. It could be Torren. I took a step, but paused. If Markens, or any of the officers, found me first, I would be out of luck, especially without a weapon.

I heard footsteps running. A scream. *I can't stay here.*

There was a dark room across the hall from me—a briefing room, judging by the table and chairs I could see. I stepped inside, then cursed. The room didn't have a door to close. I put my back to the wall next to the doorway and held my breath. Down the hall, I heard a yell. Two blaster shots. The sound of what had to be a body hitting the floor. Clear footsteps, coming closer. I swallowed, my heart racing.

I looked around the room for anything I could use as a weapon. It was bare, aside from the furniture. Carefully sliding one of the chairs out from the table, I felt its weight and lifted it as quietly as I could with the wrist cuffs on. I put my back against the wall again and held up the chair. I got ready to swing. A single pair of footsteps stalked closer. The flash of a yellow-gold uniform went past the doorway, accompanied by the distinct *clack* of a Union blaster rifle switching fire settings.

Shit. It was just one officer, but it was the gun that scared me. I held my breath and listened as he tapped a button on the interrogation room's control panel. The door hissed open. Silence, as the man presumably saw no one was inside. The alarm kept blaring, syncing with my frantic heartbeat.

I took a deep breath, causing the chair in my hands to clang against the wall behind me. *Oh no.* I closed my eyes, cringing at my own clumsiness. *Maybe the alarm cloaked it?*

The officer's boots squeaked on the floor as he turned. *Shit.* His footsteps headed for the briefing room. I felt myself begin to hyperventilate. *He'll be at the doorway in seconds.* My body tensed as the fear of being shocked or physically struck again flooded my body with adrenaline. *I would rather be shot outright than go back into that room.* As a figure darkened the doorway, I planted my feet and swung the chair with all the strength I had left.

"Woah!" the officer yelled. He caught the chair, stopping it just before it made contact with his face. Wrenching it from my grasp, he let it clatter to the floor as he advanced toward me, his face half-lit by the red glow from the hallway.

You're done. There's no way out of this. I backed away, too paralyzed by fear to do anything else. He grabbed my shoulders and I screamed, raising my hands defensively, cuffed as they were.

"Fenn!" he said over the blaring alarm. "Fenn, it's me."

I was still attempting to push him away when I recognized his voice. Torren dipped his head, leveling his gaze with mine, letting me study his face in the crimson light. I looked him up and down, my brain confused at the sight of him in a Union uniform. My hands clutched at his shoulders, making sure he was real.

"Torren…" My voice broke. We'd found each other. *Alive.*

He threw his arms around me, and we both let out a sigh of relief. I put my face into his neck and breathed, relaxing into his strong arms.

"I didn't mean to scare you," he said, holding me. "I grabbed one of the guards and took his uniform so I could blend in once I got inside. It worked. I was able to stun about half of them before they knew what was going on."

There was a Union-issued blaster rifle slung over his shoulder. He must have liberated it from its owner, along with the hideous uniform.

"Let's—" He stopped and looked up, the alarm clearly irritating him. He lifted the blaster and aimed it at the clanging speaker in the ceiling above us. When he pulled the trigger, a blast of energy punched through it. It went silent, and though the rest of the building still blared, we could finally hear each other.

"Thanks," I muttered, my ears still ringing.

"Let's get you out of here," he said. He dropped to one knee, inspecting my wrist cuffs.

"We need to find a key," I said, holding them out to him.

"Who do you think I am?" he smirked, reaching into his jacket. He pulled a small case out of his pocket; the tiny lockpicking kit Markos had found on him. Torren grabbed two of the small tines and began working the lock on the connector bar.

I swallowed the emotion rising in my throat, overwhelmed at the sight of him. We were still in danger, but I felt hope now that we were together.

When the cuffs clicked open, he gently removed them from my wrists and dropped them to the floor. *There are perks to traveling with a professional thief.* I pushed the tears aside and sobered up. We weren't out of the woods just yet.

He stood and looked me up and down. "Are you alright?" Putting his hand on my chin, he delicately turned my head, taking in the cut on my lip and the bruises already forming on my neck from Marken's hands. "Fenn..." He trailed off, his voice caught in the back of his throat. From the pained expression on his face, I could tell he blamed himself.

"I'm fine," I assured him.

"I heard everything." He shook his head at me. "Sounded like you provoked him? What was that?"

He had heard me riling Markens up, but didn't know why I'd done it. I reached down and slipped Markens' ID chip out of my pocket.

Torren raised an eyebrow as I held it up, and the corner of his mouth threatened to curl into a smile. "Look at you," he said, taking the chip and studying it. He was impressed, I could see it in his eyes.

"You taught me well," I said.

Pocketing the chip, he shook his head. "Getting out of that room? That was all you." He glanced over his shoulder, then back at me. "Listen, we need to move. Can you walk?"

I took a breath, scanning my body. "I'm a little dizzy, but I think so."

"I've got you," he said, giving my arm a squeeze. "Just stay close to me."

I nodded. Unholstering his blaster, he handed it to me handle-first. "Keep this on you," he said.

I located the trigger but held it low, muzzle pointed at the floor. He slung the blaster rifle from his shoulder and held it in both hands, ready to fire. With one final nod, he stepped out of the room. I followed closely behind, shadowing him as we crept to the end of the hallway. When we rounded the corner, we stepped carefully around two officers sprawled out on the floor. They weren't moving.

"Are they dead?" I whispered.

"Stunned," he said. "We've got about fifteen minutes to get out of here before they wake up."

We moved quickly through the hallways, illuminated by the red emergency light. It all looked identical to me, but Torren moved with certainty, no doubt having made a mental map on his way in. Eventually, we approached the doorway to the outpost's main control room.

"This alarm probably triggered an outgoing signal for backup," he said. "I need to cut it off." Torren held his blaster level, and did a visual scan on the room. "Clear," he said, stepping inside.

I waited in the doorway, gripping my blaster too tightly.

He aimed the rifle at the master control panel and pulled the trigger. A bolt of laser energy hit the equipment, and it exploded into a shower of sparks before sputtering and going dark. The red emergency lights stayed on, but the loud alarm went dead, giving the whole building an eerie stillness.

"That's better," Torren said.

I turned, ready to leave, but Torren caught my arm.

"Not yet," he said. Pulling me into the control room, he pointed at something with his rifle.

As my eyes adjusted to the dark room, I slowly made out the shapes before me. Torren's rifle pointed at two figures lying on the floor. One was unconscious with his back slumped against the wall. I didn't recognize his face, but I saw from his crisp uniform and lack of armor it was an upper ranking officer. The other figure was lying face down. Torren hooked his foot under the prone man's shoulder, roughly rolling him onto his back.

Markens. He was unconscious, but breathing. Both men must have hidden themselves in the control room while their underlings engaged in a firefight with Torren. *Cowards.*

"Is this him?" Torren asked. "Markens?"

Oh no. I didn't want to confirm it for him, but the look on my face must have.

"Torren..." I started, but he was already moving.

He stood over Marken's unmoving form and pointed the blaster rifle straight at the man's chest. There was disgust in his eyes, and a frightening calm that I didn't like.

My stomach turned as I remembered that Torren's rifle was still on its lethal setting. "Torren, don't."

He looked back at me, his eyes tracing the bruises on my neck. "After what he did to you, I'm not particularly inclined to let him live."

"I know you think you're being protective," I said, putting my hands up, trying to calm him. "But you're not a killer, you told me so yourself. Don't betray who you are for…him."

Torren looked down at Markens and tapped at his trigger lightly, thinking.

I moved cautiously and stood beside him. "In a fair fight, in the heat of battle, I honestly wouldn't care," I said. "Self-defense is one thing, but putting a blaster bolt into an unconscious man? It seems cheap. Let's just go."

He paused, still thinking it through. My heart pounded in my chest, preparing for what I was about to witness. Eventually, Torren reached down and flipped the rifle back to its stun setting, dropping his aim. My shoulders relaxed, and I released the breath pent up in my lungs.

"You're a better person than me," he said.

Drawing my foot back, I landed a hard, swift kick to Marken's ribs.

"Eh, not by much," I said, kicking Markens again for good measure. *He'll feel that when he wakes up.*

"Let's move." Torren said, giving my wrist a gentle squeeze.

We left the control room, and I followed him through the haphazard route to the exit. Everywhere I looked, I saw the aftermath of havoc. We stepped around broken glass and more unconscious Union officers—the evidence of what Torren could do when motivated.

Finally, we stumbled out of the building and into fresh air. I drank it in, grateful to be free of the place. The sun was setting, and I saw that the entrance of the outpost had been blown apart by one of Torren's detonators. *That's one way to get around a code-locked door.*

"Come on," he said. "Reinforcements from the closest outpost are most likely on their way."

He led me to our fern-shadowed hiding spot from earlier. Crouching, he reached into the tangle of fronds and pulled out our crate, along with his bag. I saw an unconscious officer lying in the shady foliage, his uniform missing. Torren wordlessly handed the crate to me. I took it without question and slung the rope handle across my chest.

"Let's go," he said, yanking my hand.

I took off toward the woods, but Torren darted in the opposite direction. Our arms stretched between us, caught in an unintentional tug-of-war. We froze mid-pull, staring at each other with matching expressions of confusion.

"What are you doing?" I hissed, already half a step into my direction.

He jerked his head toward the outpost's shipyard. "We're stealing a ship and getting off this rock."

"A *Union* ship?"

"Got any better ideas?" he asked.

I opened my mouth, a smart retort on the tip of my tongue, but I stopped myself. I *didn't* have a better idea. If we tried to journey back to Torren's ship, it would take two to three days, and they'd be on the lookout for us the entire time. We needed to leave Talar *now*.

"Torren, your Dawn-Wing…" I trailed off, suddenly understanding that we'd have to leave it behind.

"I can always get another ship," he muttered, dropping my hand.

I realized that he might have been able to get back to it if he'd left me behind. His Dawn-Wing seemed like a part of him—the vessel he and his Kedigan friends had escaped Rorric with.

"Come on. We don't have time," he said, turning away. If he was upset about the ship, he was masking it well.

I followed him into the small shipyard. He kept the blaster rifle ready, but we encountered no officers. Everyone must have chased the chaos that had broken out inside the building. There were three small observation vessels and two larger transports, both of them about the size of Torren's ship. One of them already had its boarding ramp down, making our choice easy.

"This'll have to do," Torren said, striding up the ramp. "It should just have the range to get through deep space and to our drop point."

I followed him aboard. He kicked open the door to the small lavatory, rifle up, checking that no one was inside. He then ripped his bag open and pulled his flight vest out.

I dashed to the console and checked the fuel gauge. "We're at full fuel," I said.

He ripped the Union jacket off, hurriedly pulling on his flight vest. Throwing himself into the pilot's seat, he started the ignition sequence at breakneck speed.

I dropped the crate into the copilot's seat while I looked around for a place to secure it. The search was cut short by an approaching noise—the roar of a powerful engine hummed at us from the shipyard. We looked back to see a large ground speeder pull up to the outpost. Unlike the smaller open-top speeder Markens had arrived in, this one was bulkier, and armored like a tank.

"Well, shit," muttered Torren.

This was the backup Markens had called for. I imagined the vehicle was full of Union officers, armed and ready. Torren cursed under his breath but kept working on the ignition sequence. I darted to our loading door in the back, watching as the transport slowed. It was on the other side of the shipyard from us, about eight or nine yards away.

"What do we do?" I asked.

He was configuring the ship's navigation, frantically punching in coordinates for our destination.

"*Torren*," I snapped.

"I'm working on it." He sang, not looking up from the controls. After a moment of quiet, he banged his hand on the console. "Damn Union security settings," he growled. "The ship is asking me for a pilot's code."

"What does that mean?"

"It means I'm going to have to reset the entire system to get the engines up." He pried a maintenance panel off of the foot of the console and tossed it aside. Throwing himself onto his back, he maneuvered under the exposed machinery to access the mess of cables. He pulled my shock-blade out of his pocket and began cutting into a wire in his hand.

Looking back at the transport, I clenched my fists impatiently. It came to a final stop in front of a rocky bluff on the other side of the yard. Through a small window near the front, I saw the vehicle driver looking in our direction. He held something to his mouth—a transmitter. They'd seen us. The boarding ramp was going to come down any minute now, and if we weren't in the air, we were screwed.

"We need to do something!" I shouted.

"Then do something!" Torren shouted back. "Come on, think. I believe in you."

My mind raced for an idea as I took stock of the transport again. The quickly setting sun glinted off of its shiny hull, reflecting back at me and forcing me to close my eyes. When I opened them again, I noticed something. A glittering mass marbled in the rock bluff behind the transport. My breath caught in my throat. *Moonslab.*

I still had Torren's blaster tucked into my belt, but I doubted it had the range or firepower I needed. Torren could easily hit the mark with a blast from the rifle, but he was getting the ship ready for our escape. *I* would have to do it.

"Torren, slide me the rifle," I ordered.

He looked up from the wiring, caught off guard at my request, but he grabbed the rifle with one hand and tossed it in my direction. It clattered and slid across the floor, almost falling right out of the loading door, but I stopped it with my boot. I picked it up with shaking hands. I flipped it to the lethal setting.

Bracing it against my shoulder, I put one hand under the grip at the front, and my other hand at the trigger. I spared a glance at Torren and saw he was now pressing the exposed ends of two wires together. The engines thrummed to life, giving me hope. *We're getting there.* My heart slowed enough for my hands to stop shaking.

Torren climbed into a crouch and kept the two wires pinched together in one hand, while typing a command into the ship's computer. The system began to reboot itself, and he held the wires gingerly, as if afraid to disrupt their connection.

"I've got a target," I said. "Any tips for a first-timer?"

"You've never shot a blaster?" he yelled, finally taking his eyes off the wires and looking at me.

"Will you just walk me through it?" I snapped. We were running out of time.

"Sorry," he said, taking a breath and relaxing his voice. "Stabilize the weapon. However you need to."

There was nothing near me to rest the rifle on, so I got on one knee and rested my elbow on the top of my thigh. "Walking you through the auto-targeting system would take too long," he breathed. "So you're going to have to aim very carefully."

I looked through the electronic scope and saw the hydraulic door of the transport beginning to open. *We're cutting it close.*

"Put your target in your crosshairs, then take a deep breath."

I filled my lungs.

"Relax your body."

I let my muscles loosen.

"That rifle has some kickback, so brace yourself, and don't you *dare* move just because you've pulled the trigger. Hold your position until you see the blast hit."

I made sure my foot and grounded knee were spaced apart enough to anchor me.

"When you've finished your exhale, give it one second, then fire."

The vein of moonslab was in my sights. I slowly exhaled. The transport door finished opening and an armored officer filled its doorway. When I had let my entire exhale out, I waited for a beat. Just like he had instructed.

"That's my girl," he whispered.

I pulled the trigger.

The high-powered laser bolt exited the barrel, knocking the weapon back against my shoulder. The blast hit the rock bluff, punching right through it and exploding the brittle vein of moonslab.

The officer in the transport doorway heard the impact and looked up, but the bluff disintegrated and began raining down onto the vehicle.

I took my eye away from the scope and watched as the transport was steadily buried in an avalanche of rubble. I heard a *beep* from our ship's console. The navigation screen was functioning now.

Torren let go of the wires and strode over to me, shaking his head as he watched the cascade of rocks continue to fall. Within seconds, it had slowed to a trickle, a few errant pebbles bouncing off of the top of the pile. The frame of the transport, what little we could see of it, looked slightly crumpled, but intact.

I breathed in relief. The officers inside were alive, and would get out eventually, but it wouldn't be anytime soon.

Torren pulled me to my feet, and I handed him the rifle. He took it wordlessly, setting it on a cargo shelf behind us. When I met his gaze, I saw he was watching me with a content smile. I wasn't sure what was on his mind, but I had a feeling.

We work well together.

"Let's get out of here," he said, turning toward the pilot's seat.

I took a step, but a sound in the distance made both of us pause. It was an engine, and unlike the ground transport, it sounded airborne. We locked eyes, and he joined me at the loading door, placing a hand on my arm just as another Union patrol ship zoomed into view overhead. *It must have been called in from the next closest outpost.*

It began to circle the shipyard, pointing a bright spotlight down at the scene below, the demolished front entrance and the ground transport buried in rubble. It wouldn't take long for them to notice two civilians in a ship about to take off. We were cornered, and this time, no amount of moonslab could save us.

28

———————

YOU KNOW I'M RIGHT

Torren cursed, and I heard his breath hitch. I put my hand on his arm and squeezed gently, hoping to calm him down. He didn't have his Respirin cartridge.

"Can we still take off?" I asked.

Torren ran his hand through his hair and glanced at the ship's console. It was primed and ready to fly.

"Yes, but…" he trailed off, his eyes frantic as he glanced between the transport and the controls.

"What?" I asked.

"They'll chase us," he said, "and take us down."

Looking out the loading door, I saw the other ship maneuvering over the yard. Its engine buzzed as it prepared to land. Union soldiers would be on us in a matter of minutes. I looked and saw the sun had fully set, the sky growing darker by the second. *Maybe we can make a break for the woods?*

I remembered how hard it had been to travel that morning while a patrol ship swept the area. It would be even harder in the dark. We stood quietly, both of our minds racing for a solution. *Isn't there always a way through?*

Something must have clicked for Torren, because he gripped both of my shoulders, turning me sharply to face him.

"Can you fly?" he asked with a wild look in his eye.

"What?"

"Can you fly a ship?"

"Barely," I said. "Rego taught me some basics."

"That's fine," he said. "You know enough."

"Torren, I'm not a pilot."

"No, but you're good with tech, and that's all these Union ships are." Grabbing my arm and dragging me over to the console, he pointed at a glowing panel. "Union autopilot bots are unbelievable. This ship can handle takeoff and landing. All you have to do is locate and execute the programs."

Unease began to build in the pit of my stomach.

"You're going to have to run the blockade," he said, pointing at a lever on the console. "Approach it slowly, then punch your accelerator. If they chase you, engage the nova-drive." He indicated the red, glass-encased button at the center of the panel. "I disabled the location beacon while the system was rebooting, so they won't be able to track the vessel once you get away."

"Torren?" I asked with a weak voice, realization slowly hitting me.

He ignored me and pointed at a series of numbers on the console. "This is your flight path. I've already programmed the destination, so you won't have to navigate. Just use the autopilot."

"Torren." I knew what he was planning now, and I didn't like it.

He held my shoulders, centering me in front of him and looking me in the eye. "Get to the drop point. My buyer's name is Egan Crue."

This isn't happening. It can't. I tried to break free from his grasp, but he was holding me too firmly.

"Egan Crue," he repeated. "Don't forget it."

I shoved his hands away, but he grabbed my jacket in a vice grip.

"Once you hand over the crate, Egan will give you the payment for the bounty. He can also get you back to Hadrin."

"Tor…" My voice faltered.

"Take my blaster," he said. "I'm taking the rifle. I'll draw their attention, lead them away so you can take off." His eyes searched mine for something I couldn't name. He finally let go of me, then turned around and headed straight for the boarding ramp.

I couldn't believe he was giving me this task. I couldn't believe he was *leaving.* All my fears and worries fell by the wayside as outrage took hold. I followed him, seething.

"Torren, you absolute bastard!" I shouted at the back of his head, making a note to apologize for it later. I stomped after him with a scowl so deep it hurt. "Torren—"

He stopped and turned to face me. I collided with him, my face smacking into his chest. Grabbing me around the waist, he pulled me close, pressing his lips to mine. Before I could even process the kiss, he pulled away, pressing his forehead to mine with his eyes closed. My cheeks flushed as I struggled to catch my breath.

"This wasn't how I wanted to say goodbye," he whispered, opening his eyes.

"Then don't," I begged, tears forming. "Torren, don't do this. We can figure this out, you said there's a way through anything—"

"There is. This is it." He straightened up, still holding me. "This is the best chance we have of saving Rego. You know I'm right, Sketch."

Deep down, I did. He was going to leave, and I had to let him.

"Besides," he said softly, a thin smile creeping into place, "I just stormed an entire Union outpost for you." He let out a small laugh. "All those heroics will be for nothing if you don't get out of here now." He wasn't saying it out loud, but I got the feeling this was about more than just getting the crate to safety.

Leaning back, he shot a guarded look at the Union ship making it's descent. He ripped his flight vest off and slipped it over my left arm, then my right, pulling it over my shoulders. I numbly looked down as he adjusted it into place. It was too big for me, but it would still serve its purpose.

This was happening. I had to fly the ship, travel through space, and meet Torren's buyer. All by myself.

"Where will you go?" I asked, my voice small. "How will you get off the planet?"

"I'll figure it out," he said.

He pulled his blaster out of my belt where I had stowed it, checking the settings and giving it back to me. He pulled my ID chip out of his jacket and slipped it into the pocket of my flight vest.

It all felt so final. I watched, my heart fracturing, as he slipped his bag on and grabbed the rifle from the shelf.

"One last thing," he said, fixing his deep brown eyes on mine. "Arina. My last name…it's Arina." He smiled. *Torren Arina.* "I just thought you should know," he said. "In case…" Heat flooded his cheeks.

He didn't have to say it. *In case we never see each other again.*

The newly arrived Union ship began to touch down. He turned back to face me, placing one hand on the side of my face and drawing my mouth to his. He kissed me deeply.

I grabbed his shoulders and kissed him back with everything I had. Hoping to convey everything I couldn't find the words for. Ignoring the sting of the cut on my lip. His kiss was worth the pain. *He* was worth the pain. He finally pulled away, leaving me half-dazed with longing. He primed the fire setting on the rifle, then walked to the top of the boarding ramp.

"Get this ship into the air," he said. "You can do this."

I was not nearly as convinced as he was, but I nodded.

He turned and made his way down the ramp. "And close this door as soon as I'm out!" he shouted back at me.

Every instinct told me to grab him and keep him close. I fought it, wiping away tears with the back of my hand. Once he had cleared the ramp, I shakily punched the large, heavy button near the loading door. The ramp inched back into the ship as the loading door began a slow automatic close.

The Union ship's ramp touched the ground, and I held my breath. Within seconds, armored officers began to emerge.

Torren peppered them with blaster shots, effectively turning all their attention toward him. The last thing I saw was Torren sprinting toward the woods with a handful of officers after him. The loading door shut with a resonant *clang* and sealed itself.

I stared at the metal, my breath coming in short, shallow pants. I was alone.

With tears blurring my vision, I stalked to the cockpit. *Do I have to do this?* I was so tired. As I looked around despondently, my gaze fell onto the crate in the copilot's seat. The crate Torren was risking everything for. The one that would save Rego. *Get it together, Fenn.*

Taking a deep breath, I dropped into the pilot's chair, harnessing myself in. I surveyed the grid of buttons and controls laid out on the console. *If Torren thinks I can do this, then I can.* Turning my attention to the autopilot panel he'd shown me, I found the liftoff sequence and hit *execute*. The engine thrusters fired up, and the ship lifted off the ground, beginning its climb upwards. The autopilot worked the engines methodically, but lacked the steady finesse of a human pilot.

I placed my hands delicately on the helm, but it was far more sensitive than I expected. The ship rapidly tilted to the right. If I hadn't been harnessed in, I might have fallen out of the seat. I righted the helm, but pressed too hard, and the ship overcorrected with a jerk, sending the wooden crate tumbling out of the copilot's seat. It bounced heavily against the console.

"Shit!" I yelled, realizing too late that I should have secured it. If it got thrown around during flight, it could injure me or even knock me clean out. Pressing the helm carefully, I leveled the ship. I reached my leg out, pushing the crate up against the console, and held it in place with my boot.

Once I'd cleared the height of the treetops, I took one hand off the helm and pressed the control that would execute a flight out of the planet's atmosphere. As my ship accelerated, I craned my neck to scan the shipyard below. The Union ship didn't come after me. Torren had taken the heat by firing on them.

I took a breath and gripped the helm so tightly that my knuckles went white. The ship rumbled, shakily escaping the final hold of gravity. I focused on keeping my hands steady while also keeping the crate in place. When I cleared the atmosphere, I manually decelerated the ship by easing back on the helm, starting to get a feel for the controls. The blockade barge in the space outside Talar came into view.

Run the blockade, Torren had said. I adjusted my course, aiming to pass right by it, hopefully appearing compliant right up until the moment I couldn't. My hands began to sweat, and I wiped them on my pants to ensure I could keep a steady grip on the helm. A *beep* came from the console. The blockade ship was hailing me. I searched for the receiver switch, then hesitantly flipped it on, my heart pounding.

"This is Union Checkpoint S-54," a voice said.

I made a split-second decision to pose as a Union officer. They couldn't see me, and the static of the connection would mask my voice a little. I might be able to bluff my way through. Lowering my voice, I flipped the transmitter on.

"Hi," I said awkwardly, then rolled my eyes.

"Pilot, your vessel is currently assigned to ground duty. Is there a reason you're on orbit trajectory right now?" the voice asked. I wracked my brain for a plausible cover. What kind of mainte-nance issues did Rego and the guys always grumble about?

"Yes," I said, adopting a confident tone. "One of this vessel's engines is experiencing intermittent stalling. We think the entire extraction grid needs replacing." Nothing came from the other end of the line. "I'm taking it to a nearby Union cruiser for specialty repairs." I held my breath, but the transmitter was silent. I passed the security barge, my ship heading out into open space.

"There's no Union cruiser anywhere nearby," the voice accused. *"What is—"* The pause that followed stopped my heart. Silence. I knew what was happening. Word had just been received about the situation on the ground.

"Standby for boarding," the voice came. The tone was curt. They knew the ship had been stolen.

"Well, shit," I said out loud before switching the transmitter off. I glanced out the viewport anxiously.

Two ships exited a security hangar on the side of the barge and zoomed toward mine. They were small, single-pilot fighter ships equipped with guns. *Fucking great.* They could easily hit my engines and disable my ship. *That is, if they don't get too trigger-happy and hit a fuel cell.*

I was either getting arrested, or blown up. *So close to getting away, too.* After all Torren and I had been through to get this far, I hated that it would end this way. Ignoring the tears stinging the corners of my eye, I shook my head, trying to dislodge the idea. I couldn't fail now, not while Torren was fighting for his life down there.

I watched the fighter ships approach on the console's rear view display, attempting to identify them. *What are they, anyway?* Not Air-Rooks. These were much too small. I squinted at the grainy display as they got closer and felt a ray of hope. If they were what I thought they were, I was in luck. They closed in, enough for me to see their exact shape. I breathed a sigh of relief.

The ships approaching mine were Starling fighters, Rego's favorite ship ever designed. I knew from that stupid ship game Rego loved that Starlings were built exclusively for short-range battle. Fast and agile, they boasted the tightest turn radius of any airborne craft in the galaxy. Fortunately for me, Starling fighters were too small and compact to contain nova-drives.

My stars had aligned. Lifting my boot, I held the crate firmly in place against the console, then double-checked that my seat harness was secure. I found the ship's nova-drive switch, and I lifted its glass lid.

The Starlings behind me opened fire, a few blasts hitting the exterior cowling of my engines. Taking a deep breath, I settled further into my seat. *It's now or never.*

I slammed the helm forward and hit the nova switch, launching the ship into a sudden accelerated velocity. The stars in front of me blurred into streaks. I was off.

My body had never experienced such high speed. It protested as I was violently pressed against the pilot's seat. My veins throbbed as blood surged into my limbs, making them swell and tingle. A steady pressure began to build in my chest and behind my eyes, so I forced them shut. I held the button down, ignoring the sickening groan of the ship, wondering how much force my body could take before passing out.

A metallic scraping sound alerted me that the engines were getting close to burning out. I switched the drive off, and the ship rapidly decelerated. My body strained against the seat harness, Torren's flight vest absorbing the force.

The ship returned to a steady cruising speed, and I checked the viewport displays. The fighter ships were nowhere in sight. Talar was no longer even visible. I was miles away.

I screamed, delirious with excitement and relief. I had done it. It hadn't been alone, though. My smile faded as I realized just how far away Torren was now.

"Damn it, Torren," I muttered to myself as I slumped back into my seat.

I hoped he could evade the officers, and find a way off of Talar that didn't include Union-issued wrist cuffs. I bit my lip, remembering the way he'd returned my ID and kissed me good-bye, as if he believed it would be the last time. Maybe it was the last time. I took a deep breath, steeling myself and checking the ship's flight path. *Take care of yourself, Torren Arina.*

29

THE DROP

I DRIFTED THROUGH THE EXPANSE OF SPACE FOR TWO DAYS, maybe three; I lost track without a sun to watch rise and set. With the ship's autopilot following Torren's flight path, I was able to leave the cockpit and search the vessel for supplies. There was no galley, but I found a compartment full of Union-issue rations and canisters of water. I located a med-kit, and went to work applying curative patches to my injuries.

My clothes were filthy, but I found a freshly laundered mainte-nance jumpsuit in a locker. I put it on. I had to roll the sleeves up for it to fit, but I was grateful to get into something clean. I wasn't sure what to expect when I delivered the crate, but I thought it best not to arrive covered in dried blood, sweat and dirt.

I studied the navigation panel, wondering where Torren's coor-dinates were taking me. The Union had likely already reported the ship as stolen, but since they'd lost me during the nova jump and Torren had killed the location beacon, there was a chance I could get to the drop point without incident.

For the remainder of the trip, I tried to rest. My sore muscles slowly recovered from the stress of being shocked. There were no bunkrooms on the Union ship, but sleep came easy when I curled up in the pilot's seat and switched off the ship's interior lights. Deep space is beyond dark, and it's easy to get lost in the silence.

There was nothing to do at this point but wait.

After four days, when my water was close to running out, the ship neared a planet. When its mottled green and grey surface came into view, I knew it was Laigo. It wasn't shocking that Torren's contact, a buyer of stolen goods, would be in the galaxy's largest city.

Proximity beeps came from the console, warning me that the landing protocol would begin soon. I nervously harnessed myself in and readied myself to execute the needed commands at the console. The ship entered the atmosphere, and once it leveled out, it set a course for a pinging beacon on the map.

It was evening on this hemisphere of the planet, and the city glowed in the dark like a neon jewel. I passed right over the plaza, heading toward a residential district. Civilian ships gave me a wide berth, which concerned me until I remembered that I was in a Union ship. I couldn't blame them.

The residential area I entered was a nice one, and I was so absorbed in looking at the high-rise buildings that I was caught off guard by the ship's abrupt stop.

I unharnessed and peered out of the viewport. The ship was hovering over a wide landing pad on the rooftop of a tall building. The console told me that it had reached the coordinates Torren had entered. *This has to be it.* I confirmed the landing program, and the ship executed it, slowly lowering down onto the landing pad. Touching down, it lurched to a stop.

I shut off the engines and scanned the rooftop, seeing nothing but a heavy-looking metal door I assumed led inside the building. I waited. For what, I didn't know. *I wish Torren was here.*

Pushing myself out of the chair before I lost my nerve, I left Torren's flight vest over the back of the pilot seat. I slung the crate's carrying rope across my shoulder, then hit the button that opened the loading door. The ship depressurized, and a fine mist pooled around the landing pad. It soon gave the entire rooftop an eerie haze. Tentatively, I descended the loading ramp.

A sound from the depths of the misty fog cloud stopped me in my tracks—a series of soft clicks that I assumed was more than one weapon being primed to fire.

"Hands," a deep voice commanded.

I complied instantly, raising my arms.

"I'm here for a drop," I said, squinting into the mist.

The haze dissipated, slowly revealing two figures standing stone-still, both holding blaster rifles aimed at my chest. The figures were dressed head to toe in black tactical gear. I had a healthy confidence in their ability to aim and shoot.

As the mist cleared, I saw one of them was a human male, the other a Kedigan. They both had their heads tilted down, watching me through the scopes of their rifles.

"I'm not armed," I said, regrettably realizing that I had left Torren's blaster in the cockpit. *I am really out of my element here.*

"Are you Union?" asked the Kedigan, his eyes darting to the ship behind me.

"Oh," I said. "No, I stole this. The tracking beacon is disabled, but you should probably get rid of it before the Union comes looking."

I gulped, hoping I was doing the right thing by parting with the ship. Torren had said that Egan could help me find a way back to Hadrin.

The feline took his eye away from his scope and looked me up and down. "You stole a Union ship?" he asked.

"I had help."

"What are you doing here?" asked the human man in a booming voice, finally lifting his head from his scope. He was huge, a full head taller than the Kedigan.

"I'm here to meet with Egan Crue."

"On what business?" he asked.

"I have a delivery from Talar."

The human and Kedigan exchanged a glance, their rifles wavering.

"Are you alone?" the Kedigan asked.

"Yes," I said, fighting to keep the nerves out of my voice.

They shared another look, and the Kedigan slowly lowered his rifle.

"You can give the crate to us," he said, holding out a clawed hand.

I kept my hands up, resisting the urge to grab the rope handle and hold on tight. *Torren gave me orders.*

"I'm sorry, but I believe I should to deliver the crate directly to Egan Crue."

The large human bristled, standing at full height and tapping the side of his rifle with his thumb. "We weren't asking."

"*Kiv*," the Kedigan hissed, eyeing the man's rifle.

The human relaxed his posture and reluctantly lowered the weapon.

The Kedigan gave me one more glance up and down, then pulled a transmitter out of his pocket. He pressed a button and held it to his mouth. "We have a human female here, says she has a shipment from *Talar*," he said, his eyes scanning me with unabashed curiosity. "Says she won't hand it over to anyone but you."

A garbled voice came through the transmitter, but I couldn't make out the response.

"No sign of him," said the feline, eyeing the ship.

I'd thrown them for a loop by showing up instead of Torren.

Tilting my head, I studied them both again, wondering if they knew Torren personally or just in passing. I kept my hands up, which were now ice-cold in the brisk night air flooding the roof.

"Received," the Kedigan said, putting the transmitter away. "Boss wants to see you." He slung his rifle onto his back. "Come on, arms out." He beckoned for me to approach, and I did, cautiously.

His clawed hands patted me up and down gently, feeling for anything I might be concealing in my clothes. I realized Torren still had my shock-blade, and hoped it was serving him well.

When the Kedigan was satisfied that I posed no threat, he looked at the human guard. "She's clear. You can go on in, I'll move the hot ship."

"Are you ditching it?" the human man asked.

"I'll stash it in the hangar," he called back. "Egan may want to strip it for parts." He jogged over to the ship, climbed the ramp, and disappeared inside.

The human man gestured for me to follow him, and together, we crossed the landing pad, heading for the door at the far end of the rooftop. He opened it, gesturing inside. I swallowed the worry in my throat, reminding myself why I was there. Behind me, the ship's engines fired up in preparation for flight.

The man ushered me onto a lift, and once the doors closed, he punched a passcode into the control panel, making sure to lean close to it so I couldn't read it. The lift jolted and began its smooth descent, taking us a handful of floors down before slowing to a stop.

"Not many people are invited to enter here," the man said. "You'd better not have any funny business planned."

I shrugged. The lift doors opened with a *clank,* and suddenly, I was in another world.

The large room before me was the most opulent I had ever seen. Plush rugs were strewn about the shiny floor. It was white marble, and polished to perfection. Floor-to-ceiling windows at the far end of the room offered a gorgeous view of the distant city center. This was the view for someone who wanted to be up and away from the streets, while still able to monitor the metropolis. Past a tasteful array of other furniture, I took in the centerpiece of the room—a large white sofa sitting across from a grandiose desk made of glass and metal. *Was this someone's office?*

The man gestured for me to move, so I stepped out of the lift. Colorful movement to my right caught my eye, and I turned. I stood face to face with a cylindrical glass tank of water. The tank stretched to the ceiling, and inside, a collection of exotic fish swam in lazy circles, seemingly unbothered by my presence.

"We're here," said the guard into a handheld transmitter.

We waited in silence for a few minutes. My nerves got to me, and I turned to the glass tank to distract myself. I watched the array of colorful fish, wondering what far reaches of the galaxy they had been plucked from. I would have bet a thousand credits that more than half of them were illegal to own. Whoever owned this place was just as much of a criminal as the muggers on the street; they simply had money and resources.

"It's not often someone lands a pesking *Union* ship on my private landing pad," a haughty, velvet voice said behind me.

I stiffened, instantly recognizing it. This was the voice Torren had spoken to when we'd landed on Talar. I turned to see a human man making his way across the room. His walk was graceful, more of a *glide*.

He was tall, with a thin frame and extraordinary posture. His skin was dewy and glowing, though the lines around his eyes made me think he had to be in his late forties. His hair, short on the sides with a sweeping coif at the top, was a vibrant shade of warm blue. It reminded me of pictures I'd seen of the pristine oceans on planet Okea.

Where Torren dressed drably to avoid standing out, this man did the opposite. He glided toward me in a dark crimson shirt and pants, with an embellished gold robe floating gracefully behind him. His shoes were as embellished as his robe, and as blue as his hair. His dark eyebrows knit together curiously as he scanned me, no doubt making as many snap judgements about me as I was about him. As he neared, I saw that his features were angular but beautiful, almost ethereally so.

"You really spooked my men, showing up in a Union ship like that," he said with a playful smile. He slowed as he approached, stopping a little more than arm's length away. He looked me up and down as his guard positioned himself nearby.

"You must be Egan Crue," I said, lifting my chin to meet his gaze.

"Yes," he replied, "but you're not who I was expecting. Were you working with…Kad?"

He eyed me for a reaction but I gave none.

I thought back to the conversation I had overheard between Egan and Torren on the ship. Egan had called him Tor. *He definitely knows Torren's name.* He thought *I* didn't.

"Torren? Yes. I accompanied him to Talar."

Egan raised his eyebrows.

"Ah, he said he might hire some crew for this particular job. What are you, then?"

"What am I?"

"Your profession, my dear. A wire-phaser? Mercenary? Pilot?"

"Talarian," I shrugged. "Just a native Talarian."

"I see," he nodded knowingly. "So that's how he gained entry to the planet. Where is he now?"

"He's still on Talar. We got pinned down by Union forces, but he helped me get away."

"That's discouraging," Egan said with a frown. "He had my nav-projector."

I bristled, resentful that Egan was more concerned for a piece of equipment than he was for Torren.

"He told me to bring you the shipment," I said, keeping my voice even and polite.

"This is it?" he asked, looking at the crate slung across my shoulder.

I lifted the rope and pulled it over my head, holding the crate out to him.

A flicker of amusement crossed his face before he glanced at the guard expectantly. He seemed unaccustomed to being handed things. The guard took the crate from me and held it steady as Egan delicately lifted the lid. His ocean-colored eyes lit up as he viewed its contents. Reaching in carefully, he held up one of the stunning green pieces of solcite. Gently turning the carving over in his hand, he reached for a cylinder that hung from a long silver chain around his neck. *A mechanical eye glass.* He wasn't going to take me at my word that these were what I said they were. He held it up to his eye and bent over the carvings. The eyeglass whirred and calibrated as Egan studied each carving closely.

"Well, these look to be genuine," he said.

"People bring you counterfeit items?" I asked.

His eyes flashed my way. "Mmm, more often than you would *believe*," he said woefully, still studying the carvings.

Silence fell across the room. Torren hadn't prepared me for what happened *after* I completed the hand off to Egan, but every passing second increased my anxiety.

"Beautiful," Egan said to himself, a giddy smile stretching across his face to reveal perfectly white teeth.

"They weren't exactly easy to get," I said.

Egan turned the eye glass toward me, no doubt surveying the cut on my lip and the bandage on my forearm, poking out from the sleeve of my jumpsuit. He nodded in acknowledgement. Straightening his posture, he placed the solcite back into the crate and replaced the lid. He flicked his hands lazily at the crate, and the guard wordlessly carried it over to the glass desk, setting it down gently.

"Torren said you'd give me the payment, but I only need half of it," I said. "You can hold onto his half and give it to him when he makes it back." I paused, flexing my hands at my side to stop them from shaking. "*If…he makes it back.*"

Egan inhaled, and looked aimlessly upwards as if thinking things over. "Unfortunately, my dear, I can't give you *any* of the payment."

My heart sank. "What?"

Egan gave me the performative shrug of someone who was very comfortable telling people *No* during business deals.

"My agreement was with Torren, so I will pay *Torren* when he gets back. Since he recruited you, he is responsible for paying you."

I stared at him wordlessly. *This is not how things were supposed to go.*

He gave me a dismissive smile. "You may leave now." Turning, he crossed the room toward his desk, visibly excited over his prize.

Rage simmered inside me, but I quelled it. *Maybe he can be reasoned with.*

"Listen, I brought you the crate. I deserve my part of the payment," I insisted.

Egan reached his desk and whipped around, his face pulling into a stern warning look.

"That's not how this works, my dear. I don't do deals with people I've never met."

"*Please*," I begged, swallowing my pride as Rego's safety started to slip through my fingers. "It's urgent that I get those credits. My friend's life is at stake."

His gaze floated to the ceiling and he sighed wearily.

"Sweetie, I've heard every sob story on the wire. Without Torren here to verify that, I'm afraid you're out of luck. You have my thanks for bringing me the crate. When Torren returns, you'll be paid."

"But that could take days! Or weeks! I don't have that much time," I insisted, trying to keep from tearing up. "He might not even make it back." Despite my attempts to stifle them, tears welled up in my eyes.

Egan looked uncomfortable for a moment, but cleared his throat and locked eyes with me.

"You'll have to forgive my suspicious nature, but such is the manner of this business." He looked at me with his eyebrows raised. "How do I know you didn't steal this crate from him the way you stole that ship from the Union?"

My face burned hot at the accusation. "If I had done that, why would I only ask for half the payment?"

"Who knows?" He shrugged again. "Maybe you're telling the truth. Until Torren appears and says so, farewell."

He locked eyes with the guard and motioned his head toward me. The large man dropped a heavy hand onto my shoulder. I flinched.

Egan looked past me, addressing the man. "Drop her off near the city plaza," he said dismissively. "A *nice* area, please, somewhere safe. We may be criminals, but we're not completely uncivilized." He looked down, smoothing a wrinkle in his flowing robe.

I can't believe this is happening. The entire trip, the work, the interrogation, it would all be for *nothing* if I couldn't pay off Rego's bounty. I had reasoned, and begged. I considered robbing Egan at blaster point, but realized again that Torren's gun was on the Union ship. There was no way to win.

"You're a bastard," I said, glaring at Egan, my teeth gritting hard.

"*Businessman*," he corrected me with a patronizing wink.

The guard grasped my arm and began to drag me toward the lift. I struggled, but his grip was inescapable. *I might as well fight a Cerocian.*

The lift door opened before we reached it, and the Kedigan from the roof stepped off. I saw concern in his eyes as he watched me get dragged away. As the man pulled me past, I glanced at the Kedigan and noticed something in his paws. He had grabbed Torren's blaster and flight vest from the ship. *Why would Egan's security guard have recognized and gathered Torren's things? Are they friends?* I looked him up and down as the human guard continued to haul me away.

It had escaped my notice on the dark rooftop, but the Kedigan's sleek fur was grey and dotted with charcoal-colored spots. *Is that him?* The human guard finally yanked me onto the lift, but I reached out and clung to the doorway.

"Are you Carrio?" I asked the Kedigan.

His eyes snapped to mine, his brow furrowed in confusion. He then glanced at Egan, whose eyebrows were already raised.

Egan lifted an elegant hand and the guard paused, still holding my arm.

"What was that?" Egan asked. His head was tilted curiously, and he examined me with a renewed interest.

"You must be Carrio," I said, looking at the gray-spotted Kedigan. Kedigan with spots were native to only one planet. *Rorric.*

"Where did you hear that name?" the feline asked.

"Torren told me about you. He said a group of you left Rorric after…" *After the Union murdered his family and everyone at the drill site.* "After what happened there. Torren said the five of you stole a Union ship and that *you* piloted it for them."

The Kedigan exchanged another look with Egan. It was Carrio. It *had* to be. Everyone was still and quiet. I had just thrown a vat of ice cold water over the room.

Carrio approached me cautiously. "Torren told you about that?"

"Yes."

"What else did he tell you?"

"His last name."

"Torren uses covers. No one knows his—"

"Arina," I said.

The Kedigan's whiskers twitched, and behind him, Egan glided across the room toward us.

I had definitely touched a nerve.

Egan looked at the human guard, then swept his nose in the direction of the lift.

The guard nodded and dropped my arm. I stepped out of the lift, looking at Carrio with a flicker of hope. The lift doors closed behind me and I heard it going back up, sending the human away.

Egan studied me far more closely than before, reconsidering me in light of the new information.

"Who are you?" asked the Kedigan.

"Fenn Kensie," I said.

He extended his paw toward me. "I'm Carrio Senn."

I shook it tentatively, aware that the temperature of the room had shifted, hopefully in my favor.

Egan cleared his throat and gestured at the sofa across from his desk. "Have a seat, Miss Kensie."

"What's going on?" I asked. I was glad I hadn't been kicked out, but I couldn't read the expressions on either of their faces.

"Sit, girl," Egan insisted. "I think we need to have a little chat."

30

A LITTLE CHAT

From my seat on the velvet sofa, I got a small glimpse of what a business associate of Egan's might see during a deal. The view was intimidating. Carrio leaned against the front corner of the desk, staring at me with his arms crossed. His tail flicked pensively behind him, his blaster rifle hanging from his shoulder.

Behind him, Egan sat tall and straight in his desk chair, watching me without any discernible expression on his perfectly symmetrical face.

"Where have my manners gone?" he chided himself. "You'll have to forgive me, we weren't expecting company."

Spinning his chair, he reached for a crystal decanter on the shelf behind him. He poured a blush-colored liquid from the sparkling bottle into two crystal glasses, then held one out. Carrio took it and leaned forward, handing it off to me. It smelled like a strong spirit, and noticeably finer than anything I'd ever encountered at Hollak's bar.

Egan seated himself once more behind his desk, his glass clasped between his hands as he watched me.

Is it business etiquette to wait for one's guest to drink first? I kept my eyes on Egan, waiting him out.

"Kestian spirits like this average 900 credits a bottle; don't let it go to waste," he said, tilting his head toward my glass.

I stared down at it.

"Oh for Skarn's sake," he said, rolling his eyes. Taking a large gulp of his own drink, he dispelled my suspicion it might be drugged.

"I see a bit of Tor's paranoia has rubbed off on you," he quipped. "The kid has trust issues; always has."

I glared, vexed to hear Torren judged so casually by this privileged man in silk.

"Are you going to tell me what this is about?" I asked.

Egan glanced at Carrio before leaning back in his chair, setting one velvet-slippered foot on the desk and crossing the other over it.

"How long have you known our Torren?" he asked, settling comfortably into the chair.

Our Torren? Who is Torren to them?

"Not long," I replied, deciding to keep things vague.

"Interesting," Egan hummed. "So you met on the Talar job?"

"Yes," I said, then cleared my throat. "Look, I was interrogated by a Union inspector a few days ago, so forgive me, but I'm not exactly game for another round of questions."

I saw Egan's eyes dart to the fading bruises on my neck. He held his hands up defensively and nodded.

"By all means, Miss Kensie, is there anything you'd like to ask us?"

I tried to hide my surprise that he was accommodating me and nodded. "How long have *you* known Torren?" I asked.

"Eleven years," he said, glancing at the Kedigan. "Carrio's known him longer."

Carrio didn't react. He was still watching me curiously.

"I know," I said, meeting Carrio's gaze. "Torren told me he escaped Rorric with you and three other Kedigan."

"Sounds like he told you the whole story," Carrio finally murmured, uncrossing his arms and resting his paws on the desk on either side of him. *He's probing, trying to find out exactly how much I know.*

"He did," I said, my voice soft. "I'm so sorry about what happened…at the camp."

The Kedigan's shoulders slumped and he looked down at the marble floor. I hadn't meant to make him think about his painful past.

"Well," he said, collecting his thoughts and looking up at me, "since you already know about that, there's something you need to understand about Torren." He shifted, getting more comfortable where he sat.

I glanced at Egan, who seemed to be checking his reflection in the dark screen of his console. I couldn't tell if he was staying out of this corner of the discussion or actually that vain. When I returned my gaze to Carrio, a subtly pained expression painted his feline features.

"The five of us were irrevocably altered by what happened at that work camp, but Torren...he got the worst of it. I don't just mean physically. His lungs were permanently damaged by the corrovium gas, but..." He trailed off, and I got the feeling that just like Torren, this was a story he wasn't used to telling. "Myself and the other Kedigan, we'd all grown up together," he said. "Even though our families were gone, we still had each other. We still had our tribe. Torren lost *everyone*. Every friend. Every family member. None of the humans survived what happened that night."

My heart thumped heavily in my chest, recalling Torren's harrowing description.

"After what we went through, he didn't talk. Not for a long time. It was only after we met Egan that he started to actually speak again. He stayed closed off, though. Everything with Torren is very...matter-of-fact. He doesn't talk about his feelings."

"Oh," I whispered.

"What I'm trying to say," Carrio sighed, "is the fact that he opened up to you...it shouldn't be taken lightly."

"I see," I said. My eyes drifted to Egan, who was now watching me with an amiable expression.

"You're wondering how I fit into all this?" he said with a knowing smirk. I nodded, and Egan tapped his glass thought-fully with a spindly finger. "I was running a small but successful resale shop in a shady district here on Laigo when I met their little crew. They would bring me things they had...*found*, and I'd pay them."

"So you're a fence?" I said. Torren had kept calling Egan his *buyer*, but it was becoming increasingly clear that Egan traded exclusively in stolen goods.

"Excuse you," Egan sniffed. "I prefer the term *broker*. Much more pleasant on the ears. What I do takes unthinkable business savvy, and more refinement than a mere *fence*."

"You're getting sidetracked," Carrio chided him.

Egan nodded apologetically. "Yes, as I was saying—Carrio, Torren, and the rest would steal things. I would pay them a fair price, then sell the goods. We had a nice little business relationship for a while," he paused.

Carrio's mouth twitched into a smile as Egan threw him a dramatic, disapproving glance.

"That is…until they started selling me things they had stolen from my very own shop."

"Torren's idea," Carrio beamed.

"That's quite a grift," I said, amused by the thought.

"Yes, well," Egan said dismissively. "It took me a week to catch on. They were smart about it."

"What did you do when you found out?" I asked.

"Oh, my first thought was a violent one, I'm afraid. Once I got over the initial shock of learning that I had paid them for my own merchandise, I thought about calling local Union officers. I could have had them arrested the next time they came around."

"But you didn't?" I asked, sitting up.

Egan shrugged. "I've always prided myself on my ability to see a lucrative opportunity where others might not," he mused, "and I know talent when I see it. They were skilled thieves, all of them. Torren was particularly crafty. So, we struck a deal. I put a roof over their heads, and they became my primary obtainers of new stock. As their thieving and smuggling skills grew, so did our targets. Pretty soon, business was doing so well, I was able to move shop to a nicer district, which led to a clientele with even deeper pockets." He glanced at Carrio. "Does that sound about right?"

I decided to interject. "So these teenagers drove the growth of your business while you sat back and positioned yourself as a caring father figure?"

Egan screwed his eyebrows together. "I resent that, I'll have you know." He made a face. "Father figure? The very *thought* ages me. If anything, I'm an elegant, stylish uncle."

Carrio shook his head at me. "Egan here may look and sound like a pompous snob, but there's a beating heart underneath it all."

Egan scoffed in denial, but Carrio ignored him.

"He saved us. He's always paid us fairly too. When his payouts increased, so did ours. I guarantee you, when he made that quip earlier about losing his nav-projector, he was doing it to hide how worried he was about Torren."

Egan rolled his eyes, but kept his mouth closed, not refuting it.

"My point is, Miss Kensie, we are a weird little family," said Carrio. "At least, we were, before the other three left. They flew off to join Free Sector about four years ago. Said they wanted to use their skills for something more than this." He looked around the room, seeing memories in every corner of the space.

This is why Torren had been so dismissive when I suggested he join Free Sector. He'd heard it all before. His Kedigan friends had probably begged him to come with them.

"But you and Torren stayed?" I asked.

Carrio drummed his claws on the desk thoughtfully, prompting an irritated look from Egan, who watched for scratches.

"I stayed here to keep an eye on Torren," Carrio admitted. "Torren won't join Free Sector because he's afraid of losing his independence. I don't know if you noticed, but he's far more comfortable working by himself than with others."

"I noticed," I said, downing the entire drink in my hand. I half expected Egan to scold me for not savoring it at its cost. Mercifully, he was silent, gazing at his own drink with a fond smile. I wondered if he was reminiscing about raising four young Kedigan and an obstinate teenage boy.

My thoughts teemed in my head, unable to align into anything coherent while I added more pieces to the puzzle of Torren Arina.

"Thank you for the insight," I mumbled, looking between them. "But I don't get it. You don't even know me. Why are you telling me all of this?"

Egan took his feet off of the desk, sitting up and opening a drawer. He took a small object out that I couldn't identify from the sofa. Tapping it against his console screen, he typed something into his keypad.

"Carrio," Egan murmured, holding the small object out to the Kedigan.

Carrio took it delicately in his claws, then leaned forward and held it out to me.

It was a credit marker. I turned it over in my hand.

"I'm giving you your half of the payment for the crate," Egan said, shocking me to my core. "Plus a little extra for your trouble."

I flipped the marker on its side and pressed the display tab. I gasped out loud. *5,000 credits?* It was a full 2,000 more than what I was owed. More than enough to help Rego. I stifled a cry of relief, tears forming in the corners of my eyes.

"Why?" I asked, suspicion in my voice.

"Oh, honey," Egan drawled. "First rule of business—don't question money handed to you. Do what I do and just take it."

I knew he had probably gotten to where he was by not looking at things too closely, but I also knew I couldn't do that.

"I'm not like you," I said.

The corner of Egan's mouth curled in an approving way.

"No…" he agreed. "You're like *him*."

My heart skipped a beat, aching for Torren, dying to know where he was and if he was alright. I stared down at the marker in my hand, knowing I should have been content with the credits, but all I had were more questions.

"I don't understand. You were about to throw me out, and now you're giving me this?"

Egan and Carrio watched me curiously, as if the last thing I should be was confused.

"Miss Kensie, I don't know who you are. I don't know what happened out there on Talar, nor do I need to," said Egan, lifting a hand when I opened my mouth to explain. "But Torren clearly trusts you. By the sound of things, you're apparently *very* important to him, and since Torren is important to us, we are at your disposal."

Carrio nodded in agreement. I looked down, turning the marker over in my hand, barely believing how quickly my luck had changed. Torren was still protecting me, even if from afar.

"Now," said Egan, sitting back and delicately adjusting his silky sleeves, "I think that concludes our business for the evening."

Carrio stood. The conversation was over.

"Wait—" I said. "Torren's still on Talar. We need to get him out of there."

Egan sighed and flipped his console around so I could see the screen. A series of news-wires were pulled up and playing.

"My darling girl, we are monitoring the situation. There's chatter coming from Talar, news of an assault on a Union outpost."

"That was Torren," I said.

"Yes, well, there's likely a description out on the both of you. The planet is still on lockdown. There's no way in at the moment. The best thing we can do, and the best thing *Torren* can do, is lay low and wait for this all to die down."

I looked at Carrio. He gave me an apologetic look, but nodded in agreement.

I clenched my fists, not wanting to accept it, but knowing they weren't wrong. I also knew I had to take care of Rego's bounty before anything else.

"Now," Egan said, "it's late. You may stay in one of my guest suites tonight, have a bath, a meal, and a good night's sleep. Tomorrow, one of my men will take you wherever you need to go."

"Thank you, but I need to get to Hadrin as soon as possible. Torren said you'd be able to help me book transport."

"I'll take her," offered Carrio, turning to face Egan.

"I have people for that." Egan said.

"Yeah, I'm not leaving her alone with one of your shady contract pilots."

Egan crossed his arms indignantly. "If you think you can drop all your responsibilities here to fly Miss Kensie to Hadrin—"

Carrio shot Egan a stern look. It challenged the employer-employee relationship I had ascribed to them.

"You'd be absolutely right," Egan said, softening his voice and smiling at me.

They really are family. The Kedigan got to his feet, a smug look on his face.

"Thank you both for your help," I said, standing and setting my glass on Egan's desk. I slipped the credit marker into my pocket. "Can I ask you one more thing?"

"Of course," said Egan, warmth in his eyes. The detached businessman I'd first met was gone. Somehow, I felt like I was now part of Egan's inner circle.

"What chance do you think Torren has of evading the Union forces and making it off the planet? What are the odds he makes it back?"

Egan let out a slow exhale and considered his response.

My fingernails dug into the heels of my hands as I braced for the answer.

"Torren can do a lot of things, but in a case like this…only time will tell."

I nodded solemnly, my disappointment obvious.

"Don't worry, my dear," he said. "He disappears from time to time, but he always turns up. Usually around the time you've forgotten about him."

I didn't say it, but I found it extremely hard to believe there could ever be a time when I forgot about Torren Arina.

31

PLACES TO BE

HOLLAK'S BAR BUZZED WITH THE LIVELY CHATTER OF ITS USUAL crowd. I sat alone, hunched over an untouched drink, feeling largely out of place. The last couple of weeks had been surreal. Since my return, Hollak's hadn't felt as much like home as I thought it would. Neither had Hadrin.

Back on Laigo, Egan had helped me transfer my credits to Rego via the vector-wire the same night I had arrived. Rego had taken the amount to a trustworthy broker, where he'd submitted the payment to the Hackal clan. I had Egan search the bounty wire the next morning, and he'd seen no trace of Rego's listing. Rego was safe. Carrio flew me back to Hadrin, dropped me off safely, and my life went back to normal. To a degree. Rego and I put away the extra credits Egan had given me, still undecided about what to do with them.

I heard the sound of boots in the entryway of the bar, and I couldn't help but look up. The Froxian who entered waved to their friends and rushed to join their table.

It wasn't him. *It's never him.*

I shook my head, disappointed with myself for getting my hopes up again. Torren wasn't coming. If he had managed to get off of Talar, he wouldn't be coming to Hadrin of all places. Who would? Egan had already paid me, so my business with Torren was finished. I took a little solace in the fact I had been right to push Torren away after our night together. It had been for the best.

"There you are," a voice said behind me.

My heart stopped. I sat up straight, twisting in my seat. Rego approached my table with an easy smile, barely holding in his infectious laughter. I quelled my initial disappointment. Rego was my best friend, and I *was* happy to see him. Rego sat across from me, and I slid over the drink I'd already ordered for him.

"Why'd you cut out of work early?" he asked, taking a sip from his frosty glass.

I'd feigned an illness and left work a few hours early. I'd gone home to change, then headed straight to Hollak's to lose myself in a drink or two.

"Oh, I wasn't feeling well," I said, looking down at the worn tabletop. I didn't have the heart to tell Rego that after everything I had seen and done, I was struggling to fall back into a routine on Hadrin.

"Feel better," Rego said, concern in his eyes. "But I do like you getting here first and buying me drinks. Let's keep doing that." He laughed as he took another gulp, nearly polishing off his drink.

I reached across the table and smacked his arm with the back of my hand playfully.

"Hey, didn't I just save your ass from the Hackal Clan and who knows how many bounty hunters? You should be buying *me* drinks."

He laughed giddily and rubbed his arm dramatically, as if I'd actually hurt him.

"I'm kidding!" he said. "You know that."

I shook my head at him with a genuine smile and threw more of my own drink back. Rego let a comfortable silence settle between us for a minute as he fiddled with his glass.

"Listen," he said, "I know I already said it, but I still can't thank you and Tor enough for helping me."

I made a face and shrugged at him. He'd thanked me probably six times over the last few weeks. It was starting to make me uncomfortable.

"Come on, Reeg, you gonna do this for the rest of our miserable lives?" I gestured at the dingy bar, leaning back in my seat. "We'll be eighty years old, sitting here in Hollak's with grey hair, and you'll still be thanking me."

Rego laughed into his cup, spilling a bit of the drink on himself. I laughed with him, happy to see him so at ease. He was doing so well now that the threat of the bounty was no longer over his head.

"Seriously though, Reeg, what kind of friends would Torren and I be if we hadn't done everything we could to help you?"

Torren's name caught in my throat. I had tried hard not to mention him for the past week, but I couldn't escape it. He'd gotten under my skin, and I didn't know how to get rid of him. I didn't know if I wanted to.

"I know, but I mean it," insisted Rego. "With everything you two went through out there...it means a lot."

I gave him the pretense of a smile and unwillingly began thinking about Torren again. I had given Rego a basic rundown of the trip after I'd gotten back, but I hadn't told him everything. He knew Torren had stayed behind, but I left out the interrogation, and the night we spent in the tent. If Rego suspected that anything had happened between us, he said nothing.

"By the way, have you heard anything from Tor?" I asked, taking a drink and hoping to appear like the answer didn't matter to me.

"No…" Rego said, copying my easy posture and leaning back. "But I wouldn't worry; he's probably fine. He does this. I won't hear from him for a few years, and then out of nowhere—" He gestured around the bar, as if Torren might emerge out of thin air.

I nodded. Egan had said the same thing, but it answered nothing.

"Can you do me a favor and tell me how you and Torren met? He refused to tell me."

Rego got a glint in his eye. "Tor's a good friend. Probably didn't want to embarrass me."

"Well, now I have to know."

Rego shook his head and I got comfortable in my seat. He grinned and tilted his face at the ceiling, recalling details.

"This was years ago, right after I got out of Union prison, but before Hadrin. The original bounty had just been placed, and I knew about it, but didn't think I needed to worry. I had borrowed a friend's ship and flown to Kaoss that week, just looking for work."

"Looking for work? Or sampling Kaoss's famous dura-brews?"

"I wasn't going to visit the planet with the strongest beers in the galaxy and *not* try them," he said indignantly. "Anyway, Torren was also on Kaoss. He had just robbed someone. Who was it?" He tapped his chin thoughtfully, his eyes lighting up when he remembered. "It was the Chancellor! I remember that now. Torren nicked his collection of rare artifacts from the Battle of Ravine."

"You're joking," I said.

"No, this guy had actual knives from the Boulder Wars."

"Shut up about the Boulder Wars," I said. "Torren robbed the Chancellor of Kaoss?"

"He had gotten into the Chancellor's compound undetected, but he was spotted as he was leaving. So he had a bag full of stolen relics, and now there's a description out on him. He headed to the nearest shipyard to get off-world as soon as possible."

"And you were his getaway pilot?"

Rego paused, choosing his words carefully. "In a way."

"What does that mean?"

"It means Torren stole my ship. That's how we met."

I sat back, realizing how random their meeting had been. "Wow. How did you catch up with him?"

"Well," he said, his face going slightly pink. "I was *on* the ship when he stole it."

"He didn't see you?"

"I was in the lavatory."

"Oh," I said, raising my eyebrows and trying not to smile.

"*Yeah.*" He sighed. "I was just minding my own business. Next thing I knew, the ship was taking off and I was bouncing off the walls of the lavatory."

"I'm sorry," I said, biting my lip.

"Go ahead, laugh." He rolled his eyes at me. "When I stumbled out of the lavatory, he pulled a blaster on me, and I told him I didn't want trouble. Right then, the ship started to give him issues. It was a finicky vessel, even for me, who'd been flying it for weeks. I took the controls and got us out of there. He said I was a good pilot, and that he had some work for me if I was interested. Anyway, that's how we started working together, and how we became friends."

"That's…crazy."

"Yeah. We worked together for a while, but I didn't want to chance going back to Union prison. Torren was actually the one who suggested Hadrin for me. Said it was boring, but safe."

When I thought about it, Torren had changed my life for the better *years* before I'd even met him. If Torren hadn't told Rego about Hadrin, I wouldn't have had a friendly face upon my arrival.

"You know, he's a complex guy. Cold at times, and stubborn," Rego said, watching me think. "But he's a good guy."

"Yeah…he is," I said. Torren *was* a good guy. The best I'd ever come across.

I took the final gulp of my drink and slammed the cup down. I needed to leave or I was going to bring down Rego's good mood. "Hey, Reeg, I'm gonna call it a night," I said, standing up.

Rego nodded and raised his glass to me reverently, a hint of understanding passing over his eyes.

I clasped his shoulder. "See you tomorrow, yeah?"

"Sure thing," he said smiling.

I gave his shoulder a gentle squeeze before walking out of the bar. The evening air enveloped me as I began my trek through the dusty streets. It was a cool evening, so I drew my jacket close and sped up. Lost in my thoughts, the walk went quickly, and soon I was climbing the exterior metal stairs that led to my place above the oyzo shop.

I thought about how I had left my dusty work uniform hanging up, and I groaned, remembering that my second uniform was also dirty. I needed to throw them in the wash before work in the morning.

I reached my door's control panel and punched in my code hastily, ready to close myself off from the world. The door slid open, and I stepped inside, letting it close and lock. The place was dark, so I flicked on a soft light in the corner. I was crossing the room, sliding my jacket off, when I heard a familiar voice.

"Do you have *any* idea how easy it is to override the locks on your door?"

I stopped dead in my tracks. I knew that voice, but I refused to let myself believe what I was hearing. Turning to make sure I wasn't dreaming, I locked eyes with the man I had convinced myself I'd never see again.

There, leaning against the wall with his signature smirk, was Torren Arina.

"You really should replace that control panel," he said, crossing his arms over his chest. "*Anyone* could get in here." His smirk deepened when he saw the look on my face.

I took him in with a glance. His hair was shaggy, his facial hair slightly grown out. It was smart of him to adjust his appearance for the time being. The Union was looking for someone with his description. He wore no flight vest, just a long brown coat with a high collar.

I wanted to run to him. To grab him. I wanted my arms around him so bad they ached. With an inhale, I held my composure. A nagging, insecure part of my brain told me he was only there for business reasons. Removing my jacket, I threw it over the back of a chair.

"I don't have your half of the payout," I said. "I left it with Egan."

"I know," he said. "I met with Egan as soon as I got off of Talar." Something at his hip glinted in the light. *His blaster.* He had gotten it back from Carrio.

"Oh," I murmured, unable to silence the creeping doubt in my head. "Then what brings you here?"

Lazily pushing himself away from the wall, he slowly crossed the room toward me. "You really don't know? Fenn Kensie, I thought you were smarter than that."

I swallowed, wanting to believe the man in front of me but not allowing myself to. "Tell me then," I said softly. "Tell me why you're here."

He flashed a crooked grin, then shrugged. "Do you remember when I told you there is always a way through anything?"

"Yes," I breathed, watching him move closer, taking his time.

"I was wrong," he said soberly, meeting me in the center of the room. He stood close enough for me to feel his body heat. "I've gotten myself into something I can't escape."

I looked up into his eyes, searching them for a hint of what he was trying to say. "And what would that be?" I asked, my eyes falling to his lips.

"You," he said, studying my face. My heart skipped more than a beat. "I've been in flight for so many years, searching for solid ground. I've finally found it. It's you." His eyes glided over my freckles. His *stars*.

He reached into his pocket and held something out to me. I recognized the purple-blue blossom immediately. It was a half-dried sprig of Star Bonnet.

"In the forest, I got pinned down by Union forces," he said. "I hid for hours. All through the night, I stayed quiet and didn't dare move. When dawn broke, I saw that the bramble I'd thrown myself under just happened to be a Star Bonnet bush."

I took the flower gently from him, barely believing it was real.

"I thought of you while I lay there," he said. "I promised myself I'd get out of there. To bring you one."

I shook my head, tears pricking my eyes. "I don't think you know what this means."

"I do," he said, reaching for my hand and gently closing my fingers around the flower. "I listened." He stepped closer, lowering his voice to a whisper. "*As I picked this, I chose you.*"

I knew his question, and I had his answer. Reaching for the collar of his coat, I pulled him toward me, lifting my face to meet his. When he kissed me, he hit my smiling teeth. I kissed him back, grabbing his shoulders and squeezing. My knees went weak as he circled his arms around me, removing any doubt I had that he had come to Hadrin for me. *Just me.*

He pulled away, breaking the kiss and grinning at me before leaning in again. He drew me into a hug, laughing with his face at my neck. I saw my dusty work uniform hanging on the wall across the room, ready to be washed. *Screw it.* I wouldn't be going into work in the morning. I had other places to be.

END

EPILOGUE

Torren and I sat on the edge of the roof of my building, sipping from a bottle of fermented oyzo liquor. We watched in comfortable silence as ships took off from the shipyard in the distance, their engines burning bright against the night sky. The night air was chilly, so I huddled close to him, letting our arms touch.

"I can't believe that you broke into my place," I laughed. "How did you know where I lived anyway?" I took a sip and passed him the bottle.

His mouth opened to answer, but he opted instead to take a drink, his cheeks flushing.

"You followed me around today, didn't you?" I asked.

He gave me a guilty smile, then passed the bottle back. He must have tailed me as I left the shipyard and headed home, then waited at my place while I was at the bar.

"I wasn't sure you wanted to see me," he admitted. "Not after I ran off and made you fly that ship all by yourself."

"That's a fair assumption. I was pretty mad at you," I smiled.

He returned the smile, but it faded quickly.

"I came to check on you. I had to. But I'd planned on doing it from a distance."

"What made you decide to materialize?"

He reached for my hand, holding it up between us. The moonlight shone on the carved wooden band around my finger.

"You're still wearing the ring I gave you," he said, his voice soft with amusement as he rubbed his thumb against the wood he had carved.

I wrenched my hand away and blushed. "Oh, I forgot to take that off."

"Right," he chuckled sarcastically.

I glared at him, pretending to be annoyed, but I got the feeling we were past the point of being able to fully deceive each other.

"Did you hear about Talar?" I asked.

"I read the news-wires. The Union is pulling a lot of their forces off the planet, citing that the mining industry there is no longer viable."

"Of course, they omitted the part where Canda and her team wreaked havoc on their supply chains and you infiltrated an outpost," I said.

"Of course. They can't let on that a couple of civilians got the better of them. They really don't want the rest of the galaxy to know it can be done."

"You know Markens is after you, right? He doesn't know your

name, but he's actively looking for the criminal who robbed the museum and attacked an outpost."

"I saw," he said. "I had a wire-phaser grab an internal case file from the investigation. How did *you* know about it?"

"Because I did the same thing," I grinned. "Rego knows a guy who can extract and decrypt all kinds of files."

"Look at you," he smirked, "a criminal at last."

I laughed, letting my shoulder press against his, savoring the feeling of being next to him.

"So, what's next for Torren Arina?" I asked.

He shook his head at me and gestured around us. "If I had known you were going to shout my full name from the *literal rooftops*, I never would have told it to you."

"*Please*, no one can hear us," I laughed.

He sighed and grabbed the bottle out of my hands, scoffing as he brought it to his lips.

"I'm glad you told me, though," I said, "Your name was like a magic password. Carrio and Egan were tripping over themselves when they realized you trusted me enough to tell me all the things you did."

"You really freaked them out, you know?" he laughed. "Showing up in a Union ship, then knowing *way* too much about me. Egan was impressed. I think he wants to hire you."

I laughed. "As flattering as that is, I'm still figuring out what I want to do next. It feels like I'm at a crossroads."

"Funny," he said. "For once, I feel like my path is clear." He looked down at the bottle contemplatively.

"What is it?" I asked, sitting up.

"I've thought a lot about what you said back on Talar," he said, picking at the label on the bottle, "when you asked if I had considered joining Free Sector."

I nodded. "You said you didn't want to follow anyone's orders."

He took a sip from the bottle and set it down, turning to face me. "Well…I thought about it again, and realized, *so what?*" he shrugged. "You were right. They're up against a hell of a lot with the Union. Most of my Kedigan siblings are out there, and they're risking everything. It's time I help them."

"They'll be lucky to have you," I said.

He reached over, lacing his fingers between mine. "Come with me."

"That's a tempting offer," I grinned.

"Well, think about it," he said. "It doesn't sound like a walk in the park, life on the edge of space, fending off marauders, fighting to give the galaxy a chance. But you were right about joining Free Sector."

"I was?"

"Yeah, about what you said back on Talar. We owe it to the ones we've lost to fight."

I squeezed his hand, then let go and picked up the liquor bottle.

"Well, I've been thinking about what *you* said back on Talar."

"What was that?" he asked.

I tipped the bottle back, swallowing the last of the drink in one gulp. I tossed the empty bottle over the side of the roof. It hit the street below with a melodious shatter as I looked into

Torren's deep brown eyes. The corner of his mouth lifted in approval.

"About how to honor those we've lost. I used to keep my head down, only focused on surviving. Now that I've met you, I want more than that," I said, letting my gaze fall to his lips.

"Is that so?" he said with a smirk.

"Mm-hmm," I said, reaching over and grabbing the collar of his shirt, ready to pull him in for a kiss. "I'm done with just surviving. It's time to *live*."

ACKNOWLEDGMENTS

This book would not have been possible without the help and support of many people I am unbelievably lucky to share a galaxy with.

To my parents, Chris and Diane, who encouraged me to be creative from the moment I could pick up a pencil. For letting me cut cardboard boxes into "spaceships" for my Star Wars action figures. You let me follow every weird little artistic whim I had over the years. Not everyone receives that kind of support, and I am so grateful for it.

To Heather Rhee (née Smith), my friend through many adventures, and my brother Cameron, aka my very first friendship. I have an active imagination, but I can't even begin to picture my life without either of you.

Thank you to my developmental editor, Casey Jones. Your encouragement fueled me throughout this long, intense process. Thanks for loving my story but suggesting that I delve *deeper* into the emotions of my characters. You were right.

Thank you to my copy editor Ana Hansen, for all your enthusiasm and expertise. You polished my clumsier bits of text while keeping my writer's voice intact and present, and for that, I cannot thank you enough.

Thanks to author Lindsey Clarke, who read one of the *very first* iterations of this book and made *sure* I knew how much you loved it. You made me feel like I had the start of something good in my hands, and it kept me going.

Thank you to my beta readers, Demetria Smith, Robin Wildman, Lachlan McArthur, and Abigail McArthur. I can't thank you enough for your time and opinions. Each one of you helped shape this story. You're all angels.

Finally, to my partner Sheldon Price, thank you for your endless support and encouragement. This book would absolutely not exist without you. Thank you for lending me my first book on writing a decade ago. Thank you for all the nights you did both of our shares of housework to give me free time to write and edit. And thank you, so much, for making me feel smart, and cool, and capable, every single day. You are my hero.

ABOUT THE AUTHOR

Danielle Price is a Midwest native, California transplant, and current St. Louis resident, where she lives with her partner and cats. A lifelong storyteller, she's worked in theater, special effects makeup, and the comic book industry. These days, you'll find her watching sci-fi shows and horror films while snacking on a charcuterie board that has a higher cheese content than is medically advisable.

EXPLORE THE WORLD OF THIS BOOK AT:

www.daniellepricewrites.com

instagram.com/daniellepriceauthor
threads.com/@daniellepriceauthor

9 7 9 8 9 9 9 7 1 8 6 1 7